Illumen's Children

J. Shepard Trott

Flatroof Philly Publishing
Philadelphia, PA

Cover by Blaise Vincz

ISBN: 978-0692440438

Flatroof Philly Publishing
2038 E. Huntingdon St.
Philadelphia, PA

Illumen's Children:
A Fantastic Adventure

J. Shepard Trott

Table of Contents

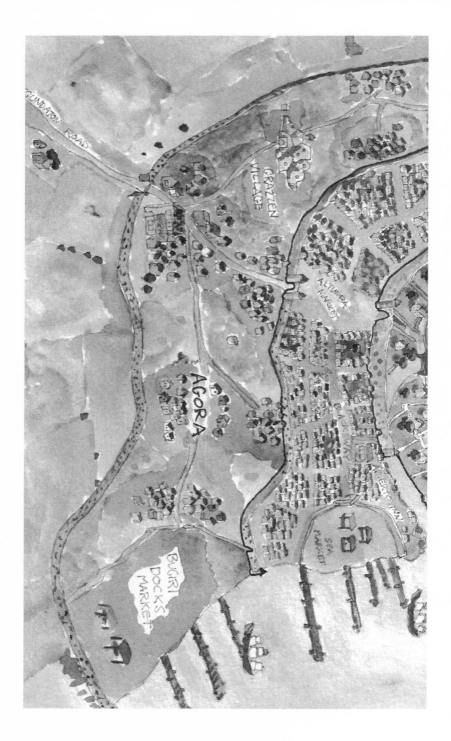

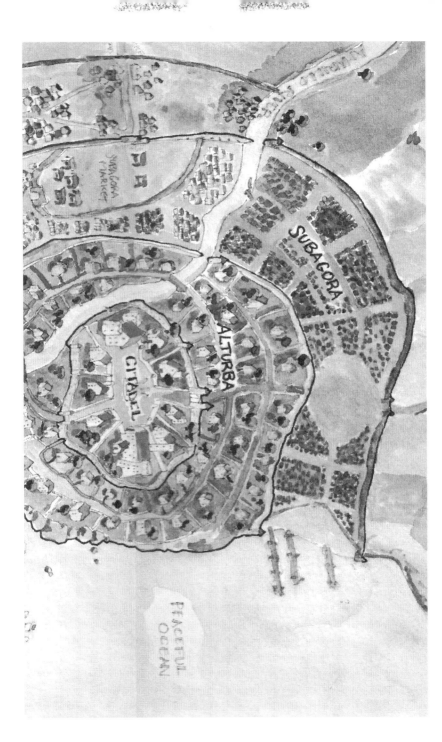

1. A Bad Day

Not so long ago, in a world not that far from ours, lived a Sub named Hands. His stomach growled at him, and he growled at the world. His stomach growled because a) he never knew his dad, and his mom died of a disease when he was three and b) nobody else gave a merd about him. Because his stomach was empty, Hands couldn't give a merd himself, no matter how long he squatted, or how loud he grunted.

Now you are asking, "Did his parents name him Hands?"

No, they didn't. I do not know what they named him. He didn't either. They may not have named him anything. They may have called him Little Merd.

"Then how did he get that strange name?" you inquire. Very justly. It was not a common name in this not-so-different world. At first glance, his hands did not look special. They hung floppy and lifeless at his sides. But if you were there and you had a careful eye, you would have seen that his hands only seemed lifeless. They were alive to everything, shook by tiny little jolts, holding energy the same way that small birds stand still for a moment, containing in their shivering little bodies the power to spring from the earth and climb into the sky.

Hands walked through the market. Pan bread sizzled, corn muffins baked. He checked each stall for vendors that were talking, flirting, or sleeping, but his eyes met eyes that tracked him everywhere he looked. If he got within a few steps of a stall, the owners said things to him. They said, "Keep your merd grippers where I can see them." They said, "Touch my stuff, I kill you, you kaMerd." They knew him. They knew he wanted their stuff, and they knew he had no money. They recognized the dirty piece of cloth that hung from his shoulders and the loose pair of shorts that clung desperately to his bony hips. They had named him Hands.

1

Hands walked along, ignoring the threats and shaking fists, as well as the growls of his belly. Then he spotted a red-faced man from the country, easily identified by his woolen gray overalls and the Humbershire accent, a slow and open way of speaking. Humbershire is a big wick, and the people there are hardworking and simple. Hands saw him the way a cat sees a mouse. His body got tense for a short moment, and then he acted as though he had seen nothing at all.

The man was selling lots of juicy looking corn and bright red apples piled high in his wagon. Innkeepers' girls and servants from AltUrba were crowding around his wagon, murmuring cheerfully about the deal he was giving.

Hands waited until the girls had all bought the corn and apples they wanted.

The farmer shouted, "I've got the best. Corn, Apples. Just look! The best corn and apples! Humbershire prices, Humbershire quality!"

Hands walked up to the farmer and asked if he needed a hand in selling.

The farmer said, "No thanks, son. If I can grow it, I can sell it. You want to buy some?"

Hands said, "No. They're rotten."

The farmer roared, "LOOK AT THIS FRUIT! BEST FRUIT IN THE WORLD. SAY ANOTHER LIE ABOUT IT, AND I'LL SHOW YOU!"

The farmer had pushed an ear of corn and apple toward the boy for examination. Hands looked at the produce. Then he shook his head as if he was sorry for what he'd said. He stepped back toward the farmer and put out his small hand, a sudden flash of movement, and patted the big man's shoulder. "Hey, man. Sorry, just a little joke. They're really good looking apples."

Hands shook his head as his hands dropped into the remnant of shirt he wore. Then he shuffled away apologetically.

Of course, in that moment Hands showed what his hands could do. Not to the farmer, who was shouting for his next customer, but you were watching. You saw how the fingers flicked into the overalls and lifted the coin-heavy purse, in the same moment delivering a pat, while our hero distracted the farmer with his concerned expression and heartfelt apology.

A few minutes later the Humbershire farmer, looking to make change, felt for his purse. It wasn't in his pocket. It wasn't on his belt. It wasn't on the buckboard. That was when he remembered the ragged looking Sub who had calmed him by patting his chest.

He roared, "Thief!"

All the merchants, as one, looked up at him. If he pointed they would send their apprentices, or if they were young they'd run themselves, and catch and beat the culprit. A thief was a threat to all of them. The farmer, however, failed to point in any direction, and the merchants and shoppers shook their heads and told their apprentices to get back to work.

Hands ran when he turned the corner and only walked when he was a quarter of a mile away. He tested the weight of the coin-fat purse, which he could use to make his belly fat. His mouth watered with the thought of thick beef stew.

He imagined that he would save some coins and buy sweet buns for Jalil and Shyheem. Not Burt, though. Burt was already fat because his dad was an innkeeper. Plus, Burt never gave Hands food, so Hands wouldn't feed him. The others, Jalil and Shyheem, would finally realize Hands was their hoodBo. They'd let him play Guard and Wendigo with them.

Hands' thoughts were interrupted by a hard grip around his neck. He had not seen the large man emerge from between two of the one-room shacks that lined the alley. The man wore the Fels' redcoat, dirty and open over a large belly covered only by his nightshirt. His tricorn was floppy and unkempt. He was armed with a club and a sword that looked like it might have rusted into its sheathe. The fat crowded his face so that his eyes were only a gleam of greed peeking through.

"'Hands," he said. Like an old friend that was happy to see the Sub. Like they were hoodBos. Like they used to run the block together.

Hands said nothing. His expression reflected an opposite reaction, looking like a man who suddenly meets a grolf on a

3

morning stroll. Grolfs come into the story later. For now you just need to know that they were monsters.

"Not happy to see your hoodBo Fel Antony?" the big guy asked.

Hands said, "I preferred seeing your wife last night."

Fel Antony punched Hands, bringing his knuckles, the only part of him with no fat, against the Sub's chin, but he did it without feeling, and Hands seemed not to notice, either. It was an old routine for both of them.

Fel Antony held Hands, and stooped, grunting with the effort, and grabbed Hands' skinny ankle. He stood up, yanking Hands' from the ground. In a whirly moment, Hands hung upside down. Then Fel Antony shook. One or two big shakes, and the purse fell from the remnants of Hands' shirt. It landed on the packed dirt of the alley with a heavy clink.

Fel Antony said, "Where did you steal this?"

Hands said, "A gift from your wife."

This insult did not even merit a punch, as the Fel pushed the boy away and stooped, with a big wheeze, for his belly was in the way, and wrapped his fingers around the purse.

Hands had landed against the wall of a shack, and the cluriKin was leaning out a small window and smacking his head. CluriKin are another important creature in this not-so-long-ago world that is not so far away. These small creatures share a life with the house they live in, and this one was unhappy that a Sub had smacked its wall.

Hands wanted to roar, to be a grolf, a mound of mountain-made muscle, stomping through people. His stomach roared, his money was confiscated, and now this little shack cluriKin was hitting him in the head with its small fists, even though he had not wanted to smack the shack wall. He'd been pushed! He couldn't touch Fel Antony, and he couldn't fill his stomach. He punched the cluriKin, sending it flying back into the shack, where it audibly smacked up against the far wall.

He turned back to Fel Antony and, trying to sound reasonable and sort of respectful, he said, "Can I at least get a penny?"

"Stealing is a crime. You're lucky I'm not locking you up."

4

Hands and the Fel both knew he only locked Hands up when the pickpocket was broke. Hands said, "You merd head."

Fel Antony pushed the purse into one of his deep pockets. Hands' insults had no force for him, because no one cared what Hands said. Hands couldn't tell anyone that Fel Antony stole from him because no one would listen. Fel Antony walked out of the alley, already planning his lunch.

Hands' stomach roared like an enraged grolf, doubly empty now because he had anticipated filling it. He considered the variety of ways that he could kill Fel Antony. He imagined paying a Bugiri mercenary to plunge a spear deep in his gut, or joining the Bellumites and mastering the art of the thunderPipe and blasting him. Of course he had no money to do these things. He couldn't even buy a piece of panbread. The thought was sweet though, and he imagined himself, well-muscled, armed with a shiny barrel of steel, and Fel Antony gasping at his feet, holding his knees. "Hands," the fat Fel begged, "Spare me. Oh, I am so sorry."

Hands would say, "You should have thought of that when I needed a piece of bread. All I wanted was one penny."

The fat merd would squeal and squirm some more, but finally, Hands would set the fire to the pan, the thunderPipe would blast, and Fel Antony would be a bloated sack of leaking blood.

Fantasy. Merd. Hands had to eat and the dumb things he made up in his head were a distraction. He stalked back into the markets where the scent of roasted meat and fried and baked bread taunted him. He tried to look sad and unfortunate by a young woman's stall but she called him a merd and threatened to throw a stone at him.

He wandered over to a pile of trash, eyeing it without seeming to. He spotted an apple core there, and, when he thought no one was looking, grabbed it.

Then he heard, "Merdy Sub, eating trash!" A little kid was pointing at him.

"Ching you," Hands said and dodged into an alley. He ate the apple core, seeds and all. Somehow eating it made him hungrier. Hunger was Hands' least favorite feeling. It filled his brain so that he couldn't even imagine a world where he was a WickBaron and he ate all he wanted. It filled his body so that there was a little itchy fire

5

everywhere, but also a slowness. He was so slow when he was hungry, he knew from experience, that if he tried to grab a fried panbread and run, he'd get caught, and beaten, and they'd take the bread back. If he tried to grab it and just shove it down his mouth, they would beat him until he puked it back up.

He walked through the back alleys, looking for a lock, but most of the houses were bolted in the back. Lockpicking was too risky at the front door. Anyway, these SubAgoran shacks probably had nothing in them.

He went toward Dark Docks. The ruffs lived in Dark Docks, and they didn't mess around with threats, skipping right to body blows, so Hands walked the perimeter, until he found Wareen, a ruff that Hands had helped on a couple jobs. Hands could pick pockets and locks, and he could wriggle through narrow windows. He had helped Wareen break into an AltUrba house once.

He found Wareen sitting in front of his two-story house, drinking ale. Two other ruffs were sitting with him, rolling dice. A bunch of money was spread on the table. Hands said, "You need a look out? A lock picked?"

Wareen said, "Get out of here."

Hands walked over and stood by the table. They rolled the dice and called their numbers. Hands stood watching, until Wareen won a roll. Then he said, "Can I borrow a penny, Wareen?"

Wareen turned on the boy, "Get the ching out of here before I fistSlap your face!"

Hands danced away and he said, "I'd like to see you try."

Wareen went to stand up and Hands took off running. Wareen's fistSlaps made Fel Antony's look like kittens. Hands would eat a kitten if he could find one. Not the best food, but his standards were low.

He went to the Illumenist temple. Lamp Kareem would feed him if he said prayers to their god.

He knelt on the slate surface of the quiet room with the wannabe lamps, the wicks, and said the words about Illumen being the power of the weak. These prayers made him angry. Did Lamp Kareem really believe there was a god who gave a ching about weak

6

people? Hands wasn't going to admit to being weak, but as far as he could see, people used their strength to get what they could.

The lamp closed his eyes, and his voice trembled when he read the words. Sometimes tears ran down his leather cheeks and through the gray stubble on his dark chin. Hands concluded that the lamp was really good at pretending. He must get more money the more people thought he believed it. Hands' belly grumbled. He hoped his stomach didn't reject the apple core. That was a risk of eating food from the trash. Sometimes he ate it, only to puke it up a few hours later.

After the service Lamp Kareem had some wicks pass out wooden bowls and small hard pieces of bread. They ate sitting on the slate floor of the one room temple. Hands had not eaten at a table in his lifetime. Another wick came around with thin cabbage soup that he ladled into the bowls. Hands asked for more but the Sub shook his head.

Hands dipped the bread and nibbled it and slurped down the soup. Even taking the smallest bites he could, the bread was gone in minutes. Once it was gone, he considered snatching his neighbor's bread, but then Lamp Kareem would not feed him tomorrow. He brought his bowl up to the lamp.

"Can I have more?"

Lamp Kareem pointed at the empty pot and basket from which the soup and bread had come. Hands looked around at the other kids still eating. He watched each sip of thin soup, each nibble of tack.

Lamp Kareem said, "You want to pray light into some baubles?" He pointed at the pile of translucent white rocks by the big double doors. Hands shook his head. That never worked for him.

Lamp Kareem said, "Illumen knows your hunger, my boy."

Hands couldn't afford to say, "Yeah, right." He nodded and got out of there.

He wandered to the docks. He was too small to work there, but he liked to look at the ocean for the few minutes after a meal. Then its great expanse, the sound of the waves made him imagine other lands, Opuland and Bugiri, where life was different. There was so much food there. There he would start a new life and become a prince among men, a hunter of tigers, and a lover of women. Respected by everyone.

The hunger returned as the markets were closing. The wickians loaded their unsold produce into their wagons and rode out of the city. The Subs moved into their homes or, if they were rich, into the inns. Hands walked the packed earth of the market spaces, hoping for crumbs, a half chewed bun. He saw one scrap of fried bread but as he moved toward it a mutt darted out from behind the market wall and picked it up. Hands slung a stone at the running mutt. He missed twice but hit it with the third; it let out a squeal. He wanted to be happy about the throw, but his stomach could only grumble about the lost piece of bread.

He considered going back to the shack were he slept but he knew he was too hungry to sleep. He wandered back to the alley behind Abierto's, Burt's dad's inn. He knew that Burt and Jalil and Shyheem would be there. Burt usually brought out some leftovers and fed them.

He hid behind the corner of the inn, listening to the other Sub's voices ringing out around the corner. They were talking about the war and Jalil was the loudest, "I'll be a general. I'll fight so well, killing those baby eaters, they'll make me general."

He could hear Burt and Shyheem, "Yeah, you'd make a good general. You're strong and you're not afraid of anything."

It made him mad because Jalil thought he was so tough because he was strong and fast, but wasn't he just a kid, just like Hands? The way those boys were all pretending that they would matter.

Hands stepped out and said, "They'll kill you just like they killed your father."

The second he said it, he knew it was a dumb thing to say. Jalil's father had died fighting the wendigo, and this comment, while true, would make him angry. Hands didn't care about that, but he saw, sitting in the middle of the three boys, a half eaten platter of bread, vegetables and meat! He wasn't getting any of that.

He still asked. They weren't eating it. None of them even responded. Jalil told him to take back what he said. It was true, and they weren't going to give him any food anyway. Jalil grabbed him and was punching him and it hurt. Hands only escaped using a clever strategy, attacking Jalil at his weak point. After that Burt chased him, yelling that he was a cheater, but that fatty would never catch Hands.

He ran back out onto the main street, Black Way, and sat in the shadows of the buildings. He ignored the warm orange lights that peaked out under the doors of the shacks and the stone houses. He ignored the soft sound of cluriSong that found its way out of the houses along with the light. Most of all he ignored the smell of baking bread. When he wasn't ignoring it he thought that all the Subs inside their houses, or hiding in the alley, refusing to feed him, deserved the worst death he could imagine. That would be being eaten by a grolf. Or a wendigo.

He was about to go and try to sleep, when he heard the clattering sound of a horse galloping on cobblestones. It rattled toward him. He slipped back behind the corner of a shack in case it was a Fel. In a moment he saw a horse and rider. The rider was wearing the redcoat of the Fel. When the rider got closer, Hands saw the rider was slipping off on his saddle, and the horse slowed to a walk. Then the rider fell off and clattered to the cobbles. His helmet rolled off. He groaned once and his head dropped onto the street. It looked like he was dying. Three thick arrow shafts were buried in his back. Hands looked around to see if anyone else was coming, and then sprang forward. He wasn't sure if he should risk a body search, trying to find the man's purse, of if he should just take the sword. He grabbed the hilt and pulled. The blade eased out of the sheathe easy as ninjas moving into the shadows.

He caught his breath when he saw it. It was beautifully worked with rivulets of dark steel. It was probably grazzen. That sword was worth more than the purses of one hundred apple farmers. Worth a thousand, ten thousand pieces of panbread! A hand caught his wrist and pulled him to the ground. He was close to the pale and taunt face of the bleeding Fel.

"Listen," gasped the Fel. "They've got a plot to kill the king. It's us. I mean . . ." and he trailed off. In the corner of his mouth, a small bubble of blood pulsed. Hands would have run, but the hand still had his wrist in an iron grip. The Fel grunted, "It's the Fels." He took a deep breath. "They got someone else helping them. It's . . ." The dying man said a work. It sounded like Miton. Hands heard many hooves cracking against the cobbles. "Run," the Fel croaked.

Hands didn't take orders from anyone. He had the sword, but he figured that this guy with his gold buttoned waist coat and yellow epaulet had some money on him somewhere, not to mention all the other weapons he was carrying. The man on the ground screamed at him, "They'll kill you! Run!"

As if to convince him of the truth of this, an arrow cut the air in front of Hands' face. Hands took the sword and ran. For the first time that day, he didn't think about his hunger.

Maybe you are worried for him. After all, he was on foot, and his pursuers were mounted murderers. The only comfort I can offer you is this. Hands had run from people intending to kill him before. In fact, most people that interacted with him ended up wanting to kill him.

On the other hand, you probably should be worried. His pursuers weren't just angry merchants, or fistSlinging Subs. They were Citan Fels, the best soldiers in Regna. They were armed with swords forged in the depths of Grek Mountain and bows curved in the shadows of Ornata. They had hunted people before, including the man whose life gurgled out on Black Way, and none of their previous quarries had survived.

2. Meet the Team

Now I want you to get to know the rest of the team.

"Team?" you ask. "Hands was alone!"

I do use the word loosely. Hands wasn't ready to play with anyone. Sometimes, your team is not the one you pick.

Burt, also known as PorkChop, pretended to work hard by dancing between the tables, gathering dirty bowls. To be entirely accurate, he was getting as close to dancing as someone with the nickname PorkChop can get. He was bobbing, like a dollop of lard in water. He had to look like he was doing something, or else Shawnee would get him. She, along with Burt's dad and the cluriKin, all worked until their bones ached and the money drawer was full. Burt didn't mind work. He just felt a break was necessary now and again, especially when he was out of breath or hungry, and since he was a big guy, he was often out of breath and always hungry.

He bobbed through his dad's inn. The big room was stuffed with tables and chairs and the tables and chairs were stuffed with men, and the men were stuffed with stew. Those who weren't stuffed were working hard to get there, shoving the famed stew into their mouths with slurpy joy.

The clients were road merchants, and they had hustled all day, yelling, counting change, and moving locations. Some of them had been working for weeks getting their wares to the Sub, traveling dangerous roads. They had earned this relaxation, and they sat expansively, kicking their feet out and throwing their arms over the backs of the benches. They ate voraciously, demanding their stew bowls be kept full, and they drank voluminously. Burt liked to listen to them talk. They talked adventurously, their words winding north into the Appalacha Mountains, and south down to Grek Mountain, and through the dark wendigo woods. These men traveled for a living, and they liked to recite the size, the possibility, and danger of their world in this fire-warmed room where every wooden edge was rounded and polished twice: once by the carpenter and twice by the passing of a thousand happy bodies. I guess you could say that it was actually one thousand and one shining and polishings.

That particular day, they boasted about their sales numbers for a few minutes and then got quiet. They glanced furtively at Sonny, planted in the corner. His face was buried deep in a bowl of stew. He had just returned from his circuit and everyone wanted to hear the news from the north. Burt guessed he had another eight bites of stew to eat, enough time.

He dodged into the kitchen, dropped his armload of plates with a clatter, ignored the beckoning fist of the cluriKin, and darted back into the main room.

Sonny wiped the back of his hand across his mouth and looked up into a room full of eyes turned toward him. He said, "What's wheat going for today?"

Someone shouted, "Half a dollar a bushel. Sonny, is the story in the paper true?"

Sonny said, "What about corn?"

Another voice shouted, "Sonny, you know the prices. We want to know the news!"

Sonny lifted up his bowl. "PorkChop, take this and tell your sister I want another bowl." Burt gathered the bowl and retreated behind a few tables.

Another voiced piped, "We want to hear about the fighting in the forest, Sonny."

Sonny said, "Isn't the custom to buy a drink for the man with news?"

Someone slapped two pennies on the counter, and Burt's dad hurried over with a pitcher and poured the dark frothy ale into Sonny's tankard. Sonny watched it fill. He took a long draught and sucked the suds out of his mustache and smiled at the bar.

Someone groaned.

He said, "I'll tell you, Regnans. It's as bad as the paper says. Worse, really. A merchant, guy I know, was taking a common load of wheat from Humberton through the North Road, and they beat him, stole his food, and sent him naked back out of the forest." His voice sounded from his black beard like a mighty stream out of the forest. His hands mimed the beating and stealing with vicious strokes.

Someone asked, "What was the Guard's reaction?"

Sonny said, "Reaction? Nothing! The Guard won't go in anymore. The last two squads that ventured in never came out. Ten Guards and a couple merchant wagons. Disappeared. Not a lot of people wondering what happened either. Those wendigo only need one arrow to kill you."

A voice called from a back table, "So those merchants and guards are all dead?"

Someone from the bar shouted, "You can bet they're wendigo food now."

Sonny continued, "That isn't the worst of it. Four Guard disappeared from the post. They found them the next day laying across North Road, right where it drops into the trees' shadow. Sunk into each body's chest was a wendigo arrow with their green leafed fletching waving like a flag."

Someone pronounced, "They're declaring war."

Another merchant volunteered, "The regnate marched out today."

"Yeah, but he's going south."

"The wendigo are acting up down there, too."

"Like we're surrounded."

Abierto said, "He should just cut down the whole forest."

Sonny said, "Cutting those woods is like stomping on a wasps' nest. You only get one stomp before they're all over you stinging."

"Wasps' stings don't kill. Wendigo arrows do."

"Not to mention, where does the forest end?"

A collective quiet came over them, as they thought of the vast darknesses that stretched around them on the new continent. Sonny said, "After all that I took the coastal road. Added two days to the trip, but at least I'm alive."

Someone asked, "I'm wondering how many of them are in those trees? If they are attacking Guard escorts, they may be ready for us. They may be planning a bigger attack."

Burt said, "Let them try!"

"Fearless PorkChop! Lead us onward!" They all shouted in laughter. Burt was not built like a warrior. He was build like a woodchuck, he moved like a woodchuck, sneaky and chunky. He looked over at his dad, who was the only one not laughing in the bar. His dad shot him a half smile and turned to fill another mug.

Shawnee's hard fingers ground the soft underside of his upper arm.

"Ouch!"

"Move, PorkChop. We're out of plates, and you're standing here talking like you were Rasheen."

Burt shuffled back into the kitchen, and pushed the plates under the hot soapy water in the large stone basin. The cluriKin Bera was standing on a tall stool, washing away, singing to itself. It beckoned excitedly for his handful of plates. He pushed them into the sudsy water.

CluriKin are not in our world, at least not that you can see. Burt paid him as much attention as you and I pay to the dining room table. CluriKin were less than half as tall as a man, but shaped something like one. They had two arms, two legs, and a square neckless head. They had hands like mittens. Their legs had no feet, but were round stumps like elephant legs.

Bera's mitten hands made the plates look enormous, but he leaned over them with his small body and managed to push them down in the suds and scrubbed them vigorously before passing them to Burt. Burt's dad and Shawnee were happy because coins were clinking into the strongBox. The merchants were happy because they had news and money, and the cluriKin reflected it all, humming as it scrubbed. It even smiled happily at him as Burt took up the cloth and began drying the stacks it had washed.

Burt tried to catch up on the drying, but in a second he was thinking about the great forest to the North, where the brave members of the Guard held back the encroaching green. He imagined how their eyes scouted the wendigo-infested forest. Soon Regnate Theodore Grant, WickBaron of Urba, would march into the darkness to punish the blood-loving creatures. At last a real war would be fought against the wendigo.

14

A smart smack to the back of his head reminded him of the dishes. The cluriKin was already scrambling off his stool and running out of the kitchen. He left a giant stack of clean dishes for Burt.

Burt dried them and then peeked into the dining room. The room looked slower, except for his dad and the cluriKin, who were both busy at the bar. His father delivered the drinks one in each hand, while the cluriKin carried one mug with both arms wrapped around it, waddling down atop the bar, and crouching from the knees to set down the mug, grinning like he was doing the greatest thing ever. Then he held out a mitten-hand for the two penny payment.

Shawnee moved through the tables, barking at the men, making sure they had what they wanted, dropping a smart smack to the hands of the guys who tried something. Everyone was occupied. Bera spied Burt as he grabbed his overcoat. It crouched to place a mug, freeing a mitten-shaped fist and shaking it at the escaping boy. Burt slipped out the side door.

He sucked in the cool air. He liked how SubAgora moved its noise from the markets to the shacks, houses, and inns in the evening. The outside was full of quiet possibility. They could fill it with their own shouts.

The stores that sold the work from far-away lands, grazzen metal work and Bugiri magics, had locked their oak doors. The potters, carpenters, and smiths had swept the shavings and clay globules out their shops, and placed the tools snug in their leather stirrups. The craftsmen had washed their hands and closed the shutters, and now, like old men sleeping, nestled into the night, the shops were quiet. The printing presses ceased the chugging of their heavy machines. The shop cluriKin had ducked their heads under chairs or pots and gone to sleep.

The idea that everything was safe and comfortable and in its place made Burt happy. He liked to imagine adventure, but he never fought in the block battles, and was the first to cry when someone accidently rapped his head in a game. He liked big bowls of stew, and extra blankets, and the thick stonewalls of his bedroom in the basement of the inn.

Burt stepped out into the alley that ran behind the inn and shops. The back of the alley went into a wall that surrounded a market space. Across from the inn there was a row of one-room houses. Beyond them rose the AltUrban wall that separated SubAgora from the upper districts. The wall rose up at an angle, towering over even the two story houses. Burt and his friends didn't see the wall; it had been there all their lives. They did not think about how thick and tall it was. They saw it the same way that a mole sees the sky, an inviolable barrier beyond which was a place they never dreamed of entering.

Occasionally Fels patrolled the top of the wall, watching for a ruff, one of Hands' acquaintances, trying to break the law and cross. It also had its cluriKin, small figures that scrambled magically out of crevasses and frowned down at passing Subs.

"PorkChop!" called Jalil. Burt's nickname was an apt one because 1) Burt was shaped somewhat like a pig and 2) he had a fondness for pork, chopped or not. Burt ignored it in hopes that it would go away, though, to be honest, his plan was unsuccessful. Subs generally believed that life was hard, and a funny nickname was good for you and definitely not the hardest fistSmack life would throw at you.

"Hey, Burt," said Shyheem. Shyheem was probably the only person who noted Burt's wince when the PorkChop name was used, and cared enough not to use it as a result.

Jalil said, "New coat?" He put out his hand and felt the dense clean wool, the closely sewn seams along the pockets.

"Yeah. Dad got it."

"Nice."

Jalil was a big kid, wide across the shoulders, with bulky arms that filled his shirt. He was coatless. He always said that he wasn't cold but Burt and Shyheem knew that he could not afford a coat.

Burt shared everything he had heard about the wendigo attacks.

Jalil had some information to add. On his way to the docks that morning he had seen the front of the column marching down Apia, the main road through the city. At the front of the column came the regnate's daughter atop a chase drawn by six white horses.

The driver was a captain of the Citan Fel, his epaulets a silver that matched his weapons. She was wrapped in a gown of white material that caught the sunlight, with a sash of purple. Perched atop her head was a silver band.

As she passed, the Subs averted their eyes. Jalil risked a short peek and saw that her face was okay but not exactly beautiful. It didn't help that Baroness Grant wore an expression of displeasure. He felt she should have been happy to lead out the brave men who risked their lives to protect them. Then he felt bad, because it was not his place as a brown Sub to criticize the daughter of the regnate. Ring respect was due.

The First Child, heir to the wick of Urba, known to her friends as Clarie, was not thinking about her dress. Unlike Jalil, the shimmering fabric was not new to her, and even if it was, she didn't think too much about dresses. She was thinking that it was unfair that she was given the opportunity to march the army to the city gates, only to have to march back to the White House and Citadel District, so that she could learn manners, and crochet, while her dad and his men marched to fight the baby eaters. Riding to the gates was festive, and it was glorious for those that the city thanked because they went and risked their lives to protect the people, but for her it was not glorious, because she was not going on the adventure and she was not risking anything but further boredom. That in itself might kill her.

Anyway, she could handle a sword and a thunderPipe. She tried to tell her dad that if she was going to head the house of Urba she should be fighting. The regnate had not listened to her, but instead lectured her on her duty to Regna and explained at length that none of this was about adventures. It was about responsibility. Her job was to wave at the troops and to look nice and remind them what they fought for. Duty first.

"Duty is booty," she whispered under her breath.

Let me return to the march. A squadron of Fels followed the First Child, strapped with their signature long swords and wearing their redcoats. They also carried different individual weapons. Some had bows. Others had spears, and most had various daggers. One or two carried thunderPipes. They all had the heavy gold tinted breastplates that the Fels wore to war.

Jalil had watched as the Guard officers, the captains and the priests followed. The Priests of Bellum wore their red cowls and many carried thunderPipes and the various powder packages that fired them strapped over their shoulders. The powerful ones had red aura circling them. The Illumenist priests wore black or navy. Their blue aura looked weaker, almost non-existent.

The main force of the Regna army, the Guard, followed in sky blue uniforms. They were many; their long spears parading by as even and endless as blades of grass. Some had swords, none had the expensive thunderPipes. Most were SubAgorans, dark skinned descendants of Bugiri. His brothers.

Some looked around at the girls and shops. They didn't want to leave the comfort of the SubAgora District, their home. Others looked at the ground, and these ones, Jalil thought, were thinking about the terrible wendigo, with their arrows and their ability to blend into the grass of the plain and leaves of the forest. These fearful ones wondered if they would have the courage to fight when the moment came. Would they march into the dark of the forest, where death was a silent as the flight of a bird? Other Guardsmen searched the horizon, already looking forward to the conflict that was coming, longing to meet the enemy. These were the brave faces. They reminded him of his dad.

Jalil told Burt, "You know I'd go if I could. We'd be the best soldiers in the whole Guard. I would chop them in half."

Bone thin Shyheem crouched in the black blanket he always wore. Actually it wasn't so much black as faded gray with enough stains to look like black. He wasn't messy, he just worked on the ground selling his baubles and he got hit by flying vegetables and the blowing dust. He also didn't have a washing machine, or the time to hand-wash his clothes. He listened to the boys' talk but did not join in. He had no interest in fighting himself, but Lamp Kareem had told him he should know what was happening in the world. Then he would know for whom and what to pray. All the people who went near the forests needed protection. It was his job to pray that the god of the weak would protect his people from the forces of darkness.

The kitchen door of the inn sprang open. Burt got up but it was too late to hide. It was Shawnee carrying a couple of bowls of stew, topped with massive hunks of black bread. She said, "Relax, PorkChop." The two other boys' eyes bulged toward the food. Burt reached for one of the bowls. She slapped his hand away, while balancing the food in the other hand.

"Like you need more food."

She handed one bowl to Shyheem and the other to Jalil. Jalil took a long look at how Shawnee's hipline popped against her wool dress, and lifted the bowl to his face. Shawnee watched Jalil shovel the pub fare into the mill of his teeth with the slab of bread. When he slowed down, she said, "I saw you walking to work today."

He looked at her, unsure how to respond. Fortunately, his mouth was full, so grunting was his only option.

She said, "Did you fight today?"

He grunted through the bread, "Yes." A bit of food flew out of his mouth. He looked at her eyes. Did she notice?

She said, "Did you win?"

Jalil nodded. "Oo ime!"

"What?"

Shyheem explained, "He won two dimes."

"Is that how you got that mark?" She bent down and ran a cool finger along his eyebrow, where the skin was darker.

Jalil nodded.

"Dollar," she said, impressed. "PorkChop's afraid to box. He's afraid of dishes."

Burt said, "You're a merd face."

Jalil reached over and pushed Burt to show his disagreement. In Jalil's opinion Shawnee was not a merd face. She had coffee-colored skin and fresh full features that had a frustrating effect on his ability to talk. He felt that the meaning of his push might be

19

unclear so he tried to say, "She looks good." Through the beef and potatoes it came out more like, "EE ooks oood."

"Good luck planning the war," she said, "I have to get back to work."

This made Jalil feel like a kid and he remembered, as he watched her turn and sashay inside, that he was two years younger than her. He wondered what she would have looked like in the white and purple that the First Child wore that day. Of course no brown-skinned kaSub would ever be able to afford such clothes. It was wrong to think it, a Sub wearing those clothes. She would have looked dollar. Brown baroness of beauty.

Shyheem said, "You shouldn't go in there." Shyheem was talking about the Hall of Bellum where Jalil had won two dimes that afternoon. The Bellumites preached that Bellum elevated those that gained their own strength, and mocked Illumen as the little brother god, the god of the weak. They had fighting in the halls. Jalil was good at fighting.

Jalil said, "Relax, Shyheem, I'm not joining. I'm just trying to get a couple extra silver."

Shyheem said, "Be careful. The path of Bellum is darkness."

The boys finished the stew and began an imagined campaign against the wendigo. They marshaled vast cavalries of Fels, and legions of Guard archers to chop down all the forests. Then they cut down the baby eaters outside the shelter of the dark trees, where they loved to hide and ambush and kill. Jalil was the general, leading a cheering vanguard. PorkChop was the master cook, and Shyheem the spiritual guide and comfort for the soldiers.

"They'd just kill you like they killed your father."

The three boys turned and saw a narrow figure standing at the corner poking his head into the alley.

"It's Hands."

"Oh, no," Burt whispered.

Hands eased out from behind the corner of the inn, and started walking toward them. He eyed the bowls. "Give me some," he said.

Jalil said, "Maybe, if you take that back."

"Take back what?"

"What you said about my dad."

"It's true, right? Your dad thought he could fight them, and they killed him?"

Jalil said, "Don't talk about my dad."

Hands said, "Don't pretend that they wouldn't kill you the same way they killed him."

Jalil stood up. He charged, but Hands dodged to the side. Their fists were up as they circled one another.

Jalil said, "Come on, Hands. You going to fight or run in lulu circles all night?"

As he spoke Hands found his moment and dived forward. He liked to grab heels and use his shoulder as a fulcrum against the shin. Jalil was fast too, dropping on the flying body below him, cinching his big arms in a ring around Hand's torso and arms. The two fell to the dust. Jalil squeezed all the air out of Hands. Hands squeaked, "Loosen up!"

Jalil loosened one hand enough to cock it back and send a punch into Hands' ribs. He did this again and again. He punctuated each punch with a word. "DON'T. TALK. ABOUT. MY. DAD."

Shyheem said, "Why do you need food? You stole that farmer's purse."

Hands normally would have cussed Shyheem out for that question before explaining his bad luck. Hands couldn't though, because Jalil had squeezed out all his breath. He was frowning like someone having a hard time in the bathroom. Then he ducked his chin and tried to bite Jalil's arm, but he couldn't reach. He looked like a chained grolf with his chomping. Jalil squeezed tighter and a sound like a bladder being squeezed erupted from Hands' lips. Then Hands twisted a bit, and reached down with his fingers, and grabbed Jalil in the groin, pinching his man parts. With a gasp Jalil released his grip and balled up, his hands plunged down to shield himself.

Hands hopped up, gulping a big breath. A smile twitched at the corners of his thin lips. He kicked Jalil in the butt. "Not so big and tough there, are you?"

Burt stood up. "You cheated!"

21

He began to chase Hands, but he only got his big frame moving by the time Hands was dancing around the corner. Breathing heavily, Burt walked back to the prostrate form of Jalil.

"You okay?"

"I'll be okay when I get that graz." He pulled himself into a sitting position.

Burt said, "You won. He cheated."

Shyheem said, "A Bellumite."

Jalil nodded.

Burt added, "He always cheats when he's about to lose."

Jalil grunted, "He always loses."

All three laughed for a moment. They tried to play Guards and wendigo. The Guard was armed with a big stick; the wendigo had makeshift bow and arrows. The Guard charged, and the wendigo hid among the rubbish and shot him. If they hit him, they won, and if not, he pounced and smacked their backs with his big stick. They got bored because there was no one else to play and Jalil refused to be wendigo. They went back to the ledge behind the inn and started talking about the war until Jalil had yawned a few times.

At that moment Hands ran back into the alley. He was not running at the dancing pace with which he had taunted Burt. His head was stretched forward, his body almost sideways as his hardscrabble feet pushed against the cobblestones, and behind him came the clatter of hooves. In his right hand he was holding a sword that caught and splintered the evening light.

"Run, subs, run," he called as he passed them. They heard the clatter of horseshoes. Instinct jumpStarted Jalil and Burt, and they took off after him chased by unknown killers.

3. Run for Your Lives

I will leave our heroes running for their lives, and tell you about the situation in Citadel District.

"Our heroes?" you are saying. "All they've done so far is argue."

Perhaps I am overstating their virtues and accomplishments by calling them heroes. They wanted to be heroes though, so maybe I'm just being polite.

The First Child was something like a princess, though not quite. She was very important, but she would not become regnate if her father died. The vice regnate would take the position until the Eight Houses could elect a new leader. Yet, as daughter to the regnate, she had a lot of appearances to make and dresses to wear, especially for the last three days as her dad prepared to lead the army. She would have the position of WickBaroness, if her father died, which was important and powerful in itself.

When night fell, her governess told her to get to bed, with the injunction not to read for more than one hour. "Beauty is the primary responsibility of an alta, Clarie, and sleep is the first requirement of beauty." Clarie was her name when she wasn't being called First Child, and it was the name she preferred. When people called her First Child they made her act properly.

She hung her dress and put on a thick wool shirt and trousers, put out the lamp, and snuck back to the door. She eased out of it and leapt past the governess' open door and ran down the stairs and through a few colonnades to the Hall of Bellum in the back of the First House. It was a large room, with no fire going and a few lamps. In it were some soldiers and WickBaron Vermont. At least that was what her governess wanted her to call him. To her he was Verms.

This was the room were soldiers and Citans practiced their skills, taking turns with wooden sword fighting. She ran down and claimed her turn in the order.

WickBaron Vermont, a tall young man with facial planes as flat and strong as a grazzen sword, said, "Clarie, we should talk." He took her a few paces away from the others. "Governess Carnegie says you are spending too much time here, that you have already surpassed the necessary training and shouldn't be here at all!"

Clarie snorted. She said, "Look, Verms." The young Citan winced at the familiarity. "I've been to boring dinners and dumb marches for the past three days. I need to just smack somebody or get smacked."

Verms said, "Listen. We have duties. I wanted to march with the Regnate, but here I am. Your dad wanted me here. Your duty is to become a lady."

Clarie snorted and said, "Duty. I did my duty, but this is my free time. Alta Carnegie said free time. This is how I unwind."

WickBaron Vermont considered sending her back to her room, but he felt genuine sympathy for her, and it was her free time.

"Okay."

Clarie knew there would be consequences but she didn't care. She only sparred with WickBaron Vermont because the non-Citan soldiers would be afraid to hit her, and they let her win which was lame. She whacked and dodged until Verms got bored. Once he got bored he went into assassin mode, disarming her with two or three twists of his wooden sword, and after her practice weapon clattered to the ground the tenth time in a row, he told her, "Enough."

She whined but only for a second. Verms was doing her a favor, and her dad had taught her that gratitude was an essential virtue. She ran off to her bedroom, her limbs aching and tired, finally able to rest.

Of course she was not aware that men were planning her father's death two districts away. She might not have slept so soundly.

Back to our not-yet-heroes. Burt and Jalil started running before they even thought. It was a short block to the dead end in the alley, but the sound of hooves was close. Burt knew that they would not catch Jalil who was already in front of Hands, his kiCalves pumping hard with each step. He was the slow one. He was PorkChop.

He reached the market wall, imagining an arrow or spearhead transfixing him before he got over. He knew the handholds from practice, and scaled it quickly. The wall was a great way to escape from Fels on horseback. On the top of the wall he caught a peek before dropping to the other side. He saw three horsemen, ajangle with metal weaponry, reining in their horses as they pulled up to the wall. He recognized the red drapes on their horses, their red waistcoats, and the precise engravings on their steel breastplates. They were Citan Fels. One leapt off his horse and onto the wall.

"Merd!"

Burt dropped off the wall and ran, following Hands, who was way in front, carrying the improbable sword. By the time the horsemen scaled the wall, the three boys were out of sight, winding their way through the SubAgora until they reached the docks. Jalil stopped at the end of a dock huffing. Hands was a little ways behind him, and he collapsed onto the wood, before Burt walked up, wheezing and gasping great gulps of breath.

Cool breeze lifted up off the river, and the water lapped against the columns of the docks. The silence helped the boys relax after their frenzied escape from the soldiers. It was not long before a quiet figure walked onto the dock and joined them. It was Shyheem. He told them he had gone unseen, draped in his dusty black, as the riders charged by and up to the wall, and then along it, looking for a way after the boys. Then they gave up and rode out of the alley.

Burt asked Hands, "What happened?"

"You'll never believe this merd." Hands picked at the wood of the dock with the tip of the sword. The wood peeled up like butter before the quadruple forged steel.

"Yeah?"

He said, "I'm sitting there, on the Way, talking to Jalil's mom."

Jalil shouted, "Shut your chinging face!"

Burt put up a hand and said, "Stop it, I want to hear this."

Jalil sat back, saying, "At least I have a mom."

Hands said, "Better to have none than yours."

Jalil punched out, but Hands held up the sword.

Shyheem shook his head. Burt said, "Just stop. Hands, tell the story."

Hands explained that had been walking on Black Way, looking for a drunk in the gutter whose pockets he could plunder. The sound of a horse galloping interrupted his thoughts. He plunged between two barrels and watched. The drum roll of hoof beats changed to a clippety clop as the horse slowed. The horse skin shone with a sweaty sheen reflecting the light that seeped out of the inn windows. The rider was a Fel, wearing the traditional red coat and grazzen-forged armor. However, he wasn't a market-watching Fel. Strapped to his back were bow and arrow, and a long spear, and he wore a gold epaulet on his left shoulder.

"Citan," Jalil said.

The others nodded.

Hands explained what the Fel had said about a plot to kill the regnate.

Burt said, "A plot to kill the regnate in the Fels? That can't be."

Jalil said, "Hands probably made it up. Hoping he'd make some friends."

Hands said, "I'm telling you, they killed that guy, and they probably want to kill us, too. Anyway, how else to explain the fact that the other Citan Fels killed him?"

Burt said, "So you saw a Fel murdered by Fels on Black Way?"

Hands said, "I didn't see him murdered. In fact, he didn't tell me that they murdered him. He told me that they were going to kill the regnate, some guy named Mic or something, that they were going to kill me, and it was obvious that someone had killed him. I figured it didn't take a watchmaker to figure out that it was probably the same guys."

The story made their minds run like the potter's wheel. Regnate Theodore Grant, WickBaron of Urba, was loved by his subjects. He defended the city and the surrounding country from the attacks of the wendigo. If someone was plotting to kill him, that person needed to be stopped. However, they doubted the story's source.

Jalil said, "Those guys were Citan Fels. If you want to get into their unit, you have to go into the mountains and kill a grolf with just a spear and bring back the horns. In battle they die first."

Hands said, "Maybe your dad was one. He had the dying first part down."

Jalil didn't take the bait; he was too interested in the discussion.

Burt said, "I thought the Fels were supposed to guard the regnate."

Jalil said, "Which goes back to the point that he could be lying."

Hands shrugged,

Burt said, "Yeah, the Fels have to pledge, 'My life for Regna and its regnate.'"

Hands said, "People lie all the time. Fel Antony don't give a merd about no regnate. All he wants is chinging food. Same as you PorkChop. I saw them. They were obviously the same guys who killed the other guy. They had all that red cloth and shiny armor." He waved the sword in front of his face. It was inlaid with intricate runes.

"You're probably lying. You probably just threw a rock at them."

"How did I get the sword then?"

"Maybe you stole it. That would explain why they chased you."

Hands laughed, "You think I'm going to steal a sword from a Fel?"

Burt said, "If they were dead you would."

Hands said, "Exactly."

He held up the blade so that it caught the moonlight. There was a picture of five soldiers, each armed with a sword, a spear, and a bow and arrow in a ring around a larger figure sitting on a great throne wearing a crown. They all looked proud and strong. Along the length of the blade were runes. The metal of the blade was mottled with rivulets of darker and lighter metal. Burt, who had seen blades and heard them discussed during the long nights in the inn, knew this was better than anything that had ever come into his father's inn.

Jalil said, "Let me hold it."

Hands dropped the blade so that it pointed at Jalil.

"You want it," he said, making the question into a threat. There was no way for Jalil to take it without putting his hand on the blade, and he didn't want to do that with Hands holding the handle. Hands would love the chance to slice his hand.

Jalil said, "I just want to hold it."

Hands smiled wickedly.

Burt said, "At least let Shyheem read it."

Hands shook his head. He didn't care what stupid stuff the writing said about honoring the regnate. He was calculating how many dollars he would get for the sword. He estimated it was worth about ten, which was more money than he had ever dreamed of having. He thought about the steak and bread he would eat, the new clothes he would buy, the nice room he would rent.

"Why did you tell us to run with you?"

Hands shrugged.

Shyheem said, "I just sat there quietly, and they didn't even see me. Didn't ask me any questions. I was praying the whole time."

Jalil said, "You're so small they wouldn't see you."

Burt said, "That robe's so dusty it fits right in with the alleyway."

Shyheem said, "Now you guys are on the run. I'm not. You should never listen to a Bellumite."

Jalil and Burt were annoyed that they had run, and also that they had been told to run. What if they'd been shot with an arrow? They reminded themselves never to listen to Hands again. Burt said, "We can't understand all this, but we have to warn the regnate."

Hands laughed. "Yeah, we'll walk right up through AltUrba into Citadel, and then into the White House. 'Uh, tell the regnate that four of his loyal subjects are here. We have an important message we need to deliver to his face.' Even if we could get that far, they would just whip us, and then toss us back out."

Jalil remembered what his father had taught him about serving the regnate. He said, "He's our regnate. If it's true we have to tell him."

Hands said, "What do we care who's regnate?"

Burt said, "He's Regnate Theodore Grant."

Hands said, "I'll see you lulus tomorrow. I've got a sword to sell." He stood up. Jalil stood up to stop him but Hands swung the sword and Jalil stopped. Hands walked down the dock toward land.

Jalil said, "He can't sell that. It's the sword of the Fels!"

Hands kept walking. The three remaining kids watched him grow small. Across the river atop a high shale wall, the golden windows of the AltUrba District mansions glowed. Far above that, enclosed in an even higher wall rose the spires of Citadel District, where the barons governed.

Burt said, "We need to find someone important, who can go talk to the regnate."

Jalil said, "Maybe we're worrying about nothing. He's probably lying. Maybe he stole it."

They made their way back to Black Way. They discussed their world, the SubAgora's biggest merchants, but none of them was important enough to go and demand an audience with the regnate. When they reached the wall that encircled the market they all stopped.

Lying naked on the ground was a man. He was light-skinned and not a Sub. His face was turned away from them, and one hand splayed toward them at an unnatural angle. The other arm was pinned under the pale flesh. It looked as though he had been thrown over the wall and landed like that. Three arrows holes, with the shafts broken off close to the body, stared at the boys from his back.

Burt and Jalil looked at the body in fear, but Shyheem walked around him and looked into the empty eyes of the man. He remembered the look of endless nothing in the eyes of his dead mother. When she was buried the lamp had read the Writ, "Death is the old enemy of the light god, but the light is not overcome."

Shyheem said, "This man is dead."

Jalil said, "I guess Hands wasn't lying."

Burt, moving away from the body toward the wall, said, "Nope. First time he missed a chance."

Jalil said, "This was the first time the real story was good enough not to need it."

They scaled the wall slowly, peeking to make sure no one was waiting for them in the alley. It was empty, and they plopped down off the wall. They said goodnight and went toward their different beds thinking they would have a think before going to sleep. It was exciting, if scary, to have such an important message.

―――――――――

The WickBaron of Segunda, Vice Regnate of the Country, John Nickson explained it again. People were stupid and needed things said many times. Even these two, whom he had personally selected for their strength and intelligence, needed repetition.

"Wait for my sparrow. Then you seize her and take her to the mansion in Segundaton. Until you hear from me keep track of her. Don't let her out of your sight. Use your subordinates and keep a detail active."

They nodded.

"Say it back."

Fel Sparks said it back to him, avoiding him with his eyes.

"Fel Sparks."

"Yes, sir."

"Are you a lulu?"

"No."

"Then look me in the eye."

Fel Sparks looked at him. His chin wavered, but he had pride. His eyes held a smidgeon of insolence in the middle of the fear.

Nickson laughed. "Better," he said. "You mess it up, I'll kill you." This last part he almost whispered. He didn't flex or go into details about how. It wasn't necessary.

They were in a SubAgora inn, one of the large ones off Apia, and he had dressed like a Fel to match them and make the meeting seem like nothing more than a common drinking night for the soldiers. He flicked the collar up with a single movement, and watched the surging pulses course through the veins of his forearms.

Nickson was not a vain man, but he was proud. His pride emanated from his strength. Not just physical strength, which took hard work in itself, but mental strength, which took pain. His pride didn't show as arrogance. Other men did not see in him a peacock, or even an eagle, which holds itself aloft. They saw in him the grace of a killing animal, a four footed predator that is natural and powerful in its own body because killing is its purpose.

He sensed that the other two wanted him to leave. They wanted to talk about women and drink. They might want to talk about him, but they feared to even touch their drinks with him present. He sensed a disturbance, and looked up.

A Fel came into the inn. Golden epaulets and buttons. A Citan. And his eye fell upon them and he advanced. Nickson would likely be known to him as the vice regnate, and this meeting, John's outfit, would be strange. Perhaps he was a friend.

Nickson tried to reach out with his mind and eye and know who it was. Albert Town. No one was more loyal to the regnate than Albert. What were the chances of Albert showing up in this inn? It was terrible luck, but one that Nickson believed, more deeply than anything, is that you make your own luck. If someone saw you doing something, you made him or her forget it. And if, like Albert Town, they would refuse, you stopped them from remembering.

Nickson hissed at Sparks and the other. "Town is here."

They were smart enough to know. They got up as one and ran for the stables. Nickson himself pushed through the bodies, sending men flying, but Town had already seen the group, the Fels with the WickBaron, meeting in SubAgora, and he knew. He was running. Nickson pushed by a few more men and vaulted a table and slammed through the swinging door.

Town was on a horse, already untethered. Nickson unsheathed his bow, and he fitted an arrow. He waited for a shot, among the late night wagons trundling out and in, but the man had lashed his horse into a gallop and merged into the traffic.

In a moment he heard the clatter as Sparks brought up the horses, and Nickson leapt upon his beast, a sleek Opuland-bred black, and slammed his heels down. The thing plunged forward, through the heavy traffic, causing mayhem and curses. He still held the bow. His shoulders shook with the pulses, the red fire, the mark of the older brother god who gives nothing. Bellum helps those that help themselves.

A veering wagon turned Town off Apia onto a circling road, and the coast was clear for his shot. It was a length of a quarter of a mile, a shot few would attempt and almost none would make. Others in this situation might consider what they had risked. They might have thought that Town's escape would mean their death, but Nickson knew what he could do. He stood in the stirrup. His arm spasmed again with the red surge when he drew the arrow back and released. The arrow itself was wreathed in the aura as it sped up, dropped down and pierced the man.

Town turned his horse, already sagging and slowing. Sparks and his little lieutenant galloped by Nickson, unleashing their own arrows. He slowed to a walk, letting them do their work. He knew that Town was dying. His shot had severed the spine. When he walked his horse up Sparks was chasing a brown who had got hold of Town's sword. He climbed the wall and chased them for a bit, but they lost him in the thousand little alleys that wended between the tens of thousands of little shacks.

Sparks said, "What if he told the Sub?"

Nickson shrugged, as if to say, "Who cares?"

Still it felt unfinished to him. Attention to detail was a form of discipline. He motioned to the two Fels and they went to the corner inn.

They tethered their horses, doffed their tricorns, and stepped into the noisy Abierto Inn. When they came in, the loud bar went silent. Nickson knew some of the merchants were silent because they respected the Fel, and that the rest of the merchants didn't follow all of the rules of Regna in regard to trading, and they were silent because they feared the law.

Nickson led the others to the bar, and said, "What's your finest, innkeeper?"

A chunky brown waddled along behind the bar, filling three pints with dark ale, placing them one by one on the bar with a small thonk. Nickson smiled and said, "Hey, we were coming up the alley here, and a couple of kids said something about the regnate, something I can't repeat, and then jumped the wall. I know you all won't stand for it, and I know we can't. Anybody know where we could find those kids?"

A murmur jumped up from the merchants in the inn. The innkeeper said, "Oh, that would be Hands. He's got no respect for anything."

The Fel nodded. "Okay. But there were three."

The people in the inn were quiet. They were thinking that the other two boys would be Jalil and Burt. Jalil was well liked on the street. He was always available to help move a merchant's wares. He worked hard and was respectful. Burt was the son of the innkeeper; he'd served them all. If it was just Fel Antony asking, they'd have said, "We don't know." The Citan Fels, however, were great warriors. The leader pulsed with Bellumite aura and had an eye that cut like grazzen steel.

The innkeeper finally spoke, "Well, there are a couple other kids, but they wouldn't curse the regnate."

Someone said, "Jalil lost his father at the Ornata border. He's a good kid."

The innkeeper said, "The other one is mine. Burt. He would never curse the regnate."

Nickson could see they would fight for the boys. He didn't feel like killing an inn full of browns, so he placated them. "What was said was a serious offense, and we'll need the witnesses. You all can help us find them; we'll take them up to the guardhouse at the AltUrba gate. Have the good ones, this Burt and Jalil, in there for only a couple of hours, but we'll keep the treasonous one for a couple of years."

The inn laughed. The cluriKin raised a fist in triumph. Most of the locals had lost something, money or goods, to Hands. They wouldn't mind missing him.

———————

When Burt stepped through the door of the inn, a hand gripped him from behind. He looked around and saw an etched breastplate gleaming between the lapels of a redcoat. He remembered the body lying in the market ground. His stomach did a flip and melted to jelly.

The Fel said, "I have a few questions for you, Burt. Your father will be waiting for you."

The hand on his shoulder steered him out the door and lifted him onto the back of the horse. His mind told him that he was going to jail or worse. He should say something to his father. As he opened his mouth, ready to shout all he knew, the Fel spoke quietly, "If you say anything to these people, I will kill them all."

Burt shut his mouth. He was too scared to talk. His dad, watching at the door of the inn, thought that this might be good for his son. He would learn about the Fels. Maybe he would stop spending time with that dirty pickpocket who plagued the street. One of these days the merchants would beat it out of that Sub. He didn't see the Fel whisper to his son. The look of fear on his son's face seemed like a normal response for a kid getting taken in by the Fels.

Meanwhile Jalil was stepping through the curtain into the one room house he shared with his mom, two blocks down, right off Black Way. He was imagining that tonight his mom had made some food for him. He always imagined this, and it never happened, but he liked the idea anyway and pictured a fried fish. When he came into the room, he saw that the table was bare. He saw his mother talking to a man.

It was dark in the room, and he walked over. He didn't like his mom talking with men but she didn't care. Then the breastplate glinted. This was one of the Fels! Without thinking he struck out, sending his right fist into the jaw of the Fel. His fist didn't even connect. The soldier caught his arm, and a moment later he was in the man's lap. Strong arms tied him up in heavy rope. The man laughed grimly.

"Not a bad try for a grazzen Sub. We should have you join up. I heard your father was a Guard."

His mother said, "You teach him respect, sir."

34

Jalil wished that she knew that he would never hit one of the regnate's soldiers unless there was something truly wrong happening. Didn't every merchant in the market know that he had respect? But his mom didn't see that.

The man remarked as he knotted the rope around the struggling boy, "Big penalties for hitting a Fel."

Jalil shouted, "What about killing a Fel?"

An elbow into his head sent a spray of stars through his brain that settled down into searing pain.

His mom said "Jalil! Threats to an officer of the regnate?"

The Fel heaved the boy atop one shoulder and carried him out. His mother called out something about having food for the soldier when he got back. As he tied the bundle that was Jalil onto the saddle, the man spoke to him.

"Friendly woman, that mother of yours. I gave her a dime and she said I could wait for you. She wanted me to give her another dime, but honestly, I wasn't interested." Jalil renewed his struggle, wanting just one more chance to fistSlap the man, but the ropes that bound him were too tight.

───────────

Meanwhile, Hands was settling into his kaShack. He lay on a board he had pulled from one of the booths in the night. It held him off the ground so that the rats that ran across the floor went under, and not over him. The cluriKin Shackin, only as tall as his knee, ran up and jumped into his lap. Hand pushed it off and it fell to the ground with a thud, squeaking. It got back up and thumped him in the groin with two hands, and he backhanded it into the ground. It landed like a gray sack and started to keen a sad high note. Hands tried to sleep, but the crying was disturbing him, so he reached over and pulled the cluriKin into his arms and gently cradled it until its high pitched keening stopped, and it burbled in his arms.

He had hidden the sword. He imagined how he would sell the sword. It was important to go to the right merchant, because the sword was stolen. Some merchants would pretend to deal with him, while calling the Fels. He wanted a merchant who was happy for the chance at a quality weapon, who was used to dealing with thieves. He knew a few guys like that down in Dark Docks. After he sold it, he would buy food for Jalil, Burt, and Shy, and he would be their favorite person. His daydream was interrupted by a heavy hand that dragged him upright.

"Where is the sword?" He was spun around to face a Fel, a young man with clear blue eyes and a jaw hard angled as a rock.

"A sword?"

"The sword."

"I wish I had a sword. Then I could be like Rasheen."

The man slapped him. "Ouch," he said.

"You wouldn't do that to Rasheen."

The man took his small arm between his two hands and twisted until Hands cried out. "Okay, okay."

He took the man to the corner of the shack, reached up under the straw thatch of the roof, and pulled the sword out from among the hay.

"See you later," he said, and began to walk away, but the heavy hand was still on his shoulder, digging in to him. He was picked up and tied to the horse's rump. A moment later and the horse was jostling him.

He said, "Last time I give you anything."

The Fel boxed his head without looking at him. A moment later and Burt was thrown on there with him. Another Fel said to the others, "Remember my words."

Then he left.

The other horse had a boy shaped lump slung over its rump. Jalil. Served him right, thought Hands. He twisted but found he was lashed to the saddle. A slap across the back of his head pounded his ears. "Don't struggle."

Hands had learned from experience that life was a merdy thing, and it didn't take much for him to figure out where this all was going. They were going to die. That stupid dead man never should have told him all that stuff.

36

Nickson rode out of the city. He asked himself whether there was greater pleasure in killing a man with an impossible shot, or fooling an inn full of Subs. He answered himself, "Both are small accomplishments. However, they are part of a great one." He looked forward to riding all night. If nothing else it would test his endurance. If he was lucky stupid bandits would attack him.

4. New Roads

Fly with me up out of the city. We glide below the stars and over a forest, brushing the leaves on the hilltops; they seem to reach out and try and snag us from the air, they whisper threats. We intrude on a quiet place, arriving at the biggest tree. We drop down through the branches. The tree remembers everything. Just a short time ago, in this very place, secret words were spoken.

Two figures sat at the base of its trunk. One was a big man, and the other was man-shaped and old, his voice whushing like wind in the leaves.

The big man said, "These are the promises of Illumen. I have to believe them."

The old one asked, "You assert that this Regnan manusignis would defend my people?"

"They fight on the side of the weak."

"My people are not weak. Nor are they human, LightTalker. There are those of your god that say this makes them not worthy."

"Even if you don't believe me, you have to believe the history. They always show up at times like this."

"I know your stories."

"They're history."

"Your history."

"Give it a try. You owe me that much."

The old man nodded his head, "If you bring one to HighSeat, I will see what I can manage with the sachems."

––––––––––––

Shyheem returned to the shack where he always slept across from Hands. The only roof that remained was in the corners. When he tried to speak to Hands about the god of the weak, he received wordSmacks.

"How come Illumen lets you live in a shack with me? If he cared about you you'd be in some AltUrban mansion eating meat."

Shyheem said, "That is not the way of Illumen."

"Illumen really helped Lamp Kareem, haha. Ching your weak god."

"God of the weak."

"Same thing."

Hands wasn't worth the words so Shyheem wasn't worried when he reached the shack that night, and he saw the pickpocket being pulled out, pinched, and pushed by the tall Fel. Shyheem ducked his small form into the shadows. Shyheem watched the Fel tie the boy to his horse. The Fel jumped into the saddle and trotted down to the corner where he met up with two other Fels. Shyheem saw that it wasn't just Hands who was caught up in this. There were two more lumps at the back of the horses, Jalil and Burt. He whispered, "Help them, Illumen."

He scampered after them keeping under the eaves of the roofs and among the used trash barrels. He saw a Fel bring a fist down on one of the lumps. He prayed that Illumen would free them. He had to speed up to keep up with the horses, and his breath came quick and hard.

Shyheem was a true follower of Illumen. He repeated the lessons he learned until he knew them by heart, and he prayed all morning. Illumen heard his prayers because Shyheem's baubles were full of light, the brightest on Black Way. Somehow, now that he had prayed the god was there, and he was working.

The houses grew taller as the horses moved down Black Way. They were in the neighborhood where the AltUrba servants lived in two story houses. Fat and happy cluriKin sat on the lawns out front, frowning at Shyheem as he snuck by. Some shook their hands at him, sure he was up to no good.

The horsemen reached the AltUrban gate, an arch wide enough for three wagons that opened into a tunnel through the stonewall. Two of the stern-faced stone-bodied wall cluriKin stood atop it. Their arms were crossed, and they watched everything. The Citan Fels barked a few words to the Fels stationed at the gate and passed through.

Shyheem took a deep breath and walked toward the gate. He saw the Fels looking him up and down under the flickering torchlight. His black blanket and shoddy pants, not to mention his brown skin, weren't going to get him through, unless he had a good story. When he got close, one of them shouted to him.

"Where you think you're going, Sub?"

"Hello, sir. I'm a wick needed for prayer at the bedside of a dying woman."

"Oh yeah?"

"Yes, sir."

"What's her name?" Shyheem paused. The clip clop of hooves against cobble was fading into the tunnel. "What street's she on?"

Shyheem began to speak but was interrupted. "Sub, I don't want anymore lies. Say another word and I'll slap you all the way down to the docks."

The man made a threatening step, so Shyheem retreated out of the square, ducking behind a barrel, and watched. He could still see the horses trotting beyond the gate, into the streets of the upper district.

"Oh, Illumen," he whispered. The god seemed to have failed him for a moment, the moment when he most wished for the fire of justice to fall upon the evil men who had taken his friends. If they killed one of their own in Black Way, what would they do to his friends in AltUrba?

"Illumen, god of the weak, best son of all-father Theom, burn away darkness with light." The Fels at the gates still stood there, and the faint sound of hooves on cobbles still echoed out of the tunnel. Nothing good was happening, and there was nothing he could do.

He sat there for a minute, feeling powerless and abandoned, when he felt a tingling in his hands. He looked down at them, flexing them, but the tingling grew. His hands became hot. They started to glow then, and if he'd be in the habit of swearing, he would have. As it was, he said, "Illumen!"

The glow grew, an eerie blue. The clay surface of the road and the barrel he was behind lit up. He worried that the Fels at the gate would see him, and he buried his glowing hands under his shirt. At first he put them against his belly, but they grew hot and hurt his skin, so he held them under his shirt but away from his body. The tingling had grown into a painful burn bringing tears into his eyes.

What was going on? Was something wrong with him? In all he had learned about the giftings of all the gods, he had never heard of blue hands. And while his hands burned his friends were being dragged off into the higher districts by murderers.

He felt a surge of pain, and then it dropped off. In a short minute the strange feeling had faded and left his hands. He pulled them out of his tunic slowly. They looked like normal, brown hands. He could no longer hear the hoof beats of the Citan Fels.

Shyheem needed help, and he knew only one adult, Lamp Kareem.

When Lamp Kareem talked about Illumen, his old eyes lit up, and his voice trembled. The years had cut black ravines through his face. He still tried to help people with heavy jobs whenever he could, and they said that Illumen allowed him to keep his strength into his old age because he loved the god so much. He listened to the Subs when they had problems, and would feed any Sub who needed it when he had food.

Shyheem figured if anyone would or could help him, it was Lamp Kareem. He ran back past the two-stories down through the shacks to the temple on Black Way.

There was a man sitting on the steps of the Hall of Bellum next door. He grinned at Shyheem. "Hey, kid, still holding out for the Big Light?"

Shyheem had enough problems without listening to the jokes from the Bellumite, so he kept running. The Bellumite reached into the bag around his waist and pulled out a spark of red fire.

The Bellumite flicked a drop of fire at Shyheem. Shyheem dodged between the square pillars into the quiet of the temple. The lamp was still awake and praying for his people. Their life was full of hardship. The temple cluriKin kneeled by him, emphatically closing its eyes, and humming along with his prayers.

The lamp's prayers were interrupted by the gasping breath of the wick. The kid was shaking and wide-eyed. He dropped a second blanket over the boy's shoulders and sat him down while the cluriKin danced between the sleeping figures spread around the fire, and hung the clay kettle over the fire. The cluriKin went over and sat by Shyheem, rubbing his shins. When the tea was ready, the lamp asked Shyheem what was bothering him.

Shyheem said, "My friends, they're going to kill them!"

Lamp Kareem said, "I'm going to need more."

"They discovered that Fels did a murder, and then the Fels grabbed them, and they took them into AltUrba. Come on, we have to stop them."

"Fels that have gone into AltUrba?"

Shyheem nodded.

Lamp Kareem shook his head, "Shyheem, I can no more pass that gate than you, and what would I do against Fels with murder on their minds?"

This was a shock to Shyheem. He thought that the lamp, by virtue of his service to the god, was allowed into AltUrba District. Now it looked like his friends were going to die.

Lamp Kareem said, "Take a deep breath. Tell me the whole story."

Shyheem told all about Hands' story, his friends abduction, and his glowing hands at the AltUrban gate. It took a while to tell, and the lamp listened patiently. He continued nodding his head when the story was done.

He asked, "What color were your hands when they glowed?"

"Blue, Lamp Kareem."

The lamp nodded. "How did it feel?"

"I was crying because it hurt so much."

"What were you thinking when that happened?

"I wanted Illumen to do something because they were taking my friends. I prayed, but it didn't help," Shyheem said.

The lamp nodded. He refilled the wick's cup with more of the clippings tea and this time dropped in a precious chunk of sugar. The cluriKin continued to warm his feet.

"Thank you," said Shyheem.

The lamp put a plate of bread in front of the child. He said, "Eat up. You're looking thin."

Shyheem said, "How can we save my friends?"

Lamp Kareem found this difficult to answer. He believed Illumen cared about Shyheem's friends, but he could not be sure that the god would save them. Perhaps they would die. He said, "I don't know." That uncertainty hung there for a moment; the boy's eyes large with fear. "This is what we will do. We go north and tell the Firmament. Maybe they can help." The Firmament was the group of leaders at North Temple.

Some excitement had crept into his voice when Lamp Kareem continued, "The other thing, your strange hands, is a wonderful occurrence. I do not wish to say too much, for I am only the lamp of one small SubAgoran temple and barely know the legends. I will say this. You say it hurt, but it may be a blessing. We both know that your prayers create the brightest baubles in the SubAgora. Legendary lamps had a gift like what you describe."

Shyheem thought about the searing heat that had roamed through his hands. It did not seem like a blessing. Regardless, this was the only way he might help his friends, and Lamp Kareem suggested it.

The lamp hurried back into his small room, packing some food and his extra tunic and his handwritten pages of the writ. His old body shook. He had the cluriKin rouse the young lamp and told him to run the Temple until he returned. Shyheem felt relaxed from the tea and relieved that something was being done to save his friends' lives.

They walked to Apia, the wide street that ran from the outer gates of the city up into the Citadel. They walked to an inn, The Running Horse, close to the Agora gate. The inn, a loud, big place, was surrounded by empty wagons. When the lamp entered, the room quieted down. The crowd turned toward the lamp.

The barkeep said, "Something I can do for you, lamp?"

The lamp said, "I need a driver to take me to the North Temple, one who has a set of fast horses. He will be well paid."

Most of the guys in the room turned back to their drinks, but a small man got up and walked to the lamp. His hair was a curly mix of brown and red, and he wore simple north country boots and a heavy cowl.

He said, "I'm Eire. Was going north myself."

The lamp said, "We need to go now."

"How much are you looking to pay?" asked Eire.

"What do you think is fair?"

"Let me see. I got to go fifty miles on the North Road, and back. It's a dangerous road. I think three dollars should cover it fair."

"Three! I heard it was a dollar and eight dimes."

"When was that, lit one?"

The old man said, "Let me see, hard to remember. Lamp Harin visited me, let me see, sixteen years ago."

Eire shook his head, "Lit one, the road has changed in sixteen years. Three dollars is a good price, which I'm giving you because I'm an Illumen worshipper myself. You can ask anyone here and they'll tell you it's a good price."

A few of the wagon drivers at the bar grunted in agreement. The lamp said, "I will pay you when we arrive at North Temple. I don't have that much now."

"I need two dollars to start."

The lamp looked surprised.

"No offense, lit one," Eire explained. "Lot of people dress one way and act another."

The lamp searched in his small moneybag. He counted out nineteen dimes onto the bar. "I'm a silver short."

Eire counted them and remarked to the inn, "I was always told it was bad business to work for the temples." A few of the men laughed.

Shyheem noticed the men looking at them. Shyheem thought that they stared at them because they were holy people in a bar past midnight. Later he realized that they were staring at him and the lamp because of the road they were traveling.

Eire went back to his seat. He drained a large glass, his adam's apple hammering forward against his skinny neck, and picked up a beat-up canvas bag. He led them out through the back, pushing through the crowd of men. "This way to the wagon. Excuse me."

In the dark of the stable, the driver lit a candle and led the Illumenists to a wagon. He told them to get in. They couldn't see it very well, but while he tied the horses into their harness, they could smell the odor of mildew. They pushed aside some canvas bags, which rattled with bits of metal, and sat. There were two horses in the harness and a third tethered to the wagon. All three horses were built like the man, thin, short, and wild maned.

The lamp remarked, "Mister Eire, are you sure this wagon and these horses will reach North Temple? I did ask for a fast wagon."

Eire said, "Fastest wagon in the east. Wouldn't take the job if I couldn't do it."

Shyheem didn't like this man. He felt that Eire should have given the lamp a better price. Also, he made a joke about the lamp and the money he had after saying he followed Illumen. He should know that followers of Illumen were never rich, and Lamp Kareem gave away money as fast as he got it.

A stable hand swung the doors open. Eire flicked the reins, and the horses leaned forward. At first the wagon didn't move. He whispered something, and the horses leaned harder. Still the wagon stood there. Eire jumped off the box and threw his shoulder against a wheel. The wagon creaked into motion, and the driver leapt back up.

When they emerged into the streetlights, the lamp looked around at the beat up wagon-sides, rustily joined together. It rattled onto the broad and well-lit Apia Way. He considered stopping and trying to get a different wagon, but there had been no other drivers willing to take him. There was nothing for it but to pray that Illumen kept the wagon from falling apart.

The lamp said, "Tell me, bright wick, what do you know of North Temple?"

Shyheem told him what he knew. It was where the Shining One and the High Firmament had their seat. It was in the northern section of Humbershire. Some believed that Illumen himself lived to the north of it. It was where the best lamps learned the Writ.

"Good. It is also said to be very beautiful. North Temple touches the stars, and it was made by old craftsmen whose skill died with them. Set in its windows, carved into its walls were images of the great torches and manusignis.

He asked, "What is a manusignis?"

The lamp shook his head. "I am not the one to answer that question. You will learn soon. All my life I have longed to go to North Temple. It is like a little town. Around it grow carefully tended orchards and farms that feed the wicks and the lamps that teach them.

"Also, it is a pilgrim's destination. People come from all over, even as far south as the Great Desert and as far East as the Isles of the Peaceful Ocean. It is as far north as men go. Its back is against the mountains. To the north are only grolfs, wendigo, and wild animals. When the pilgrims arrive, they enter into the sanctuary of light, and they greet the Shining One. I hope you will receive a blessing from him."

Shyheem thought about the reaching the main temple of the Illumenists. All his life he had struggled against distractions to see the god, to hear his voice. He felt flashes of true sight as he prayed the light into the baubles, the light formed into the figure of a gentle man moving against the dark sky. He thought that when he prayed at North Temple, he might completely transcend the world of darkness and be pulled up into the star fraught arms.

He was afraid to meet the Shining One. The Shining One could see everyone's dark corners. He had heard that the words of the Shining One were strong and biting. Grown men cried in shame before his chisel-like brightness. He hoped that there were no dark corners in him. He hoped that the Shining One would see how he had tried as best he could.

They rode through the sprawling chaos of Agora. Unlike SubAgora, where business occurred in streets and market spaces, the Agora was a wide field dotted with large shops and groups of houses, surrounded by fences and angry cluriKin.

During the day, Agora was full of grazzes and Regnans selling, and even some people from the ocean. Right then, as they trundled out of the city, it was past midnight. The late sellers were packing up carts. Grazzes, small figures with lizard eyes and skin like sandpaper, loaded carefully worked swords, spoons, and metal plates into their strongboxes. The shopkeepers, who had worked late trying to sell to the war-bound soldiers, grabbed the shutters of their mobile shops, slamming them to, and sliding in their bolts, before they harnessed their ponies and set out. Eyes were wary for it was the time of night when the robbers were about, and Fels were rare. The many inns, in thick clumps of buildings close to the outer gate, held all the life. Music and voices and light streamed out of them. The men in the streets stumbled and muttered toward wherever they would sleep that night.

When the wagon drove in among the bunch of inns, they found themselves in middle of a wild party. Women were screaming. Music was pouring through the windows there. A graz ran zigzag across the street hissing some song. Past the inns was the last wall of Urba. It was only as tall as a man, and the Fels bunched by the gate paid no attention to who passed. They were watching the excitement in the inns.

The wagon rattled through the gate into the open beyond. Immediately, the landscape changed. There were few houses, all spaced out, and between them squares of uniform grasses, gray under the moonlight, check-marked the wide land. Shyheem noticed that the skinny horses had sped up, their broomstick legs clip clopping away at the stones of the road. The repeating squares of fields and the rhythm of the hoof beats and his long night had him nodding soon, and he collapsed into the mildewed burlap on the bed of the wagon.

They drove through farmland for two days. Each farm was centered around a huge stone house with high walls. In the fields were huts where the workers lived. Many of the workers were dark-skinned like Shyheem. Following them on horseback around the fields were bosses, pale men, barking orders, pushing the shoulders of the workers with boots. Neither the bosses nor the workers looked up at the passing wagon. The lamp explained that every house-holder in AltUrba owned a farm like this.

The lamp and the wick passed the time reviewing the Writ and the Truths. The driver didn't seem to love this recitation, but he put up with it. Halfway through the second day, green hills were visible far away. As they got closer, the hills grew until they could see millions of trees spread over the hills like carpet. They were looking at Faunarum Forest. Shyheem had never seen a forest. In the back of his mind, he was remembering that this was a place of the wendigo. The road they were on burrowed right into the high and leafy trees that blocked all the sunlight.

At the forest edge a fortress with a tower stood sentry looking out over the woods. Atop the wall and in the tower sat Guardsmen with arrows strung to their bows. Above the tower fluttered the red and blue flag of Regna.

The lamp said, "Where is the escort?"

Eire spoke for the first time since the inn. "They went to the west. The only army here is in the tower protecting the road."

All this while the wagon trundled toward the trees. The lamp said, "Stop. Where are we going?"

The driver reigned in the wagon and looked up into the forest. He nodded his head forward. "To North Temple."

The lamp said, "Wait here. I'm not going in there without an escort. We're going to talk to whoever is in charge of this outpost."

Shyheem got off the wagon first and tried to help the lamp get down. They trudged up the hill. The lamp walked through an open door into the front room, where a large man was sitting. He was cleaning his fingernails with the point of a short sword. He looked up when the lamp entered.

"Hey, lit one. Going to North Temple?"

The lamp answered, "Yes, but we need an escort through Faunarum."

The man shook his head. "First of all, I've got strict orders to keep all of my guys here. Second, I'm just a lieutenant so if I go around changing orders, I'll get whipped. Third, you heard anything about them woods?"

The lamp said, "Illumen does not forget a kindness. We need an escort."

Shyheem looked over at the window, where a big cluriKin was perched. He looked out at the dense leafy darkness and threw a stone into it. Then another.

The man grunted. "All right, lit one. I'm going to do you a favor. I'll give you some advice. Don't go in there. Even if I didn't have orders, there's no way I'd be found under those trees. Last two escorts that went through never came out the other side. Those wendigo hate us, and once you're in the forest, they're chinging fantastic at killing. A lot better than any of us Guardsmen. You're dead before you see them. Go around to the Coastal Road. There aren't any woods there. Tell North Temple to get the news out. I get four or five different people everyday with the same problem. There's no escort."

The lamp said wearily, "Illumen bless you."

The man shrugged. He said to the cluriKin, "Bobo, stop throwing stones in there. You'll just piss them off."

The cluriKin looked at the soldier, turned, and threw another stone.

The Illumenists walked back down the hill to the wagon. The lamp said to Eire, "What was your plan? You knew it was like this?"

"Yeah. I drive through here all the time. Nobody stops me."

The lamp shook his head and said, "Take us to the Coastal Road."

Eire said, "I'm okay with that, but it's going to take us three more days. I will have to add three dollars to the price, and there is a toll over there. Two dimes."

The lamp paused. He didn't know how much money he could ask for at North Temple. He had never been there. He imagined arriving, and the Stars and the Lighted One scorning him because he forced them to pay for his expensive journey. He wanted to serve well, not waste the Temple's money. That money was for helping people. On the other hand, the forest was dangerous.

"You think we can go straight through?" Lamp Kareem asked. "What do you do about the wendigo?"

Shyheem peered into the forest. It invited him into its darkness like the Bellumite house. He did not want to want to go under those trees where the wendigo waited. He had never seen one, but he had seen the paintings and heard the stories. He imagined their eyes of fiendish green and their teeth like the wolf fangs, peering back out at him, in the dark.

Eire gave his mop of hair a shake. He said, "The wendigo? I usually leave them alone."

The lamp grasped Shyheem's hand with his bony hand. "Illumen, we are but children, shot into the dark. But for your light we would still wander blind. Today, we ask you, guide us in the dark. Protect us from the creatures of darkness. Give us light."

Eire watched him, waiting for his say so. The lamp nodded, and Eire flipped the reins. The horses began to move into the wood. Soon the trees shrouded them in dark, and the road was barely visible. The darkness to the left and the right of them was full of little noises. There were many legends and stories of the things that lived in the forest, and all of these stories went through Shyheem's head.

Eire kept his back straight, and his face directed on the road. The lamp was murmuring an ongoing prayer, but Shyheem looked hard into the wood. As they progressed through the morning, and sunlight began to puncture the leaves above, sending shafts of light into the forest floor, Shy saw nothing in the forest but small birds and rabbits. The morning was cool. Streams chortled by, reflecting triangles of sunlight. He felt safe then, like the wendigo were somewhere else, or they were letting them pass.

The trees swayed in the gentle breeze, the branches of one tree scratching his neighbor. The leaves turned up and reached for the sun, and the roots turned down and gripped the soil. Among the branches of these tall brothers, the birds made their nests. The mice made holes between the roots. Some trees lay on their sides, laid to rest by lightning or bugs. Moss grew green and red along their trunks. These trees fed the bugs and fungus as they rotted slowly, until they returned to the dirt. In a thousand ways the forest worked in on itself, green to brown to a more glorious green.

His reverie was broken by a face in the branches of a tree, close to the road, staring straight at him. Its eyes were hard green. Then the face was gone. He peered closely at the underbrush and the trees, but saw no more.

He hissed, "I saw a face!"

Eire, unconcerned, said, "That's why I look straight ahead."

The lamp said, "In the trees? What did it look like?"

The face was different than anything Shyheem had ever seen. It was like a human's but wilder, the eyes glinting with instinct, the foreteeth curved and sharp as a cat's. The driver didn't like how curiously the kid stared at the forest. He should leave well enough alone. The lamp thought about the horror stories. It would be alright if he died in Faunarum and became a meal for the wendigo. He had lived a long life in service to Illumen, and if the time had come for him to die, he would go gladly. But the little wick was far more important. The idea of the wick's death, now, when the lamp had brought him there, made Lamp Kareem tremble. What a failure it would be.

He said, "Don't you think we should speed up?"

The driver turned around and looked at the lamp. "The wendigo will stop us if they want. Right now, they don't. You being quiet would help keep it that way."

The path dipped down a hill, and the trees seemed to lean over it further. Shyheem imagined that the trees were speaking to him. "You do not belong here, city boy. What are you doing in the forest?" The lamp shook his head, his lips still moving in prayer.

The driver said, "Shut up with that praying merd, too."

The lamp looked angrier than Shyheem had ever seen him, but he held his tongue, looking up among the branches for the patches of light. Shyheem trained his eyes on the branches and trees. He thought he saw more faces among the brush and branches.

Then they turned a corner and looked up a little hill toward a sunlit clearing. The lamp thought that they were looking at the end of the forest, and his aching heart eased as he thought about the open spaces of Humbershire. Then he saw he was wrong. He was looking only at a small gap in the forest. As they got closer, he saw the meadow was occupied by shadowy figures.

After a moment of terrible calculation, in which the lamp considered trying to ride them down or fight them and the inevitable loss and capture, and what would follow, the lamp said, "We need to turn and ride back."

"No." The driver continued on up the hill.

The lamp whispered, "You are killing us."

The driver said, "These are their woods. There is no escape."

The lamp shook in anger and reached for the reins with a shaking hand. Eire pushed the old man back into the wagon with one hand. He whispered between his teeth, "Just keep calm."

The horses strained in their harnesses, and the wagon popped over the roots and weeds in the path, approaching the clearing.

As they neared, Shyheem saw that two or three creatures loped around the figures, and birds were flying in varied loops all around them. Two of the animals were wolves; another was a squirrel. The figures' faces were like the one that he had seen, flinty green eyes. Instead of hair, their heads were crowned with leaves. On some, the leaves fell and rustled freely, while others tied it back in tails. These were the wendigo. They each had a bow and a quiver of arrows. They wore outfits of woven green, with brown hoods, and they were speaking in a language that Shyheem had never heard, but it sounded like the rainwater in the Urban gutters, gurgling and jumping and flowing.

They were thin and wiry and had ears that stood out from their heads like wolves. They were Shyheem's height. When they reached the top of the hill, the driver pulled the wagon to a stop. The wendigo, continued talking, the one in front angry, his teeth flashing like a barking dog's, but the other five answered him tonelessly. Behind the angry one sat another animal that Shyheem had not noticed for its stillness. It was a cat, but it was not. It was as tall as two cats and as long as three, with tufts of black hair at the end of each ear. It sat back on its haunches, heavy fur flowing off its shoulders and haunches, looking Shyheem in the eye imperiously.

A wendigo came forward and took the reins from the driver. Another came forward, and got hold of Shyheem's hand.

Shyheem pulled his hand away. Before he knew what was happening, strong hands took him and threw him from the wagon. He sprawled out on the ground among the underbrush of the forest. He got up running, but in a moment, he found himself down on the ground. A sharp pain bit him in the ankle, and he twisted to the see the big cat standing over him, her teeth set in Shyheem's foot, lips peeled back, revealing canines the size of a man's finger.

The angry wendigo walked up to him. "Lynx no like run. No run."

Shyheem nodded, and the wendigo said something in a bark to the cat, which released his ankle, but remained in a crouch, ready to pounce again.

"You follow." The angry wendigo, who seemed to be the leader of this group, started into the trees. A hand pushed Shyheem, and the cat-thing nipped at his calf and ankles and he followed. The wendigo spoke in their strange language, and the only thing Shyheem understood was the hate behind his words.

5. Words with the Enemy

Nickson had to make it to Segundaton before the regnate. His horse tired after ten miles. He rode up to three travelers, merchants, no doubt. He discharged his thunderPipe into the back of the one. The other two wheeled, drawing steel.

He said, "Bellum saves those that drive away death by themselves."

He rode in, parrying the blows with such strength that the men's blades were still knocked down as he stabbed the one and, with a great swashing blow, hacked down through the other's shoulder so that the blade clove his heart. He took the three new horses, already saddled and rode on. He left the road to pass the Regna army.

Nickson had little pleasure in killing the travelers. They did not have enough strength to challenge him. Still, it was a chance to exercise, not in the Bellum Hall, but in the field, where the strong thrived and the weak died.

———————

Shyheem followed the wendigo deeper into the woods. He was carrying himself to his own death. When he figured this out, he sat down, but the cat nipped his behind. He started up, holding the puncture wound, and sped up to get away from the needle teeth. This was the magic of the wendigo, controlling the minds of the beasts and even men.

Soon, though it was Summer's Last Moon, drops of sweat began to drip down his face. They were climbing up through long silver trunks, under the leafy canopy. They followed steps beaten into the hillside clay by the passage of feet. It was steep, but the wendigo chanted, and though Shyheem's legs ached, they still stepped in time to the rhythm of the chant.

Shyheem wondered if they would kill him and use his body for dark magic. Would they eat him? Would he be cut into parts, here a shoulder, there a ham, and spread down a long table, which the wendigo would watch with bright eyes and eager stomachs?

After a while he remembered Illumen and began to pray. He first prayed for forgiveness for all his dark. He could not think of any right then, but he had learned that dark was often hidden. He was about to die, and he wanted to be right with the god. But the longer he prayed, the more his prayer turned into a question. "Illumen, you are supposed to protect the weak and innocent, but you allowed the traitor Fels to capture Burt and Jalil. Now you have allowed the wendigo to capture Lamp Kareem and me. Are you sleeping? Maybe you don't care? Or maybe the Bellumites are right, and you just aren't powerful enough to fight the darkness?"

And this doubt grew and shook the wick so much that he forgot the pain in his legs as they climbed, and forgot to pay attention to the landscape. He stopped and stood when the wendigo stopped and stood, unaware that he was being told to do something. The cat bit him, but he didn't notice, so it bit again, this time breaking the skin. He cried out and started forward.

He found himself climbing up a hill covered in short grass. Scattered through the field were animals he had only heard of, their legs thin but strong, with large eyes and ears. Atop their head, some had horns of many branching points, called antlers. Shyheem had heard of these animals. They were called deer. He stopped when he came to a lamp's robe spread on the grass. Surrounding it, squawking, were buzzards. They flapped their black wings, and stretched their pink necks toward it, dipping their ripping beaks between the folds of the robe.

Then one curved beak flicked aside the material. As Shyheem approached, the birds started and fluttered up and away. He saw that the robe still was being worn, but the one who wore it was not the man that he had been. He was a pale body with fleshy holes picked open by the buzzards. And the robe itself was caked with dried blood around small holes. The arrows of the wendigo had killed him.

Shyheem fell on his knees, muttering the prayers. He was afraid and couldn't move. Then a whisper floated down from the top of the hill, speaking to him in wendigo, and he rose to his feet and climbed toward the top of the hill again. At the hillcrest a giant tree rose up into the blue sky. Shyheem saw that it was the tallest of the trees. He did not know that it was an oak tree. Throughout the tree, a million different birds were flying and singing.

Sitting at the base of the tree, leaning against its great trunk, was an old wendigo. Standing by him was a deer that was taller than any of the others, with innumerable points on his antlers. The wendigo rested one wrinkled hand on the shoulder of the beast. The wendigo wore a thin beard that covered his neck, and his head leaves were pale and faded. He turned and looked at Shyheem and beckoned for him to approach. Shyheem walked forward.

The wendigo spoke in Shyheem's language, "Sit down."

Shyheem's legs responded to the command, acting independently. He found himself looking down a cliff that started only a foot away from where the wendigo sat. Far down below them flowed a river. The water was crystal clear. He could see fish swimming, little dashes of color, as the sun flashed off their scales.

"I am Kikimensi, the sachem of this forest. And you?"

"I'm Shyheem, a wick of SubAgora."

The wendigo said, "They tell me you saw them among the trees. Is this true?"

"I saw a wendigo face."

"This is difficult to believe. Only one who knows the forest can see its people. And you are from the city."

Shyheem didn't know what to say.

The wendigo whispered, "Why do you travel through here?"

Shyheem found that just like his legs before, his tongue wagged on without his control. "We go to the North Temple for help. We need to talk to the regnate, but we're not important enough. The Shining One will listen to us, and then tell the regnate what we need to say."

"What is it you need to tell the regnate?"

"There is a plot to kill him."

The sachem asked, "Who tries to kill him?"

Shyheem blurted, "The Fels."

The sachem looked out over the green canopy of trees dotted with red, yellow, and copper. He said, "Then it seems likely he will die. I want him to die. If you were he, you would not be speaking now. Mishipeshu would be eating your arrow-ridden flesh."

Shyheem shrunk from the angry eyes of the wendigo, whose voice had turned bitter and rough.

The sachem said, "But this is no concern to you. Your path is roundabout, and the Illumenists are no fonder of him than I. What concerns you is that you and your companions have trespassed in my forest. Death is the punishment for this crime. Why should I let you live, wick of the SubAgora?"

Shyheem looked up into the gray eyes of the sachem, which were turned out over the waving branches of the forest. He tried to speak. He reached down inside his throat and tried to find air. There was nothing there.

The sachem continued, "No human has passed through these woods and lived in over a year. It would be easy for you to die. I only need to nod toward the guard down the hill, and an arrow will fly into your neck. Or, more terrible still, I could call Mishipeshu."

Shyheem looked back down the hill and saw that the wendigo that had brought him was standing in the shade of the trees, an arrow notched on the string of the bow. He saw the lamp's corpse lying in the field.

Shyheem found his voice and began to speak. He said, "You should let me live because I am innocent, and Illumen says the lives of the innocent are sacred, and those who hurt the innocent shall pay with their own lives. The lamp who traveled with me is even more innocent than I, he is the kindest man in the whole SubAgora."

The sachem looked away from the woods to look in the eyes of the wick. He said, "You really believe that the god cares about your situation?"

The boy nodded.

The sachem said, "Why then has he left you here, in my hands? In the hands of Mishipeshu?"

The boy said, "I do not know."

57

The sachem laughed. "Rest your heart. I will not kill you, nor the lamp, or the driver. You see us, servant of the Light God, and this has made me merciful. Go. But warn the Shining One that it is unlikely this soft spirit shall take me again. In my old age, I rejoice when men are slaughtered."

Shyheem got up and went down the hill, carefully avoiding the throng of buzzards. The wendigo at the bottom of the hill barked at him, and they started back down through the trees.

When he reached the wagon, he saw both the driver and lamp. The lamp was weeping, "I have failed. Oh."

"Lamp Kareem, I'm here. I'm fine."

The lamp grabbed the boy, pulling him into the wagon. He held him for a long time. Shyheem repeated, "I'm fine."

"Shyheem. I feared the worst." Eire flicked the reins, and they lurched into motion.

The lamp was crying and talking, until Eire hissed, "Let's not disturb these woods anymore." They rode out in silence, hoping that the wendigo would not change his mind and decide that they should die as well. They saw the trees end and finally escaped from under them. Going on a little further they came to a walled town with an iron gate and many battlements. Guardsmen stood at the gate and watched from the battlements. It was when they passed through this that they breathed a sigh of relief.

The lamp bent his head. "Illumen, thank you for saving us from the great evil of those woods."

Eire interrupted, "Don't know how you're calling him evil. He let you go, didn't he?"

The lamp shouted, "You took us in there. You're crazy."

Shyheem said, "He didn't let that last lamp go!" He told them about the corpse on the hill.

The driver said, "Likely he deserved it. You're safe and the road saved you two dollars."

The lamp said nothing. If he'd had more strength, he would have attacked the driver. But as he sat there, his anger turned in on himself. He had wanted to save embarrassment at North Temple. That was why he had chosen the quicker route even though it was dangerous.

People were friendly in the town, and the lamp and wick ate free food at the Illumenist temple. After a night in an inn for the driver and in the hay of the stable for the lamp and wick, they trotted on through the open plains of Humbershire for some time, before the driver returned to the discussion of the wendigo.

"Everybody is always talking bad about the wendigo. But what do they do that's so bad? That is their forest, you know. The sachem's got every right to make sure you aren't spies. You think spies don't go through there in lamp's clothes?"

Shyheem said, "You're saying they're not that bad?"

Eire nodded. "Never hurt me once."

There was a silence in which both Lamp Kareem and Shyheem considered that this might mean that the driver had some dark alliance but saying that was likely to get them left on the road, miles from their destination.

Shyheem said, "What was that cat, the big one?"

The driver smiled, "That creature is a rare sight. It's called a lynx. Ferocious when it wants, a silent hunter, but it can purr like a housecat."

"They all have animals?"

Eire said, "Yes, if you're talking about the Faunarum wendigo. Each one of them has always got an animal with them, like a pet, but better trained. But wendigo in the West, it's said, don't always have animals, and some of them out there ride on the creatures of the forest like they were horses."

The lamp said, "That's enough of this talk. I think you are a lover of the wendigo."

The driver nodded his head.

The lamp said, "Do you love them when they kill farmers?"

The driver said, "Don't like anybody killing farmers. But I'd have to see that happen to believe it."

The lamp shook his head. "Don't listen to him." It was bad for the boy to hear this crazy talk. If an Illumenist believed it, he'd be on the verge of going against the truths.

Before them spread a great plateau, cut into squares of golden fields and pasture. On the far horizon, faint blue mountains were visible.

The farms in Humbershire were each centered around a single small house. In the fields men and boys, and sometimes women worked bringing in the harvest. The farmers turned when they passed and waved enthusiastically. The boys ran out of the fields and greeted them, jogging along beside them, asking them for news. The lamp told them about the possibility of war. The driver insisted there was no need for war. All the while the horses trotted along, until the boys, breathless from keeping up, and full up on news, stopped, and the wagon trundled on into the flat expanse of the northern plains.

Baubles, small stones holding Illumen's light, sat next to the road. In the darkening dusk they lit the way like a line of earthbound stars. Some were faded, holding but a glimmer. The lamp had the driver stop and told Shyheem to get down and hand him the dark baubles. The lamp prayed the light back into them. Shyheem followed his example walking by the wagon.

They saw the three spires of North Temple a mile ahead, reflecting pink light as the sun dipped below the mountains. When they grew closer, Shyheem saw the stone buildings laid out. Surrounding the structures were green fields and orchards. They reached the carved stone gates, which showed a man standing against a group of Bellumites armed with swords and pitchforks. In one hand he held the Writ, and in the other a flame. The Bellumites fell away from him.

At the gate they stopped. A lamp emerged from the guardhouse and Lamp Kareem got down and walked to him. Shyheem continued staring at the vast grounds.

The driver spoke to him. "Have fun in there, kid."

Shyheem said, "I will."

He watched a line of wicks walking in bright blue robes into the Sanctuary. Each one carried a bauble, and they sang a hymn that was eerie in the evening quiet.

The driver said, "Not everyone who talks about light, has the Light."

Shyheem looked at Eire in surprise. He had just quoted the Writ. He hadn't thought that the driver cared at all about Illumen or the scriptures.

The driver nodded, "I love the Light too, kid. But these people, "And he nodded toward the North Temple, "They have all the truths, and they have nothing. Just remember the basics. Protect the little guy at any cost. Fight the big guy. It ain't about you. That's what the Writ says."

Shyheem was staring at the driver curiously, when Lamp Kareem returned and dropped a dollar and a dime into Eire's palm. The driver dropped the lamp's bag into his arms and flapped his reins.

Lamp Kareem said, "Welcome to North Temple, my son."

They walked through the entrance gate straight down the main road toward the temple. Inside the ceiling was higher than anything Shyheem had ever seen, which really isn't saying much, since Shyheem had lived in a shack. The airy triangles of rafters and beams held up a plain wooden roof. The walls were plain stone and unremarkable, so that his eyes were drawn to the height and the windows. The late sun streamed through them, filling the room with many colors.

On the west side they were bright, catching the remaining sun. They were pictures of the torches and lamps in the Writ.

One window depicted the Writ, hardbound, with light flowing out of it in streams of blue and white. Another depicted Illumen himself walking across the fields; his hands sending life light into the tiny, tired and hungry workers. The most outlandish showed a wick whose hand was raised in the air, holding a cord of vibrant blue that plunged out of the sky. From his other hand blue flame sprang, caught and burned a group of evil-looking soldiers.

6. Manusignis

In SubAgora the day had collapsed into night. Jalil's mother was slumped over the Abierto bar, fingering an empty mug. The innkeeper had given her a few on the house. After all, her son was missing. She leaned across the bar and looked at the innkeeper. "You told them where he was," she cried.

The innkeeper shook his head, and walked to the far end of the bar. He wiped up some imaginary wet spot.

She leaned forward and shouted, "Don't walk away from me. Don't walk away! You gave them my son!"

He walked back to where she was, and whispered hotly, "Yeah? That's what you're telling yourself between drinks, Tamar? 'Cause the way I heard it, you got a silver out of the deal."

Traveling merchants eyed this exchange curiously, while the regulars concentrated on their drinks and food.

She shouted, "You traded your son to keep your inn!"

A regular interrupted. "The boys might be fine."

She turned and shouted, "They said they would be back that night. It's been a week. He's never coming back!"

She dropped her sweaty head onto the bar, and began to weep. The innkeeper nodded to a big guy at the door, who came over, and gently picked up the woman. He carried her in the basket of his big arms. He usually tossed drunks out the door to sleep where they landed, but she had lost a son. A son that everyone on Black Way liked. The kid was strong, fearless, and loyal even to his wreck of a mom. The bouncer carried her down the street and dropped her on the pallet in her shack.

The bar had discussed the Fels arresting the Subs for the first few days. Why hadn't they gotten the boys back? Then, as they became more worried, they discussed blame. Why had the innkeeper told the Fels anything at all? He had no choice. It wasn't as if he was the only one who had talked. If they had all said that

62

they knew nothing, did anyone really think that the Fels wouldn't have come down with a squad and knocked heads, and destroyed merchandise, until the boys were handed over? That was the second and third day. As time dragged on, the absence of the boys grew in their hearts. Talking about it lessened and then stopped.

On the fifth day, the innkeeper had walked up to the gatehouse. He asked the Fels there about his son. They took him in and showed them the Subs that they had in the cells. None were his son. He became angry with them, and they made fun of him, before pushing him out and telling him that he was crazy, and that they would lock him up, too, if he kept making noise.

He went to the neighborhood rep. The rep said he would send a message to the Citan Fels. He asked how long this would take. The rep said it would take a few days; they would send a messenger to him. They understood his situation, but Citadel did what it did when it wanted to. It might take some time. He'd have his boy back soon. It wasn't as if the Citan Fels ate children; they weren't wendigo. The innkeeper walked back to Black Way with sagging shoulders. He was afraid. He tried not to think about where Burt was, because the remaining possibilities were horrible.

He rubbed the bar into a gleaming shine. He tried different spices in his stew. He didn't talk to the customers; he listened to orders. The regulars in the bar knew better than to talk to him about their problems, and those passing through didn't expect him to be talkative.

In the kitchen, the two sisters tried to talk about it. Sherise said, "KaBro shouldn't have hung out with Hands."

Shawnee said, "It's not his fault. It's those Fels." She missed Burt. She missed Jalil too. She missed the slow way he said, "Hi, Shawnee." She missed seeing his square back walking to work.

Lamp Kareem nudged him and he looked forward. At the front of the temple sat seven people robed in bright blue. The floor of the room was littered with kneeling pilgrims. Some sang, others trained their eyes adoringly forward at the person in the middle of the seven. Crowning his head was a silver disk out of which rose a flickering tongue of blue flame.

You probably would have said, "Dude's on fire!"

In fact all seven figures were shrouded in wreaths of blue light that seemed to coalesce in the crown of the Shining One. Shyheem knew that this shining was a sign of Illumen's presence. He had seen it for a moment in the temple on Black, when Lamp Kareem was most carried away with his reading. Then a brief shimmer of blue had swirled and disappeared. Here, the blue light stayed, eddied in the air, disappeared for a moment, only to reappear.

This was the Firmament that led all the Illumenists in Regna. The seven people on it were called stars. They made the decisions regarding right teaching and any other issue. Seated in the middle was the Shining One, the leader of the Firmament and the whole Temple. He turned his blue eyes on Shyheem. The Sub shivered.

The seven persons of the Firmament were used to the expression of admiration that they saw in Shyheem's eyes. They were honored throughout the campus of North Temple, but something was lacking in their leadership. Fewer and fewer pilgrims arrived at North Temple every year, and throughout the nation of Regna, more and more people were forsaking their teachings for the self-reliance taught by Bellum. They grasped as they could for some sign that would draw the people back to them.

The Shining One nodded to an orange-robed youth; the youth rang a bell three times. At the sound of the bell, the blue robed wicks behind the Firmament quietly filed out of the temple hall. The orange robed youth went to the pilgrims seated on the floor and spoke quietly. They rose and shuffled out, until the only people in the room were the stars of the Firmament, the lamp, and the wick.

He said, "The Firmament is called because Lamp Kareem brings news from Urba. Lamp Kareem is new to this place; he was trained in SubAgora and served there his whole life. Welcome. How are our brothers in the city?"

Lamp Kareem told them the city's big news. Three farmers had been killed outside of Ornata. Two escorted wagons had disappeared in Faunarum along with the escorts. The Bellumites had taken the opportunity to urge war against the wendigo, while the Illumenists of Urba said it was a time for contemplation and preparedness. The Bellumites had swayed the Citans, and they declared that Regna would punish the wendigo, and then the regnate, the Fels, and the Guard had marched out. They were probably, at this moment, a week's march from Ornata.

"Did you encounter the wendigo in Faunarum? Our people tell us that you came that way."

"We were stopped, and they took Shyheem. He saw how they had killed a lamp and left his corpse rotting in the field. The sachem there let him go because the wick could see the wendigo in the bushes. The sachem attributes this to some kinship with them, though Shyheem stuck to his truths. The sachem also warned that other Illumenists would get the same treatment as the dead lamp."

The Shining One said, "Does anyone know who that lamp was?"

No one spoke, each wondering if it was their friend.

The Shining One said, "Can you describe him?"

Shyheem shook his head.

"At least, young wick, something about him," the Shining One said. "Was he brown skinned, like a Sub, or white, as a normal Regnan?"

Shyheem spoke, "Bright one, he was mostly eaten."

The room went quiet. Each of the stars' minds traveled to that awful hill in the forest. The wendigo had recently captured, harassed, and even killed a number of travelers, but no pilgrim to North Temple, before that moment, had been known to die.

The Shining One spoke, "Illumen, light has been extinguished by darkness. Come and bring justice."

"By your light," echoed the Firmament.

The Shining One said, "Why have you come here?"

Lamp Kareem said, "Your brightness, this wick, who has studied with me for four years, came to me with his problems. I did not feel I had the knowledge to teach him, so I brought him to you. He can tell you what happened, how his hands were filled with light."

The Shining One said, "Shyheem, tell us what happened."

Imagine that you met the person you admired most in the whole world. Actually, the seven people you most admired, at once, and then you were told to speak to them about something that happened to you that you didn't understand. That was the situation in which Shyheem found himself and he was speechless. He thought, "I'm a SubAgoran wick, not worth the Firmament's time!" He peeked up and saw all seven pair of eyes turned on him, waiting patiently. He realized that in his embarrassment at wasting their time, he was wasting even more of it.

Though his voice quavered, he forced himself to speak. The Firmament listened patiently while he told the story of the plot against the regnate, the kidnapping Fels, and the blue glow that had seized his hands.

When he had finished, the Shining One said, "Lamp Kareem, can you add anything?"

"Your Brightness. This wick has been faithful in his prayers and Writ memorization, though we did not have time for a serious course. He, like most SubAgoran wicks had to pray light into the baubles most hours of the day, to feed himself and others. His prayers produced the brightest and the longest lasting baubles. With his contributions, more than one orphan was fed. I was happy, but not surprised by the advent of the fire hands, though I have not spoken to him about their meaning. I have only the most basic of lamp training and did not feel it was my place."

The Shining One nodded to the lamp. "Thank you, Lamp Kareem. You have served the people of the light. You were right to keep the secret of the manusignis and bring him here.

"We face two questions here. The first is what to do about this plot against the regnate. I suggest that we send a lamp to speak to him. However, it should be said that regnate has not been friendly to the Illumenists. He may not want to hear us. Many say he is of the Bellumites. Others say he worships whichever god suits him. If he does listen to us, he may be able to save himself and free your friends.

"Next, there is the thing that happened with your hands. We are going to ask that you demonstrate. All you need to do is close your eyes, and imagine that you're back there behind that barrel, watching those men take your friends. Remember how you felt and pray as you did then."

Shyheem nodded. He closed his eyes and tried to put himself back in that situation. He prayed but it was weird to pray for them now. He didn't know where they were, or really, though it was hard to consider, if they were alive. He remembered he was trying to show the Firmament his gift though and concentrated. He felt his hands tingle, then burn. Shyheem opened his eyes. His hands were faintly glowing.

All the stars were nodding their heads and murmuring. The Shining One said, "That is impressive. Few not initiated into certain secrets can do anything like this. Though it was painful to you, it is a blessing. We are about to reveal a secret of the Temple. It must never be told to any outside this place. First you must swear to tell no one outside of North Temple of these things. Do you promise to keep the secret?"

"Yes," Shyheem said. His voice came out like a squeak.

"Star Hampstead, read him the story of the first manusignis."

She stood up. Shyheem was surprised that someone so young, a girl almost, could be a star. She opened a large book, the Writ. Shyheem stared at the book, remembering that at the temple on Black Way they had no more than five pages, each brown and hard to read. Shyheem had been frustrated with how little of the Writ they had. Sometimes half a book, usually Cantos, was on loan to them, and then the more serious wicks gathered round, while one read aloud, and now he was hearing a secret book.

"From the book of Sarah Hope, 'Before there was a regnate, when the Opulanders were clearing their land, each did what he wanted to, and every man carried a sword. Bellumites rejoiced for their swords drank blood, and they drank the wine of the bleeding, and they ate the bread of the fallen. Everything belonged to the strong."

The star continued, "Illumen's people said, 'Why are you far, Illumen? Why is the world awash in darkness? For my hope is far from me, and the light of the morning has been swallowed by the night. Those who love violence pursue me, and my eyes are eaten by the servants of Bellum.'

"In the hills of Desicca there lived a man Thom and his family. A band of robbers came into his homestead, and they killed him and his sons, and only the women were left. And the strongmen said to the women, 'Come back into the shelter of the cabin, and we will let you live.'

"And the women went one by one, while the youngest daughter, Sarah Hope, waited. She cried out to Illumen. Her hands glowed with light. She shook and was afraid that she would be consumed by the flames that spun from her hand. She heard the voice of Illumen.

"'Do not fear. The light is mine. With it, you will save my people. With this flame burn away those who delight in eating dead men's bread.'

"Her hands flared, and she cast the flame against the men. It reached out and touched them, and even their bones were consumed. Her sisters ran over the hills to share the story. The people of light went to where she was. She settled with them on the Amarillo River, near the Peaceful Ocean.

"All those who feared the sword gathered, and Sarah Hope waited for the army of Bellum. She knew that they would come when their hunger outgrew their wisdom. They came like locusts, covering the plain, for they heard that many people hid in the city, and that the people were weak with no army, but only a woman lamp to defend them. And when they assembled and waited for the sun to set, she came out to them, standing on a high hill. They looked up and saw that a halo of light surrounded her.

"They shot their arrows at her, and threw their firebombs, but she was already alight, and the arrows burnt away, and the firebombs did not hurt her. They said, 'Who is this woman, who burns but is not consumed?'

"But others answered, 'Why are we standing and doing nothing? She is just a woman, and we are warriors!' They charged up the hill. She unleashed her fire, and they were consumed. Yet when the fire burned she felt the pain herself, and as her enemies were turned to ash, her own heart was drying up. She cried out asking for the pain to be taken from her, but the pain remained.

"She collapsed, and the Bellumites sent up a yell, for they thought she was dying. They charged. They lifted their swords. Sarah Hope screamed and the last gust of wild blue flames swept through her veins like desert wind. They leapt from her hands and seized the remaining warriors like hearth fire lights on straw, and in the moment they flamed up, they were gone. The Writ of Illumen, from the Narrative of Sarah Hope, Chapters One and Two."

Star Hamstead closed the book and sat down. Shyheem was amazed. They seemed to consider him as a possible manusignis himself. Maybe he would someday use his power against those Fels that carried off his friends! However he had nothing like the powerful flame of Illumen that Sarah Hope had wielded. If he had, his friends would be safe, and the regnate would know everything.

The Shining One spoke. "This is the book of Sarah Hope. Illumen promises that when there is need, he will send a manusignis. Those with hands of fire are still given to his people. Now is a time of need. The wendigo kill pilgrims. We have lamps and wicks with gifts like yours, but none have yet loosed flames that could consume an army. In the years since the second manusignis roamed the land, respect for, and belief in, not to mention followers of, Illumen have dwindled. The followers of Bellum strut arrogantly through the city. So we wait, and hope for the next one. You may be him."

Shyheem thought about the long hours he spent in prayer. When he prayed, it wasn't about putting power in the bauble. He was lifted up close to the moon, its cool light surrounding him in ebb and flow. It became easy for him to shine rather than be dark. This was the moment to which all his prayer had led.

The tall man next to the Shining One stood up. The other stars looked a little surprised that he interrupted, "May I, Shining One." His shoulders were broad and his arms were large. His serious face was worn by many thoughts, while the jutting fix of his chin showed a man of action.

The Shining One shrugged his shoulders, made delicate by the years, as if it was just as well that someone spoke for him.

He said, "Welcome to North Temple, wick of SubAgora. I am Star Tenace, from Montanawick. We call those who train to become manusignis parwa. We have only one class for parwa. There you will learn how to pray and how to deal with and use your gift. You will also be enrolled in regular lamp courses for learning the Writ and the Truths. Wicks and parwas have household duties as well.

"I must say one more thing. The greater the fire strength of the manusignis, the greater the pain that comes with its use. In the book of Sarah Hope, she collapses after the battle, and the people think that she is dead. It takes her months to recover. There is a lot of pain in the path of the manusignis. Many start, and have great gifts, yet they quit, because the pain is too great for them. The hands of light that you have don't mean you have to train. You could go back to SubAgora and sell baubles."

Shyheem nodded.

Star Tenace said, "I should add that we need hands of fire. We need people to know about the light god. Belief in him dwindles in every corner of Regna. The parwa are our hope of returning the people to Illumen. What do you say? Do you want to become a parwa?"

Shyheem didn't answer right away because he was too excited. "Yes, Star Tenace."

The Firmament nodded, smilingly.

The Shining One said, "Welcome to the temple. Star Tenace will show you your lodging. The Firmament is dismissed."

The stars got up and walked out. Lamp Kareem put his hand on the wick's shoulder. The wrinkles around his eyes were wet.

"I have dreamed that one of my wicks would become a parwa. This is a great honor; they accept very few."

Star Tenace appeared between the lamp and Shyheem. Up close he was even bigger, wide across the shoulders, towering over Lamp Kareem, who looked tiny and old.

"Thank you, Lamp Kareem," he said. "You have brought this one far. Now I must take him even further. Shyheem, follow me."

Lamp Kareem opened his mouth, as if to say something else, but then closed his mouth.

Shyheem followed the star. Behind the temple he got an even better view of the mountains. Their white caps reflected the sun's waning light. Star Tenace led Shyheem through trees whose branches dipped toward the ground with the weight of fat green apples. They were not like trees in the forest, which grew close together and wrestled upward for sunlight. They were set apart at even intervals, and below them grew a closely clipped lawn that looked like an inviting bed to Shyheem, who was used to sleeping on a plank in a shack.

Star Tenace pointed out the workshops. Even these were made from cleanly cut stone, so the walls were flat and strong. Inside he could see wicks working on desks and benches. Next door was a smithy, where a forge flared and the gong of the hammer echoed. Shyheem saw that the temple was a complete city. Food was grown, and everything necessary was made here.

They walked through another orchard toward a long building that was underground except for the two sides of the pitched roof. Star Tenace climbed down steps to a door that was half below ground. Seated at a small desk was a young lamp studying the Writ. He looked up when the star and the wick entered.

"Lamp Obsur. This is Shyheem, from Urba. He will be in this class as a parwa. Shyheem, this is your house father. He will be like a parent to you. You will come to classes tomorrow, the other wicks and parwas will show you the way. I will see you tomorrow."

He left. The young lamp looked over the wick. He sighed and pushed his desk aside and got up like he had a big burden on his shoulders. He walked Shyheem into the second room.

The room was warmed and dried by a large fire though it was underground, with bunkbeds made of feathered mattresses and stone bases. The windows were tucked below the low rafters. Behind each bed were shelves. Some shelves had toys, wooden soldiers, or carts, and others had books. The walls were covered in paintings of lamps and manusignis serving people and protecting them. There was a great hearth, and several desks.

"That's you."

The lamp pointed at a lower bunk with an empty shelf behind it. Shyheem sat on it. It was soft.

"You from the Sub?"

"Yes."

"You aren't going to see a lot of browns here. I guess that you're the true manusignis?"

Shyheem felt more out of place than he had with the mention of his Bugiri skin. Shyheem said, "They said I might be."

"Yeah, we get a new one every six months. They're pretty desperate for him to show up. Think it will make some folks bring some offerings again. Ha."

Shyheem said, "I have the light."

The lamp said, "Great," exactly as if it was not great at all. "Here are two blue robes." He tossed two robes on the bed from a stone shelf. "Always wear these, unless you're playing in the mud. Then you can go naked, or put that thing on that you're wearing now. Not like it could get dirtier. That reminds me, the bathing room is in the back. Clean yourself up; this isn't the SubAgora gutter. You better keep the robes and your skin fresh. I find you stinking and I'm giving you toilet cleaning. You'll find some wicks training to be lamps and manusignis in the bunks next to you. Everyone of them thinks he's Illumen's own moonbeam too."

The lamp continued, "Keep this space neat, and make your bed every day. Remember nobody likes a crybaby and you and I will be fine."

7. Illumen's Own Moonbeams

The scary part was that maybe he would fail. The Shining One and the stars believed he could have that power, and they spoke for Illumen. He felt so shone-on that he wanted to dance in hilarious circles, but he was pretty sure that Lamp Obsur would disapprove.

Shyheem looked at the neat little beds and wondered what the other boys and girls would be like. He had never met real wicks. The wicks in SubAgora only prayed to get enough light in the baubles so they could sell them. They only took wick classes so that they could become lamps and get paid. Burt went to Temple because his dad made him.

He'd always felt separate from them. Shyheem prayed and he felt the presence of Illumen. Sometimes he saw visions of the god, a distended blue giant walking over wheat fields, or sitting on the mountains. When he tried to talk about that, the other wicks called him a moon freak.

The house cluriKin interrupted his thoughts, crawling out from a ball of blankets on the bed next to him. It walked over and stood squarely in front of him. It was built like the dorm, low, thick, and comfy looking. With its small arms crossed it looked him up and down. It shrugged and walked off. Not very welcoming, Shyheem thought.

A bell rang. The walls of the room seemed to vibrate, and he heard lots of talking. Lamp Obsur yelled, "Hey, Brown, it's time for dinner."

He walked outside. All around him, robed wicks and lamps moved toward the same long building. Two green robed wicks held open double doors. Carved into the door were chickens, cows, wheat, and apples. The room smelled deliciously of roasted turkey, and this made him hungry. There was a table in front of him, and he sat down.

He looked down the table. Every wick at the table had on a green robe.

Said one, "Check your robe, Blueby."

Another joked, "He gave himself a promotion."

The table laughed. Shyheem stood up, hoping that his dark skin didn't show his blushes. A quick scan of the room showed him that the Firmament had their own table, the lamps had two of their own, and that the wicks sat at tables according to the color of their robes. He moved to the long table of blue robed kids. They looked younger than he was. One kid moved over a little, and he sat.

The kid who moved said, "Hello."

"Hello," he said.

One whispered, "He's old for a blue."

Shyheem looked to see who said it. None of them said anything else. Everyone got quiet while one of the lamps gave a blessing. Two Orange Robes came over and put a roast turkey on the table. They carved off meat and dished out potatoes and carrots. The aroma of hot food in front of him made him forget everything else. Compared to the stale bread and leftovers he got in the Sub and the oatmeal they'd eaten on the road, this meal was a king's feast. When he'd eaten all of his food—too fast—he leaned back and looked around.

The kid next to him said, "I'm Boniface." Boniface was as round-faced as the moon, and not much thinner than Burt.

"I'm Shyheem," he said.

Boniface said, "Where are you from, Shy?"

He said, "SubAgora."

A girl with freckles said, "Ooo. City boy."

A small wick with a pointy nose said, "Think you know about Truths?"

Shyheem shook his head.

The girl said, "Wait until he meets Star Tenace. Then he'll know Truths."

Shyheem said, "I already met him."

The boy laughed. The girl said, "Isn't he nice?" The boy bent over his plate of turkey, laughing very hard.

74

Shyheem said, "What's funny?"

Nobody answered that question.

Someone said, "How old are you?"

Shyheem said, "Thirteen."

The boy said, "You just started? You'll make lamp when you're an old man."

"Yeah," someone else said, "he'll have a beard when he gets an orange robe."

"Grandpa Sub. Ha ha."

After dinner, the blue robes had to wait for all the other Illumenists to leave. Lamp Obsur met them as they entered the dorm. "Get in bed and shut up, and leave the new kid alone. Don't want you all to go the path of Bellum and annoy him to death. Then I'll get in trouble."

Shyheem pulled the heavy blankets up to his chin and felt the down surround him. He'd been sleeping in the bed of the wagon on mildewed sacks. Before that, he slept on the ground on a pile of rags and a board. This was the first time he'd been in a real bed, and he liked the way it felt to nestle in something soft, with the sheets and blankets cocooning him against the chill of the night.

When the room had been quiet for a while, someone whispered, "Hey, Sub. Why'd they take you, Sub?"

"Yeah, he's old for a blue robe."

Someone said, "He's supposed to be a parwa."

"Oh, a parwa. Can you do this?"

Suddenly at the near end of the room there was a stabbing blue flame between two glowing hands. The flame lit up a small pointy nose face. The other wicks oohed and aahed. The cluriKin, which was walking the center aisle, stopped and clapped ecstatically. Someone said, "Awesome, Gladius."

Shyheem said, "I can't do that."

Boniface said, "Show us what you can do."

A chorus of voices echoed this.

"Are we supposed to just do it any time?" Shyheem asked.

"Call on him at all times, and he will hear you."

"That's the Writ."

"Can't argue with the Writ."

75

Shyheem asked, "How do you do it?"

"It's easy," Gladius said. "Think about those wendigo killing that lamp, and think about Illumen at the same time."

Shyheem tried to think about the wendigo killing the lamp. He thought about the body in the grass, and then he thought about Illumen, but nothing happened to his hands.

Somebody whispered, "Come on, already."

Gladius said, "He can't. He's not a parwa."

Shyheem thought again about his two friends and Hands being carried away. He thought about how he couldn't do anything; he thought about how Illumen should have helped him right then. His hands glowed faintly in the room. He felt a faint heat in his hands. He waved them around. The kids murmured in mild approval. Then the light died.

Gladius said, "That's nothing. I can't believe they let you in."

Shyheem thought about his friends then. They were Subs; they liked to fight and steal, and sometimes they went into the Bellum Temple to watch the fights or joke with the Bellumites, but they accepted him just the way he was. He hoped the lamp hurried with his message to the regnate. He hoped they were okay. The next morning the bell rang loudly and all around him he heard bustling. The bed felt warm, and the air outside was cold. He pulled the blanket tight around him. Boniface grabbed his blanket.

"Move," he commanded.

Shyheem grunted something and curled into a ball. Boniface said, "You have to make your bed before the check."

Shyheem got out of bed. He hugged himself against the cold. The blankets were a mess. Boniface made his own bed. Shyheem watched what he did and tried to imitate it. Somehow the blankets stayed wrinkled no matter which way he pulled. The other wicks had finished making their beds. They were putting away their things and leaving for breakfast.

Boniface looked at his neighbor's bed and shook his head.

He said, "I've got to go. Sorry, Sub."

Shyheem saw that only four other kids were left in the room. He started trying to tuck the corners of his covers back under the bed, but it looked wrong. He pulled them out and smoothed the top and tried again.

"I guess browns don't make their beds."

Shyheem turned and saw Lamp Obsur.

"You got work duty now. Go to dawn service, and see me after classes."

Every weekday went the same. All the wicks gathered on the dining hall roof for Dawn service. The sun was rising over the Humbershire plains and reflecting off the mountain peaks to the North. They sang some hymns and an orange robe read from the Writ. A lamp explained the meaning of the text, while Boniface nodded. After that they had breakfast, something more like what Shyheem was used to, often oatmeal, but also a cup of hot cider. The cider was delicious, and Shyheem found that he drank it too fast.

Then they went to class. All their classes were conducted in the same room. There were three long benches with a desk connected. The seats were ordered by the standing of the students, so during the breaks between classes, the wicks might move, but in most classes the order was pretty similar. Gladius was first in every class. The freckled girl named Jany was second. In Writ Studies, Shy was put in the last seat, number twenty-five. The middle-aged, middle-fat teacher was Lamp York. Lamp Kareem had told him that Illumenists weren't supposed to be fat, that was the way of Bellum, but this teacher was.

In this class, students recited chapters that they had memorized from the Writ. The other Bluebies told him that Orange Robes actually got up and recited whole books, but he couldn't believe it. A chapter in itself seemed like an impossible string of words to memorize.

While the one wick recited, Gladius, as number one, held a copy of the Writ, checking for any mistakes. Every word missed, every word added, Gladius' hand shot up, and the lamp made a tic. If you got no tics, that was good.

If a wick made a single mistake, Gladius would correct it, but if he made a lot, the lamp just told him to reread it. It was the third day of class when Shyheem heard a chapter from the Book of

Origins that excited his curiosity. His friends in SubAgora always talked about the monsters that the wendigo worshipped, but he'd never taken it seriously, until he heard the trembling wick recite.

"Origins, Chapter Twelve."

"When Theom all-Father made the Humans he asked his sons to watch them and help them. Bellum strong-Son looked at the creatures on the earth, and he laughed at them. Illumen infinite-Heart took pity on them, when he saw how they were helpless before floods, fires, and droughts. He listened to their cries, and helped them survive the harsh world, teaching them about light.

"Theom sky-Father made the grazzes next. Again, he asked his sons to watch them. Bellum looked at them, and laughed as well. "Smaller even then humans." Illumen looked at them. They did not call out to the sky, but looked down at the stone they lived in, and Illumen said, these ones need me less. Still, if one asked for help, he helped him.

"Theom sky-Father next made the wendigo. He asked his sons to help, but Bellum said, 'What can I do?' Illumen had been answering the cries of humans, so he arrived later. He said, 'I am too busy with man.'

"Said Bellum, 'If they need help, they are not worthy of it.'

"Illumen said, 'I am too busy.'

"Bellum offered, 'I will make them their own gods.'

"Illumen agreed, and he left Bellum to work. When he returned Bellum showed him the Mishipeshu, the gods of the wendigo."

Shyheem leaned forward. He heard Burt talk about this, a monster that lived in the forests. Burt believed in them, but most of the men didn't. Here, the name was in the Writ. He waited to hear the description of them.

"He said, 'They will not be able to speak to such terrible animals.'

"Bellum spoke to the first Mishipeshu, and it moved, running on the face of the earth, and swimming through the water. It moved with power and great speed, it was not like a thing already on the earth. Its full-toothed mouth gaped with hunger.

"Illumen said, 'Is this a creature of the sky?'"

"Bellum said, 'This is a creature of power; that is what gods are.'

"Illumen said, 'Now I know you love power over light. You have made the wendigo people of dark. They will have claws and fangs, not hands and teeth, if this thing is their god. Fear and power will be the only language that they know. They will war with everything.'

"But he had let Bellum make the gods, and he watched as the Mishipeshu moved out to the shaded places where the wendigo were waiting for a god. They saw it a long way off, and they were filled with awe and fear. It galloped in among them, and they waited for it to speak but it rose up and fell, ripping a wendigo in half, and began eating him. The others ran back to the trees."

The wick reciting this chapter sat down, examining his tics for mistakes on the board. Shyheem stood up to ask a question.

Lamp York said, "Yes, Shyheem."

"Lamp York, what are the Mishipeshu?"

The lamp said, "There are ignorant men who say they have seen them. The wendigo, back when we spoke with them, describe them as a great cat mixed with a crocodile, and say that they travel both in the water and on the land. They worship them in that they give them carcasses to appease them. They receive no words from the Mishipeshu, nor do they direct any words to them, for they describe them more as great beasts than as thinking beings. However, if these monsters exist, why is it only drunk farmers who report seeing them?

"Some say that Mishipeshu refers to grolfs. However, grolfs do not look like great cats with lizard parts. We can't say they don't exist, here it is referred to in the Writ. Thus, whatever the wendigo think, or drunk farmers see, there is a question, what is this Mishipeshu referred to in the Writ?

"After considering that the belief in this thing's presence would make the wendigo people of dark, scholars have decided that Mishipeshu is a word for Bellumite thoughts. Loving power, and worshipping that which is not of the light, are a few examples. Those that look on the gods as chaotic and opposed to them have that kind of bad thought. The meaning of the story is that the wendigo are separated from Illumen because of the bad spirits, Mishipeshu that they worship. They wanted more than was right, and so they sought the help of Bellum."

Shyheem was disappointed that the monsters were not real. It would be dollar for such things to exist. He would have to tell Burt and Jalil when he got back. He hoped that they would be there.

He wasn't seated last in every class. In Prayer Class, Star Tenace said, "Shyheem. I want you to sit in the twenty-second seat. Boniface, and Nord, both of you move down one."

Boniface said, "But he hasn't done anything yet."

Star Tenace walked back to the front of the classroom. Shyheem thought he was going to ignore Boniface. He picked up a chalk and looked at the board. He remarked, "There is no way, Boniface of AltUrba, that a parwa could be behind you in prayer."

Boniface turned red. A few of the kids laughed. Shyheem took the seat and gave a mini-shrug toward Boniface, who shook his head at the world.

Once Star Tenace started to lecture, the words came fast and logical, and the wicks wrote notes quickly on their papers. He gave them examples from Cantos and stars gone to the light, of prayer. Shyheem already knew some of them from his work as a bauble wick. Then there was a quiet time for practice. They were supposed to call to Illumen.

Star Tenace's loud voice interrupted Shyheem's meditation, "Boniface, you are not to construct projectiles during prayer time. I will see you after class. Now, hard as it may be, please close your eyes and call."

The front row turned and looked at Boniface before going back to their prayer.

Later, in the break after classes, Boniface explained in their bunks, "I pray a little, then I find myself doing something else. Today I thought it would be dollar if I made a paper castle. Next thing I know, I got double duty."

Shyheem said, "Illumen hears even simple cries."

"Tell Star Tenace that. Anyway, it's okay. I'm here because my father sent me here, not like you other kids who actually are special."

80

"At least you're nice."

"Thanks. You should have met me when I lived in AltUrba."

"What were you like then?"

He paused. "I never talked to SubAgorans. I used to throw pebbles at them."

AltUrba boys would often climb the wall, which wasn't guarded on their side. They hurled pebbles down at the Subs. The wall cluriKin would join in. The Subs would try and throw back, but the wall was high, and by the time pebbles reached that height, they didn't have much speed. They were easily dodged, or caught, and thrown back. Shyheem didn't play this game, but sometimes he watched. If Jalil wasn't playing, the game was one-sided, with the Subs retreating eventually with welts on their heads.

Jalil. Shyheem had forgotten him, the way he carried himself like a small god. He changed the game. He waited until the AltUrbans were in mid-throw or not paying attention, before he ran and threw. He ran two steps before his arm lashed out, unleashing a good-sized rock. His rocks hurtled with debilitating accuracy, smacking the AltUrbans in their boy parts or their heads, and they fell down crying. Even Shyheem had permitted himself a smile. The altas would get down off the wall, and then the Subs would run, because they knew the Fels were coming.

Boniface said, "It was just what we did. You ever get hit?"

Shyheem nodded, "A couple times."

"I'm sorry."

"You don't seem like a boy who would throw pebbles."

Boniface shrugged, "Everyone did in AltUrba. We'd say 'Dirty browns, that'll teach them.' I thought Subs were a bunch of merds. Here it doesn't matter where I lived. What matters is that my prayers suck."

Shyheem whispered, "You should start with a low hum and open your mind toward light . . ."

Boniface said, "It's okay. I'm not good at prayer."

Star Tenace taught Truth Class also. He said, "Today's truth is the oneness of light. All light has common qualities and all light is from Illumen. This means that there is some good in even the worst, because light is reflected off everything." He paused. "Shyheem. Give me two implications of the oneness of light."

Shyheem didn't know what implications meant, but he went ahead and said everything that he'd understood from what Star Tenace had been saying.

The star said, "Where did he go wrong?"

The round wick stood along with the four kids in the front. "Yes, Nord?"

"He said light was everywhere."

Star Tenace said sternly, "He did say that, but it was correct. Listen better, and until you do, keep your hand down."

Nord sat down and stared at his desk. Boniface reached over and patted his arm. Star Tenace was always telling them that the survival of Illumen worship depended on their studies, and he had no mercy for the slow.

Jany was quaking, her hand cleaving the air, eager to correct Shyheem.

"Yes, Jany?"

"He said that Illumen is all light. Just because all light comes from the light god does not mean he is all light. He should have said that Illumen is never dark."

The star said, "Thank you, Jany. Shyheem, listen more carefully. Every part of the truth matters. When you say that all light is Illumen, you open up the possibility of heresy. There is light in the temples of Bellum, in the pots of their fire. Is this light Illumen?"

Shyheem lowered his head and stared at his desk. Star Tenace had been so nice when he came, but now he made a little mistake and the star spent half the class correcting it. Part of him didn't think that any of this mattered. Did these people know that kids were starving in SubAgora? Wasn't that supposed to be Illumen's concern?

Anyway, it made sense to him. When he prayed, that light was all around him. What other way was there of knowing the god?

The star went on and explained the lies. One was that light was a sign of goodness. Though light gives life, and darkness kills, darkness can shroud itself in light, just as light can be shrouded in dark. He gave examples from the Writ. He said, "Boniface? What is the first lie related to the Oneness of Light?"

Boniface mumbled something.

"I didn't hear you."

"I don't know, Star Tenace."

"But I just said it. How can you not know, when I just said it?"

Boniface mumbled, "I wasn't listening."

The star said, "Interesting. This new student can at least try to put a thought together, but you don't know anything. It's not because you're stupid. You may or may not be, but we don't know, because you've never tried. It's because you're lazy. Now, can anyone help him?"

At the end of the class Tenace called on four students, and they had to review a truth from the last classes, its lies and references in the Writ.

After classes, every wick had a daily job. Some went to kitchen to help prepare the evening meal. Others had to work in the orchard. Many were assigned to fields, and many went with the shepherds. A few kept up the grounds, and some did housework. Shyheem got kitchen. He reported to Butter, the head cook.

Butter said, "You the new worker?"

Shyheem nodded.

"Say what?"

Shyheem said, "Yes, I'm the new worker."

The cook took Shy's thin upper arm in the fingers of his fat hand. "What's wrong with your arms?"

Shyheem shrugged.

Butter grumbled, "Always the little ones. Is this not work?"

While Shyheem was still coming up with a reply he was directed to an Orange Robe who was slicing off the tops of the carrots and carving off the sides. Orange shreds flew fast. The older wick showed him the process and gave him his own knife. He tried to work on the carrot. He looked over at the older wick fifteen minutes later. The older kid had a pile of clean carrots in front of him and was watching Shyheem with a small smile on his face.

Shyheem said, "What?"

"Nothing," said the Orange. He started laughing.

"How do you do it?"

"Just like that, but hopefully about ten times faster." He was still laughing.

After work there was free time. The first day Shyheem reported to Lamp Obsur and had to sweep because of the unmade bed. He swept and got Boniface to teach him how to make the bed.

He went back to the dorm room. The other Bluebies were seated in groups on three different beds. He moved toward one group, standing close to them. One of the wicks was saying what he remembered about a truth. The others interrupted him if they thought he made a mistake. They stopped after he stood there for a minute.

"You want something," one said.

Shyheem shrugged.

They said, "Leave us alone, brown."

He studied on his bed by himself. Boniface would try to study with him, but would get bored. He tried to convince Shyheem to go outside. He had a castle he was building from mud in the orchard. Shyheem refused, insisting that this was his only time to study. After a week, Shyheem had climbed a few places in each class, but the other wicks still wouldn't let him study with them.

"Shh! Here comes Grandpa Sub."

Lamp Kareem found him in the dormitory.

"Walk with me, Wick Shyheem."

He had his bag slung over his shoulder. They went out walking through the orchards, stepping over the fallen apples.

The lamp said, "I must return to SubAgora. There are other wicks there that need training. There are people who need to know the ways of Illumen."

"Yes, Lamp Kareem."

"I asked the Firmament about the man they sent to tell about the plot to kill the regnate. They said they would send him soon. I said that they should hurry, because Hands, Jalil, and Burton are in prison right now."

"What did they say?"

84

"They said everything in its time. I was angry then, and they reminded me of my place. I am only a lamp. But you will need to check, to see if they have sent someone."

Shyheem nodded. He felt bad. He had become, in only one week, so intent on showing those altic wicks the true light by passing them in class that he had forgotten his friends who were in prison, waiting for him to help.

They had reached the gate out onto the wide plains of Humbershire. Lamp Kareem turned to him and put a hand on his shoulder. "I will miss you. I have been in SubAgora for forty years, and all I wanted was to shine the light in that place. Never was there such a special wick as you, in all my years. I knew that you were different. They say you are shining here, rising in the class, doing well."

"I'm twentieth out of twenty five."

"You have risen five places in one week! I would never be able to even study here. And that is just wick classes. You are also a parwa. They tell me only ten here study under Star InSpent."

"I have not started Parwa class yet, Lamp Kareem."

"It will be soon. Just stay in the lighted way, and I know you will make me and the whole Sub proud."

"The other wicks won't let me study with them."

"It will take them time to get used to you. North Temple does not get a lot of Subs."

"But they're Illumenists. It shouldn't matter where I'm from."

"Well, we see the light darkly, as in a mirror. They will see, but you must give him time to shine into their hearts. Pray for him to move."

Shyheem said, "Yes, sir."

"Shyheem, what a joy this has been. I have seen the windows recording the histories, the carved reliefs telling the story of the manusignis. I have seen the light of the Firmament, the shining crown of the Shining One. Now I will die in peace. Goodbye, Shyheem. I'm going by the Coastal Road this time."

"Goodbye, Lamp Kareem." He felt like he should say more. He should say 'Thank you.' He should say, "All the learning here, Lamp Kareem, has no more to do with Illumen than the crusts you hand out to the Subs." He couldn't though, and he realized that he looked forward to the old man walking away. Then he would be able to give his all to becoming the best wick and parwa in North Temple.

"Keep making me proud, and when you finish, however old you are, please come see me in SubAgora."

The lamp turned and walked away. Shyheem watched him walk through the gate and out onto the plain. The dark robe dwindled out into the vast and growing darkness.

8. Aeternanox

John Nickson rode one horse after another, exchanging them at the inns. He had to take to the shore road to avoid the army, which was also marching south. He prayed for a bandit party, or a herd of wild cluriKin to try him. He had but a single sword and the aura of Bellum.

While he rode he thought about Regnate Grant, and why he deserved to die. Grant had stolen the election from him.

Grant had allowed the wendigo to grow strong.

Grant was soft, oblivious to threats in general, including John Nickson. Did he think that Nickson forgot those slights? And didn't he know that soldiers need to exercise their abilities?

Hands twisted his head halfway off the horse's haunches. He saw large houses with firm stonewalls and bright windows looking out into the night. He imagined what it was like to live in such houses. Big fires must warm the rooms. KiBaubles must hang on the wall. Best of all, meat, dressed in apples and oranges, would be heaped on the table every night.

Hands bounced on the horse's merdup. With each bounce his stomach growled. The streets in AltUrba were paved with cobblestone, and the horses' hooves rang out clearly in the night. When they passed AltUrbans in brightly colored robes and elegant leather shoes, or in carriages bedecked in lanterns, they bowed their heads to honor the Fels. On the lawns fat cluriKin watched the trussed up SubAgorans suspiciously. One threw a small stone that hit Hands' shoulder. The rope cut into his wrists with every bounce.

"Excuse me," he remarked, trying to get the attention of the Fel. "I feel like merd."

The Fel slapped Hands' head again. Hands didn't say anything more, partly because he didn't want to get slapped, and partly so he could concentrate. Hands knew about pain. He had been beaten before. He had been locked up in uncomfortable places, and he had definitely been hungry before. That was just the life of a Sub.

Hands had a trick to deal with beatings, lock-ups, and hunger. He would switch everything around in his head. Hands was regnate, and he had a mighty army at his command. He had the Fels pick up Fel Antony by the heels. He had Jalil beaten up on a daily basis. Then he would go to his hall and eat from a magnificent feast and invite friends, all of whom were much nicer than Jalil, Burt, and Shyheem.

Hands also imagined that it went differently with this Fel. Somehow Hands pulled the sword from its spot and wounded the man, forcing his surrender. Then Hands would tie him up, and throw him over the rump of the horse like a bag of oats. Hands would become as famous as Rasheen. Then Hands would say, "Ha, ha. You're just a puny Fel, I'm Hands, the KiBaron of the kiSubs."

While Hands was daydreaming, the procession progressed upward, and arrived at a gate that was set in a wall rising high above the great houses of AltUrba. Standing on each side of the gate were ten Citan Fels. They spoke briefly with the two that bore the boys, and in a moment they were being carried into the grand square of the Citadel. The broad street was lit up on each side with lanterns hung on posts inlaid with interlacing stalks. The boys twisted their heads to see the great halls and towers populated with detailed statues, covered in arches, and full of bright windows. The buildings rose up toward the stars. Before one building ended, the next took up. Citadel District was stone and mortar knit together, the center of Regna's Eight Wicks.

The prisoners were lifted off the horses and pushed through a low stone arch into a dark room. The sergeant grabbed a torch and told them to follow him. Down a dark passage, into a hole in the wall they went, before the torch plunged down stairs. Hands felt Burt fall into him and he fell over too. The Fel following them propped him up and kicked him hard enough to sting, but not hard enough to knock him back over. The sound of their steps echoed back and forth and up and down the spiral stairs. He started to count the stairs, but he wasn't very good at counting. He lost count around fifty and started over. He was at twenty-eight when the stairs ended.

They entered a room with a group of Fel guards sitting around. Fel Starks said, "I've got three for cell eight."

One of the men in the room responded, "Pretty fearsome bunch. You guys pull them in yourselves, or did you have help?"

"SubAgorans. Don't be fooled by their size."

The Fels laughed.

Fel Starks then got serious. "These browns talked some lip to Vice Regnate Nickson. I want them in the back corner, near it." He said the word 'it' with a spooky emphasis.

Their captors shoved the boys through the room and down a long corridor. The darkness seemed to grow, hemming in the light of the torch. The sounds of coalescing water drops echoed faintly. A heavy smell filled their noses, like the smell of a bull. The Fel in front of them paused.

Hands said, "You could have just killed us up there, and dropped us down the stairs. Save us the walk."

A deep growl came out of the wall next to them. The stonewall seemed to shake.

A hand reached from behind, grabbed the pickpocket's ear and twisted. "Quiet," the Fel hissed. They walked around another turn. The Fel stopped and used a key off a large ring on his belt to open a door of hickory that was as thick as a man and encrusted in iron fastenings.

He whispered, "Welcome to Aeternanox. Enjoy your stay." Then he laughed. The three boys stared at the dark entrance. The Fel kicked Hands in the merdup, sending him sprawling into the room. Burt and Jalil came tumbling after, falling over him.

The ponderous door creaked shut behind them, thudding into its casement. They heard the key turn and the lock click home. It was pitch black and freezing cold. Hands felt around. His head was wet, probably with blood. He found no furniture, just the walls. They were in a box of stone. He tripped over something soft and round. "PorkChop?"

Burt was crying on the ground.

Jalil said, "It's going to be okay; they made a mistake. Come here, Burt."

Jalil felt bad for Burt, but the crying made him feel awkward. He patted him on the back, and said, "It'll be okay. Your dad will come and get us. They'll figure out that my dad was a Guard. It won't be long."

Hands drew his knees to his chest. He said, "They are going to kill us."

Burt said, "But my dad knows they took me."

Hands said, "This is Aeternanox, the deepest, darkest prison in the country, for the kiBads, but your dad is coming to get us. I feel relieved now."

Jalil said, "Shut your kiMouth before I shut it for you."

Then nothing happened for a long time. The door opened and a torch-bearing Fel toed in a thin, twisted cluriKin, who came in and dropped three dishes down, all the while eyeing them from underneath a cliff-like brow. As the dishes clattered on the ground it retreated to the door. From there he pelted the boys with small stones. He seemed to aim especially for Burt. Hands remarked that this was because Burt was easier to hit. When, on the third day, Hands threw a handful of pebbles back, the Fel told them they would miss their next meal.

The gray stuff delivered in moldy wooden bowls was not really food. The first day, Hands ate Burt and Jalil's when they refused it, but after a day they became hungry enough to eat. The first day in there Jalil wrestled with Hands, hoping to shut him up. He pinned him, his arms tight around the pickpocket's neck, his body twisted so that Hands could not cheat and grab his privates. Then he punched him for a while.

"Lulu kaSub," Jalil said.

"Your mother likes them lulu." Hands replied, after Jalil released him. "That's why she married your dad."

Jalil felt around in the dark, but couldn't find him. After that he swore he would ignore the insults. Later, he didn't need to swear, because the only things he cared about were when the cold and hunger were going to end.

They counted the days by the meals. Hands said they were getting fed twice a day, but Burt swore it was only once a day, so every meal counted for a whole day in his system. Jalil let them know that he would rather be in prison alone than with a lulu and a merdup. Hands remarked that he'd rather be in prison with Jalil's mother.

Jalil sent out a punch in the direction of his voice, but hit nothing but air. They lay on the cold wet stone. Burt prayed to Illumen because that's what Shyheem would have him do. He didn't pray out loud, because Hands would make fun of him, and Jalil might join in. Hands was counting two weeks, Burt had reached four, when the door creaked open.

It was Fel Starks carrying a stool. He nodded at some others, who came in and dragged out Jalil and Burt, leaving Hands. He shut the massive door behind him, and sat on a stool.

He said, "I'm Fel Stark."

Hands said, "Great to meet you. I'm Hands."

The Fel leaned back and sighed, "I'm probably going to kill you."

Hands nodded, "I thought so."

"But if you're really helpful, I might let you live. I'd even let you out of here someday. Just tell me everything he said."

Hands launched into a detailed account of his meeting with the dying Fel on the middle of Black way. He watched the face of his interrogator, and saw a ridge of anger emerge across his brow.

When he was finished, the Fel said through his teeth, "Did he tell you how he knew?"

Hands shook his head. The man stood up and grabbed the Sub, shoving him up against the wall, his hard soldier hands clenched around the Sub's throat. It hurt badly and Hands could not breathe. "Tell me what else he said."

Hands' mind worked through the possibilities. If he pretended the man had told him something he hadn't, the Fel would find out, and that would just get Hands killed faster. At the same time, it didn't seem like he had any other option.

But Hands got a glimmer of hope then, even though he couldn't breathe, pinned up against the wall. His hand, clutching frantically at the uniform of the Fel, found a clasp on his belt. While he choked, he tried to smile. The Fel didn't like the smile, and he squeezed harder. He was so intent on squeezing the smile out of Hands that he didn't feel the fingers twisting the clasp back and forth, back and forth, until it broke. He didn't hear the little tinkle it made when it hit the floor. After that Hands stopped smiling.

The Fel let up and said, "Did any of you tell anyone else?"

Hands said, "Yeah, we told half the boys in the Sub."

The Fel laughed. "Nice try, Sub. We may kill you if you can't remember more about that graz and his friends."

He dropped Hands and exited the cell. A few minutes later the guards threw Burt and Jalil back through the door. The boys looked scared before the door shut them back into blackness.

Hands said, "Told you we're not getting out alive."

Burt said, "If you just ran by us, we would still be back home."

Hands said, "Stop being a lulu."

He crawled toward the door. He felt against the wall until he found the clasp that he had torn from the belt of the Fel sergeant. He inserted it into the lock, feeling the tumblers for weight with the tip of it. Burt and Jalil heard the sound of metal ticking.

Burt said, "Even if you open that, which I doubt, where do we go from there? There are like ten soldiers in the room after the stairs. Not to mention that growling thing."

Jalil said, "Don't get us into more trouble."

Hands said, "You idiots. We're in so much trouble, they will kill us once they figure out we don't know anything else."

"That's not true. I told them my dad was a Guardsman. They're going to let us out. This plot will get uncovered, and we'll go free, if you don't get us into more trouble first."

9. Strangers in the Dark

They'd thank him later. He kept working. It was not ideal, using a clasp. The tumblers needed to be at different heights. He sat back, feeling the metal that he had in his hands. He was lucky it was thin and he could twist it. A few twists. Try again. Feel the parts move, feel the tumblers click up. The twist was limited, but he could also use the rocks in the wall of the cell as rasps against the thin piece of metal. Scrap. Scrap. Feel it. That was the contour.

Two minutes later the lock clicked open. He reached under the door with both his pinkies and ring fingers, and pulled up, and slowly in. The door creaked, but he didn't stop. The long squeak echoed into the darkness of the dungeon halls. Jalil thought he heard shuffling and movement, but wasn't sure if it was the beating of his own heart. Burt was sure that the soldiers and the creature called 'it' had heard them.

Burt said, "Hands, you're going to get us into trouble."

"Lulus." Hands said, as he eased through the door. The hall was pitch-black and he moved like a blind man, his hands in front of him, feeling with his toe before stepping down. The stillness and the darkness eased up his spine and rested its eeriness against his neck. This was not the stillness of being alone, but the stillness of being watched and listened to, of being next to large and lurking murderers and monsters. He told his legs to be firm and continued forward. When he felt the doors in the wall he moved into the middle of the hall, listening to the breathing of the other inmates. They were not his friends.

Eventually he got to a point where he could see light, and he knew that this was the beginning of the hall that led to the guardroom. He peeked down the hall. It was long, and the room at the end was bright and full of talk and red-shirts. There was no way past them. He turned back until he reached the open door of their cell. He went further into the dungeon. He turned a corner and heard a deep and sonorous snoring that filled the hall. His terror grew. The heavy animal smell grew stronger, and as he moved on, the snoring became louder until it seemed that the floor was vibrating with it.

Behind that door slept a creature with excellent hearing and a sensitive nose. Usually, it would have heard the passage of anything in the hall. Then it would have roared loudly, again and again. The guard would have rushed to investigate. They would have caught Hands, returned him to his cell, and cut off his hands to avoid further lockpicking. Hands was very quiet but mostly he was very lucky.

He continued until the wall on his left opened out. He turned left with the hall and felt his way with hands and feet. After some time he felt another wall and he was forced to turn left again. He saw again the light emanating from the guardroom. He now had a rough mental map of the dungeon. The hallway formed a square, lined with the cells. Branching off from the middle of the front hall was the passage to the guardroom, and through the guardroom was the stairs. That was the only direction out. There was no possibility of escape. He sank to the floor of the hall.

That was when he heard the voice. "Hello, prison friend."

"Huh!" Hands jumped and stared but he could see nothing beside the faint glow down the hall. The voice that he heard came out of the darkness only two steps away.

"I here, friend." The voice was quietly distinct, almost like a bell. Hands was shaking. "I friend."

Hands trained his eyes in the direction of the voice, but he still couldn't see anything. He flattened himself against the wall. "Nobody is my friend."

"Two came with you?"

"They're not my friends either."

"Question please. You not big, and you here in Aeternanox. What you do?"

Hands said, "I'm not telling you."

"Why tell me, you no know me. You want out. I help you. I want out Aeternanox too."

The voice sounded like the wind in the trees. He didn't like talking with someone he couldn't see who apparently could see him. It scared him that the owner of the voice knew how many people were in his cell. Still he sat there and listened.

"How you out your prison?"

Hands didn't say anything.

The voice continued, "I wendigo. Wendigo see, hear in night like animal. My hands ironed behind me, and my feet ironed together. They fear me. I kill three mans. He, in back hall, the roarer, him they fear most. No know how many he eat."

Hands thought, "Great, a murderer."

The wendigo said, "Okay. I kill. Now kill me. Maybe cut me too. But no. They know I want die. No want cold dark place, no trees and rivers. No birds, no bugs. Just dark. You free me. I run and fight them, then they kill me. Good death then."

Hands said, "You might just eat me."

"Wendigo no like man for food. Roarer like eat man and wendigo. My name Seketeme."

Hands paused for a moment. Finally he spoke, "I'm Hands."

"Hands, ha ha. Hands good with the irons. Okay. I plan this. Upstairs there is man river."

"Man river?"

"Um. Place for use from eat?"

"A bathroom?"

"Yes, river from bathroom. It go to big river. Go through mans, upstairs, in water, free! Question? The guards. I kill maybe five. They maybe twenty, thirty upstairs. They come and come. You kill maybe one. Need kill more. Need help from roarer in deep."

Hands thought about the roaring growler in the back hall. He shivered. "We shouldn't let it out."

"It not bad. It hungry, strong, angry angry. I say, 'Roarer, bad mans put you here. Want eat?'"

Hands asked, "You can talk to that thing?"

"Seketeme is wendigo. Can talk to all wild things. Hands, you get me from irons and you, I go."

The thing wanted him to take off its chains. He did not know what to do. The option presented was terrible. He did not want to free the wendigo. He was even more afraid of releasing the thing in the back hall. At the same time, there was no other way out. He knew that it would only take the Fel a day or two to decide that the boys knew nothing of use, and then they would be killed.

"You do plan now?"

Hands didn't say anything. He was thinking it through.

The voice continued, "I want get back. We use roarer for out, roarer get back much more. Mans talk, NO NO." The wendigo laughed quietly to himself.

Hands said, "What is it?"

"His name wake him. He big, long hair, from mountains."

Hands knew then that must be a grolf, the monsters of the mountains. They ate everything that lived, the wendigo included. He shook his head. "You can get him to do what you say?"

"Yes. You get me out?"

If Hands were offered a chance to bet on the situation, he would have bet against the trustworthiness of the wendigo. He had heard of their charm. They could talk to you, and the singsong of their words worked a spell, so a person agreed with them, even when they were clearly being walked into a murder.

Also, Hands knew that everyone was selfish, and the idea that somehow this wendigo was an exception was improbable. Nevertheless, Hands decided to release the wendigo. It was only a small chance that the wendigo would help him escape, but it was the only chance he had. Hands shook his head and got up and tripped quietly across the hall. He stuck out his hands feeling for the keyhole. "To you left, Hands."

Once Hands found the keyhole, the door was quick work. He'd already picked one of those doors that night. He eased it open, happy that it swung silently. He walked into the cell.

"My feet right there."

He found the great thick plate of iron that wrapped around the ankles of the creature. He sat down and took the padlock in his hands. The padlock took some time. When he popped it open, and carefully opened the shackle and set it on the floor, the wendigo sighed. In the dark, he heard him stretching. "Thank you."

Next he moved to the manacles. He felt the metal with his makeshift pick, plucking and pushing the tumblers, until he was removing the second shackle. It came off faster than he expected, clattering to the stone floor. The noise of metal on stone echoed down the halls.

"Quick." The wendigo forced him under a stone bench, and closed the cell door with a quiet click. Then he positioned himself in front of the hiding Sub and draped the chains over himself to disguise his freedom. A moment later light filled the hall, and then a Fel walked up to the cell, holding a torch.

"What you doing now, LeafHead?" The Fel looked up and down the cell. Hands worried that his heels were visible. He stayed still, holding his breath.

The wendigo said, "Prepare to kill you, TreeCutter."

The Fel laughed. "You're in a cell, LeafHead. Shut up, we're playing a game and your noise isn't helping." He stomped off. Hands knew that this was the moment when he would be eaten. He waited.

The wendigo said, "Come. You all bone; no good to eat."

They walked silently toward the back hall. When they reached the corner, the heavy smell of musk was everywhere. The wendigo spoke in a guttural hum. "No afraid, Hands. He grolf, you small man, but he think you afraid, he eat you. He no like afraid."

The wendigo went back to growling. A syllabled murmur answered him from the middle cell. When they reached it, the wendigo pushed Hands toward the door. The voice of the thing beyond the door shook the walls with its depth, and the boy's hands shook as he tried to work on the lock. He kept himself going by imagining that even if the grolf ate him, it would eat Jalil, Burt, and the Fels too. His hand was steady, and the clasp conformed to his wishes, and soon, the great lock clicked open. He pulled the knob, but it did not stir.

"I can't open it," Hands whispered. The wendigo grabbed the bars at the small window and pulled, making a whispery grunt as he exerted all of his strength, but the door did not move. He growled something, and the door opened slowly, pushed by a great force. The wendigo growled some more. It sounded like a song played by muffled drums, deep and rhythmic. A deeper growl hummed from the blackness of the cell.

"Hands, irons on him, too."

Hands forced himself to follow the wendigo into the room, where the goatish smell was so strong it hampered his thought. He felt fur and then the metal of the padlock. The band of steel was as thick as his arm. The room vibrated with the breathing of the grolf, and he imagined its teeth the way he had heard them described, great grinding blocks. He told himself to concentrate on the lock. Locks were something that he could spring. As he concentrated, his hands slowly stopped shaking, and his mind reached inside the mechanism, creating a picture of the tumblers.

The lock fell open. Great stony things grabbed his shoulders, and lifted him up. Then hairy limbs surrounded him, crushing him, and he knew that all his air would be squeezed out. The voice of the wendigo growled a song. The grolf released him, and he plopped onto the floor. He was petrified.

"Leg iron, leg iron, Hands."

Hands said nothing.

"Leg iron." A toe, the wendigo's toe, prodded Hands. That brought him back to reality. Oh, yeah. He had to get the leg shackle off. He crawled forward, pawing at the musky air. He felt a hoof cloven like a goat's, but bigger than a man's head. It was the foot of the grolf. He felt up for the iron shackle with its dangling padlock. The plates of steel were thick. No part of him was thinking any longer, he only acted. He did not hear the garbled speech that went back and forth between the wild creatures. He only opened the padlock, and carefully pulled open the shackle.

The wendigo said to him, "Good. Get friends, go toward mans."

He stumbled out of the cell, happy to be alive, and skipped down the hall toward his original cell. Behind him he heard footsteps in the stone hall heavy and fast. Hoofsteps. He stepped into the open door of his cell.

Jalil whispered, "Well?"

"Follow me." He moved into the cell and grabbed them, pulling them by their shirts.

98

Burt said, "Where are we going? What was that . . . noise?"

Hands hissed, "We need to go now."

Burt said, "Tell me where we are going first."

Then the roar went up and Hands heard the guards shout in response.

He said, "I'm going." He walked out of the cell. They weren't following him. Another roar, even louder, sounded in the dungeon. He heard Burt gasp.

He ducked back into the cell and hissed, "I let that thing loose. So now we're in more trouble. You better take the chance now, or else you'll die tomorrow."

Jalil said, "You graz."

"Just come on." After a few moments he heard them coming after him. Why he wasted his time on grazzen altas like them, he didn't know. They followed his voice down the hall and around the corner. The sound of shouts and screams mixed with the smashing of wood, stone and bone and echoed through the dungeon.

They watched as the grolf, tall as two men, whirled, struck and threw the Fels. The redcoats jumped in, only to fly off him, slamming into the wall, and the grolf's once white fur flowed like the snow-bound fury of a winter storm. The staircase entering the room was now full of red-coats and armor, the Fels there crying out for others to fall back, almost falling over one another as they retreated up the stairs.

The many years of his torture were with him. His torture had not been to his body but to his mind, for he was a creature that ruled the mountain slopes. There among the goats and the deer and the bear, he ran for days, leaping from crag to crag, the whistling winds alone keeping pace with him. When he rested it was on peaks, his eyes galloping across pine-covered slopes and river-sliced valleys. They had held him a prisoner in the bowels of the earth, laughing at his growls and mocking his glory. They had sought, with knife, magic, and metal, to bring him under their sway.

Heavy were the days on his great shoulders, until the recollection of those places where he had come from dimmed, and all he could think of was dark and damp, and he forgot the sun. He remembered only that this was wrong, that Fels had done this to him, and that he hated them. This deep anger flowed through his mighty claws and gave them for a moment the strength they had had when he was the king of a mountain. The chance to destroy those who had broken his heart gave him no joy. He no longer hoped for happiness, but only that there be some justice, that those who had broken him would also be broken.

The soldiers had heard the roar and seen his charge. One braver than the others had unleashed his spear, which now was lodged in the grolf's fur, but the thrower was broken against the wall, and seven others were dead in the room. An eighth pretended to be dead, while the cluriKin wailed in a corner of the room, expressing the general distress of the dungeon. The main force rallied in the room above, knowing that they needed to fight in numbers to bring down the mountain king.

The wendigo, standing next to them said, "Come." He loped down the hall, and found the remaining guard, who jabbed a spear at him. The wendigo dropped, allowing the spear to slide through the air above his left shoulder, and grabbed the guard. He used his teeth. A second later, the Fel was lying on the floor with the others. Burt gasped.

The wendigo turned to the boys, who watched him in varying degrees of amazement. Hands saw that his skin was dark and dirty, and instead of hair, a bunch of brown, shriveled leaves topped his head. He was shorter than a man and thinner, but his body had the electric poise of a wild animal.

The wendigo pointed toward the stair that the fight had moved up and said, "Go up, look for river. Breathe, jump, swim." Sharp teeth flashed in his mouth.

Burt said, "Who are you?" But the wendigo was already climbing the stairs. A chatter sounded next to them, and Hands felt a pain in his leg. The prison cluriKin had sunk its teeth into his leg. Hands pounded down with a fist on it, and its jaws released. Then Hands sent a ferocious kick into it, and it flew across the room and into the far wall, letting out a keening series of screams.

Upstairs the Fels were trying to stop the grolf. They spread themselves in a semi-circle, their spears pointed like wheel spokes toward the grolf, who roared and waited for their advance. Behind them was a small channel way of water set in the stone of the floor. The wendigo pointed with a clawed finger, "See?"

Hands said, "There are about twelve Fels between here and there."

The wendigo roared something and the grolf roared in response, charging into the redcoats. The wendigo leapt up the remaining three stairs, grabbing a spear off the floor. He threw it in among the soldiers, who were falling back and falling down. The grolf had two spears sticking out his chest, his fur was now striped with spurts of red, but he was still up. His roar was seismic, and his flashing hooves struck like Bellum's own hammer.

The boys jumped up and danced through the room toward the water. Hands felt his heel grabbed and fell down. A fallen soldier had a hold of him.

"I'm taking you with me, you little merd," the soldier said, dragging Hands to him. There was a dagger in his other hand, and blood coming out of his stomach. Hands tried to pull free, but the grip was too strong.

A moment later a great cloven hoof slammed down on the soldier. His eyes went dark; he released Hands. Hands looked up at the great beast above him, and the grolf looked down at him and roared, and Hands was not afraid because he understood that the grolf sounded a thanks. Then the wendigo scooped him up, shouting, "Breathe," and as he sucked in air, they dove into the murky trough and felt the current sluice them down and out of Aeternanox.

10. Fourth Blueby

The old sachem stood behind an oak trunk, in the southern slopes of Faunarum. He listened to the frantic murmurings of the trees. He watched the Regnan soldiers below, slamming their axe blades into a tree's flesh. The trunk snapped, and slowly leaned, dropped, and crashed through the shrubs below. Bursting forth squawking and squealing came the small animals of the forest. His hands trembled; his eyes narrowed.

"Sachem."

A young longeye was behind him, breathing heavily. He had run far to find his leader.

"Yes?"

"The MishiMaster is at your seat wishing to speak with you."

The sachem took off running, quick for one so old, the buck leaping at his side. When he reached the high meadow, he saw the MishiMaster lying flat by the great oak, watching the clouds meander across the blue sky. The sachem walked up to the crazy haired man, breathing heavily, and stood, waiting for the man to speak.

"Please sit," he said. "You breathe like you've run from the southern slopes."

Taking a seat by the green-eyed man, he said, "It is rare for us to have two visits from you in such a short time."

"I have come to ask your help. The LightTalker that came through here will arrive at the HighSeat soon. You must advocate for him so the wendigo hear what he has to say, regardless of the boy and his attitude."

"Why won't you go? They will listen to you surely, but of the sachems, I am the least."

"If by least, you mean oldest." The man chuckled. "I'm busy, old leafHead."

102

The man got up, and walked into the trees. The old sachem wished that for a moment he could lie as the MishiMaster had, against the grass, looking at the sky, every limb relaxed. He had too much to worry about.

Pilgrims arrived at North Temple every day. They first appeared as black specks and grew and took shape. The wicks sat on the ridge of their dorm roof and watched them arrive. They guessed why each traveler made the pilgrimage.

One pilgrim walked awkwardly and Gladius joked that the man had a groin itch he wanted the Shining One to pray over. One kid with the broad forehead of a Humbershire farmer walked up, his eyes bulging at the ornate architecture, his mouth slack so that he looked always surprised. They guessed that he wanted to become a wick, but would start crying after one class with Star Tenace. Dusty and tired looking farmers marched forward to get prayer for their dry fields.

Shyheem had admonished the wicks, "These are pilgrims. You guys are going the way of Bellum, making fun of them."

"They can't hear us, Grandpa Sub."

"It's your heart you should worry about," Shyheem countered, "not their ears."

"Whatever," said Gladius, "I'm not the one with darkness for skin."

Shyheem said, "This is the way Theom made me. If you think he makes mistakes, we'll go talk to Star Tenace about it."

"Theom just had off days. He made the wendigo, right? And then he made Subs. It was a bad day for him."

If only Jalil were here, Shyheem thought.

One day they spied a man in a lamp's black tunic coming up the road. Beside the tunic, everything else about him was unlike a lamp. His arms bulged in the sleeves of his robe; his calf muscles clenched into a big ball with every step, and his hair was a black bush. He wore a fierce beard. The least lamp-like thing was that, next to an ironbound Writ on his belt, he wore a large sword.

103

When he got close he saw the wicks sitting on the ridge of their roof, pretending to recite their writs to one another. He shouted, "Tell me a truth, you Bluebies."

They couldn't think of anything to say, and he laughed. "You must all be at the bottom of the class. Don't any of you want me to carry a good report to Star Tenace?"

They all started saying one truth or another all at once, and he laughed again. "No, I won't be able to test you, for I've forgotten them myself."

The Bluebies looked at him with their mouths open. Either he was joking about forgetting truths, which was something they couldn't imagine, or worse, he had actually forgotten the truths. They watched him walk away. He did not march toward the pilgrim lodging, but went straight into the temple hall, even though it was late afternoon, and the Firmament were in their meeting. The Orange at the door didn't try to stop him as he marched in.

Gladius said, "He's a torch."

Shyheem said, "What's a torch?"

Gladius said, "How can this fake parwa be number twelve in our class? He doesn't even know what a torch is."

Jany said, "It's a traveling lamp who shines where people forgot about the light."

Gladius said, "There are only four torches left."

That night Wick Boniface popped into the dorm when Shyheem was reciting to himself. "Ultima is out there. She says you're supposed to go with her."

"Where?"

"I don't know, go ask her."

When he got out to the front room Wick Ultima was standing there. She was one of the smarter wicks. "Come on, Grandpa Sub."

"Where are we going?"

"Parwa class."

"You're a parwa?"

"I'm better than you."

"Sorry. I didn't know."

They walked up the stairs onto the roof of the dining hall. The mountains shone faintly in the dusk light, reflecting the old light of the day and the new light of the evening's stars. Seated on the benches was the class. It was small. There were four orange robes, two green robes, and Gladius. Star InSpent looked at them.

"Today, we welcome a new parwa. That is good because the rest of you are not doing what we hoped. The light is small and without power. Star Tenace let me know that he is saddened that you can't do better."

She talked about magnitude of flame. It was said that the flames of Sarah Hope and Anstabt had spanned up to one mile. The magnitude of the flame came from the strength of one's relationship with Illumen. It came from being clean. This quality, this cleanliness, should be understood as translucency. A dirty or dark glass does not allow light through completely; it lessens and distorts it. Thus, the serious parwa needed to be in constant prayer.

They took turns praying and producing the flame. Shyheem was shocked to see that almost all his classmates could produce a flame that was about two hands high. She corrected some and directed others how to pray and study in order to improve. The youngest kids in the back tried first, while the Oranges and Greens prayed. Gladius and Ultima had around the same size, one foot. The best that Shyheem could manage was glowing blue hands.

Shyheem noticed that the wicks in Parwa class were serious. They never made fun of one another. Even Gladius said, "Nice light," to Shyheem. It didn't sound sarcastic.

The green robes went next. A girl produced a two-foot flame that crackled and shot. Applause erupted from around the building and Shyheem looked down. Surrounding the dining hall were wicks, watching the flames of the Parwas.

They clapped even louder and let out oohs and aahs when one of the Oranges sent up a four-foot display. It lit the ring of smiling faces on the ground. They did one more round, before Star InSpent dismissed them. When he stood, Shyheem swayed, and Ultima pulled him back to his seat.

"Give it a minute, Grandpa Sub."

He looked around and saw that all the other parwas were lying on the benches, breathing heavily. After a quarter of hour they got up, and Shyheem watched them shuffle like old men who had used all their strength. He got up and felt his limbs pull him toward the ground, and barely made it into his bed before he was sleeping.

In wick classes, he found that his hard work was giving him success. He had climbed to fourth in the class after only three weeks. He had passed a wick or two with every day, but he didn't know if he could rise any further. The top three studied hard. They were smart. Gladius was first, followed by Jany, and then there was Rojo, who was third. They were neck and neck with one another. Some days Jany was first, and some days Rojo made second, but even on his best day, Shyheem was nowhere near breaking into their group. In Truth Class, Jany was called on to explain the truth of nature.

"Nature is lit because Theom has made it. It is neither a god, nor is it darkness, because it is made by the good god. It is made for man, but man was also made for it, so that he could be served by it.

"Here is an example from the Writ:

'These waters are like light,

They flow wild and capsiezmic over me.'"

She went on and repeated everything that the star had said. When she had finished with her summary, she continued.

She said, "The twenty first Shining One said this, 'Nature is all things, those made by man, and those not, for all come from the Light. Yet that which man has not made, the earth, the rivers, the trees, and the ocean, is better nature, for it proceeds more directly from his light, and does not pass through man, who has both dark and light, Bellum and Illumen, in him. This is why sometimes we gaze at workmanship, and see some Light, but the reaches of the Ocean always blaze like the sun in our hearts."

Star Tenace nodded. "Excellent, Jany. You have chosen an excellent source by reading the Twenty First Shining One. He loved nature, and wrote the best commentaries on the nature truths."

Shyheem was amazed that she had read extra, and actually memorized a whole passage from a commentary. Shyheem didn't have time to do extra reading beyond rereading the things covered in class. He read and recited until lights out, and felt like he was never up on all the class work. He could not understand how the top three managed to read beyond the assigned material.

He said to Boniface, "How do they do that? Where's the time?"

Boniface said, "Who cares? You're number four, that's great."

"But how do they do it?"

"It's not like they started four weeks ago." Boniface answered, "When we have days off, holy days, or breaks, they keep studying. They know the order of the truths, and they figure out which one they're going to have to do. They read up on that one. What they don't do is have any fun."

Shyheem was so wrapped up in making a success of North Temple that he had completely forgotten that Lamp Kareem asked him to check with the Firmament about the message to the regnate. After asking the lamps if anyone wanted to journey to Ornata and getting no volunteers, the Firmament had also forgotten. They did not like to try to interact with Citans and be reminded of how unimportant North Temple had become. Nobody wanted to travel three weeks in order to be ignored.

Shyheem figured that currently, he was number one in the second group. He wanted to bridge the gap, become number four in the first group. He didn't need to pass them; he just wanted them to feel his breath on their heels. He got his first chance that week with the Harvest Feast. There was a long Dawn Service, and then a classless day until the feast. He worked two hours in the kitchen and escaped.

He went into the library. There were no chattering blues and green robes. Long windows let the sunlight in to light rows of tables. A number of orange robes and lamps sat at tables reading. Even the motes that swirled in the sunlight did so with a somber, intelligent air, as if they too considered eternal truths.

Gladius was seated with two Greens, and piles of books were on their table. Rojo and Jany shared a table and even a book. Many lamps and orange robes studied at the other tables. Nobody noticed him as he walked quietly along. The shelves ran far back, and there were many sections. In the Sub, books were rare and highly valued, and to see so many excited him, but it also daunted him. How many would he need to read, in order to be taken seriously as a wick? He needed to find a commentary on the Truths. He searched through the rows but could not find what he wanted. He realized he had no idea how to start looking.

He went to Gladius. He climbed the bench and sat next to the top student. Gladius turned and glared at him. Shyheem whispered, "Can you help me?"

Gladius put a finger fiercely to his lip, as if Shyheem had just been shouting, and turned back to his book. After a few moments, Shyheem got down and went to Jany and Rojo. They looked at him and pulled the text closer. He wandered back into the tall shelves, preaching against them in his head. "It's wrong not to help another Illumenist. I'm trying to get light; they should want to help me. The more light, the better for everyone. I don't know how those altics got in here."

The books were set in wooden shelves that stretched up to the ceiling of the tall room. Shy pulled one out and looked at it. It was in a language he didn't know. He wandered through the shelves staring at the books. He knew that they were going to be doing the Truth of the Sun when it was his turn, but he didn't know where to find commentaries. He didn't know which ones would be important. It wasn't as if quoting a random text would impress the star.

He ended up pulling out a book and reading the title and then moving on. He thought he could do this all day and not find a volume even mildly relevant. He saw a man standing by one of the dark shelves in the middle of the stacks. He walked closer and saw the black beard of the torch.

"Hey. Looking for something, Blueby?"

"I'm new here, and I don't know how to find a commentary."

The blue eyes twinkled under black eyebrows, "What truth are you studying?"

"The truth of the sun."

The bearded torch said, "I've just the thing."

He fished a small red book out from the shelf. "These are all on the Nature Truths. Third chapter."

Shyheem said, "This is an important one?"

The torch said, "That's Lucius. Very important."

"Thank you."

The torch smiled through his beard. "It was my pleasure."

Shyheem sat down and opened up the little book. He paged through until he got to the third chapter. "The truth of the sun, as given to us by the Third Shining One. The sun is a symbol of Illumen, because it gives light to all, and from its light comes life. Without the sun, we would all perish. It is held in a crystal sphere; it is a disk of light. The Third points out that the sun is used often in the Writ as a symbol of Illumen. Therefore, the truth of the sun is that it is a symbol."

It went on like this, and Shy was confused. When he had read the whole chapter, he felt more confused. He went back to the beginning and started reading again. Eventually he pieced this much together. The Third Lighted One had said that the primary thing they should know about the sun was that it was a symbol of Illumen; whereas Lucius felt that the primary thing was that the sun was in fact the face of Illumen. It shines on the world, giving life, and if this was not Illumen, then what was? Further, the idea of symbol made no sense. The god was physical, and existed. If the sun was the best symbol of the god, then in fact it was he.

"How does the third Shining One know the sun is held in crystal, that it is a disk of light always oriented on us? For Illumen is not held in any sphere but his light burns like flame, sudden, unpredictable and uncontrolled. The sun itself burns in like manner, for it is given as an image of the god through out the Writ. The sun is a ball of flame that stretches toward us and draws back from us on its own accord."

Shy memorized a passage that he felt the author himself would have felt was vital. He repeated the words, his lips moving, but no noise coming out. When he looked up, he realized that the library was almost dark. He walked back among the series of wooden bookcases, but he could not find the correct one. In the end he shrugged and tucked the book under his robe. He went out and found that the campus was quiet.

The feast! He was late for the feast! He ran through the orchard, which was almost completely dark, toward the lights of the mess hall.

He heard the feast before he got inside, the loud happy conversation of a couple hundred people relaxing together after a long harvest season. Inside the three robe classes were eating, and even the lamps and the stars were kicking back. The tables were piled with meat that filled the room with savory smells. Bowls were overflowing with apples roasted with cinnamon, and many other green and yellow vegetables filled every little space at the tables.

He went to tail end of the lamp table where his dorm father was. "Lamp Obsur, I am late."

"I see."

"I was studying truths in the library."

"Ah, yes. You are a parwa, and therefore you need extra time in the library, even when the whole of North Temple is at a feast. Perhaps I should make an exception for you. You are such a brightness."

Shy felt the lamps and blue-robes watching his shame. Gladius would be laughing at his botched attempt to compete in Truths Class. The half of the class that he had passed in two months would be happy too. Shyheem shouldn't think he was better than them, or that he was as good as the top three, they would all think with satisfaction.

Lamp Obsur said, "Tomorrow you will be digging. For now, you should go back to the dorm and continue your important studies. No time for dinner."

Shyheem walked out with his head down. He could feel the lamps and wicks eyeing him. He didn't mind missing the feast, because it was his fault. He just didn't want the lamps to think he was disrespectful, or the wicks to think they were better than him. He had not done it on purpose. He wasn't proud; he just wanted to please the star.

When he got back to the dorm, he put his head in his hands. He knew that other dorm fathers would have let it pass because it

110

was a feast day, but not Obsur. Obsur never missed a chance to punish him. Then he felt the aching hole where food should have been opening up in his belly. He had barely eaten lunch, he'd been so eager to get to the library.

Back in the Sub, he'd be fed by friends, even when he was broke. That thought reminded him how far he was from true friends, and he let out a choked sob. He was more alone than he had ever been, despite being among fellow Illumenists. The house cluriKin was watching him. It laughed when he wiped his cheek, but then, when the crying didn't stop, it started to sing in its gobbly gook language, grabbing his knee in its mitten hands and rocking it back and forth. He pushed it away, and lay down.

He was awakened by a gentle shaking. Boniface whispered, "Here."

He gave him a balled up napkin which flapped open revealing a meal of pork, apples, and buns. Shy said, "But I was late. I'm not supposed to eat."

Boniface said, "You're so skinny, you might starve to death tonight. That won't make Illumen happy either, so shut up and eat." The cluriKin, which always followed Boniface around and did whatever he did, had gotten beneath the napkin and was lifting it up with two arms, bearing it toward Shyheem.

The smell of the food made him hungry, and even though he didn't feel it was the right thing to do, he had a kaTaste of the pork, and then some more. Pretty soon he'd eaten all of it. He lay down and felt the darkness of his disobedience. He was sure that Star Tenace would know.

The next day he was in the field, ready to dig his punishment. An old man gave him a hoe. "Dig up three whole rows." The old man lifted the hoe over his head and brought it down. It lodged in the dirt, and the old man gave it a twist. The earth came up and broke into pieces. He did it again. "Like that."

At first Shy enjoyed the work, but soon his arms began to hurt, and his hands developed water blisters. The sun shone down. He was only done one row and felt like he had no energy left. The water blisters broke open, and the wooden handle stung as it rubbed the raw skin. As he worked he swore that he would show them all, Lamp Obsur, Gladius and Alta, the kind of student he was. He wouldn't be stepped on forever, treated like nobody, and called Grandpa Sub. They would see. He would squash them, put them in their place.

11. Heresy

Parwa class was on Teraday so that the parwas had all Theoday to stay in bed, letting their drained bodies recuperate. When it was time for class, many of the wicks and lamps would come out and sit on the lawns below. The lights often made beautiful shows, and of course, this light was the hope of the Illumenists, so all of North Temple was excited when the Parwas demonstrated power or control.

Star InSpent talked about the connection between control and intention. She demonstrated by praying. A blue flame sprung from her open hand and rose into the air, where it slowly spun. A perfect sphere of flame hung and spun, small flames licking the sides. The audience below applauded. She opened her eyes and the flames returned to her hand and died.

"Now, remembering your own limitation, remembering that the flame is not yours, but a gift from Illumen, try to do what I have just done."

Shyheem watched. Gladius and Ultima only succeeded in creating the same one-foot flame that flickered around. The green robes looked a little better, with flames that stood up, but failed to actually leave their hands. The oranges were trying hard. The tall girl sent a flame up nicely, that turned into a ball at its height. The crowd below clapped for a moment, but it extinguished before returning to her hand. She slipped down onto the bench and closed her eyes, breathing heavily.

Star InSpent looked at him. "What about you, Shyheem? You're expected to try as well."

After two tries, all the other parwas were exhausted. They turned heavy eyes toward the new kid. He closed his eyes and began to pray. He tried to remember that Illumen was the source of light, and he was just the air through which the light passed. He remembered the Lucius passage, the strange idea that Illumen's face was the sun, and he recalled the SubAgora, with all its people, the strength of Jalil, the kindness of Burton, and the cleverness of Hands, the thousands of people, all the things they sold and bought, the curses and blessings they exchanged, and saw Illumen in it all. Then he called the light and asked that it do what it had for the star. He opened his eyes. He was shocked to see, suspended six feet above him, a tight ball of blue flame, which rotated for a moment, before slowly descending to his palm, dispelling in a bubbly flash.

It was dead silent; even the wicks and lamps that normally talked and laughed among themselves during the light show were completely quiet. Then as one, applause and roars of approval erupted from below. Shyheem smiled slackly at the other parwas who were staring at him. The star looked at him in disbelief. The wicks down below continued their cheers.

When the star had recovered she said, "Very good, Shyheem. Very good indeed."

The next day, as he sat in class, ate in the dining hall, and walked through the grounds people pointed at him. The story of his control and power as a parwa was whispered over and over again. Nobody called him Grandpa Sub, and some called him Parwa Shyheem. Gladius glared at him; Jany asked him to study with her.

The next week Star Tenace called Shyheem to go over the truth of the sun. Shyheem had planned for this moment. He was ready to move into the top of the class. He started by quoting lines from Cantos in which the sun was mentioned. He reviewed these, and listed the historical Writ references. He explained these for about twenty minutes, and he could see that the class was impressed. Gladius was frowning while Rojo nodded in appreciation. Boniface was listening for once, smiling as if it were he himself who was kicking merdup on presentation day.

Then Shyheem mentioned the book by Lucius. Star Tenace started. Shyheem figured he was surprising them all with his additional knowledge. He carefully explained how Lucius said that the sun was not just a symbol. After all, it was real, everyone saw it and felt it everyday. Its effects spread through everything. In fact, its effects, that of giving life-giving light, were not just like Illumen's effects. They were his effects; therefore the sun was the face of

Illumen. He had been concentrating on explaining this introduction, and he knew that his explanation of Lucius was thorough. He checked the faces in the room, to see how he was doing.

Tenace's jaw was locked, and his massive hands gripped his chair like he might pull it apart. Gladius was smiling ear to ear, and Boniface was looking at him in horror, shaking his head, and mouthing, "No." He must have misunderstood what he read, even after three times. He had grown to even like the difficult sentences. He began to recite the quote he had memorized, "From 'On Nature' by Lucius, Chapter Three, line thirty two through fifty one . . ."

"Stop." The star interrupted him.

The room was taut; not a whisper, not a rustle was heard. Even Gladius was looking fearfully at the star. Star Tenace spoke in a strained voice. "Lucius said nothing that was truth or light. After he had written two books, he was thrown from the temple into the darkness. His books are darkness; his words are heresy.

"Can a true worshipper say that the sun, which is just a thing with no face, is Illumen, who is a god? The sun goes down and is gone for the night. Is Illumen gone for the night? So this is an untruth of the most evil nature, for it seeks to limit the power of Illumen."

"Beyond that, Lucius sought to say that the others, the grazzes and even the wendigo were the same to Illumen as humans. This goes against many passages in the Writ. Can some of you give me some?"

The class responded, trying to assuage the anger that was between the star's teeth. They gave the creation in Origin. They also brought up the history of Rasheen. Shyheem wanted to bury himself in his desk. After dismissing the class, the star said, "Shyheem, I will speak with you further."

Shyheem went up to the front and stood by the star's desk. His classmates walked out some nodding sympathetically, others laughing.

Star Tenace said, "Where did you find out about Lucius?"

Shyheem told him how the torch had handed him the book in the library. Star Tenace instructed him to follow, and they marched straight to the temple. Two stars were blessing pilgrims.

Star Tenace said, "The Firmament must meet at once. Wick Oppurtune, please clear the temple hall, then get the Shining One and the stars. Then tell Torch Angen to come at once."

The Orange Robe ran out of the room. Shyheem sat and waited. Torch Angen was the first to arrive. He walked in and sat down next to Shyheem, facing the seats. Shyheem thought he saw a smirk on the torch's lips underneath his beard. How could he laugh? Shyheem had worked hard, missed a feast, for nothing, all because of the torch's evil joke. Star Tenace glared at the torch. When they were all assembled, Star Tenace spoke.

"Today, I was treated to a lecture on Lucius' reading of the third Shining One's commentary on the sun. This was not in an Orange class, where the heresies are discussed, but in a blue class, and the student did not know that he was reading from the worst castOut in history. He was lecturing on Lucius as a commentary on the truth of the sun! When I questioned this student, he told me that Torch Angen was responsible for handing him the book."

Shyheem bowed his head in shame. The Firmament murmured among themselves.

The Shining One said, "Torch Angen, is this true?"

Torch Angen said, "Yes. My addition to Truths class."

The Shining One turned to Shyheem. His eyes were burning blue. "You had no knowledge that Lucius was a castOut?"

Shyheem nodded. He glanced over to see a cool expression on Angen's face.

The Shining One said, "The parwa did not know what he was doing. He was trying to succeed in Truths."

Star Tenace spoke, "I agree. Yet, it is important to see the damage that was done. He is our most promising parwa, and he has committed Lucius to memory. Now it is there."

The Shining One nodded. "You are right, Star Tenace, to point out this evil, but we must never forget the power of light. Shyheem, you are new here, doing your best to study, and suddenly you find yourself in this problem. It is a great danger to read Lucius. We do not want you to take these words into your heart. Begin now to forget what you read there.

"Lucius is only one hundred and forty years gone from North Temple. He was a great student here, the best, and in fact he was thought to have the wisdom, humility and compassion necessary to join the Firmament and perhaps sit in this seat. Yet his scholarship took a bad turn, which finally became perilous. This bit on the sun is what he always did. He took a truth and made it into a lie, by stretching and rewriting it. He did not respect the commentaries, but thought that he could make new truths.

"He was castOut as a shrouder, but he always used Illumen's name. He said that Illumen was present in all things, in rocks, in the sea, in the sun, in grolfs, in wendigo, in grazzes.

"When the Firmament saw the way he was thinking, they took Lucius into a meeting, and they tried to speak to him. But he would not listen, and he said that the Firmament wanted to keep Illumen in books. When he refused to turn, he was cast out. His books, the two he had written, were placed in a special shelf in the library, the shelf of heresy. We keep those books to remind us of the perils of certain thoughts, but we do not intend that wicks and parwas still in blue robes should read them.

"Lucius wandered alone, and became friends with lovers of darkness, wendigo, wild cluriKin, and some even say he spoke with grolfs. He is shrouded in the darkness. You also, forget him, and his words. Memorize instead the truth of the sun reading by the one hundred and ninth Shining One, my predecessor and teacher."

Shyheem nodded. They dismissed him. He found the wicks waiting for him in the dorm.

Gladius said, "You're a follower of Lucius."

Jany said, "Shut up, Gladius. Why did you read Lucius?"

Shyheem told them his story. He told them that the torch was there in the temple hall, standing before the Firmament. The wicks had always thought the torch was funny, and joked around a lot, but it was too much to make a joke like that. He would be in trouble. They wondered if a torch got the same punishment as a wick. Would they see him in the cornfield tomorrow, harvesting ears and shucking?

The Blue Robes would have been shocked to see how calmly the torch gazed up at the Firmament. They wouldn't have been able to return glares from stars. Maybe he could look that calm and direct because he had studied with three of those stars, and had finished ahead of them. Maybe it was because he felt less respect for the Temple than he once had.

Star Hamstead, the historian, spoke first, "How could you give that book to a Blue Robe?"

He said, "This was coming all along. I have seen, in my travels, many new lights. I have gone places that no living Illumenist has. I have learned of the shrouded days of Lucius. He wandered among the wendigo, and they still speak of him with respect. As I learned his history, I came to believe that he should not have been cast out. I tracked down his writings, and read them again, and through him, the light is renewed in me."

Star Tenace was out of his seat. "Send him into darkness! He praises the shrouder. He has become a shrouder! He is a friend to the murderous wendigo. He gave Lucius' book to a Blue Robe. And this Blue Robe is a parwa who could have been reading something of light! A parwa that has genuine power!"

The Shining One spoke, "Angen, think about what you are saying. Lucius denied the transcendence of the human. He equated light with darkness. If you can't remember the truths about these things our hearts will be overcome. We do not want to see you walk into darkness."

The torch said, "It did not seem likely to me that you would see my way of thinking. Yet, things being as they are, I will speak, and say what I have come to believe. I can only hope you will see."

Star Tenace shouted, "Don't let him speak. Too many untruths have been proclaimed already."

Star Hamstead said, "That is not how we make decisions, Star Tenace."

Star Tenace sat, smoldering, to listen to the darknesses of Torch Angen. "Every time I return to North Temple, I hear the same stories. The Parwas have only small flames. We remember that there were manusignis, but today there are none, and it is mourned, because our influence dwindles, fewer and fewer follow

118

Illumen. You sit and ponder old writings and create more rules and more commentary, and you wonder why there is no flame.

"The parwas need to be where the needy are oppressed for their gifts to shine. The needy are in Ornata and Faunarum. They are in the streets of SubAgora. They are not here. This studying in this safe place is not the way of Illumen. He came down off the clouds to be among the people. You guard truths that are no longer true, and therefore are blind.

"Consider my words."

After a brief discussion the Firmament ruled that Angen had gone the way of darkness. The Shining One offered him a final chance to return to the light. He asked the torch to think of the love that the Shining One had for him, and listen to the truth and light. The Shining One spoke about when he had taught the torch, then a wick, the Truths, and how then he had loved them. How had he gone so far? Still the torch would not turn from his darknesses, and the firmament convicted him of shrouding. He was commanded to leave North Temple, and not step into any Temple of Illumen. He was a castOut.

The torch asked for a night to gather his things. They granted him this, and asked that he leave with food as well, for they did not want him to leave life though he had left light.

The Orange Robe who kept the door of the Sanctuary told the wicks about the meeting. They meandered over to the lamp dorms, a line of one room apartments half embedded in a hill side. They had never seen a castOut before, and they expected to find the torch weeping. They saw him in front of his quarters. He was moving his possessions onto a sheet, which he then tested for weight. He would remove something, and then stare at it. All along he was whistling songs to himself, and glancing up at the mountains in the northwest. When he saw the wicks staring at him, he asked them if they wanted to come with him.

A green robe said, "You're going into darkness, why would we want to go with you?"

The torch said, "I'm going into darkness?"

"You're a castOut."

"According to the Firmament, I'm a castOut. According to me, I'm full of light, fuller than I've ever been. If you come with me, you'll be able to see the same light."

A lamp emerged from the adjoining room. "All of you get back to your dorms. Shame on you, Angen, to abuse the graciousness of the night the Firmament granted you."

Back at the dorm, seated on the spine of their roof, the wicks consulted. They asked Shyheem to rehash his version of events. All the Orange Robes and Green Robes laughed hilariously when he confessed to quoting Lucius in Truths Class. They did impressions of Star Tenace that shocked the Bluebies.

Gladius said, "I wonder if those words will slowly twist your soul. They are in you now. Even when you dream, Lucius may speak to you, and call you to go with him to Bellum's darkness."

Shyheem looked at him. He said, "The Firmament cleared me. They see the power of my light, and figure a little thing like that won't mess me up. It would be different if my light had less power."

Gladius shut up. He may have been a better wick, but nobody cared about that. What really mattered was the skill of the manusignis, and everyone knew about the fireball that Shyheem had created. That night after everyone got in bed, Rojo asked from across the room, "Ready for the recital in Writ Class, Shyheem?"

He said, "I don't know, I'm a little nervous."

"Yeah, me too."

Boniface said, "Only person not nervous is Gladius. He knows it all!"

All the boys laughed. The cluriKin laughed and turned somersaults down the center aisle. Gladius growled something about burning them all with the flames of Illumen.

Boniface said, "You going to get Shyheem to burn us for you?"

Everyone laughed. Gladius didn't answer again. They all thought about the recital due the next day. Even though it was going to be hard, they would face it together. Shyheem pulled the covers tight against the crisp fall air and snuggled into the warmth.

———

120

Shyheem woke up and tried to yell. Rough hands forced a rag into his mouth. He couldn't move his tongue to yell. Ropes were lashed around him. He was being carried out of the dorm, and through the orchards, toward the wall behind North Temple. He was pushed over the wall. He fell onto the grass and bounced. He got to his feet and started to run but the man jumped on him.

"Damn Blueby. Never figured a Sub would be a singer. I'd have told them, but I needed time to get a little support."

Shyheem gasped on the ground, looking up at the wild beard of the castOut. The shrouder had not been content to leave, but had decided to take a parwa from the North Temple, a final act of dark revenge. Shyheem threw out his hands and kicked, energized by the fear.

The man whispered a laugh and unsheathed his sword, a heavy blade. "Walk," he said.

"Where?"

"North." Away from North Temple. Away from Regna. Into the haunts of the grolf and the wendigo.

12. LeafHead

Years before Hands met the dying Fel on Black Way, another person from this mostly-the-same sometime-ago world was reaching the age where everyone in the town could see what he was. They remembered that his mother's pregnancy had been nervous. Of course it had been nervous. She knew she was not carrying a human, not the child of her young husband all along.

But when he was born, he looked perfectly human, only large, and covered in pale hair. No one said anything about the quickness of the marriage, or the nerves of the mother. It was a little after his fourth birthday when the two protuberances pushed at the upper right and left corners of his forehead. It was as if he had received two solid, symmetrical knocks. As time wore on, the skin broke around them and everyone could see that he had horn nubs.

Her husband knew why she had been so eager for marriage. The village knew that his wife's love for mountain jaunts was more than natural affection. They saw the horns, the child's wide nostrils, and the strange white hair that covered his arms and back like thatch. They drove the mother and her abomination out with stones, leaving them collapsed, half-dead, in the cold and windy heaths of Humbershire. She sat there thinking that she could not go to another town, for it would be obvious to them as well. She thought about returning to the mountain, but she knew that the mountain kings would have no more place for the half-breed than the humans.

She despaired, weeping tears of defeat. The child nestled his strange head against her neck, vainly seeking to comfort her. In the distance appeared a wagon, trundling along at a good pace. She ducked into a ditch, waiting for it to pass, but its rattle stopped, and a voice called out, "Woman! Come out from that ditch with your kid."

She rose, pulling the terrified child with her. "If you kill us, we will thank you for it."

The wagon driver, a man with a bush of wiry hair, laughed. "Killing is not my business, but you are the ones I am looking for. Come over here; get in the wagon. I know a place and a people that can be home for you."

And what could she do? He might have been searching for slaves, he might be a labor man, but in the end, he was something other than the Humbershire wind. They got in the wagon, and prayed that the driver was good.

The water around grew gray as they moved from Aeternanox and then black as Burt swam deeper into the tunnel. He wished for air until he was sure he needed it, that without it he would die. He wanted his lungs full of it. He thought about breathing in the water. At least it would fill his lungs. He thought, "Maybe it's best if I just drown here."

Someone, most likely Jalil, pushed him from behind, and he surged forward through the murky soup. He spied a small gray light far in front. This restored his motivation and he cupped the water with his chubby hands and pulled. The light grew, turning from gray to bright yellow. In another second, he shot out.

He was twirling through the sky, sucking in great chunks of air. So bright. Blink blink. For a moment he caught a glimpse of the city as seen from Citadel District, the green yards and strong stone houses of AltUrba, and then the wall, and another circle where the houses were close together, pooled around the markets, that was SubAgora, home. Beyond that was the wilder Agora, open space dotted with random roads and houses.

Directly below him coming up fast was the river. He tried to hit feet first, but it was hard to control himself while falling. His feet broke the surface first but he was sideways and the side of his legs and bottom smacked hard against it. He plunged deep into the river, before the drag of the liquid slowed him. He swam up to the surface. He sputtered when he got his head back above water, because it felt as though half of the river was up his nose.

He could see three heads bobbing in the river, Jalil, Hands, and the dark leafy mess of the strange man. He looked back to where they had fallen from and saw, high up the cliff, the water spouting forth. Towering above the cliff rose the massive stonewall of the Fel Bastion.

They struck out for the opposite shore. The Subs were good swimmers. They spent most of their summer diving off the docks into the ocean, but the creature quickly outstripped them. He wriggled through the current like a fish, and was pulling himself out and shaking droplets off in a fine spray, while the Subs had only swum halfway.

When they reached the shore, they found themselves in the garden of an AltUrban house. The garden was dotted with small trees and shrubs. They lay on a recreational dock, breathing in the sunny air. They could hear the horns of the Fels and the roar of the grolf, echoing out from the rocky cliff, as he battled on against his captors, paying them for their tortuous experiments.

Burt said, "Whew, that was crazy. Crazy dollar."

Hands said, "Do you think the grolf will live?"

The stranger said, "No. He strong, but they many many. He fight, fight, kill, kill but then he die."

Jalil and Burt were examining their new companion. He stood breathing deeply on the dock, his eyes greedily eating up the trees, the grass, the yellow river, and the blue sky. He was clearly not human; the mass of leaves worn down to the skeletal veins atop his head proved that. He had teeth like a cat, and fingers like claws. A wendigo. Although he couldn't quite figure out what was going on, Burt didn't want to be rude, so he introduced himself. "Hey, wendigo. I'm Burt."

The wendigo took the boy's hand, "I Seketeme."

Jalil didn't mind being rude at all, and continued staring at the wendigo. Burt saw the look, and tried to smooth things over by changing the subject. He said, "What was that thing? What just happened? All I remember was running, peeing my pants, and then someone was pushing me into that toilet water. My pants were already merded so no big."

124

Hands explained that Seketeme had helped him free the grolf. He said they were going to the wendigo's contact in Agora who could help them reach the regnate. Burt nodded.

Jalil said, "You going to listen to the baby eater?"

Hands said, "He's our friend."

"No! He's wendigo. He can't be our friend."

Hands said, "Shut up, Jalil. We need to get to the regnate. Deal with it."

Jalil shook his head and spit, "Baby eater."

Ignoring this, Seketeme said, "You need regnate? I owe this one," and he dropped a claw on Hands head, "so I tell you. I know one man maybe help. Orpan in Agora. Right now we need go. When grolf die, Fels come for wendigo and little mans. Then we no here."

Burt said, "He's right, we need to get out of here."

Hands said, "Back on the river?"

The wendigo shook his head. "They boats many. No river."

Burt said, "We've got to go out through the streets."

Burt was the only one of them who had been in AltUrba before. His father had been asked to cater a party. He had brought Burt along. They had been stopped multiple times by Fels. Their dark skin and inexpensive undyed clothes made it obvious that they were not AltUrbans. The Fels asked where their badges were. They showed the patch badge the merchant had given them and were allowed to proceed.

The four escapees' clothes were soaked, but even if they were dry and their skin was peach, they wouldn't have passed for AltUrbans. Burt had the most respectable outfit of all them, including a blue tunic, breeches, and a pair of soaked shoes, but that was grimy after living on the floor of a Aeternanox cell for weeks. Jalil was wearing a pair of pants and a used shirt, but he had no shoes. The rags that hung off Hands weren't anything, but they might have been shorts a few years ago. The wendigo was naked except for something like pants made of animal skin. The wendigo pointed his claw across the river as a small galley launched from the far bank.

Mounted on the boat's prow was a great thunderPipe, used to break the hulls of smugglers' ships. It would splinter a Sub's ribcage. The escapees crept toward the front of the yard until they were hidden among the branches of a small maple.

Burt said, "We need clothes."

Jalil didn't say anything; he was busy staring hard at the wendigo. Hands shrugged. "This was the best I could afford."

Burt looked around, as if clothes might be behind the bushes. His eyes rested on the AltUrban house. It was a large structure, with windows on top of windows, holding as many rooms as a whole block's worth of SubAgoran shacks.

Burt said, "Hands, get into the house. We need nice clothes."

The back wall was covered in ivy that worked like a perfect ladder, especially for a Sub who had entered second floor windows uninvited before. In a moment Hands was slipping his knife thin body through a second story window. His brown feet plopped onto a floor. He flexed his toes and pressed them against it a few times, enjoying its smooth cool feel beneath his feet, before he heard a thumping coming up the stairs. He ducked further into the room, sliding behind the door, but the thumping came right in. The door shut. The house cluriKin turned slowly, until it faced him. This was no teddy bear sized Shacko. It was as fat as Burt and almost as tall. It saw him.

"Merd," Hands remarked.

It charged him; its arms open to tackle him. Hands stepped forward and aimed a kick at the side of its head and made solid contact. It went spinning into a pile of clothes. Hands stayed on his toes, ready for a second onslaught.

He heard a keening sound from the pile of clothes. He kicked into the clothes and the sound got louder. He pulled the clothes back. The AltUrban cluriKin had balled up, covering its eyes with its mitten-hands. It was crying like a baby. AltUrban cluriKin might be bigger and fatter than SubAgoran ones, but they had no rah.

The room was painted yellow; curtain of green tickled the breeze. A bed big enough for ten Hands-sized kids filled a corner, heaped with pillows and quilts. Hands forgot his mission for a moment and sprang through the air and fell on the soft down,

126

twisting his wiry frame in among all the cotton stuffed bedding. It felt magnificent. He only lay there a moment before springing back up. He had a mission.

He grabbed a pile of clothes out of an open bureau. It was fortunate that it had been left open because Hands wouldn't have known where clothes were stored. He always wore all his clothes.

The three in the yard were listening to the bugle of the Fel galley as it moved across the river. They looked up, wondering where Hands was, and saw a rainstorm of brightly colored clothes twirling down. Hands might be a pain in the merdup, but if you needed someone to steal something, he was nice to have around.

They tried on different things. Jalil's shoes were tight, and Hands' were loose, and the wendigo was too thin for his overcoat, it billowed around him. AltUrbans were not built thin, and no one but Burt had the proper belly. Burt stuck extra shirts under their belts. They all popped the collars, pulled on a tricorn, or covered their heads with hoods. Seketeme had to hide leaf hair, the Subs had to disguise their dark skin. Burt looked at them and decided they would pass at first glance, and that was as good as it was going to get.

They didn't have a lot of time. The Fels' citywide organization was efficient. As they dressed, trained sparrows had winged the news of the escape to the AltUrban company, who quickly moved to deploy mounted troops toward the river.

They scaled the sidewall and found themselves on a lawn by a main street that descended toward SubAgora. It was evening and the AltUrbans strolled by in their bright coats and tricorns. Though many people were out, it was quiet. When people were out in the Sub, you heard them talk.

Burt hissed, "That way, and spread out. They'll be looking for four of us."

They spread apart and walked downhill toward the gate of the SubAgora. Burt led the way, and Hands was some paces behind him. Jalil found himself a few steps behind the wendigo.

Just then the mounted Fels appeared on the street. They rode quickly, and even the important citizens of AltUrba found themselves diving for the side of the street to get out from under

127

the hooves of the galloping horses. As the Fels approached, Burt found himself holding his breath, but they rode by him, fooled by the bright yellow of his coat, and then by Hands, their eyes passing over his forest green cloak. They continued on, and were almost by Jalil and Seketeme. It looked like the stolen robes would work. They were focusing their attention on the houses on the riverside of the road. They thought the fugitives hid in those buildings or were still in the yards behind them.

Jalil watched the Fels as they rode by. He was thinking about his dad. He used to watch for his return. When Jalil saw the sky blue shirt, he ran and his dad caught him up, threw him through the air, "Hey, little warrior." At home everything was okay when his dad was there. His mom didn't drink, she cooked, and together they bought new clothes for Jalil. Then he remembered the tears of his mother, while Jalil had just stood there. The Guard sergeant said, standing there in the doorway, "Your dad is dead, son. Fought hard, good soldier, but the wendigo crept up on us in the night. By the time we knew what was happening, he was gone."

That was the wendigo. Sneaky snakes that slithered through the grass and killed sleeping men. His sleeping father. Not even fighting face to face. A man, a soldier, stood and faced his foes.

The Fels were about to go by, and the disguised wendigo was about to escape! Jalil ripped the wendigo's hood back, exposing the forest-like head with its pointed ears and leaf hair. He screamed, "This is the wendigo!"

The Fels wheeled on their mounts toward the scream, as every AltUrban on the street turned and stared. The wendigo took off running in the opposite direction. The mounted Fels charged after him amidst the terrified screams of the rich people. He sped up the hill, his feet almost as nimble as that of the horses, but then more Fels emerged at the top of the hill coming down toward him. Arrows whistled toward him from every side.

13. Get Your Rah Up

Two arrows skimmed him, almost hit him. Then a thunderPipe cracked. The wendigo ducked, throwing himself under a wagon that was making a full turn in middle of the street. The arrows thudded into the wood side of the wagon, and the driver stopped, turning his green eyes in surprise toward the attack.

"Out of the way," roared the Fels, momentarily blocked from their pursuit. The driver nodded and flapped his reins, but by then the Fels had ridden around the back of the wagon and were charging after the wendigo, who was vaulting the garden wall, smooth as a cat.

Jalil grabbed Burt and Hands. "Come on," he said.

Hands didn't move, transfixed by the wendigo's flight. Seketeme was going back toward the river, where the Fel Galley and its horrible thunderPipe waited. He was going to be killed. Hands felt anger boiling up inside him.

"You graz!" he yelled at Jalil.

The AltUrbans turned to see who had shouted. They saw nice coats, but deep hoods and darkish faces beneath it. Then another thunderPipe cracked, and their heads swiveled back toward the chase.

Burt hissed, "Shh. We still need to get out of here."

Hands knew that Burt was right and pushed his anger down for the moment. He turned from watching the Fels pour over the garden walls and followed Burt and Jalil. They approached the tunnel out of AltUrba, gearing themselves up for questions there.

There was only one Fel at the tunnel, a young soldier who was watching what he could of the chase, which was now only the sergeants bellowing orders. They tried to walk normally as they descended toward the tunnel.

Anybody could leave AltUrba; it was getting in that was hard. They walked through the down slope of the tunnel, out the gate into the Sub. Burt felt relief at seeing the familiar low and nestled structures. When they got past the first turn in the road, they looked back to see if they were out of sight. Then they turned on Jalil.

Burt said, "That wasn't kiDolla. He got us out of prison."

Hands said, "That was my friend, you graz."

Jalil said, "I would rather die than be saved by a wendigo."

"But you're still alive, aren't you?" retorted Hands. "He's the one who's going to die."

Burt added, "Even if you didn't like it, you can't just choose to betray him like that. We were working with him, as a team, and you just decided to do that on your own."

Jalil pushed Burt and said, "What are you going to do about it?"

Hands was waiting for this, already behind Jalil. He threw his arm around the bigger Sub's neck, and kicked out so that Hands' whole body weight pulled down on Jalil's neck. Jalil fell back on the floor with the snake like arm tightening around his throat. He coughed, choked, and finally got his hand under the arm, and struggled to his knees. He ducked and pulled, and Hands went flying over his shoulders. He ran over and planted a knee in Hands' back and twisted an arm. Hands cried out and a few Subs looked over at them to see if it would turn into a real fight, but Burt pushed Jalil off, and tried to punch him a few times. Jalil pushed him away, and swung one hard punch into Burt's ribs. Burt sat down gasping. Jalil looked at them lying in the dust. He burned where Hands' arm had tightened around his neck.

Jalil said, "I'm going back to Black Way. Later, lulus."

He stomped off, thinking about home, and getting away from them and their dumb plans. He had just saved the city from having a killer loose in it, and all they could do was criticize him.

The other two boys caught their breath. Hands wondered whether he should have topped off falling five stories into the river and kicking the hard head of an AltUrban cluriKin with a fight with Jalil. He knew he'd done some damage, though, with his forearm choke-hammer, and that lessened the pain in his arm and back.

Burt said, "I want to go back too."

Hands said, "They will be waiting for us there."

Burt said, "Just to see my dad and get a kaBowl of stew."

Hands shook his head. "We can't ever underestimate the Fels again. Them guys are looking everywhere for us and next time they aren't going to waste time putting us in prison."

Burt felt tired and hungry and dirty. Home was, in his mind the answer to all those problems. "If we just go quick. Or in disguise!"

Hands stood there, shaking his head.

"Fine," Burt said, with a tone that suggested it was not fine at all.

Hands said, "Look, at least we have a mission. Seketeme said we should go to Orpan."

They turned and got back on Apia Way, winding their way down toward Agora. They looked around them and saw their people, the brown Subs, moving toward the markets, shouting across the streets at one another. They relaxed a little, losing their hats and hoods, and popping their collars down. The only time they tensed was when they saw a Fel patrolling the crowd but he was too busy checking for illegal products to notice the nicely-clothed Subs.

Hands was silent, chewing on his loss. He had trusted the wendigo. That wasn't something he did everyday. Then the wendigo did everything he said he would, got him out, saved him. A guy, or whatever he was, that Hands could really trust. A warrior too. And just like that the wendigo was gone again. How come Hands wasn't allowed to have one good thing for a minute?

Burt saw the heavy way Hands was walking. He owed Hands a lot for the way he had saved him and Jalil, and he didn't like seeing the anger and sadness smack each other across his friend's face.

He said, "How big do you think that grolf was?"

Hands laughed, "Like as heavy as four men!"

"KiDollar. He fought thirty of them."

"That was what we saw! Probably killed another thirty after we left."

"And Seketeme. You let him out?"

"He said he wasn't going to eat me, but I was scared merdless. My hands shook like a sail in the wind while I picked his locks. Then he didn't eat me."

"How high were we, popping out the cliff like that?"

131

"I felt like a bird, saw the whole city!"

"That river."

"Hurt!"

"I'm not scared of no river though. But it hurt."

"I can't believe Jalil. Seketeme just risked his life to save us, and he sings on him like that?"

"A Sub singing like that is not dollar."

"I hope a Fel finds him on Black and they take him right back to Aeternanox, he said that's what he wanted."

"It would serve him right," agreed Burt.

Hands felt warmly toward Burt, which he thought was probably because Jalil wasn't around telling everyone how he was such a kiSub. They wondered if Shyheem was still back at the alley.

When they went through the SubAgora Gate, twenty feet tall and manned by a squad of Fels, and entered Agora, the market was still running, for Agora never slept. The grazzes called out, their voices creaking like metal, that they had necklaces that guaranteed love, and rings that gave the wearer pride. Their large eyes were set wide, and shifted about quickly. Their skin was almost scales, rough, and brownish green. Rather than hair, they have rougher scales atop their head and down their neck. Their bodies were wiry and their legs short. Armored mannequins were positioned by the stands and wagons in battle-ready poses, while the grazzes themselves spun the various swords and axes so that they caught the light of the torches and lamps that lit the market at night.

"There's a war on! Be armed against the evil wendigo."

"Trouble finding love? Try this potion. Tastes like crap, but it's worth it. I'm not too good looking. Greenish, hey, I'm a graz. But you should see the girls I get after drinking this stuff."

"Got your swords cheap. Grazzen forged."

"Cuts wendigo like butter."

They didn't talk to the grazzes because they were liars and cheats. Instead Burt walked up to a group of Humbershire farmers who wore overalls. He asked if they knew Orpan's Inn, but they didn't. He found a shop with a human keeper. The keeper said, "Two nice AltUrbans such as yourselves don't want to go there. Not a good place for Urbans, you got grazzes, even wild cluriKin in

132

there. Something happens and your mom will have the Fels in my shop, asking me questions." They walked on.

Burt found a smiling graz counting dollars. "Orpan's?"

He said, "Wait a minute while I lock up these fine weapons. You need fine weapons? Got biting little knives perfect for smaller AltUrban warriors such as yourselves." Hands enjoyed being mistaken for an AltUrban that could afford such fine weapons. He did like the daggers. They were inlaid with fine rune-work and the handles were wrapped in strands of soft leather. Too bad he was broke.

The graz finished putting his sharp wares in a great chest, which he eased onto his back. Because grazzes are the height of a man's shoulders, they couldn't see him above or around the chest, so they trumped along, following a chest with two little legs.

He led them down Segundaton Road. They found themselves in a wide circle of inns, ranging from the ramshackle to the luxurious. Music, yelling, and fighting spilled out of the inns into the street where the rest of the district was also talking and hanging out. At the end of the street was a great three-story building of stone. "ORPAN'S" was written with fat letters on a heavy sign. Beyond it was the gate out of Urba.

The graz marched in and slammed his box down at a door on the floor where a young man hefted it down into a storage closet and gave him a ticket. Grazzes perched two to a bar stool, chatting wildly in their strange hissing language, their hands jerking in time with their words. Ponderous Segundawick farmers, wider than tall, sat at round tables that crowded the room, talking to one another in sonorous tones. There were humans from far places, their clothes strange, their skin rough, and their necks unshaven. Some were Urban, but they were also rough looking. Some were sailors with purple scars across their faces. Others had the violent eyes of mercenaries, marked by their profession. Some were thieves missing a hand.

Two bare-chested men were slugging at one another on a roped-off stage near the back of the first floor. One swung, and the other stumbled out of the way. The swinger swayed. The fight was slow, and Hands figured that neither of them really wanted to be in

133

it. Someone yelled at them to hit one another, and one renewed his effort launching a windmill attack that was more about energy than injury. Burt looked around for a seat, but found none. He motioned his friend toward the bar. The place had a second tier, a balcony from which chicken bones flew occasionally.

Burt leaned across the bar and shouted, "Two cocoas here."

A giant of a man under a white mane of hair dropped the heavy mugs on a small open section of the great bar and collected their coins. He moved on down the bar, filling orders and collecting coins in a flurry of motion.

The farmer next to them was talking loudly, and the whole bar was listening. "Yup. A wendigo. Running right through the middle of the city. Yup, AltUrba. They say he killed three Fels today." Loud exclamations of shock, indignation, and general interest answered this.

"Serves them right."

"Vultures." Everyone at the bar nodded. Nobody explained exactly whether they thought the wendigo or the Fels were carrion. Based on the generally wild outlaw look of the customers, Burt guessed it was the Fels.

"They said they caught him in one of the backyards by the river. The rumor is that he escaped from Aeternanox, but the Fels are saying that he was an assassin sent to take the regnate's life. As if the whole country and the next one over doesn't know that the regnate marched out toward Ornata two weeks ago."

"The AltUrbans are angry. You should have heard them whining, 'Who let a wendigo into High Hill? What happened to protection?' They say that the reason they have walls is so this doesn't happen."

Hands said, "Ah, those Fels."

The giant behind the bar was in front of the kids again. His hair was a snowy pile of white that tumbled from his head, sprouted from his chin, and gushed out from the collar and sleeves of his shirt. He leaned over the bar and shouted loud enough to be heard above the general din, "By your skin, you kaMen are either Bugiri, or SubAgoran. Which is it?"

Burt said, "Sub."

"And what brings you out of the safety of the man's city into the wide world?"

Hands said, "You Orpan?"

The big man said, "Some call me that."

Burt leaned over the bar. He whispered, "Seketeme sent us."

Orpan's head twitched the mildest bit when the name was dropped. He rubbed a section of the bar vigorously with a rag that had been slung over his shoulder.

He said, "You guys had trouble with the law lately?"

14. Wild and Wide Agora

"Would you like some tea, Alta Clarie?"

No. I want to skewer you with a sword. "Alta Carnegie, thank you but I do not care for more tea."

"Perhaps, Alta Clarie, a small cracker would please you?"

Shut up! "Alta Carnegie, it is kind of you to offer, but I must refuse. I am sorry to be inopportune, but I must excuse myself briefly."

Alta Carnegie smiled at this bit of nicety. She had been reciting mantras for weeks. Everytime the First Child said, "I've got to take a piss," Alta Carnegie suffered another heart attack.

"Enjoy the walk, Alta Clarie," said the governess.

Clarie started up and moved out past the three footman who held the tea, the crackers, and the napkins. Alta Carnegie didn't hear, when Clarie gathered the voluminous skirts and took off running. One of the footman gasped, and the alta heard it and turned. She saw the young heir to Urbawick running at top speed, in a fifty dollar dress!

She shouted, "Clarie Grant, First Child, Heir to Urbawick, stop this instant!"

Clarie didn't hear, or didn't want to. It doesn't really matter which. She kept running.

It requires not just skill, but commitment to vault a three and a half foot stonewall while wearing a dress, but Clarie had all of those, and she sailed over the garden wall like she was a bird wearing a four-skirted dress.

Shortly she was disguised as a houseboy, her hair tucked up under a shaggy tricorn, her legs in pants, jogging through the back yards toward the House of Plainwick. She stalked the WickBaron Vermont these days. Not because he was cute, although he was, with his blue eyes and brush thick hair. She stalked him because he was talking and thinking about the war, and most of the people in

136

Citadel were trying not to, either because they were squeamish, or because they didn't want to be reminded of their own cowardliness in staying home behind the four rings of walls that guarded Urba.

Today she stalked him because she knew something big had happened yesterday. She heard commotion coming from the Fel Bastion, and she had seen the Fels moving quickly out through all three gates. She figured he was her best bet at getting real information.

She found him in his yard, loading a thunderPipe. Then a bird plummeted out of the blue sky and bobbled to a stop on his shoulder, hopping close to his ear. He reached up and carefully grasped the fine boned thing, removing a bit of paper from its leg. Clarie ducked behind a bush, because it was obvious the news was important. Vermont read it, looked up, and walked around his house and out the front gate. He breezed through the gates, the Fels fading back before him. She pulled her bonnet forward and followed him out of Citadel.

Orpan was asking if they'd been breaking the law. Burt looked around, checking for a clear path to the door. Was this guy going to have them arrested?

Orpan, seeing the skittish look of his undersized customers, said, "I meant to say, you were underground with the gentleman we were discussing?"

"Yeah, I didn't know there was that much ground to get under."

Orpan looked at them and shivered. He moved down the bar and grabbed one of the fat maids who moved through the crowd. "Get these two the upstairs corner booth. Give them some of that beef stew too."

The girl nodded, and they were led upstairs to a full booth. The five men in it were engaged in chewing through some gristle, and calling each other's mothers names, when the maid walked up.

She said, "Hey. Orpan needs this booth."

They muttered to themselves, "A free man moving out for two Sub boys." They moved right out anyway, and the two boys slipped

137

in. They were sitting for a moment when two steaming bowls of stew arrived. The steam that rose from the bowls reminded them of the way Shawnee made it, and soon they were slurping at the spicy broth and chomping on the hearty beef and potatoes.

Hands said, "Dollar!"

Burt said, "It's not Abierto's, but I'll take it right now."

The giant man from behind the bar scooted in, pushing them firmly up against the wall. He was hairier than most people, with great thatches of white beard covering his cheeks. Even his eyebrows were big bushy growths.

He spoke loudly, "Welcome, brown travelers. My inn is the best. We have the best entertainment, the best food. If this is your first night in wide Agora, you picked well. I rarely have young people in here, Agora is a place for the full grown."

Burt said, "The food's good. I like the rosemary in the stew, but the entertainment," he nodded over the railing at the big drunk men who were boxing the air between them, "is not the best."

The big man laughed, but then his voice dropped, "The last time I saw the one you mentioned he was enchained, bound for a place from which none return, especially his kind. Until today."

Burt nodded. "That's where we met him." He went on to tell their entire adventure in a whisper. Orpan seemed less interested in the bit about the Fels and the plot to kill the regnate. He asked more questions about how Hands and the wendigo had released the grolf into the guardroom and escaped into AltUrba.

Orpan chuckled and said, "Grolf loose in Citadel; wendigo loose in AltUrba. The wickBarons will question themselves tonight, little Subs. They will ask questions."

Burt added the story of Jalil's betrayal of the wendigo. Hands muttered curses to himself at this point. Orpan asked, "How long ago did you leave Seketeme?

Burt said, "It was around three this afternoon."

"Where?"

Burt said, "In the main way of SubAgora, about thirty minutes walk up from the SubAgoran gate."

"And what about this friend? He went to Black Way in the Sub?"

They nodded.

"Okay." He stood up and walked to the stairs, somehow moving easily through the throng of talkers around the bar, despite his big frame.

Hands said, "What do you think?"

Burt was swallowing a mouthful of stew. He said, "He's not bad. He seems to know Seketeme, so that's good. I think he'll help us."

Hands said, "I don't know. Where is he going now? Probably to sell us to the Fels. You can't just trust people." Hands wanted to get up and run, but Burt held him.

Burt said, "Seketeme sent us here. We trust him."

They heard a hullabaloo from downstairs and from their perch saw one of the farmers stand up and pull a club from his back, while a largish graz unsheathed a dagger. Tables and chairs fell around them as they lunged.

The man screamed, "Shouldn't let you lizards in the city."

The graz rasped, "You stink like rotten milk."

A roar came from behind the bar, "None of that merd in my place." Then, leaping, his feet somehow finding stepping places on tables, men, and chairs, came Orpan. In a moment he was upon them, grasping the farmer and the graz by the heads, shaking them vigorously so that their weapons skittered to the floor, before popping their heads together. The brawlers slumped.

He marched to the door dragging a combatant in each hand and flung them out one after another, their limbs flying in aimless circles, their bodies slack as used dishcloths. The Subs could not say what it was, but they recognized something in the way he moved.

He returned to the table not long after. "So now you kids want to contact the regnate?"

"Yes," they chorused.

Orpan shook his head. "Here's the thing. The regnate doesn't deserve help. He's the one that put Seketeme and the grolf down there. He doesn't care about people in the Sub, whatever you've been told, and he definitely doesn't care about people in Agora. I don't want to help him, and if I help you get to him, I might be helping him."

139

Burt said, "What happened to loyalty to the regnate?"

Orpan said, "This is the Agora, the wide marketplace. Somebody helps me, I help them, but the regnate hasn't done much for us out here. I wouldn't say that to a Fel, but you guys are escaped criminals, real Subs, so I can trust you."

Burt said, "But Seketeme sent us to you. He said you would help us if we helped him."

The giant said, "I don't know about that. Seems like he's probably dead because of your help."

Hands said, "Yeah. We feel great about that."

Burt said, "He told Hands he would rather die free and fighting. Letting that mountain monster loose and getting a spear back in his hands, he would have said it was worth it. We still helped him, and you still owe us something."

The big man ran his big fingers through his coarse white beard. "I can only imagine the suffering of a wendigo in Aeternanox, they're not made for the dark. They need sun and rain. I'll get you someone who can get you to the regnate. But you got to know the regnate isn't the nice perfect guy they think he is up in the Sub. You guys are brainwashed by all the returning Guard guys. He started some of these tree-cutting projects, and that's why the wendigo attacked. Not only that, he's been taxing people pretty hard. Some folks are hungry, and he doesn't care."

The Subs weren't used to hear the regnate criticized. Burt found it upsetting, while Hands felt that it was the most intelligent thing he'd ever heard an adult say. Both were fascinated that Seketeme, a wendigo who spoke barely any Regnan, was friends with an innkeeper in the Agora.

Hands said, "Mind if I ask how is it that you owe Seketeme anything?"

"I'm not going to answer today, but if you make it out to Fort Ornata, and get back here, we can have a talk, and you can trade your tale for mine. Now I'm going to find someone that can take my message, and by tomorrow you should have what you want. All the rooms are taken, but you guys can sleep in the stable."

The giant slid away through the tables. They found themselves starting to drift off. It had been a long day, and they were full of

140

beef stew. At some point, the giant barkeep lifted them up with gentle hands, and carried them to the stable to nestle them in a bit of hay for the night. They were friends, but beds were for paying customers.

They woke to a Citan accent saying, "They're in here?"

Someone was holding a lantern over them. They heard the deep horn of Orpan's voice, "This is them. They can tell the story better than me. If I hadn't lived the life I've lived and seen the things I've seen, I would say that they're nothing more than excellent storytellers."

A girl's voice chirped, "They're very dirty."

"Please wake them up, and direct them to come inside. The alta can't tolerate the smell."

Orpan said, "I should have thought about that; I'm not used to entertaining altas in my bar, Vermont."

The lantern and the dim faces moved away, and the boys sat up, brushing the straw from their hair. Orpan came back in. He said, "Come on, Subs. This is what you wanted. Don't ask me why."

They walked back into the inn, which in the early hours was empty and smelled like sour beer. The shutters were thrown open and sunlight lit the tables. Seated in corner were a young man and a bright haired girl the same age as the Subs. The man wore a bright green tunic over a brown coat. His shirt was bright white, crenellated with ruffles. The girl wore plain brown breeches and a shirt so white snow would have made it dirty. Burt and Hands, natives of the market district, priced the visitors' clothes as much nicer than the their own borrowed AltUrban threads.

He was armed in the Citan still with a small, beautifully engraved thunderPipe tucked on his left and and a sword on his right side.

Hands said, "This the two-bit woke me up talking about her fine nose?"

Orpan was sweeping the place, and he snorted.

The young man spoke first. "I'm WickBaron Vermont, head of the house of Plainwick, a true servant of the regnate. You are Hands and Burt from SubAgora?"

141

Burt stood at the end of the table, but Hands, who didn't know how Subs were supposed to act in the presence of Citans, crawled into the seat next to the girl. She stood up quickly, turning her green eyes on him with surprise.

The young man said, "Hands, you are not permitted to sit next to a Citan." His skin was smooth, his hair a tufty mess that looked too good to be accidental. His face was angular, like a cut jewel, and his blue eyes were direct and confident.

Hands said, "Merd face. I'm leaving."

He got up and headed for the front door. Burt caught up with him, "Hands, this is just how they act. To them we're Subs, they wouldn't sit with us even if we were AltUrbans. Anyway, this isn't about that, this is about getting those Fels, right? We alert the regnate, and his executes those guys. We can watch it and comment on the size of their tears! We can charge these Citans for the story."

He dragged Hands back to the end of table, where Orpan had pulled out two footstools.

The WickBaron said, "I would like to hear your story."

"What will you pay?"

"You will be well rewarded for your service to the regnate, rest assured," the Citan said.

"In the Sub, we are sure when we got money. Ten dollars sounds good."

The man shrugged. "I can work with that price, though it will lessen the commendation I give the regnate on your behalf."

"Whatever, we want money."

The man reached inside his vest and pulled out his purse. The girl voice chimed in, "Maybe you should ask them to wash, as part of the deal."

The man said, "Clarie, be quiet." He handed over the gold pieces, which Hands counted meticulously.

The girl declared. "Someone needs to declare a citywide bath day."

Hands said, "You can't put a leash on that?"

The young man got very stern. He said, "You don't talk that way about her, she is a Citan and you are a Sub. Remember your place."

Hands said, "My place is about to be sitting on her head."

Burt took over the storytelling from Hands, who was occupied mouthing curses at the alta. He told about the Fel Hands found in the alley, and the plot, how they were chased, captured, questioned, how they escaped.

The man said, "So you are the ones that loosed a grolf and wendigo upon Aeternanox?"

Burt grimaced.

The man said, "You realize helping an enemy of Regna escape carries the penalty of death." Now Hands not only disliked these Citans, he was afraid of them. He wanted to ask Orpan why he didn't know anyone else who could help beside these altas. WickBaron Vermont continued, "I'm joking."

Hands said, "Ha ha. I love jokes about getting arrested."

Vermont ignored this and continued, "Anyway, your story corresponds with too many details for it not to be true, and I can't think of another reason why they would imprison Subs in the Fel Bastion. Who was the dying Fel?

Hands shrugged.

"Did he say anything about the identity of the assassins?"

"He said something like Mic was in it. It was hard to hear with all the blood in his mouth and the grunting wheezing dyingness of the man."

Vermont shook his head. "This is bad. The Fels are all around him, and now he is moving toward war. That is when they will strike."

He pulled a paper from inside his tunic and inked a short message onto it. "Alta, the bird." The girl took a small wicker cage from the floor, in which was a small, brown bird. She reached in, cupping it in her hand, where it tweeted happily. She pulled it out, holding it firmly in one hand, while with the other she wrapped the message around its leg and tied it with wire. She moved to the window and tossed the bird out. As it left her hand its brown wings stabbed the air, triangles propelling it into the gray dawn sky.

"The bird may give him warning, but it may be caught by a hawk, we will go ourselves as back-up. We will go as soon as the horses arrive. Do you have any baggage?" He rose from the table.

143

The girl asked, "They're coming, too?"

WickBaron Vermont said, "They have seen the conspirators. We need their eyes."

Hands said, "You are altic merdups. No way we're going with you."

Burt said, "Where will we go if we stay?" Hands remembered that Fels were stationed on Black Way, waiting for them. They couldn't go home."

Hands shrugged and looked at Orpan. The big man said, "I gave you one favor. I think you picked poorly," he nodded toward the Citans, "but I'm not offering you anything else."

Hands said, "So I got to go with merdup and his little girl?"

Vermont looked angry. "That is not how you talk to a Citan."

Hands said, "I do what I want."

Vermont shook his head, deciding to confront Hands' attitude later. Vermont said, "Think of it this way. It's an adventure. You have an important part, identifying any of these Fels. The regnate will probably make you a neighborhood rep as a thank you."

Hands did not look forward to more time with these people, but he would be fed and as Burt had pointed out, they had nowhere else to go. He said, "Okay."

Vermont said, "You guys got bags or something?"

Hands spread out his hands as if to say this was all they had.

"It is just as well. Money is the best luggage. It's light, and gets anything else you need?"

Vermont said, "Good. Can you Subs ride?"

The boys shook their heads.

"Ah. They do not teach riding in SubAgora." Hands could not believe how dumb these Citans were. Did they think the Sub was a bunch of horse-riding lessons and tea parties? Vermont continued, "We will find easy beasts, and buy new ones when you have become proper horsemen."

The girl said, "Are there any sacks in here? Maybe if we drop a few sacks over them, they won't smell so much."

Hands said, "Maybe you should do something about your wig, too. It makes you look like a labor girl."

She said, "This is my real hair."

Hands said, "Just like you were born in those clothes."

Burt said, "We're dirty because of sleeping in a barn, and all the other things that happened to us."

Hands added, "We wrecked your district, then we escaped out of a sewage drain, and washed in the river. You try it, altic-nose."

WickBaron Vermont said, "Alta, you aren't doing a good job of making friends."

Clarie said, "Well, it's going to be strange. We'll look strange traveling with them. We'll smell strange, traveling with them. We don't match. People will ask questions."

WickBaron Vermont said, "I'm sure they can be cleaned. Orpan, how much do you charge for washing SubAgorans?"

They heard a snort, and the giant moved back into view. He dropped a large mop and said, "Come on, kids. Let's get you a bath. The sun is almost up."

He led the kids to a series of stalls on the second floor. He opened one, and pointed them toward a bath of steaming water. Burt stripped and jumped in, and started scrubbing himself, but Hands just looked at him.

Burt said, "Come in." Hands didn't move. "It's like the ocean except hot. You'll like it. Then you use this." He held up a washcloth and then scrubbed his chubby stomach. Hands took off his clothes and carefully tipped his toe in the bath. It felt hot and good, and he got all the way in and followed Burt's instructions. They emerged from the tub after about a quarter of an hour, shining clean. They found the two Citans at the table, eating great plates of fried eggs and bacon, along with loaves of bread.

Orpan put some plates at another table for them. "Eat up, Subs, it's a long road to Ornata."

The girl said, "Okay, they look nicer. Next we teach them how to eat."

Hands said, his mouth full of eggs and bacon, "I'll teach you how to eat a fist in a second."

WickBaron Vermont said, "Hands! I cannot permit you to speak that way to her."

Hands looked over at Orpan who was standing at the table, watching them eat. The big man was back to mopping up the spilled beer.

Hands said, "I don't know if I can do this."

Orpan put the mop down and took a seat next to him. He said, "Look. They are the way they are, and it's going to be tough, but I got two things that make me feel good about you getting it done."

"Yeah?"

"First, you're tough. Like you, I saw some merd in this life. When problems come, I didn't cry, and I don't see you going lulu either. Second, when it really matters, the gods show up and help."

Hands said, "You were making sense until you started talking about the gods."

Orpan said, "How else do you explain this: all that talk about them capturing the wendigo is a lie. They think they hit him with arrows after he knifed a few Fels and jumped for the river, but they haven't found the body. My money is on the wendigo making it."

The girl said, "I wish the wendigo was here instead of these Subs. It would smell like rotting flesh, which isn't nearly as bad as SubAgoran gutters."

The WickBaron turned to her. "Enough. I'd like you to remember that you are only here because I let you."

An older man stepped into the inn. "The horses are ready, WickBaron." They hurried outside. There were six horses out there. The servant picked up Hands and settled him on one horse. He put Burt on the next. He showed them how their feet fit into the stirrups, and told them how to tell the horse what to do with the reins. He told them that they had to be confident bosses or else the horses would do what ever they wanted.

The old man looked at Vermont and murmured something. Vermont said, "They'll have to figure it out."

Hands was, in a few minutes, able to convince the horse to walk in a circle, stop, and go. Burt tried to flick the reins, but the horse wouldn't move. He kicked his heels, like Vermont had told him, and the horse jumped a little and stepped sideways, and Burt bounced, rotated, and crumpled to the ground. The girl laughed.

146

Burt got up and dusted himself off. He said, "I'm going to walk."

Vermont laughed and said, "That's ridiculous. You'll slow us all down. Today you can ride behind me, and get used to the movement of the horse."

Burt shook his head, but he was hoisted up by the servant and was shortly astride the great horse behind the WickBaron. He looked down and found that he was higher than he had been on the other horse. He grabbed Vermont around the waist and thought fondly about waiting tables at the inn of his father. He wished again that Hands had not told him to run in that alley.

The WickBaron said to the servant, "If I do not return, or the regnate comes to the city and I am not here, remember what I told you."

The servant nodded, "Of course, WickBaron."

They rode toward the gate. The wide strong oaken doors swung open, and farmers and craftspeople and merchants moved in and out. Shortly they too went through the doors and looked out on the broad plains of the wide world. They were bound to find the regnate, in the western reach of Regna, in the shadow of the Ornatan trees.

The WickBaron said, "This road is dangerous. Stay behind me, and alta, keep your sword loose in its sheath."

147

ORNATA

FORT ORNATA

N OUTPOST

SEGUNDA-TON

TO GRAZZEN MOUNTAINS

RED RIVER

AMARILLO RIVER

SEGUNDA ROAD

City of URBA

Peaceful Ocean

148

15. Mountains

In a large room, Vice Regnate Nickson and Arch Bellumite Potens stood above a map, splaying their fingers over it like spiders. They discussed with calm tones the position of the army, the possible placement of wendigo troops. They looked up when Fel Starks entered the room.

"WickBaron Nickson, I have two pieces of bad news. We lost track of the First Child."

"What do you mean?"

"The girl has run away."

"What?"

"No one knows where she is. Citadel District has been turned upside down, but she is gone."

Nickson said, "You did your job well."

Potens murmured, "She won't matter if you take care of the father."

Nickson said, "I'm disappointed, though, to make a plan with a soldier I believe is capable and have him fail."

Starks tried to explain, "No one thought she would run away."

"What else?"

"I left the three Subs in the bottom level of Aeternanox. The guard there was lax, and they have escaped."

"Escaped Aeternanox?" Nickson was surprised. He did not like to be surprised.

"Somehow one was able to get out of his cell. He freed the wendigo warrior and the grolf. The guards were overwhelmed by the grolf. By the time they had killed it, the wendigo and the Subs had swum out the sewage channel. We tracked the wendigo down in AltUrba, got him in the river, and the guard was able to put down the grolf after some casualties, but the three Subs are gone."

"Some casualties?"

"Thirty two Fels."

"Who do you think, Starks, should bear the responsibility for this escape?"

"WickBaron, I am sorry."

Potens said, "We will need to move sooner than planned."

Nickson asked, "How can Subs get word to a regnate?"

"You didn't think that they could escape Aeternanox, when I counseled you to kill them. You are creative and self-sufficient, but it's not enough. You must learn the third virtue: ruthlessness." Potens pointed at Starks. "Start there."

"No, Vice Regnate. No!"

Nickson had met Potens at the end of a three hour ring fight in the AltUrba Bellum Hall. Nickson had beaten about fifteen boxers in a row, and the red haze wavered around him. Then the clamoring crowd of fighters parted and an older man, bald, hopped up on the platform.

He heard the whispers, "That's Potens." Later he would learn that Potens was the foremost Bellumite in Regna. Then, he didn't think the older man had anything for him, but he'd gotten in the ring.

The older man said, "You think following Bellum is all about fists?" Nickson charged, found himself caught, lifted in the air. Red flame crisped his arm hair. Potens remarked, "Bellum is not the god of fists. He is the god of strength. True strength is of the heart and mind."

Since then, he listened when Potens spoke. Potens said he needed to be more ruthless. He stood and walked around the large table toward the Fel. Starks drew his sword. "I will fight for myself." Nickson nodded as if this was to be expected, but it was not important. He watched the Fel, who lunged. Nickson ducked and dove. His strong hands flipped the Fel onto his back. His fingers ground into his throat.

Nickson said, "Your weakness has destroyed you."

Starks' wheezing and struggling subsided, replaced by the sound of sizzling, as Nickson's red aura singed the neck skin. His hard fingers squeezed out the last bits of life.

Potens said, "You should have done that with those Subs."

Nickson said, "I just need to find them."

151

Shyheem woke and found himself slung across a shoulder, bouncing along. His view was of a broad back, big legs, and rocky ground. Once his mind cleared enough to remember his situation, he screamed, "Help! Help me!"

The man dropped him. The fall took his breath. Black beard and white teeth filled his vision as Angen stooped to him.

"Silence," Angen hissed. "Look around." Shy twisted his head and saw that they were surrounded by rocks and blue sky.

Angen said, "Nobody is going to hear you. Men's noise is not welcome here. We will talk when we are off this mountain. Right now we need to keep moving, with our mouths shut."

Shy shouted, "You kidnapped me, you shrouder!" The words echoed off the mountains' faces, and came back to him, "Shrouder!"

The man said, "I warned you. Now I'm not staying around to get eaten with you." He released the boy and took off plopping down a series of rocky ledges. His feet were nimble for such a large man.

Shyheem stood after a moment. He couldn't believe the shrouder was just going to let him go. He looked behind them, and saw a mountain that stretched toward the sky. He looked back at the man who was walking down toward tiny trees that lay like carpet over the lower slopes. Shyheem wondered what his chances were of making it over the mountain back to North Temple. He thought about Gladius and Jany studying as hard as they could, getting further ahead of him by the hour. He'd done all that work to get to fourth, and now he was losing his place.

A creature walked out on a ledge twenty paces above him. Shaggy white hair blew in the wind off massive limbs with cloven-hoofed feet, and two curling horns framed a nose like a goat's. It was looking at him, examining the thing that made all this noise in the windy heights of the mountains.

Suddenly it rose on its hind legs, its silhouette cutting off a ragged chunk of blue sky. It let loose a great snort-like roar that echoed down the mountainside, and Shyheem's legs melted beneath

152

him. A hand caught him under his arm, and dragged him away. Angen moved quickly down the mountain. "From the Sub, but you don't know when to run away."

"What is that?"

Angen said, "That is a grolf."

Shy tripped after the man, his anger momentarily replaced by fear. He looked back to see the monster eyeing them from the ledge. He could have been killed and eaten. "You kidnapped me from North Temple."

"We'll talk when we get into the woods. This is still grolf territory and while Kikimensi gave me a bag of herbs that is supposed to keep them away, he wouldn't guarantee it. He told me that it'd been known to fail." Shyheem thought angrily that it was not the way of light to get a kaWick killed.

The path down wound its way over rough terrain. At certain points the path led over sheer drops, the height of a man. Shyheem skinned his hands and strained his knees jumping from these ledges. He had never been a physical boy, and the last few months he had used all his free time for studying, and his breath came hard. At other points the path led over dirt slides. He struggled to find footing, more than once going into a slide, bumping and bruising his merdup, before the hard hands of Angen caught his robe.

"Don't touch me, you Bellumite," Shyheem said. Angen smiled. The mountain was bare, without any shade, and though it was late fall, he was sweating. Ahead of him, the man's feet were tireless, his stride vigorous. His eyes were surveying the forest that filled the land below them all the way to the horizon, and he remarked, "It's good to be out of that stifling place."

Shyheem heard the roar again. Then the echo returned from the ledges and hills below them. This time he did not look back but continued moving, trying to not to think what the way it would rend him with its knobbly hands, gnash him with its great teeth, stomp him with its heavy hooves.

The path became less rocky, sloping down into the wood. They passed a tree, small and stunted from thrusting roots through stone. Below them, a line of trees signaled the beginning of the wood. Shyheem did not ask himself what forest it was, but if he had, he would have heard that it was the legendary Magnasylva, the wood that was rumored to be North of the Northern Mountains and West of the Aerie Lake. It had no limits, but stretched to the northern edges of the world. When they passed under the boughs of the trees out of the sun Angen sat down and pulled Shyheem down with him.

"I said not to touch me, Bellumite," Shyheem gasped out between breaths.

"I suppose I deserve to be called names, but I prefer castOut to Bellumite," Angen said. "I'll give you a solid truth that shows I'm no Bellumite. Illumen hates the oppressor and humbles the proud through his servants the manusignis. Here you are, a real manusignis. Summon the fire of the younger brother and burn me with your blue hands."

Shy recognized a truth, regardless of its source and took Angen's suggestion at once. He called out in his mind, waiting for his hands to fill with heat. After a few minutes of contemplating the injustice that Angen had done to him, his hands were still cold and covered with sweat. Then he thought about the Fels who took his friends and his hands lit up almost instantaneously. He opened his eyes to see each hand filled with stabbing blue flame. He reached to grab the man next to him, but by the time his hands got there, they were cold again.

Angen laughed quietly, the dark bulk of his chest and shoulders shaking. Shyheem was enraged and unable to speak. He should have known that Angen had some trick to protect himself or the castOut would never have taunted Shyheem with the idea of using the god fire. The torch knew the lies of Lucius and all the mysteries of the North Temple library.

Angen reached into a green bag of hard cloth and pulled out a handful of wheat kernels. He poured the dry fare into Shy's hand, and got another handful for himself. He cupped one hand and dropped some of the grain in his mouth.

Shyheem was hungry, so he tried it. It was dry and flavorless. He had to grind the kernels in his teeth for a while before they broke open. He thought about the roast chickens dressed with apples at North Temple, and he looked at the black-haired man and imagined once again the flames of Illumen consuming him.

Angen said through his mouthful of grain, "You can't burn whom you want. You can burn true oppressors. It's Illumen's flame. If you can't burn me, it means I'm not oppressing you."

"But you stole me!"

"This is true. But I did it for your own good."

"My own good? You stole me!"

"No real manusignis ever came out of North Temple. Just a bunch of talking lamps. I got you out of there before your faith was replaced with secret knowledge."

"What are you talking about?"

Angen didn't answer. He tied the bag, stood up, and they continued on the path, which dropped into the forest. The trees at first were spread apart, and the sun made its way through regularly. The trees were different than any he had ever seen. They had short wide trunks that rose only a little above the height of a man before they split apart into many branches that supported the foliage. Angen pointed at them and said, "These trees are called StrongBoughs. They only grow in Magnasylva." The StrongBoughs were so wide that four blue robe wicks joining hands would not be able form a ring around the tree.

The further they went, the closer together the trees stood. Sunlight penetrated the canopy only as dappled splinters, and soon they were walking in a green drenched darkness. Rasps, squawks and screams burst from the dense foliage. Shyheem remembered the life of the wood that he sensed in Faunarum, and here too he felt it. The forest yawned and looked down at him, and there were faces in every tree.

He whispered, "Where are you taking me?" He knew there were wendigo among the trees. Kikimensi, the Faunarum leader, had coldly told him not to expect to pass safely through his woods again. Shyheem thought that, were he to be captured again, they would remember their warning. He said, "Don't you know that there are wendigo here? They won't like us entering their forest."

"Ah. Kikimensi told me that you had the eye for the forest, and I told him it was not possible."

155

"You talked with Kikimensi!"

"Yes. He was interested in you. He felt you had a particular gift. That, much more than the ball of flame you produced, convinced me you were the one."

"You talked to that lamp killer!"

Angen just laughed and kept walking.

Shyheem looked back, considering which was a greater danger, to go forward to this meeting, or back up the grolf infested mountain. He thought he heard the trees whisper to him, "Go away, go away, go away." He stopped walking and sat down. He was off the mountain, away from the grolfs, and now he was in the territory of the wendigo. For some reason, the flames didn't work, but Angen was definitely a bad man. He was trying to kill Shyheem, and he was going to laugh and smile the whole way there.

Angen turned round on him. "I could coddle you, and tell you I understand your anger and your fear. But I won't." His loud voice was drowning out the animal noises. "You loved North Temple, but not because it was a place of Illumen. You loved it because it gave you a place to be better than others. Down in that SubAgora, you were the holiest kaBeggar, but no one cared except to buy your baubles. At North Temple they could recognize how light-filled you were, how good an Illumenist. You aren't crying because you lost Illumen. You're crying because you lost your place in the pecking order of the little birds."

Shyheem said, "And what about you, playing games with a wick, making me read a shrouder, and saying you know better than the Firmament?"

Angen smiled. "Such a quick tongue. But it is true that I should not have had you read Lucius, however amusing it must have been for the new bright hope to be quoting the old shrouder in Truths. I would've given anything to have seen Tenace's face.

"I am not without faults. Your eyes' ability to see this, like your eyes' power to see the wendigo, gives me hope for you yet. I am not so different than the Firmament, kaWick. I also long to see a manusignis in our day and age, a wielder of his flame. I want to see flames as big as those that arced Bellum's Field. I have done my own studies. The Firmament believe that a great manusignis will

156

come through careful teaching of the scriptures and the truths. They have been doing this for a long time yet no manusignis has emerged.

"I asked myself why it has been over three hundred years since we had a manusignis. It's not as if we're missing talent. Anybody who creates a blue buzz ends up there, training. At first I told myself, the reason was because there is no great injustice in our age. There are no bands of robbers that roam the country, killing for joy. The regnate rules the land with something like justice. I thought we didn't have real manusignis because there was no need. The Firmament talked to me about the wendigo. 'Look,' They said, 'these creatures kill farmers. They worship dark gods. They are the injustice. We need to train the parwas to fight them.'

"At first that story worked for me, but I went around, I asked. The more I learned the more it seemed there was another side. Yes, the wendigo killed people, but most of the time, the people they killed were crossing boundaries that were agreed upon long before our time. The more I learned about the situation, the clearer it became to me, that the real injustice was not done by the wendigo, but to the wendigo."

Shyheem gaped. "Did you see that lamp in the field in Faunarum! He was killed and left to be eaten by the vultures."

Angen ignored the boy's argument, "The manusignis needs first to have the heart of Illumen, before he can channel the fire. If the manusignis are told to summon flames against the wendigo their flames will never work."

Shyheem said, "But scripture never refers to them as creatures of light."

Angen said, "Cantos says, 'Shine your light on all people.' It says 'all'. Here's another: 'The light shall fall on you and you will blaze like suns on earth, and the grolfs will shout in the mountains, and the wendigo will call the trees to lift their branches.'"

Shy shook his head. He knew those were scriptures, but Angen was twisting their meaning. "People" did not refer to wendigo. He said, "But the whole temple has agreed that Illumen cares for humans. How come all the scripture writers and all the manusignis were humans?"

157

Angen said, "Humans have the light, but they have chosen to hide it from the world. So the temple is separate from the power of Illumen. It has failed to find its purpose."

Shy said, "You kidnapped me to explain all this?"

Angen said, "You've got the signs of being the real thing, kaWick. You can see the faces of the wendigo in the trees, which means you have compassion. I don't see it but that's hard proof. Then, you've got the fire hands."

"So you kidnap me?"

"If you really are a manusignis, you need to learn about the oppression that's happening in the world. Then maybe you can throw some real flames."

It was wrong he knew, but it was so new and surprising he had to think about it. The wendigo worshipped a thing called Mishipeshu, which was even darker than Bellum, demanding the sacrifice of living things to feed its appetite. The lamp at North Temple had taught him that Mishipeshu was not real, but an excuse that the wendigo leadership used to sacrifice both wendigo and human for their own evil hunger.

His attempt to sort Angen's lies was interrupted by something moving in the murky brown horizon between the dark leaves of the trees and the dark earth. As it approached they could see many thin running legs as if a giant insect had somehow jumped the gap from Sheol to haunt the darkness under the StrongBoughs and now hunted them. Perhaps the lamp was wrong and this was Mishipeshu.

Then a gust pulled back a bough, and a slim shaft of sunlight broke through the darkness. He saw it was not one creature but many deer. They were far bigger than the deer he had seen in Faunarum with antlers that spread wide. Their necks were covered with dark shaggy fur. Astride them rode wendigo with oval-shaped leaves on their heads and the bows and arrows that hung over their shoulders. Three carried long spears. They encircled the two travelers. The animals stood high above the seated pair; the riders stared down at them.

Shyheem clenched his teeth, and sunk down toward the ground as if somehow he could blend in with the forest earth. One wendigo spoke. Angen replied in the same language. Then the wendigo held out his hand and pulled the man up behind him on the creature. Another wendigo rode up and held out a hand to Shyheem. Shyheem looked around, but there was nowhere to run. Angen spoke in Wendee and they laughed, and the rider stooped and grabbed the shirt of the boy, pulled him forcefully off the ground and plopped him on the back of the mount. "Once again," he thought to himself, "I am kidnapped and manhandled."

Another one of the animals sidled forward, and all the wendigo turned to its rider. The wendigo was younger than the others, skin as smooth as a young birch tree. She carried no weapons. Her leaves were different, five pointed and red tinted. They stopped laughing abruptly as she rode forward. The wendigo picked up Shyheem and dropped him behind the unarmed girl wendigo.

The wendigo spoke to their animals, and the whole herd took off through the forest. Shyheem was jolted into movement, and soon he was flying through the StrongBoughs. He saw only glimpses of the other mounts flashing through the leaves. He clung to the waist of the wendigo, smelling too much wild forest in the dark thicket of her leaf-hair. They ran straight toward a StrongBough as wide as a house. He closed his eyes before the crash. He opened them in surprise a few moments later; they were still galloping along.

Somehow, the animal and the rider were able to run through the dark woods as quickly as Hands danced between booths in the market after the call of "thief" had been raised. The twigs didn't even scratch them. The branches seemed to twist away before the riders contacted them. Shyheem thought that the power over living things was dark magic, from dark pacts with darker gods. If they could control the trees, what couldn't they control?

The wendigo in front of him smelled something like the SubAgoran Livestock Market where the cows lowed before the butcher got to them and the goats munched on sundries. The Illumenists taught that wendigo were just a little above the animals, for they didn't have any sense of right or wrong. They killed to eat and protect territory, eating all kinds of flesh. They worshipped

159

something that by their own testimony was just a mishmash of other animals.

You smell bad to me. It was not his own thought. A soft voice entered his mind just like something he heard, but he knew he hadn't heard it. The voice was clear; if anyone had spoken to him during that helter-skelter dash through the trees, he would have barely heard them. He knew, somehow, that it was the thought of the wendigo in front of him spoken into his mind.

He had heard of wendigo who could look into minds. They had the power of Bellumites, reading thoughts, and some said, even controlling thoughts. This meant that everything he thought, how bad she smelled, how terrible the wendigo were, and any way he might escape, would all be known. So much for any escape plans.

"You can't just come in my head," he thought.

You have come into the forest of the wendigo. I don't need to go into your head because here your thoughts are louder than shouts to me.

"You think I want to be here? That man took me from my bed at night, and dragged me all the way across the mountains."

Sound like you've been mistreated. That's something wendigo can understand. Let me introduce myself. I'm Kwenemuk, a mindscout of Ornata (this came to him as a flash of a vast forest, made of trees with five pointed leaves), *a people that are now besieged by your leader. I'm in your head because if I talk aloud you won't understand, and I couldn't understand you either. In the mind, it is thought to thought.*

"Fine. Let's talk. Or think. I hate you; I hate this smelly animal. This is all wrong. I've been stolen, kidnapped. If you people were any good at all, you would let me go."

The Light Talker has said you are not happy about the sudden departure from the Light School. If you will listen though, maybe I can show you why the wendigo leaders want to talk with you.

"Angen told me your reasons," thought Shyheem. "You want me to use my fire for the wendigo against the regnate. He is crazy. I would never pray for you leafHead babyEaters to be protected from the punishment you deserve. Don't waste you witch talk on me."

They said that you were a student of light, but all I see in your mind is pride and hate. Here, the trees teach us the value of patience, for to make

160

something great, even your understanding, is the act of many years, and great patience.

"You're wasting your time with this witch talk. You might as well let me down, and I'll walk out of here."

Mishipeshu would find you long before you got out of here.

'Mishipeshu' didn't come to his head as a word. It came as a flashing picture of forest-green scales, teeth as long as thieves' knives, and movements as graceful and terrible as a cat of great size.

If you got off this wapiti he would be here. He does not like things that don't belong in the forest.

They rode on, and Shyheem resolved not to talk with her anymore. He turned his thoughts instead to the Cantos. He had memorized the eighth one.

"Shall my enemy overwhelm me and put his hands on me,
And shall the little brother be strangled by the older?
I have seen that dawn still comes after the night,
I know that Illumen will wrestle and pin Bellum.
Even in the dark cranny where the snake's fang finds flesh,
I am comforted by unfurled flight,
The blue fledglings flung across the sky."

When he had recited it a few times she asked him, *Who do you think is the little brother in the war between Ornata and Regna?*

He snorted. He tried to push her out of his mind, but it was like trying to push a bird out of the sky. He remembered SubAgora, the dead Fel, the other Subs arrested. *What happened next?* He remembered the journey through Faunarum to North Temple, and how he became a Parwa. His mind opened up to her questions like a flower budding, revealing everything. He tried to stop it, to concentrate on the things he knew about wendigo witches, and how they controlled thoughts before harvesting body parts for their potions. *What happened next?* He remembered North Temple, the cruelness of the other wicks, how hard he had worked, and Angen.

I see that the regnate is not kind to your people either.

"The regnate protects us from you!"

He makes you stay in the one part of the city. You can't be leaders even though your place is called the Free Country, because of your skin.

161

"The regnates gave us SubAgora, after we helped him in the Long War. It is a better place than Bugiri, where we lived without knowledge of Illumen. We are protected by the Fels, and we can trade."

What a place to give you. It has no trees, too many people, and the stink of rot.

He said nothing, glowering into the leafy mess around them. The journey moved through the hours, and his bottom hurt from the bouncing.

Near the end of the day they passed out from under the trees onto a pebbly shore. A great lake stretched almost to the horizon. The water was clear as the sky, and little and big fish were visible chasing one another in the shallows, while great eagles wheeled overhead, watching and waiting for the silver flash. In the middle of the lake rose up a few islands, and in the center was one that towered above the others, like a small mountain, covered by StrongBoughs.

The wendigo dismounted. A long canoe was resting with one end on the gravel beach, the other floating in the lake. In it were two wendigo, each bearing a wooden paddle. The leader of the wapiti riders spoke to the water-bound wendigo, while the other riders escorted Shyheem and Angen down to the canoe. Angen got in the canoe. Shyheem stepped in after him and the whole thing tilted. The wendigo at the back shifted his weight quickly, while the foremost wendigo forced Shyheem down with a hand, barking something in Wendee.

"Stay seated," Angen translated.

"Like I care if this boat sinks." The wapiti riders disappeared back into the forest, except for the wendigo witch, who also climbed in the boat. The boat wendigo spoke to her, their tone deferential, as if they also feared her. Shyheem got a better look at her in the full sunlight. Her body was erect and supple like a young tree, clad in leather, and her eyes, turned upon him, had the same innocent boldness of a deer's. Shyheem knew that the appearance of health, the show of strength were Bellumite qualities, and that he must be careful of such power. He asked, "The witch is coming with us?"

162

Angen said, "Kwenemuk is a mindscout, not a witch. She traveled all the way from Ornata to help you. She hears the voices of the forest, and speaks for it to the people. She is here because we need someone to translate Wendee for you. That's her job. It's a pretty terrible job, getting a little merdFace like you to understand."

"I understand you're a shrouder and kidnapper." The taunt did nothing to remove the smile from the castOut's face. The wendigo at the bow shoved against the gravel bottom of the lake with his paddle, and the canoe eased out into the water. It turned slowly in response to the wendigo's strokes until it was pointed toward the great island. The wendigo did not seem to strain, steadily dipping the paddles into the water and pulling, but the bark-craft was slicing through the lake. The witch said, *Come and help, water creatures.* In a moment two otters emerged, swimming behind the canoe and nudging it with their noses. Joining them came great black fish, longer than his arm, and smaller trout, their rainbow skin reflecting sunlight. The water around the canoe roiled, and the canoe surged forward, and the water plants below the surface of the lake passed in a blur.

In minutes they reached the central island and shot up out of the water onto a beach. The canoe made a hollow grinding as the bark ran up onto a sandy cove. The mindscout got out, and the two humans followed. The oars pushed the canoe back into the water and it moved back across the lake. *We will wait here for our guide.*

The wood was quieter here, as if they were in a holy place, and the animals and birds whispered rather than shouted. Out of the trees walked a wapiti. His antlers rose up like a many-pointed crown. Astride his massive shoulders perched a giant wendigo. Kwenemuk explained, *This is Aihum, the greatest longeye of the Magnasylva.* The word "longeye" was a flash of images, strong wendigo, armed with bows, axes, and spears.

Aihum carried a spear of oak that rose into the air like a threatening talon of the forest. His eyes took in the humans and his nostrils stiffened as if he had smelled something rotting. He nodded to Kwenemuk, saying a few words.

"Walk behind me, humans." His voice was deep. As he spoke, Shyheem heard the voice of the mindscout translating. "Go neither

163

to the right, nor to the left. This is a sacred place, and if you leave the paths, you will die."

Based on his expression, Aihum would be doing the killing.

16. HighSeat

The humans tried to keep up with the wapiti, which walked calmly, but a single swing of its leg was the same as four human steps. Every so often the rider would stop and wait for them to catch up. The path climbed up steeply through towering trees. Once again the wick found himself huffing and puffing. He grew tired of staring at the hindquarters of the king wapiti. They finally saw sunlight ahead, and climbed out of the trees. Above them was a meadow. Wildflowers of yellow and purple rose out of the green grass, and bees and butterflies flitted among them.

Atop the hill four wendigo sat on a circle of large stones. Spread around them beyond the ring of trees was the blue lake. Beyond that, stretching to the northern and western horizons, was forest. To the south there was forest and, glistening with reflected light, another lake. To the east, whence the humans had come, the woods bordered on the mountains.

The tallest wendigo wore his leaves wrapped around his head in braided strands of copper colored oval leaves, matching the leaves of the Magnasylvan StrongBoughs. Shyheem realized that wendigo headLeaves matched the trees of their forest. In Faunarum, the wendigo had oak leaves, longer, with many points. The Magnasylvans all had oval-shaped leaves with edges like a small saw blade, just like the StrongBoughs.

The leader nodded to Kwenemuk. "We are honored by your presence, mindscout of Ornata. What do you hear from the mothers?" Shyheem heard the translation in his head, almost as if he understood the wendigo.

She said, "They bear a weight far greater than that of ice and snow."

The wendigo turned to Angen. "You come to my forest for the first time, Light Talker."

Angen answered, "Sachem Tenaxen, your forest is alive with the people and their trees. Never have I seen so many trees."

The sachem nodded toward Shyheem. "They tell me you are a friend to the wendigo, and that you bring the hope of Kikimensi?"

Shyheem stared sullenly. Angen said, "Yes. This is him."

Other introductions went on. An old lady wendigo from Desicca, the young one from Southern Ornata. Shyheem found his eyes pulled to a wendigo glaring at him.

"And this," Tenaxen turned toward the angry wendigo, "Is Askasktuhon. He is the sachem of Ornata." He had five-fingered yellow leaves on his head.

Angen said, "We are heartbroken by the injustices done to your forest. We are sorry that men destroy your trees."

Askasktuhon said, "I do not know why humans are allowed at this seat. Yet you are here, and I am told that you will be present for this meeting because of what you know. Know this, human. If you were in my forest you would be food for the Mishipeshu, not sitting in the seat of sachems."

Angen spoke solemnly, "Were I in your place, would I say anything different? But consider, if not for thinking outside the realm of your normal allies, what hope have you? Can you win this war without help?"

Askasktuhon said nothing. In the angry silence the bees buzzed, and the birds sang.

Tenaxen picked up the thread. "We still wait for Kikimensi, Sachem of Faunarum. I'm told the boy has already met him." At that moment three wendigo emerged from the trees below. Shy recognized Kikimensi, because of the gloriously antlered buck standing by his shoulders, and the pale oak leaves on his head. The two longeyes with him stopped, and he strode up through the meadow, followed by the deer, and sat on an empty rock. He looked tired when he reached his seat, and Tenaxen took a leather pouch and passed it to him. He lifted the bag and squeezed it, and a green stream shot into his mouth. Tenaxen said, "Welcome, Kikimensi. How do you find Magnasylva?"

The pale-leafed one said, "The StrongBoughs are tall, and the water clear. The wendigo are like the trees, straight and true."

166

Tenaxen said, "These trees grow straight remembering your coming, and we also lift hands in welcome."

The old wendigo nodded. He turned to Angen who stood and embraced him. Shyheem and Askasktuhon turned away from this disgusting show of affection.

Tenaxen said, "How was your journey?"

The pale-leafed wendigo shook his head. He said, "We took canoes, for this is the quick way, though Faunarum wendigo are no water people. The soldiers of Regna on the Aerie Fort thought they would stop us, and put out their longboat in pursuit. We had thought they had no chance because our longteeth would find them long before they could hit us."

Longteeth are arrows, explained Kwenemuk.

Kikimensi told them how the boat had a Bellumite on it, equipped with a larger thunderPipe. It cracked and a great dollop of red flame spun toward the last canoes. The wendigo were too surprised to move before the second shot struck, and one of the canoes was hit. The two fire covered longeyes dove for the water. The wendigo recovered them but the canoe was lost. They shot their arrows, and summoned the lake creatures for help. The fish and otters sped them along, helping them escape. The two longeyes who had been hit died from the burns.

Tenaxen said, "This is ill news. Since when were the Fire Warriors stationed in the North at the Lake Aerie?"

Angen said, "They have more and more of the Bellumites in the Regnan Army."

Askasktuhon said, "These things are true. There are many, some twenty of the Fire Warriors at the Fort outside Ornata."

Tenaxen asked, "Twenty? Are they as strong as it is rumored?"

Askasktuhon hissed sharply, and said, "Before we waited in the shallow woods, and when they set to with axes we sent our longteeth to bite them, and they retreated. Now, when we attack, they unleash their redFire, and many longeyes die, and the trees continue to be consumed. They are strong."

Sachem Tenaxen said, "We are moving to business without a proper beginning. The Five Sachems of the Five Forests, or their deputies, are now gathered at the High Seat. It has been long since

167

we gathered here. I was but a sapling on my grandfather's knee, and there was only joy in sharing the events of our separate forests. Sachem Mahtaksen and Sachem Kikimensi were young, and Sachem Askasktuhon was still a sachem's son. Ahilensu Xinkwelepay was here then, and his youth was glorious in its strength. For sport he chased the wolves upon the meadow, and he would catch them with great flying leaps, and growling they went rolling, until they rested in a heap, he pinching soft whimpers out of their throats.

"Now Ornata is threatened on all sides by fire and axes. Faunarum is besieged by stone creations. Askasktuhon's longeyes take ten men for every wendigo lost, but more men come everyday. Ahilensu Xinkwelepay is old. The Ornatan wendigo are shrinking into the core of the forest. It is at the call of the sachems of Ornata, Ahilensu and Askasktuhon, that the High Seat is called. What the High Seat decides, let all wendigo follow."

The yellow-leafed wendigo did not look up from his hands when he spoke. "We need more longeyes. The humans come forward in a line of thousands. The Fire Warriors shoot thunderPipes and fire rages through the forest. We fight the fire and the men. The men are merciless. When they capture a wendigo, the wendigo never sees the sun again, but he is pent up to die slowly in the belly of the earth."

Shyheem knew the wendigo killed any human they could. He had seen the proof, the lamp, poor pilgrim, rotting in Faunarum. Why were they surprised when the humans killed them? High-sounding words did not change the truth that it was just repayment.

Askasktuhon said, "See. It has no compassion."

Shyheem looked up and saw the wendigo staring at him, his gimlet eyes glittering hate in the leaf shadows. He realized that Kwenemuk was sharing his thoughts as well as translating their words.

Kikimensi said, "Give him time, Askasktuhon. He has a mind and he belongs to the Light Talker's god. The other Light Talkers have filled him with their hate, and told him it was truth. You must give his mind time to understand."

Askasktuhon snorted. "You talk about time, Kikimensi, but you know that the more time passes, the more trees die. I did not come here to listen to fantasies. I came to ask the sachems for longeyes."

Tenaxen said, "Askasktuhon, we shall discuss what to do after we know how things are. First, we will establish the situation. Kikimensi, what news of Faunarum?"

The pale-leaved wendigo spoke slowly. Beside the woman, he was the oldest, and calm, for he fought a losing battle against despair. "They are mining on the southern slopes of Faunarum, and we can't fight them off. I have too few wendigo. I send out parties in the night, and if the humans push further, which they always do, we attack them, but they have infinite reinforcements. Now they have built forts surrounding the wood, and we have less and less refuge. My young longeyes are angry because we do not fight. They would rather die than see the wood be cut and stand by. I also long to punish the humans, but I can see no chance of victory. I cannot sacrifice my people for a meaningless gesture of resistance. I wait. If the situation were not desperate, I would not have heard the words of Light Talker, or the other. The MishiRider."

Shyheem wondered how the wendigo thought that an appropriate punishment for chopping down a tree was taking a human life. What truth said that the life of human was worth less than the life of tree? Illumen made trees, yes, but he made them to be good for man. They were good for the fire, for buildings, or for tools.

Tenaxen said, "Let us discuss what to do. For this purpose Angen has traveled here, let him speak."

Askasktuhon barked, "Why is the human first to speak? Is not the problem mine?"

Tenaxen said, "I am the sachem of Magnasylvan, and I preside over the High Seat, Askasktuhon."

Askasktuhon shook his five-pointed yellow leaves and turned to look at the sky.

Angen stood. "Sachems of the High Seat. I am nothing among such leaders. I was a servant of the temple of the Light God, but even this position is stripped from me for I pleaded the case of the

169

wendigo in their council. I believe that the Light God still lives and sees, and he hates what the humans are doing to the forests. I wandered many roads, and pondered the written words of the dead Light Talkers. I asked myself, 'What did Illumen do when people were oppressed?' He sent the men with hands of fire. If I was right then one would emerge in this day, and he would be called to fight for you, and the army of Regna would be destroyed."

Askasktuhon interrupted him, "The men with fire are there already. They are the ones destroying the mother trees."

Angen nodded. "Those are Bellumites, servants of the older brother. They love strength first and last. War is their way. The servants of the younger brother resist them, and the manusignis that I speak of have power that makes the power of the Bellumites seem like nothing. The legends tell of manusignis who destroy entire armies."

Askasktuhon shook his head at this story.

"To find if any with the fire hands had come, I visited North Temple often. I walked through Faunarum, and risked my life to speak with Kikimensi, and he decided to trust me, though he, like Askasktuhon, had learned to hate all men. He was the one that told me that a new manusignis was going to North Temple. He was impressed, because the child had the eyes of the wendigo mindscout, for he could see the faces among the trees.

"He has no sympathy for the wendigo, but both Tenaxen and Kikimensi will tell you he sees the faces of the trees. He has great gifts with the fire, and this tells me, despite his hard heart, that he does have the gift of the Light God. I bring him here hoping you will accept his services in your defense."

Kikimensi leaned against the buck that stood patiently by him. He saw the disgust in Askasktuhon's eyes and the reserve in the others. Tenaxen said, "And you, Shyheem of Urba?"

Shyheem said, "Illumen cannot love wendigo for wendigo are of the dark. You value nature over human life. Even if I could wield Illumen's flames for your cause, I would never do it for you are Bellumites, lovers of slaughter and eaters of flesh."

Yellow-leaved Askasktuhon spoke. "Why should I have to listen to this, when my heart is already broken for one hundred

170

trees, and my tears cannot bring Spring to a million leaves that have fallen?"

Angen spoke, "Can not one of you speak to him of your cause?"

Askasktuhon said, "You would have us beg a boy that you dream has power even as he insults us?"

Kikimensi reached out a hand and rubbed the head of his buck. He said, "But he does not know about the trees and the wendigo."

Tenaxen said, "Since Kikimensi calls for it let him speak."

Kikimensi nodded. "Shyheem, I had mercy on you once, so you owe me an open ear. You feel that wendigo attack men for nothing more than chopping at grass. Yet that is not why we fight so desperately for the trees. The life of the wendigo is bound close to the life of the wood we live in. We do not tell our secrets to men, but I will say that when a tree falls it is the same as a wendigo death. Maybe now you can see how a wendigo killing a man for killing a tree is not an injustice but only self defense."

Shyheem said, "Your thoughts are a perversion. There is no way that the value of a tree can be equated with the life of man. I long for fire to fight you now so that I could punish you for your crimes. These woods too would not be safe from me. I would kill them all had Angen not taken my flame."

Askasktuhon shook his head.

Tenaxen looked at Kikimensi. "Surely you know I cannot let such words be spoken in my forest. I will give him one more chance. Boy, you come here at the request of this one. I love him well, but you mean nothing to me, and I will feed you to Mishipeshu if you cannot show these StrongBoughs the respect they deserve. You apologize to the trees of Magnasylva immediately."

The boy laughed. "I will not join in your mindlessness. I won't talk to trees. I will pray against these trees after I am dead."

Kikimensi said, "He is a boy. He has only thought one way all his life. He needs time."

Tenaxen stood up. "Youth will not excuse these words delivered like a knife into the heart of the already sick. He will meet Mishipeshu. Aihum, take him."

Angen stood up, pulling the sword from its sheath, but three longeyes were already surrounding him with lowered spears at his throat. He dropped the weapon back into its sleeve.

"You are too quick in this, Tenaxen." As he spoke his Adam's apple bobbed against the spear tips. "Can't you see that the boy would rather be martyred than continue on his journey?"

Tenaxen said, "These are my woods, Light Talker. I do not care what the boy wants, only that justice is shown. Be happy that you have pulled out metal in the HighSeat and live."

Askasktuhon, for all the loathing he had showed for the boy, seemed to find no pleasure in his execution. Angen and Kikimensi watched helplessly as the giant longeye seized the boy and dragged him up onto his wapiti. Shyheem did nothing to resist. The pair rode quickly through the forest, until they reached the water's edge. The sun was dipping toward the trees.

The longeye lifted the wick off the wapiti and dropped him on the bank. Running out from it was a fallen trunk that extended far into the darkening water. The wendigo pointed down along the log. The boy looked out the log. The longeye wanted him to walk along that thing into the lake. He wasn't interested, so he sat down. He wasn't going to help them hurt him. The longeye prodded him with the tip of his spear. It cut through his robes and bit into the flesh of his behind.

"Ouch," he said, standing up quickly. He took six little steps out on the log, and stopped, feeling his behind. There was definitely blood. He looked back, checking to see that he was beyond the range of the sharp point. The wendigo reached calmly into his quiver and pulled out an arrow, notched it to the string, and drew it back. With one finger from his bow hand he motioned for the boy to continue down the log. Shy didn't doubt he would shoot. The wendigo had had no problem stabbing him.

The log bobbed up and down under his weight until he reached the end. He looked back, and saw the mounted wendigo watching with the arrow drawn. Was his punishment standing on a log in the middle of the lake? This wasn't too bad. He could do it for at least four hours. The lake was Mishipeshu? He remembered how they had spoken of it in Writ class. It was nothing but a myth and a symbol.

Then he felt something like a fingernail scrape his neck and a splash beyond him in the lake. He saw an arrow sinking into the water. It had nicked his neck as it flew by. He felt something cool on his neck; it was wet. He checked his finger, and saw blood. A fat drop fell from his finger into the brown water. He looked back at the longeye, who was watching him impassively from atop his wapiti, bow in hand.

Back atop the high hill, Askasktuhon said, "Tenaxen, I ask you for longeyes. How many can you send me? If you would send us one thousand longeyes, we could fight them in the open, drive them back out of the fort and destroy them, and they would not be able to camp within five miles of Ornata."

Kikimensi said, "You know I do not have enough to defend my own borders. I can offer you this. When you are ready to fight, I will fight as well, and the resources of the Regnan army will be stretched. This is all I can do."

Mahtaksen spoke like the chirping of a small bird. "We are few in Desicca, but I will send three hundred young wendigo to help, but we are not war-like, as you know. Healing and building are our arts. It will take at least three weeks for them to arrive, for I must journey to Desicca, equip them, and they must march back to Ornata."

Askasktuhon nodded. "These are great gifts. What of you, Tenaxen? You command the greatest force of longeyes."

Tenaxen shook his head. "Your claim that one thousand reinforcements will give you victory in this war is wrong. You underestimate them, not knowing their numbers or what weapons they have, and what powers that they have gained. You sit in the forest, believing that you can fight with the same bows that your grandfathers fought with. The humans are not so simple. They make new weapons, all the time. These thunderPipes are one example of the new terrors.

"I have counseled with the fathers. They have turned their vision toward the Regnans, and they have seen the visions of the Sachem of the Fire Warriors. He has shown them twenty more Fire Warriors for every one stationed at Fort Ornata. They have sent machines to be used against trees that make axes look like children's toys. But the Sachem of the Fire Warrior offers mercy. If the wendigo retreat to Magnasylva, leaving him Ornata he will let you live."

Angen had been sitting without speaking, angry that they had taken the boy, and prayerful, for he had brought the boy here. The talk about the Bellumites brought him out of his head. "You listened to a Bellumite? Surely you know that they seek power with all their words, and he will have brought you under his spell. You must not seek counsel from such a one without a friend that understands his lies."

Tenaxen said, "I am the sachem of the greatest forest, and around me are the oldest fathers of the wendigo. Together we are able to seek the mind of any in the known world and search it. Askasktuhon, there is no meaning in a hopeless fight. We offer you Magnasylva as a refuge."

"Refuge?" Askasktuhon spat the words, his yellow leaves shaking about his head. "Taking refuge in Magnasylva would be death for the Ornatan wendigo. We will die before we leave our trees."

Tenaxen shook his head. "I fear for the Ornata wendigo. Your anger makes you forget reason."

Askasktuhon spoke bitterly, "I have asked for help, and you have given me a coward's counsel. My fight is not yours because the brotherhood that so long joined Ornata and Magnasylva is broken. Today we are separated, and I will pray that Mishipeshu smells your cowardice and roots out with badger claws the sickness that the human has planted in your chest."

Kikimensi leaned against the flank of the buck. He said, "Askasktuhon, you are young and you speak too quickly. Tenaxen, don't you see that we are joined? If Ornata and Faunarum are cut down they will come to your forest next. We should fight now, together, while we still have strength."

174

"Ah," said Tenaxen, "This is a better point. But if you come now bringing all your longeyes, your treetenders, we will have the same strength, all in one place."

"You speak like a human, and not a wendigo." Kikimensi's voice had lost some of its calm and he draped his arms around the neck of the buck that stood rigid like it was about to run away. "What is my strength, away from the mothers? What wendigo does not value his father? Under the boughs of the oak, I am stronger than ten men, but in the flat of the plain I am smaller and weaker than one. Magnasylva is not Askasktuhon's forest. StrongBoughs are neither the Oaks of Faunarum, nor the LongBoughs of Ornata."

The copper leaves on Tenaxen's head glowed in the evening sun, as he gazed out on his forest. He said, "We must think differently for it is a new time, and we have a new enemy. Your people's memory is not what you think, and there are trees enough here to share. In a few generations, your forests will be completely intermingled with mine, and we will truly be one."

Kikimensi turned to Mahtaksen, "Can you speak to this wendigo, and tell him his responsibility?"

The old wendigo looked out across the forest, and down at the lake. When she spoke it was almost a whisper, "Tenaxen, now you are strong, but a worm is in your wood. You have asked your fathers to look into darknesses. The Fire Warrior Sachem is a twister of truth. He raised up the Fire-Warriors that burn the mothers and the children in Ornata. Even now your heart is gnawed through by the lust for power. You are taking the calamity of these forests as an opportunity to grow your own people."

Tenaxen stood up, and he was tall and strong, and his voice was deep. "I have let you all speak your piece because I hoped to save you. You have not listened; you have sat here and insulted me. Because of the friendship my grandfather had with yours, I give you today to leave my forest, but if you come back, the longteeth of Magnasylva will remember your insults."

They all stood. Askasktuhon clenched his hands, and heaved a sigh as heavy as a toad's squat. They felt a presence that changed the forest. Wind whispered among the trees, and lake glinted in the

175

sun, and a sound like rushing water came from the lake. They saw the movement of some great fish in the water, and with it visions of the snow falling, the streams freezing. The Mishipeshu came for the offering.

———————

Shyheem watched the drop of blood marble in the water. Then he saw a churning bump far out in the lake that grew larger and larger. He heard it next, a shriek like an eagle, a growl like a bear, and then the water erupted and he looked upon the flashing forest green of a million scales and clawed limbs. He was caught and dragged under water. He tried to shout, but instead of words going out, water came in and he snapped his mouth shut. He was being dragged down and away, gripped by claws, teeth, and talons.

The water rushed about him, pulling him under and spinning him around and around so he didn't know which way was up. Water was up his nose and in his mouth, and he had lost most of the skin off his knees, but what was most terrifying was that he had no control over his body. He was caught by something that didn't care about him at all, and it was so strong that his little arms and legs and their silly paddling were nothing.

Then the thing released him, swimming around him. In the middle of the brackish swirl he only glimpsed parts of it, the eyes that flashed the knowing yellow of the lynx, then green evil like the alligator. The white teeth lined up evenly like a great lizard's jaw. When he saw them next they were four yellow canines of the wolf. The scales or fir changed from brown to green. He glimpsed the antlers of the deer, the paws of the lion, and the webbed hand of the otter. Each moment he saw something different and could barely hold the idea of what he had just seen. It was every creature of the forest. Shyheem would have thought someone was crazy if they told him there was a creature that was every creature in the forest at the same time. This then was Mishipeshu.

The water rushed about him, pushed by its mighty limbs, and he felt the hot hunger of it as its jaws closed slowly over his shoulders. He would be a victim of this forest, fed to its monster, never to see North Temple again, never to learn another truth,

176

never to be a manusignis. This was how he died. Suddenly, in the midst of the storm he was calm. He no longer thought about how he longed to burn the beard off Angen's face. He looked in awe and wonder at the thing before him, and prayed, "Oh, Illumen, what a wondrous thing!"

Suddenly he was warm, and then the water all around him boiled up with blue flame. The great creature released him, its yellow eyes glowing angrily as it gazed at the spikes of blue heat that curled around the boy. It opened its jaws, and snapped forward, but the blue light reached out and seized it. A loud hiss of singeing sounded, and the thing howled, a roar turned keening that echoed off the hills and pulled back from him. It slowly backed away through the water, and then it disappeared into the deep lake.

Atop the High Seat, the four sachems watched the approach of the forest spirit, how it carried the boy to the middle of the lake and prepared to eat him. They saw the lake erupt in blue flame and the retreat of the monster. They stood silently for a long time.

It was Askasktuhon who spoke first. "I will take the fire boy. If he can stand up to Magnasylva Mishipeshu, he should be able to do something against the Fire-Warriors. We only need to convince him."

Tenaxen said, "This flame is nothing, just one small boy's. The Fire-Warrior-Sachem would destroy him."

They ignored him. "You do well," said Mahtaksen. "I think his heart is softer than he knows, and, in time, he will see wisdom."

Angen said, "Thank you."

Kikimensi said, "I am overjoyed that you have changed your mind. He will not fail you."

Askasktuhon shook his head. "I clutch at grass blades, when the strength of the tree trunk would not be enough to hold my weight."

17. Altic

I have seen Death stroll into our forest and walk among the LongBoughs. I look down and see him at the base of the tree, waiting for me to invite him in. 'Climb up," I say, "Sit," I say, "here on the roundest branch. Let us observe together the slow passing of the moon."

Death has been a stranger for too long. If he will dwell with us, then let us practice hospitality; we should be his friends. Where he goes, we will also go. These humans have brought him into our forest, we will bring him back out when we go to meet them.

When the Citans and Subs found themselves on the open road, WickBaron Vermont took stock of his ragtag party. "We aren't exactly war-like," he thought. "I can't even escape quickly, with this fat brown riding double and clutching me, and the other barely able to sit on his horse." He had, when he received the bird-note, considered putting together a squad, but his own troops were with the regnate. The assassins were among the Fels.

It wasn't ideal to have the First Child with him. He had agreed because he knew she wasn't half bad with a sword, but mostly because she had threatened to use her authority to have him stopped. She would have done it too, and while it wouldn't have stopped him, it would have created too much chatter, and the assassins might have figured out what he knew.

He was wanted to reach the regnate quickly because a) he admired his national leader and wanted to do his duty protecting him, and b), the big reason, he also was stung when the regnate asked him to stay in Citadel. Showing up and saving him would show WickBaron Grant his skill, and guarantee that he was never again given the boy's job of watching the Citadel while a war was on.

He grabbed the reins of Clarie and Hands' horses and pulled them close. He said, "Now, we can't trust people out here. We need a story that explains why a wickBaron and an alta are traveling with two SubAgorans."

"Two smelly SubAgorans," added the girl.

The wickBaron continued, "We will tell people that we are taking you to a home for orphans down in Segundawick."

Hands said, "Thanks so much for saving me, WickBaron and alta. Without you, I'd be nothing more than a common Sub."

Burt whispered, "Show them respect."

Hands said, "Yeah, 'cause they show me so much."

Vermont shook his head. This Sub had no understanding of ring respect. He made them listen as he explained that, if they were attacked, they should get behind him. Hands made some silly comment about his ability to defend himself, which the wickBaron ignored, as it was clear the brown had a comment about everything.

He led them south on Segundaton Road. Hands saw huge fields of waving beige grass. The houses stood by the fields all alone, surrounded by tall hedges. Dotted around them were smaller buildings. In the Sub, the big houses were by the AltUrban gate, and then the rest were small. He asked, "Why are the small houses around the big ones?"

The girl laughed. "You've never seen a farm before."

WickBaron Vermont explained with a chuckle, "That big building is the barn, and the tiny one is a chicken coop. That long one is the workers' house."

Hands thought about the stupid questions the Citans would ask in the SubAgora like "How come people keep hitting me on the head and taking my money?"

They trotted along for a day, switching horses as they could. He encouraged the fat one to try his own horse more than once, but the kid quaked at the idea.

Late in the day the girl convinced the wickBaron to pull two wooden staffs from under his saddle. He handed one to the girl, holding the other in his left hand. She commenced to attack him with a flurry of blows, which he parried casually. Burt shrank down behind him, hoping to avoid being whacked by the whirling weapons.

After minutes of trying to break down the wickBaron's defense the girl tried a desperate lunge that he soundly smacked down. Before she could recover, he swung his weapon back up and tapped her head.

"Patience, Clarie, is mental strength."

She had scrambled from the saddle and recovered her stick. She went to work on him again, this time going for much longer before she once again leaned too far out, committing to the strike. Again, he disarmed her, and thwacked her head.

"Ouch!" she cried.

Hands laughed loudly. "He's thumping your merdup."

She turned coolly on her saddle. "Perhaps you would like to try."

"You got to be kidding me," said Hands. "I will destroy you."

She reached for the staff in the wickBaron's hands, and reined in her horse, waiting. When she was abreast of Hands, she handed him the weapon with a small smile. He took it, waving it about fiercely. "On your guard," she said.

Hands held his weapon at ready, and then attacked with a big downswing, but with a clever twist of her wrist, his staff went flying into the bushes on the side of the road. She rapped him smartly on the shoulder.

He dismounted quickly, fished the stick out of the hedge, and pulled himself back on his mount. "I need to get warmed up," he said.

"Whatever you say," she said. In a moment she went to it again, beating down the stick, and tapping him on the head. "When are you going to destroy me?"

Hands didn't say anything. He was thinking hard about how he might get an advantage. She was too good, she had practiced too much for him to beat her.

When her horse drew near, he threw the play sword at her, and lunged from his saddle, grabbing her and pulling her off the horse so they fell together with a plop onto the dusty road. There Hands pinched and punched, and the girl yelped like a puppy, before the wickBaron was upon them. He pulled the boy up, and delivering a series of emphatic slaps to Hands' face and merdup.

"Back on the horses, and no more of that. We're trying to get to Segundaton, and you are wrestling altas in the dirt. In Urba you could be executed for that."

"She started it," Hands murmured.

The girl was dusting off her cloak, and shaking out her mess of blond curls. Dust fell from her like rain. She mounted lightly, while Hands was set back on his horse. When Vermont cantered back to the front of their little train, he turned an evil grin on her, letting her know that there was plenty more where that came from, regardless of what the wickBaron said.

She leaned over toward him and remarked, "Cheater."

He said, "Told you I would destroy you."

She didn't say anything, and he saw a bruise was growing on her right cheekbone. They rode on. His thighs, stomach, and back were aching with the riding and bruising. The farms looked different. No longer did they have the fences and hedges around them; they were open. He saw cluriKin far rounder than any he would see in the city, happily tending the gardens alongside gardeners. The cluriKin waved their mitten hands, the gardeners waved their gloves at the passing group.

She said to him, "See, we're in Chestershire. No more fences."

He didn't want to ask what Chestershire was, so he looked around, and memorized the landscape. This was Chestershire.

She laughed, "You don't know what Chestershire is, do you?"

"I know what it is," he growled.

"There are eight wicks of Regna. Chestershire is the one immediately south of Urba."

He said, "I knew that."

"Then you must be able to tell me the name of the wick west of here."

Hands did not know the name of that wick, or any of them. To show her that it was not a good idea to make him look stupid, he leaned out in his saddle, and grasped a handful of blond curls. He gave them a good tug, and pulled back his hand. She didn't yelp this time, but struck out with a fist, catching him on the jaw. He hadn't

181

expected that, and he didn't sit that firmly on the horse yet. He found himself sliding down the side of the horse's belly, and hitting the ground. WickBaron Vermont heard him thump into the ground and turned.

"What are you doing now?"

"Fell off the horse." Hands said. "He walks funny."

The wickBaron shook his head. "They can't even ride a horse. What do children do in the Sub?"

Hands remounted, running through possible retorts. He came up with some good answers like picking the pockets of Citans who had more money than was fair, and amusing Citan mothers. He didn't share his answers though, not out of respect, but because he'd felt the stingy slaps of WickBaron Vermont. The girl said, "Why didn't you tell on me?"

"He wouldn't have believed me. Anyway, real Subs don't go singing, but don't worry, I'll get you."

The girl pulled her horse away from him. She asked, "Why don't you show respect for Citans like your friend? You're supposed to. It's a crime against Regna to fail to show ring respect."

"I respect people who respect me. Plus you don't deserve respect. All you ever did is order cakes and lie in a bed and get your hair dyed yellow."

In a way, it was true that she did not work for her bread, but on the other hand, she had worked hard. She had studied everyday for hours, and knew the history of Regna, the worship of the five gods, the culture of the graz, the wendigo, the Opulanders, the Bugiri-Men, and their languages. Also, her skill with the sword came from hours of practice, over many years. Most of those practices had been stolen during free time, and sometimes she got punished for them. But trying to tell Hands about her life seemed hopeless so she just rode on, glancing curiously at the brown boy who had so much pride in himself and an illegally small amount of respect for Citans.

They rode on and on, stopping only for a moment to buy some roadside bread and grilled meat, before rotating onto fresh horses and continuing on. When the sun dipped below the horizon, the wickBaron said, "We stop now, before the dark of night."

182

He took them into a grazzen inn, a brown monolith that shouldered up to the road. He ordered three rooms for the night. After dropping off bags they came down to the main room for a meal. Everything was finely cut stone in the room even the tables and chairs.

"Welcome, welcome," the leathery green owner said, bowing low when he saw the finery of the Citans. "Alta, shall I sit you here?"

He indicated two finely carved and padded seats that were clearly the best in the place. The wickBaron nodded, "Bring two more seats for the Subs."

The graz objected, "The browns can sit at that table," and he pointed to the corner.

WickBaron Vermont said, "I need to keep an eye on them."

"As you wish, Baron."

WickBaron Vermont rattled off an order in Grazzen.

The first dish was a plate of red vegetables smashed together. WickBaron Vermont and Alta Clarie spooned themselves some of the brightly colored food and started eating. When they saw that Subs were not eating but staring at the food, they spooned them each a helping. Burt tried some, and so did Hands. Burt chewed on it a while. It was spicy and he thought he was going to cry from all the heat in his mouth, but he kept chewing it. After his mouth cooled a bit, Burt decided it was not that bad, and helped himself to more. Meanwhile Hands turned and spat the food on the floor.

WickBaron Vermont said, "Hands!"

Hands said, "You're trying to kill me?"

WickBaron Vermont said, "You're the one who is going to annoy me to death. Listen carefully to these rules. You may not spit out food. If you are not sure of how to act, please look around and copy the manners of those around you. If you do it again, I will have to deal with you. Now, would you like me to order you some bread?"

"I don't care."

In a moment the graz was back at the table mopping up the red spittage.

The wickBaron said, "Would you fetch us a basket of bread. The Sub doesn't like grazzen spice."

"Right away, Baron."

Hands said, "I'll take a double ale too."

WickBaron Vermont shook his head, "No, you won't."

Hands pretended not to want the bread when it came, but when the rest of them were eating a strange green meat, he grabbed three buns and the butter, and set to cramming them in his mouth.

Clarie said, "Do you think we could teach them about utensils?"

The wickBaron looked over at the way the Subs used their hands to shovel the food into their mouths. "SubAgorans, you are now in the presence of an alta. The tools you find to the right and left of your plate are called your knife and fork."

Hands grunted through a mouthful of bread, "We know what they are."

The wickBaron continued, "In the presence of an alta, you do not grab your food with your fingers, but use these tools to bring the food from your plate to your mouth. It is also correct not to lean forward but to sit up straight while eating."

Hands laughed, "Well, your WickBaronship and alta-ship, you are eating in front of two Subs. Subs find forks offensive. What? It isn't good enough to touch? And as for sitting up like that, it looks like someone stuck something up your other end."

Burt tried to stifle his laugh. It was the practice in the Sub to wash one's hands before eating, and to use the fingers to eat. Some said this was because the Subs had been in the wars, and there was no room to carry utensils. Others said this was a tradition that they carried with them from Bugiri.

The alta said, "Your WickBaronship, clearly manners have different expressions in different places in the wide city of Urba."

While forcing a whole bun in his mouth, Hands made a face at her. It was meant to say, "I don't need your help," but the effect was lost because his cheeks were bulging like a squirrel's.

When Vermont got up to use the bathroom, Hands grabbed his ale. Burt said, "Hands!" Hands tilted it back, and in three great gulps emptied the stein.

Clarie told Vermont when he got back, "The Sub stole your ale."

The wickBaron looked at the empty stein. "Which one?"

"You have to ask?"

Vermont turned to Hands, "I'm buying your meal, and you disobey my orders?"

Hands said, "Why you got to be stingy, I know you got more dollars than chest hairs." The chest hairs were a sore topic. Vermont was now the leader of the Plainwick family, and he was the youngest wickBaron in Urba at twenty. He awaited eagerly the signs of manhood in his body, but they came grudgingly. His chin was smooth with a few wispy sprigs waving like solitary flags of surrender.

The wickBaron stood up, grabbing the Sub, and sending two punches hard into the boy's ear. Hands turned and would have punched the wickBaron in the groin, if the wickBaron had not been quicker and caught his arm. Then he pulled him up and twisted him in the air, before he sent a flurry of smacks into Hands' bottom. Then he flung the boy onto the floor.

"Go to bed, and think about showing me a little respect."

Hands said, "Like I want to eat the merd you buy me anyway." He walked up the stairs to bed, mouthing curses.

When Vermont settled into bed, he found himself tossing and turning, replaying the events of the dinner. The boy deserved discipline, surely, but as he replayed his actions in his head, he was not happy.

The next morning he knocked on the First Child's door, and she told him she was dressing. He knocked on the Subs' door and got no answer so he went in. The heavy kid snored, while the thin one made no noise at all, barely breathing from deep in the pillow. He looked down at him, and saw how his eyelashes lay against a cheek that still, despite his scrawniness, had a child's roundness. He was just a boy, and the wickBaron realized why he had been unhappy with himself. He had lost his temper with a boy, which was not dignified, and therefore, not Citan. He resolved to be patient, and in control with the brat.

185

When they got outside, Hands sat on the steps of the inn and refused to get on his horse. The wickBaron rode over to him, and said, "I lost my temper with you yesterday. As a wickBaron, I should be honored. You could help by showing ring respect."

Clarie came out, wearing a green riding cloak, and looking bright. The wickBaron had a serious expression on his face, and the boy was looking up at the sky as if he had not heard a word.

She sparkled, "Hey, sillies. Let's go!"

Hands didn't say anything. The wickBaron murmured, "Morning," and walked to his horse. He set Burt on his own horse while Clarie checked the cinch and reins on hers. She mounted; the wickBaron mounted; Hands was still sitting on the steps. They all turned and looked at him.

The girl said, "Did you say sorry for going grolf last night, Percy Vermont, WickBaron of Plainwick?"

The wickBaron shrugged. "He's a Sub."

She turned in her saddle focusing her green eyes on him. The wickBaron did not try to meet her gaze but bent his head. She was a strange girl, he thought. Usually she was determined to avoid even a hint of maturity, but every once in a while there was the stern face that her dad made, and it said all sorts of things about what was right and honorable and Citan without saying anything at all.

In a moment he turned his horse, cantering back to the angry boy, "What I meant to say was, you know." He paused. "You're a Sub, I'm a Citan, but I still shouldn't have done that. I'm sorry. Okay?"

Hands scowled up at him. Vermont turned and rode off. Hands watched them for a while. He thought that it was a fake apology. He wanted to go home, anywhere away from this altic merds. He told himself that the main thing was getting some dollars and revenge on the Fels. He would get the Citans after he dealt with the Fels. He shrugged, untethered the frisky black horse, now mounting with some ease, and dug in his heels. The horse started into a fast trot that had Hands slipping to the right and the left. He passed the group, waving excitedly, and gave the horse another hard dig with his heels. The horse jolted into a gallop and Hands was rocked out of the saddle, onto the rump, and then he was falling, hitting the dusty road.

Even Burt laughed, but the laughter of the girl galled Hands the most, the way her blonde curls shook as she leaned back and gave herself to it. The wickBaron took off, chasing down the runaway horse. Hands imagined learning to ride as well as a general leading the Guard and the Fels out into battle. How gloriously he wheeled and reared, perched atop his powerful beast like an extension of it, and then her alta-ship would squeal with wonder at his horsemanship. She would beg him to teach her something of what he knew. He would say, "Alta, have you seen what I've seen, and ridden where I've ridden? How then can you ride as I ride?"

The next day they found themselves entering a dry area, where brown grasses spread far, occasionally dotted by straggly trees or pillars of rock. There were no houses, no businesses, and little water. The wickBaron had prepared; they were all carrying large water bags lashed to their saddles.

Vermont dismounted and spread out his thunderPipe on a piece of silk. He said, "This is wild cluriKin territory. They take advantage of travelers who are not up to defending themselves, so be prepared."

He primed his thunderPipe, using a long wire cleaner to plunge the barrel before reassembling it and carefully packing in a scoop of black powder which he followed with a small handful of metal bits. He rapped the flintpan with cloth.

Hands said, "You have a sword and a thunderPipe. The alta has a sword. What about us?"

The wickBaron reholstered his thunderPipe and pulled the wooden swords from his saddle and handed one each to the SubAgorans. Hands said, "This won't cut anything."

The wickBaron said, "If you get a good hit on a wild cluriKin with that, it'll run away."

Burt asked, "How do they become wild?"

Vermont said, "If a household stops being a home because the people move or split apart or die, the cluriKin normally pass away along with their household. The exception is when the household is destroyed by violence. This place used to be full of farms." He pointed out the roofless shell of a small building. "Troops of robbers and bands of wendigo took to attacking the farmsteads. They killed the people. The cluriKin did not die but instead absorbed the horrors that were visited upon their households. Now they wander the dry lands seeking to recreate the dark deeds done to their households. They band together in herds that are as fearsome as the wendigo."

Hands said, "Isn't there another way to go?"

WickBaron Vermont shook his head. "All the other roads take much longer. Anyway, they say the Fels have been hunting them down, and there aren't any left."

Hands thought about Shackin, the cluriKin who had inhabited the home with Shyheem and him. Shackin was runty, and had three different personalities. He turned blue and prayed sometimes, other times he hit anyone he could reach, and other times he was cuddly. Hands hoped that Shackin hadn't died because he was gone. He was probably just blue all the time, on bent knees mumbling things to Illumen, trying to be like Shyheem.

The Citans and SubAgorans traveled through the dry lands quietly. It was a long hot day. They saw no signs of life and bedded down in the shell of a house. Hands was fine on the floor. The blanket he was sleeping on was softer than any he ever found in the Sub. The others tossed about, unaccustomed to hard ground. The tossing woke Hands. In the moment between waking and sleeping, when he was remembering where he was, he thought he saw a round head with a glint of teeth in the window frame. He started, looked again. As his eyes opened, he saw only an empty rectangle of moonlit sky. Just a dream, he told himself. Still he remembered the talk of wild cluriKin and found it hard to go back to sleep.

The next day they continued on through the dry heat, the alta was less talkative, and the main sound was Burt protesting. "You know, you guys could have only brought Hands. He has a better memory than me. How much further to the inn? Was that a wild cluriKin?"

The wickBaron was testy, watching the rocks that stood out against the flat land for any signs of movement and directing the others to watch as well. Hands thought about telling him of his dream last night, but he figured the alta would make a bunch of jokes about him being scared of the dark.

A mile ahead, a ribbon snaked across the brown flat. As they came nearer they saw it was a small canyon. "That's the Red River Canyon," said the WickBaron. The road narrowed and wound down among the cliffs toward a small wooden bridge across the brownish red river.

The wickBaron told the alta to draw her sword, and drew his thunderPipe. He explained, "The rocks are close to the path, it's a good spot for ambush." As they climbed down between the red cliffs, Hands thought the wind between the rocks sounded like whispers, but he saw nothing moving. When they got to the canyon floor, he breathed a sigh of relief, and started after the Citans onto the bridge. Burt came whining behind him. "If I was home right now, I'd be having fried potatoes, some greens, and at least three pork chops."

Suddenly the wickBaron's horse reared, flailing the sky with its hooves, and screamed a high-pitched whinny. "Merd!" The wickBaron had forgotten his manners in the presence of an alta because five thigh-high men stood in the middle of the bridge, having quickly crawled from its underside. Behind them, more and more were running from the cracks in the cliffs and behind the rocks. They massed at the far end of the bridge, a sea of angry round heads. Their hands and faces were stained rust red. Needle-like teeth glinted in their mouths.

Hands tried to turn his horse, but Burt whimpered, "They're behind us. They're everywhere." Twisting on his horse, Hands saw another crowd of the small blood-speckled creatures emerging from among the rocks behind them.

He said, "Thank you, WickBaron Vermont, for leading us. You led us into a trap set by creatures too dumb to talk."

The wickBaron ignored the comment, and commanded, "My lady, fight in the back with Hands. Burt, come up and fight with me."

The wickBaron fired his thunderPipe, "CRAKOW"

It blasted a triangle shape gouge into the mob, but in a moment more cluriKin crawled over the fallen. The wickBaron

189

charged his horse in among the little creatures. They chattered and jumped, sinking their teeth into the horse's belly. Again it reared, this time throwing the wickBaron, who twisted in the air, catlike, and landed on two feet, his sword already unsheathed. He stabbed and slashed at the small gray attackers.

"Dismount," ordered the girl. Hands slid down his horse. She stood next to him, and he smelled the flower fresh smell of her hair. What was it that she washed her hair with? She said, "Just keep swinging." An angry line of wild cluriKin advanced, their eyes red, darting forward and back, all the while growling and squeaking their rage. It was hard to think that they had once been household spirits.

Suddenly the line of them broke forward. He caught three or four with the stick. Out of the corner of his eyes he saw her sword twinkle among the little monsters, skewering them. Whenever she pierced them, they turned into wisps of reddish smoke. Suddenly keening pain shot up through his leg. A round head was latched onto his calf, and he dropped to the ground, grabbing and pulling it, trying to get it off and stop the spasms of pain. When he tried to pull it, he felt his flesh tear and the pain increased so much he dropped to the ground. Then another was on his shoulder, and he saw his brief life skip before his eyes.

18. Wild CluriKin

Hands wished for a moment that he was back in the Sub hungry and alone, but not dying. Then he just thought how much the bites hurt. He didn't see Clarie dance through the grasping paws of the beasts, making her way to him. When she reached him, her quick weapon lanced the creatures, one, two, and three, that bit him.

A shiver of relief shook him as the needle teeth dropped out of his flesh.

He hopped to his feet, accepting the stick she handed back to him, thinking, "Survive!" When he looked out, he saw the bridge was still covered in a sea of thigh high attackers. They hadn't made a dent. Those he had knocked off the bridge were climbing back out onto the bank, and running around to get back on the bridge. Others crawled over the bridge sidewall from the underside.

The wickBaron was yelling behind them, "Fight for your lives. Don't just wait for them to eat you, Burt. Fight!"

Burt had collapsed in a heap, weeping loudly. Hands redoubled his swinging, his stick plopping one then another of the waist-high creatures. They came from all sides, crawling from under the bridge. He felt teeth in his bottom, and then his knee. He looked over and saw that the girl was covered in them, her sword unable to kill as fast as they came. Already two had their teeth in her. He fell, feeling as though the teeth were everywhere, and before he was overrun, he saw even the wickBaron going down, his sword twinkled like a trickle in desert sunlight, too little to give or save life.

Through the flashing of small gray limbs, Hands saw the girl again, down on her knees, swinging desperately, and then he just thought how much the needle teeth of the wild cluriKin hurt. They hurt worse than Wareen's punches, than an empty stomach at midnight. It was like a thousand splinters.

Another sound, the creaking of something wooden and mechanical, was growing into a great rattle. Then a shout erupted, "Get back, you holes!" Standing up in the front of a wagon rode a man, his two horses galloping down the far side of the canyon. The cluriKin jumped back, retreating at a run. Those on the far bank that the wagon thundered toward dived into the river, or sprinted along the bank away from the bridge. Those on the bridge tried to climb over one another to get away. Some spilled over the sides of the bridge into the river, all the while shrilly screaming.

By the time he reached the middle of the bridge, all of them were gone, their wild murmurings anxious and unhappy as they disappeared behind rocks, or up the road out of the canyon. The man was smiling widely, "Well, travelers, seems you've stumbled into Red River Crossing unprepared."

The wagon stopped in the middle of the bridge, surrounded by four prostrate, bleeding figures. Vermont was groaning, and Burt was weeping loudly.

Hands thought he recognized the wagondriver with his wild head of curly hair, but he could not say where he had seen him. All the horses except the wickBaron's were down, lying in puddles of their own blood. The wiry man jumped from his wagon, and put his hands on one horse, whispering into its ears. The animal gasped. He cajoled and the beast struggled to its feet. One after another, he coaxed them up. Then he led them back up the cliffs they had come through. They were a sad looking train, stippled by bites. The travelers just watched him, in shock that they were alive.

Burt said, "I thought we were going to die."

The wickBaron nodded, "So did I."

The man returned from the turnings of the road. "By the looks of it you could use a ride. I'll give you a good price." He applied some herbs to their wounds that burned, and bound them with brown cloth he pulled from the wagon. He helped them into the wagon, putting Hands on the buckboard. He took it across the bridge, and turned it, before setting out back the way he had come, which was the way the travelers were headed. He said, "I'm going to take you to the next town down here. No big hurry for Eire."

"What did you do with the horses?" said the wickBaron.

"Oh, they were tired, those horses. They didn't deserve to be carting around humans who took them into a mess like that. I put them to pasture. You all will have to walk now." The girl started crying, and Vermont patted her back.

"Now, I don't think I need to say it, but you all are god-blessed. Another five minutes and I'd have found four dead travelers, and another twenty and I wouldn't have found your bones. You need to know how we prevent the Wild cluriKin from hurting us. You need protection, see." He shook a small leather bag that hung around his neck.

"Is protection why they run from you?" Hands wanted to know.

"That, and other things," said the wagondriver. "They know not to mess with Eire. The most important thing is peace. It's an easy thing to say, but a hard thing to have. If you resting inside, see, at peace with all of Theom's green, or brown, earth," and he laughed at his own joke, "the Wild cluriKin can't even find you. They got no nose for a peaceful heart. Now, anger, hate, they can smell that a long way off."

Hands felt that this was directed at him. "You try riding across the country with those two altic snobs."

Eire laughed. "You are the strangest group of travelers that ever rode in my wagon, Hands. How did you all come to be traveling together?"

Hands looked at the driver. He was built small with glowing green eyes. He wanted to trust him, but there was too much, escaping Aeternanox, making friends with a wendigo, in the story that any Regnan might use against him. He said, "Long story."

The driver smiled. "I know more than you think. Matter of fact, someone told me I should get over here, that Hands and Burt were in trouble. You two by name, that was my concern. These others, they've got their uses," he turned toward the Citans, "But you two are made for bigger things. Well, I should say, you four."

Hands looked back in the wagon, hoping someone would chime in with how weird the wagon driver's statement was, but the rocking of the wagon, along with the extremity of their wounds, had put his three fellow travelers to sleep.

193

The driver said, "I know you're not much for Illumen, and that's probably because most of those that say they follow him go in for being more altic than those Citans. But he's the one that had me here, saving you from those cluriKin."

"You're telling me Illumen talks to you? About me?"

"Oh, Illumen is a talkative god, if you know how to listen. He's got plans for you four."

Hands scoffed, "What's the special plan for us? And why do you keep saying four?"

The driver said, "One question at a time. Four, I'm talking about the Subs of Abierto's alley, Shyheem, Jalil, Burt, and you."

"Jalil! He's a snake."

"But you, Hands, you're a good Sub? Do you think it's right to take a farmer's money, money that he worked all year to have. Yup. Going to take that home and buy his kaBoy a pair of shoes."

Hands glowered at him, "Maybe you're one of those Illumenist Citans yourself, telling me what's wrong with me."

The driver ignored him. "Now, regarding the plan for you four. There is some bad merd happening. Some red burners are trying to take over, and Illumen is using, everywhere, silly little people to fight them. You four are a big silly part of that."

"So now I'm little and silly."

"Well, don't forget bad. You're bad, too." Hands couldn't muster up any annoyance. The driver was calling him bad, but back in the Sub, calling him bad always went with shooing and throwing rocks. The driver looked over at him, smiling. He seemed to enjoy talking to Hands more than any adult ever had.

"It might seem like I'm dropping a lot on you all at once. The reason why I'm telling you anyway is, when things seem really bad, you need to remember that one of Illumen's servants showed up and helped you, and ask if maybe it can happen again. I'm not asking you to go all Shyheemy all the time. Just know that the guy watching out for you, he's real."

Hands nodded. The man continued, "Now, you're doing good. You got a quick head, even if your heart's a little hard. Course, after a life like yours, kaSub, it ain't easy to keep soft. Anyways, good job back in Aeternanox. They'll be telling that story to your grandkids.

194

And you keep this Citan," he jerked his thumb toward Vermont, "on his toes. Without you, he'd be up Merd's Creek without a paddle."

The driver put one of his hands on the boy's shoulder and squeezed it so it hurt. "Look." The driver fished in the leather pouch around his neck and retrieved a stone. "Take this bauble. It will become special when you need it to be."

Hands felt the rough stone in his hands. It looked like it came from the side of the road. The driver had saved his life so he put the stone in his pocket. "Thanks, I guess."

The driver said, "Don't sound so thankful."

Hands said, "No, it was a nice speech, but then you gave me a rock."

The driver beamed at the dry countryside that they passed, not saying anymore. Hands thought about everything the driver had said. For some reason he wanted to believe it. It was weird that the mission of talking to the regnate had fallen to them. It was weird that Hands had decided to take the mission; it was impossible that they had escaped Aeternanox, and special that they had met Seketeme and Orpan, and, even if they were altic Citans, WickBaron Vermont and Alta Clarie. The driver had said that he was special. He was important.

This thought surrounded him in its warm glow, and he nodded off, slumping down on the buckboard. It was evening when the wagon pulled to a stop outside an inn. The driver helped them get situated in a room, carrying up their stuff, because they were still hurting from the needlelike teeth of the cluriKin.

Vermont realized that he had lost his purse in the attack. "We can't pay for the inn!"

The driver waived his hand. "This is on me."

Vermont said to the wagon driver, "We are very thankful, and I, as WickBaron of Plainwick, want to extend you any service. You may pass any gate in Urba with my name, and, when I am able, I shall reward you, just tell me where to send the dollars."

The driver chuckled, "Nice of you. I don't really have an address though." The WickBaron would normally remonstrate a

Regnan for not addressing him as WickBaron, but it was hard to do when the man had just saved his life.

Vermont said, "Would you take us on to Segundaton? I could pay you back in time?"

The driver shook his head of wild curls. "I've enjoyed my time with you, really, but I've got to be traveling on now. Lots of things to do."

The next day they woke and felt their wounds healed enough to move on. They set off, walking this time, with only one horse.

Hands said, "WickBaron Vermont, did you enjoy leading us into that trap?"

The WickBaron walked on. The girl said, "Shut up about it."

Hands said, "I just want to know if he thought he did a good job of leading us."

The girl said, "He's a lot older than you, and he's been through here before. If it was you leading us, do you think we would have survived? Anyway, how many wild cluriKin did he stop compared to you?"

"I had a wooden sword! Of course I didn't stop any."

She said, "I had to save your life."

Hands said, "I was just resting, letting them get a couple chomps in, when you interrupted."

The alta let a half smile onto her lips. She had to admire how, regardless of the facts, he never admitted to weakness. He smiled, too, and looked ahead, feeling pleased with himself. He was not expecting it when the girl landed a punch on his shoulder. He stumbled up to the ditch and caught himself before falling in. She giggled at this, and walked quickly, so that she was next to the wickBaron, and safe from revenge.

Hands said, "PorkChop did pretty good in the fight."

At this the WickBaron, who had appeared to be ignoring them, chuckled. Burt looked down at the ground.

Hands added, "You were crying in a ball."

Burt said, "Whatever, I knocked three or four of them in the water, and then one got me so I just balled up and got ready to die. I had a few prayers to say before I passed."

"You mean you had a few tears to cry."

Everyone but Burt laughed. The wickBaron said, "This country is pretty peaceful for the next day or two, just the well-run farms of Segundawick. We'll stop with the Vice Regnate in Segundaton and he will give us new horses."

Hands said, "Who's that?"

Burt, happy to recover some dignity after the battle, laughed. "Everybody knows he's the regnate's number two. He helps him do everything."

"Well, I don't want to stop there," said Hands. "We can't trust anybody, and we're not far if we just keep walking. Or you could buy a horse with all your dollars."

The WickBaron said, "I'm not going to debate the course of action with Subs. We need an escort to go into wendigo lands, and the vice regnate can give us that."

"We can all relax," said Hands, "because we all remember how you led us into the wild cluriKin ambush so well."

The wickBaron contemplated various ways to punish the boy, but he could see how lightly Hands stood on his toes, and knew that the boy would scamper if he tried to catch him. He did not want the indignity of chasing a Sub around in circles on a highway. Anyway, he was supposed to stay in control of himself. He would punish this kid when they got to the regnate and had found whoever was planning the assassination.

On the seventh day of their journey, they entered Segundaton. They approached the town through amber fields, ripe with grain, and large well built farms. The walls around Segundaton were as high as three men, and atop them Fels patrolled. The wooden gates were open, and a few well-dressed persons were leaving through them. The travelers walked through the gate and into the market.

Hands knew markets, but this place did not make him feel comfortable. It was different than the SubAgoran market where the succulent smell of pork frying mixed with the tree-breeze smell of ripe fruit that mixed with the odor of rotting discarded fruit, the public toilets, and the sweat of thousands of people. The SubAgoran markets boiled with life, the stalls packed so close together that the apples on one stall overflowed into the pile of axe heads at the next. Broken pots, bruised fruit, and dirty children were kicked about under the stalls by the rolling crowds. Beautiful women picked through piles of silk, while gutter beggars squawked their needs at a heedless world.

The stalls in Segundaton were built out of straight wooden beams that held up little roofs. Each stall was painted carefully with yellow, orange, or red. They were in even rows separated by a walkway wide enough for many shoppers to walk down without bumping one another, and the floor beneath them was clean paving stones, not the beaten murram of Urba. There was no trash under the stalls. Hands wondered where they put it. At each junction of the larger streets there stood a group of Fels, who watched as people shopped.

Hands watched as the girl examined some apples. She spoke to the shopkeeper, a sturdy woman with gray hair and brown eyes. Hands pointed out a bruise on the apple she held with a sudden stretch of his arm. The farmer's wife, and the lady's eyes followed his sudden motion. Meanwhile his other hand tucked two apples under his cloak. He listened as the farmer's wife explained how shallow the bruise actually was, and he nodded, but insisted that Alta Clarie choose another.

She said, "Like you know how to choose an apple."

It was true that Hands would eat any apple he got his hands on. He shrugged, no longer concerned with whether the high and mighty listened to his advice, and walked away. The two little bumps in his cloak made him feel better about this neat little market. They might have Fels at every corner, and keep the floors clean, but a Sub could grimy them easily. Somebody pinched his arm. He turned and found Burt breathing hard.

"Why did you do that?"

Hands shrugged. "You want one?"

Burt said, "If you wanted one, WickBaron Vermont would have bought it. You are risking everything for two apples."

Hands said, "I don't need his money, I can get my own apples."

"You got something wrong with your head."

"At least I didn't start crying when attacked by little cluriKin."

Burt stomped after the wickBaron, who was waiting at the top of the market. The little group passed through the town. Flowers were planted out front of the houses. The houses were painted pastel yellow and green. They reached a large open field, the commons. Across the commons was a gate, and a green hill rose up beyond the gate. Atop the hill stood a great house that rose behind a high wall topped with sentry towers. A lone tower went up beyond the battlements so high that the mist of the clouds shrouded it.

WickBaron Vermont said, "That's where we're going."

Hands didn't like the look of the house. It was too tall, too perfect. More altas would be in there, lecturing him about ring respect. He said, "If he's not the regnate, what's the point?"

WickBaron Vermont shook his head. "Just try and be respectful for once."

Hands continued muttering to himself as they crossed the commons and came to the door in the wall. A Fel bowed as the walked up. "Baron, we have sent for the vice regnate."

They went through a yard with a stables and neat rows of flowers. He directed them to tie up their horse outside the stable, and brought them into the house. They found themselves in a large anteroom lined with slippers. A reddish cluriKin, both muscular and elegant, helped the wickBaron and alta out of their dusty shoes, and into soft slippers with firm mitten-hands.

The servant said, "You Baron and Alta, come with me. You browns will be taken to the servant quarters."

Hands said, "I'm not a servant."

The servant sniffed, "No, of course."

Nothing more was to be said, and another servant led the two Subs off.

The house they walked through was magnificent. Huge tapestries hung from the ceilings, telling stories about rock lizards, grolfs, and the heroes that fought them. Beautiful swords and thunderPipes hung from the walls, and one fine weapon glowed with magic that was either grazzen or Bellumite. They were led up broad stairs of the smoothest dark green stone Burt had ever seen. His feet seemed to slip and slide on it as if it was ice. He gripped the handrail, a curving piece of the same green stone. The Citans walked right ahead underneath a magic rock lizard statue that roared as if it was alive. It sent fine puffs of sweet smelling smoke out its flaring nostrils.

Hands said, "Let's take that."

Burt said, "They'd kill us."

"We'll ride it out the window. Then they won't be able to get us."

"I don't think it can fly."

"I'm going to grimy something from this place."

They were led down a hall that stretched as long as a SubAgoran block, and up a bunch of stairs. Burt said they were servant stairs, which left Hands to wonder what the alta stairs looked like.

Hands entered a room with a bed as large as the shell of a house he and Shyheem had shared back in the city. He rolled back and forth on it, while the servant got a hot bath ready for him in the next room. When the servant told him it was ready, he danced into the bathing room. He slipped out of the dusty clothes and dipped his tired body into the hot soapy water. He took the sudsy bubbles and placed them on his head so that he was wearing a crown, and admired the look of it in the mirror set in the wall.

When he got out of the bath, food was delivered to the room. Hands asked why he wasn't eating with WickBaron Vermont and the Clarie, and the maid said no Sub servant ever ate in the dining hall. Hands said that he thought he was higher class than them, but he had allowed them to eat with him up to this point. The maid smirked, but didn't make any comment. Burton dove into the fried potatoes and kaSteaks. Hands didn't wait much longer, fearing Burt would eat it all. When they had finished and were lying on their beds groaning contentedly.

Vice Regnate John Nickson, WickBaron of Segunda stood when Vermont and Clarie entered the room. "Welcome, WickBaron Vermont, and First Child, to the second house."

They greeted him.

He said, "You brought the First Child without an escort so far from the city? So close to the wendigo lands? The birds fly every which way; Alta Carnegie has heart attacks. What are you doing? When the regnate hears about this you are going to be in it."

Vermont said, "You will understand my reasons soon, Nickson. I have heavy business."

The vice regnate said, "SubAgorans are strange companions for the First Child and the WickBaron of Plainwick."

Vermont said, "They are part of my heavy business."

The vice regnate said, "We have stabled your horse. Take these ones to the guest rooms—put the First Child in the Freeland Room. You must all wash up and eat and then we will have your story. The road is still on your cloaks, and your limbs hang like willow trees."

They washed and met Nickson in his dining hall. The food was wonderful after the inn-fare they had been living on. Nickson turned the conversations to Clarie's mother.

The vice regnate said, "The dresses she wore. She was the most elegant alta I ever met. And it wasn't just because she was the regnate alta. There was something about her, a sense of adventure."

Vermont said, "He hasn't been the same since she died."

"Of course. The whole country hasn't. He hasn't had the same focus since then. But this is enough talk of the past. Tell me your story."

Vermont told the story as best he could, and Clarie filled in the details. The vice regnate seemed curious about the whole story, peppering them with questions. He said, "So, there were in fact four SubAgorans who learned of the plot? What happened to the other friend, the bauble wick? What was his name again?"

Vermont said, "We don't know his name. We can ask the Subs."

The vice regnate nodded. "Now you need to go to the regnate, and warn him that some of the Fels are plotting against him. You need an escort. This mission is a serious one. What I will do is this. In the morning we will set out for Fort Ornata. I will take you, WickBaron Vermont, and the Subs, so that they might identify any of the Fels responsible. I can't take the First Child though. It is too dangerous to risk her."

"No," said Clarie. "I came to help."

The vice regnate shook his head. "I do not understand why you brought her."

WickBaron Vermont said, "I have no excuse, but that she insisted, and she is the First Child."

The vice regnate nodded. "I see. I should remind you that, as an adult, you may tell her what her duty is as heir to the Wick of Urba and to that, though not your word, she is bound. She will stay here, and we will go. It is a dangerous two days ride to the west, and in a few more we shall return with the regnate."

Clarie said, "I want to go."

The vice regnate said, "Alta Clarie, I am not your father, so I can only give you counsel. But you know that your father will expect you to take my advice. It is not wise for the country that you be exposed in the same place as the regnate, especially in times of war. Should an arrow somehow pierce the regnate's grazzen armor, and, Theom, Bellum and Illumen prevent it, he died, you would be WickBaron. What if you died as well?"

Clarie looked unhappy but said nothing.

"Now," continued the vice regnate, "you all need rest. In the morning we shall depart for the west." Two servants stepped forward and escorted Clarie away to her bedroom.

The Subs were awakened by an iron voice outside their room. "The SubAgorans will come with me."

Burt tried to get up but Hands snuggled further into the ocean of a bed. After a minute the big voiced servant marched in, set his lattern down, and pulled Hands from bed, and forced him to get into a proper shirt. Halfway down the stairs they realized that the guys pushing them were Fels. Hands sort of smiled. It was the smile of someone who has had so much merd piled on them in life that they see more merd as a kind of cosmic joke (on them) that they have learned to see the humor in. They were pushed into the War Room. There was Vermont. And there was the vice regnate.

202

Hands gaped. Burt said, "No!" Before him, he saw the same man that had taken him from Abierto's and Black Way, and sent him to the dark depths of Aeternanox. He was not in the redcoat of the Fels, but wore an intricately brocaded coat and vest. Hands jumped up and ran for the far door of the great room, but two Fels stepped through it blocking his escape. Hands sprinted for the next door, but it too was filled with grinning redcoats.

Vermont said, "What's going on?"

The vice regnate laughed, "It's a good question, little wickBaron. What's going on? Some things you already know. Someone is plotting on the regnate's life. You know that some of the Fels are involved. You seek to warn him. And these little merds you escort have seen a few of the involved Fels including," here he paused, relishing the next word, "myself. They've put together what you still can't seem to figure out. I am the one who will kill the regnate."

WickBaron Vermont stood up, and unsheathed his sword. The Fels leapt forward but the vice regnate waved them off and slid his own weapon out of the sheath.

"Ah, the WickBaron of Plainwick draws his weapon on the vice regnate, WickBaron of Segunda. Your optimism and idealism amuse me."

Vermont charged. Hands had been impressed by what the young wickBaron had done against the wild cluriKin. His sword was quick, his movement faster than the pickpocket's eyes could follow. Vermont was just as fast in his attack of the vice regnate, but Nickson was unconcerned, his blade casually meeting and parrying each thrust and hack, until, with a quick twist, he disarmed Vermont, and placed the tip of his weapon against the young man's neck, and with a series of small steps prodded him back into the waiting arms of the Fel.

"Disappointing. I thought you would be better," the vice regnate remarked.

"Treason! I will kill you all!" Vermont's face turned red as he shouted. The Fels laughed. One of them stuffed a cloth in the wickBaron's mouth.

The vice regnate turned to the boys, "So you are the ones that escaped Aeternanox, letting a grolf loose in the Citadel, and freeing a wendigo warrior. It caused quiet a mess."

Hands said, "Not the first mess I made, and it won't be the last."

The vice regnate said, "Take off your clothes. I have heard about your gift for lock picking."

Hands said, "What, no sweet talk first?"

A heavy hand struck him in the mouth. The blow sent him down into the carpet. He stood wearily, being no stranger to the fists of soldiers, and wiped the blood that seeped from his cut lip. He worked on the twine knot that held up his rags. The Fel picked up the crumple of clothes, and felt through them. He found something in a pocket. He pulled out the smooth stone that Eire had given him.

"What's this?"

The vice regnate looked at it and laughed. "That is an Illumenist stone, commonly called a bauble. The Subs pray, and light shows from the stone. Some of them are pathetic enough to believe that the stones give them protection. Much good Illumen has done you, Hands."

"I'm get you by myself," declared Hands, "I don't need a god."

The vice regnate laughed. "Your bauble indicates you believe otherwise, Sub. Give him back his stone. His pathetic dependence on the younger god amuses me."

He felt the stone forced into his hands. They pulled his arms behind his back. The shackles clicked coldly around his wrists.

Nickson spoke, "I want you to think very carefully about what I'm going to ask you. If you answer well, and truthfully, then I may let you live. What is the name of the bauble wick who also knows the plan?"

Hands said, "I forget." He received another heavy blow for that.

Burt tried, "Rasheen. His name is Rasheen."

Nickson laughed, walking over to Burt. "You are no liar, Burt."

Burt looked extremely nervous.

Nickson pulled out a knife from some hidden pocket. The thing was grazzen, rivuleted with metal from the earth's hardest veins, and its curve held the stinging promise of a snake's cocked head. It twinkled and jumped in his hands, and then it nicked Burt's brow, and the single slice turned faintly white before blood made it red.

Nickson said, "Burt. Let us not play games. You are not built for torture, and the torture of lulus offers me no challenge. Tell me his real name."

Hands said, "Don't tell him, Burt."

Burt didn't hear Hands. He was watching the knife. It was now hovering by his finger, advancing toward his fingernail, incising the sensitive skin beneath it.

"Shyheem! His name is Shyheem. He makes the best baubles on Black Way." He started weeping.

Hands said nothing. Pointing out that Burt was a lulu was about as useful as pointing out that Vermont was an idiot.

"Thank you, Burt. That wasn't hard. Is there anyone else, beside the Subs Shyheem and Jalil, that you told about this plan?"

Hands said, "Yeah. We told half of the Sub about the plot. Also, we met twenty Guardsmen in an inn, told them about it."

"You're lying."

"I told your mom, too. I saw her on Labor Street, working the late shift." A Fel slapped Hands.

Hands said, "You know his mother?"

He got two slaps. The stream from his nose dropped splashes of crimson onto the marble floor. The soft sound of Burt weeping filled the silence.

Nickson looked at Burt, and said, "You had no time to tell anyone. Before you leave, I just want to say what a pleasure it is to see you again. When my Fels failed and you escaped, I was so disappointed. I thought we'd done such a clever clean job of catching you. I did not anticipate that you would come to me. I have to thank you for that, Vermont."

Vermont said, "What are you doing with the First Child?"

Nickson smiled. "In time, I will tell you. For now, I have business, and you have captivity."

205

He waved his hand and the soldiers escorted the three prisoners out.

Hands asked, while they were being pushed and pulled along, "First Child? Like the child of the regnate?"

They were pushed down long ornate hallways. The castle cluriKin walked by them, his head down, and his hands behind him like he too was bound for prison. Then it lifted up its face, grimacing wickedly at the prisoners. Hands kicked at it, but it dodged his foot and punched his leg. They went up stone stairs that followed a curving wall. "The tower," Hands thought.

Burt said, "WickBaron, is Clarie the First Child?"

Vermont made a face, which Hands and Burt took as a confirmation.

A Fel banged Burt's head against the stonewall. Hands whispered, "These Fels don't like talk." He heard Burt behind him quietly sobbing. Crying was bad because it made them look weak, but Burt was going to be Burt.

Hands found it pretty amazing that Clarie wasn't just any Citan. He had tackled the First Child, only daughter to the regnate. He had pinched her, and called her all sorts of names. This did not embarrass him the way that it would have embarrassed a respectful boy. Instead, a smile curled up his face, as he wondered how many people in the country could boast about how they tackled the First Child off her horse. Probably only him.

He wanted to tell her that he was surprised she was the First Child, because he thought heirs to wickBaronships were nice and good and boring, but she spoke up for herself, and had fun along the way. Now he wouldn't ever get to talk to her again.

The three prisoners' thighs and calves started to burn as they climbed higher and higher, until they were shoved up through a thick wood door into an empty room. The door shut behind them, and Burt lay down on the stone floor. Vermont sat in a corner and covered his head with his hands. Hands went to the window of the room, a small slit, and looked out.

The moonlit estate was spread around him, a beautiful expanse of fine lawns, carefully trimmed trees, and strong hedges. It was dotted with small structures and encircled by a great strong wall,

206

broad enough to have a walkway atop it. A few Fels walked the wall in a circuit. Behind it grew a small wood. Dotting the field in front were the tents of the Segundawick army. Hands considered the possibilities of escape. A rope would have to be extremely long. He estimated that they were the height of ten shacks from the ground. He looked around the room, wondering if there was anything with which to pick a lock, or attack a jail keeper, but the room was bare. Two stone benches, built into the wall, were the only furniture. He went and laid on the empty one.

Hands said, "Looks like we die here."

Burt said, "Why are we doing this?"

Hands said, "I just want to get revenge. These Fels slapped me, this vice regnate had us arrested twice. I want to see their heads cut off."

Burt said, "No, I mean, why would it be us? We're kids, and when we talk nobody respects us because we're from SubAgora District. We picked stupid people to help us."

Vermont said, "I'm right here."

Burt continued, "Now we're stuck. There is no way out of this place. And we've brought the First Child into the clutches of the kiBad."

Ignoring him, Hands answered, "I don't care about that two-penny First Child. Anyway, that's his fault," Hands pointed at Vermont. "I told him we shouldn't come in here, and he wouldn't listen. He's a wickBaron, so he knows everything; I'm a Sub, I don't know merd from flowers."

Vermont said, "Shut your mouth, and stop your disrespect."

"Disrespect? Me telling you the truth about what you did isn't disrespect. It should help you realize the truth, and then you should admit it. It doesn't matter that you're a Citan wickBaron, and I'm a Sub, because we are both locked up, and we're only here, and not dead, because that nut likes to talk."

"There is a way that you must talk to me."

"You holding on to that stuff still? Your dumb ring respect? I'm going to come over there and head butt your face in."

207

The Citan smirked at this threat, but Burt, who knew that Hands never backed down, tried to intervene. "Don't fight him, Hands. It doesn't matter if he admits it or not."

Hands said, "If he thinks he's going to tell me that I'm supposed to call him WickBaron and all that, when all he did was almost get me killed and get me captured, I'm going to fight him."

The WickBaron said, "What are you going to do? You're half my size, and you've got your hands chained up." Vermont forgot that his own hands were locked up too. Hands got up on his feet, and bounced once or twice. Then he ran across the small room, and dove through the air, head first, smacking Vermont's temple with his skull. Hand fell to the floor, twisting in the air so that he landed on his bottom, and rolled back onto his feet. Vermont groaned while the Sub ran across the cell, ready to charge and head butt Vermont again.

"Ouch, stop," said Vermont. Burt was laughing.

Hands said, "Now what? This isn't sword fighting; we are watting it out now, KaWickBaron of the Citadel, and I'm kicking your merdup. This is how we do in the Sub."

A thin line of red was oozing from Vermont's forehead. "Calm down," he said. "I was just teasing. You guys can call me Percy until we're out of this tower."

Hands said, "I'm calling you Percy until we die. Of course that will be when we get out of this tower."

Hands returned to his seat, satisfied that Percy had given up his insistence on ring respect. It was a small victory that had nothing to do with the bigger problem. Hands knew they were in a desperate place. He would not get his hands on something to pick the locks with this time, and even if he did, there was no Seketeme, and no grolf to help them battle their way out of the tower.

Burt said, "Let's ask Illumen for help."

Hands thought about the wagondriver's words, and he tried to think about talking to the invisible gods and he knew he couldn't. He used to pray when he was younger. He'd cry because he was hungry, and he'd ask that if there was anyone out there that cared, could they please just send him a bread roll. The roll had never come, and Hands decided that if someone was out there, they didn't care about him. He wasn't going to waste his time crying to those gods anymore.

Vermont said, "That's a good idea, Burt."

Burt mumbled "Illumen, Shyheem always says you care about us, so, if it's true, do us a favor and get us out of here alive, and help us find the regnate."

Vermont said a few words to Theom All-Father about wanting to have a chance to fix his mistakes. They waited, but nothing happened. Hands shrugged, looking sadly out the window.

After a long silence Percy wanted to talk. "Hands, I should have listened to you. You were right about the vice regnate. I had no idea about the scale of this plot. I guess it was just a bit of fun for me, until this."

"Lot of good apologizing does," said Hands. "We're still in this tower, we're still going to die here. Your First Child is still in the hands of Nickson, and he's still going to march out tomorrow and finish his plot to kill the regnate."

19. SubAgoran Return

Mishipeshu, what do you ask from us?
The wolf's tooth is long in the shadow of the moon.
The moose bellows his loneliness to the swamp loon.
Mishipeshu, is your beauty greater than your terror?
The evergreen is a jagged promise in iced snow.
The mountain breaks the earth like god's own backbone.
Mishipeshu, do you accept my sacrifice?
The deer runs but the panther's claw still catches.
Balance the ice knives with the sunlight.

Jalil couldn't believe that Hands was angry. All he had done was save them from being wendigo food and create a diversion that got them out of AltUrba. The biggest surprise was when Burt joined with Hands and tried to fight him. Of course Hands ruined everything and befriended a wendigo. He was almost a wendigo himself. He grimyed people just like the wendigo. Of course he found a wendigo in prison, where thieves and murderers are locked up. Of course, the thief and wendigo ended up killing more of the regnate's soldiers, and escaping from prison. Hands was always doing wrong and saying stupid things. That didn't make him mad. Burt talking Hands' side made him mad.

Anyway, they wouldn't try that again. He rubbed sore knuckles and thought with satisfaction about the blow he had landed on Burt's stomach, and the twist he had given Hands' arm. That's what his father had taught him: stand up for what's right.

He walked down Black Way. The houses around him grew shorter and closer together until they snuggling shoulder to shoulder against the street. He kicked a few busted barrels across the road.

"Yo." He looked up and saw three Subs walking toward him. He was still blocks away from home.

"What you doing here, Jalil?"

"Where your friends, kaSub?"

The three boys were about his size, maybe a little older. He recognized them as AltUrba Market Subs. They were smiling evilly at him, filling the space in front of him so he had to stop or risk walking between them. He stopped.

"What do you Subs want?"

"You got a dime for me?" The largest one asked. "Cause you know you got to pay to walk through here."

"And that nice new coat." The thin one next to the largest one reached out and ran the altic silk through his hands. "Nice."

"Take it off, kaMerd."

There were three of them, and he was alone. He didn't care much about the robe. Normally he would have given it up, and maybe come back with some Black Way Subs, but right then he wanted to grind his fist into someone's face, and these guys had just put their faces in front of him.

"Hold up," he said, stepping back as if to remove the robe, and then he pounced, sending his right fist into the nose of the big one, followed by a left to the chin. The others pushed him off. One grabbed him around the waist and the other tried to punch him, but Jalil dodged it and hammered his elbow into the side of his skull. The big Sub was back up though, and punched Jalil in the back of the head, which knocked him forward into the third one's clutches. Jalil jerked his knee up into the kid's belly, before a tackle from behind put his face in the dust.

He struggled but they had him pinned. They ripped the coat off him, and took turns punching him, while he told them that they hit like lulus. A shopkeeper ran out with a stick and chased them off. Jalil had a bruise on his left cheek, and his right eye was swelling shut, and his mouth tasted bloody.

The shopkeeper said, "Come in, I'll help you."

Jalil got up, dusting himself, and shook his head. "I'm okay." He walked on down Black Way. He planned how he'd find them alone, and when he did, give them a watting. He saw Abierto Inn in

211

the distance, its windows bright, and music wafting out of its windows.

"Jalil!"

Standing in the middle of the street, smile blazing, was Shawnee. Her hands on her hips, the wool of her dress lying against that body that Jalil found so bewildering that he didn't want to look at it, but he did. Then she took off toward him and embraced him.

He flinched. He had belly-flopped into water from some forty feet in the air, and he had a couple tussles since then, all of which left some bruising. She leaned back and examined him, as if she couldn't believe it. "What happened to your face?"

She kissed his cheek, as if to make the dark bruise better, and it worked. The cool soft pressure took his mind off the pain.

She leaned back, keeping her arms around him, and shouted to anyone who would listen, "Jalil's back!"

"Hey, Shawnee."

"Where have you been? Where is Burt? What happened? What happened to your face? You're back. I can't believe it. You're back. We thought . . . Well, you're back. Come on, let me take you to the inn."

"I've got to see my mom first."

"Oh, yeah. I'll go tell everyone you're back. Is Burto here?"

"It's a long story."

"Is he here?"

"No. But he's okay, I think."

She grabbed him and squeezed again, and then she was off, running toward the inn. Jalil went to his house. He paused in the door. His mother was sprawled out on the bench. The cluriKin Yako was comatose by an empty bottle on the floor.

"Mom!"

She turned over slowly, "Huh? Jalil?"

"I'm home, Mom. It's me, Mom."

She looked up, bleary eyed. "Jalil?"

He spoke patiently, "I'm home. Mom, it's me."

She jumped up. "We thought you were . . . And with your dad gone, I was all alone. All alone. All my boys gone." She started crying on his shoulder.

212

"But I'm here, Mom."

"You're here! That's right. Why am I crying? It's wonderful. Let me just make you something, I've got some nice beef broth stored somewhere in here."

Yako was up too, running in circles around Jalil's feet, punching him in the merdup and hopping on his toes. "Hey, Yako."

His mom bustled around, cracking open earthenware. She murmured to herself suggesting various meals, before vetoing them because of missing ingredients. Jalil said, "Don't worry about food, Mom. I saw Shawnee in the street and she went to the inn, and she'll bring some food around."

"She's a nice girl. I hope she brings a drink. This calls for celebration." She grabbed the boy holding him tight. "It was so hard with you gone."

A moment later Burt's dad popped through the door. He was out of breath from running. The first thing he said was, "Where's Burto?"

Jalil shrugged. Burt's dad put a hand on his shoulder.

"Where's Burto?" he said. He was gripping his shoulder hard.

Jalil said, "It's a long story." He didn't want to tell Burt's dad that he left him with Hands, on his way to talk to some guy that a murderous wendigo had told them about.

Burt's dad shook his head. "I need to know where he is, right now."

Jalil said, "Somewhere in the Sub or the Agora. They're going to a place in the Agora. I can't remember what it's called."

While they were talking, Shawnee came in and placed a steaming bowl in front of Jalil. The aroma of beef and sage filled the room, and Jalil was drawn toward it.

"Where were you?" Burt's dad said, "You escaped?"

"Yes. Aeternanox. Pretty great story. Can I eat first?"

"No. The Fels put out a price for you. A lot of money. You're not safe here. You need to come with me. Now."

Jalil said, "But I . . ."

Three men ducked through the front door. The one in front had shoulders so wide he stepped in sideways. He swung his eyes

213

around the room and smiled when he saw Jalil. "KaChing," he said, already counting the dollars they would get for turning Jalil in.

"Back door." Burt's dad didn't need to say it twice. Jalil jumped across the table and went out the back door. A second later he flew back in and thudded onto the clay floor. A mustached man walked in after him.

"No exit this way."

The big one walked over and picked up Jalil by his shirt. "One hundred dollars right there." The two behind him laughed. They held clubs in their hands.

The big one continued, "Thought you might be going to see the boys when you rushed out, Abierto."

"This isn't right, Sheem. Subs stand together."

"Depends how much money is involved."

"Singers." Abierto flung the word at them.

The big man Sheem shrugged. "Where's your boy, Abierto?"

"Not here."

"I guess you aren't going to tell me where he is."

Burt's dad said, "You Subs don't bother coming to the Abierto anymore."

"With this kind of money, we won't need to. But thanks for all the drinks."

They laughed. Sheem walked over to the boy. Jalil grabbed a chair and brought it down on his head. The chair shattered. The mustached man wrapped his arms around the boy from behind. Jalil swung an elbow low and caught a groin. Mustache released him.

Burt's dad moved toward the scuffle, yelling for help, "Subs, Subs, at Tamara's house!"

One of the club guys clubbed his head, and he went down. The other one reached the scrum around Jalil. He jumped on him. Sheem piled on top. When the two of them had Jalil squashed on the ground and breathless they were able to tie him up. Yako was running around them, trying to sink his teeth into their calves until the big one landed a kick that sent him flying across the room. Jalil was yelling "Subs, Subs." A gag was stuffed down his throat and he was carried out the door.

Four of five people were coming in off the street. "What's going on," they said.

"Little tussle in there, Tamara had too much to drink. I think she hurt Abierto," the leader said. They walked off with the boy struggling between them, as the local Subs rushed in to find their innkeeper unconscious, and Tamara in hysterics, "My boy, my boy."

By the time the facts were clear, the kidnappers were in the shack alleys blocks away. Jalil still twitched and kicked between them. Mustache remarked, "Didn't they say that the reward was for dead or alive?"

Sheem said, "He's worth more alive."

Jalil thought about the bowl of stew he had lost and the sudden warmth of Shawnee's hug and kiss. He desperately wanted that bowl of soup, and to tell his story to a grown-up, someone who could tell him he was right to point out the wendigo. Burto had told him that they couldn't go back to Black Way. He would have listened if they hadn't just tried to beat him up. He smelled the ocean's fishy breeze, and heard the easy lap of water and the sound of feet on the wood. They were at the river docks.

Sheem said, "Kid, if you don't stop struggling, you're going to fall into the river, and then you'll drown."

"I don't know. He wiggles like a fish."

Sheem said, "Stomp on him a couple of times."

Mustache said, "You should have said so sooner."

They dropped him, and something crashed into his head.

Sheem said, "Not his head. You'll kill him. In the ribs."

Mustache said, "That's where he hit me."

"He's a kid, stupid."

"A little graz is what he is."

He was stomped a moment later on his thigh. It didn't feel too good, and it was persuasive. He stopped struggling.

"Okay, he stopped."

"I was just getting started."

"This is about money not about stomping on kaSubs."

"He watted me."

"We saw. If we weren't there he'd have kicked your merdup." This got a laugh from the other two. The four men pulled a large

215

rowboat to the dock. Two held ropes while Sheem and Mustache pushed their bundle into the boat. Mustache got in, putting his foot on Jalil. Sheem came after, and the boat sunk a few inches under his large bulk. The other thugs were about to get in when a thunk sounded in the night, and one of them dropped onto the planks. The other one looked over at him.

"Hey, Tono, you okay, man?" Tono didn't respond. He just lay there. His companion looked wildly about, searching for what had struck his friend. "Hey boss, I don't see anything up here."

Sheem said, "Get in the boat."

"What about Tono?"

"He picked the wrong time to go sleep. Let's go." Sheem's voice rose in a note of panic.

The last ruff turned toward the boat. His toe dangled, searching for purchase, when a loud tonk sounded in the night air, and he too fell onto the wooden planks like a sack of meal.

"Forget this," said Sheem. He dipped his oar in the water and the rowboat surged out into the river. Mustache saw a wiry figure suspended from the bottom of the dock crawl spider quick atop it. In his hand was a rope that he swung around his head and released. It whistled through the air before clonking Sheem's head. Sheem released the oars and sagged forward in his seat. A heavy steel hook attached to a rope fell from the shoulders of Sheem and caught on a strut. The rope went taut, and the figure began to pull the boat back toward the dock.

Mustache cried, "Stop. No. It's him. It's the thing." His voice rose with fear.

The boat reached the dock. Mustache threw his club but the silhouette dodged it as casually as a man ducking through the low door of his own home. Then the figure jumped into the boat and shoved Mustache into the water. He lifted Sheem's heavy legs and dropped them over the side of the boat, shoving the man's big torso next, splashing him into the brackish water. The night attacker grabbed an oar, and pushed the rowboat back out toward the middle of the Amarillo. Then he turned and pulled the sack off of Jalil's head. All the gratitude Jalil felt washed away, when he saw that the leafy head of his rescuer. It was the wendigo. He tried to

216

growl but the cloth in his mouth stopped him. The wendigo smiled. Jalil knew he was ecstatic to capture the boy that had sung on him.

20. Ocean

The wendigo plied the oar with the river currents, his arms working tirelessly, stroke after stroke, and the boat swept out into the river and turned with the easy current toward the ocean.

The wendigo said, "It no easy me getting out from Urba. More men die. You quiet, not so many die."

Jalil interpreted this to mean that Jalil was responsible for more deaths, because he had tried to stop the murderer. He growled again. By now they were far out in the river's delta. Behind them the city lights spread horizontally. To his left the many small windows of the Sub created a polka dot pattern of light. To the right the solitary houses of AltUrba lit up the trees and lawns around them. Atop that rose the Citadel district, where all the many windows of the high houses shone brightly. As he looked, the distance grew, and the ocean spread its waves between him and the city he called home.

The wendigo made his way down the center of the rowboat toward the boy, who tensed as a clawed hand reached toward him, but it was only to untie his hands and hand the boy a paddle. He said, "We keep moving. Fels come after us."

Jalil stared at him. This wendigo thought Jalil would help him. Jalil would always stand up to evil, just like his father. The wendigo had made a mistake by handing him the oar, a weapon. He used both hands to swing the paddle at the leafHead.

The wendigo caught the paddle with one hand. Jalil tried to lean on it, and push the creature out of the boat, but the paddle only quivered as the boy exerted all his force. Jalil couldn't move him.

Seketeme slowly stood, still holding the oar. Suddenly he sprang forward stopping inches from the boy's face. His narrowed eyes boiled red. His lips were peeled back, revealing wolf like teeth. A low growl rumbled in his chest. Jalil dropped the paddle and it clattered to the wooden floor. The wendigo picked up Jalil's paddle and put it in his hand. "Slow, stupid, little, man. Row, or I eat you."

Jalil was impressed. The thing he most respected was physical strength and skill. He had sincerely swung the paddle, careful not to telegraph his intention, and the wendigo had not looked at it, using only one hand to catch it, while Jalil had swung it with the force of his whole body. After Seketeme caught the paddle, Jalil knew he was going to attack, and Jalil was ready to fight back, but the leap of the wendigo had been too quick for any reaction.

The wendigo turned and made his way back to the other end of the boat. The starlight lit the creature's back. Three broken arrow shafts protruded from it, two in the right shoulder, and one in the right lower back. A stream of dark liquid flowed from each hole. Underneath them was a bluish tattoo, a wolf, that covered the width of its back. The wendigo sat down, and picked up the oars and continued to row. He gave no sign of pain, and if Jalil had not seen his back he would not know he was injured.

"How did you escape?"

"I run. Jump wall. They wait in river, shoot more, I jump other wall, more there. One try spear, but no, I kill. I jump in river, they shoot bow, thunderPipe, hit, but I still alive. I swim down, down, far, far. They everywhere, on all banks, but Mishipeshu hear me, send catfish big as me. He pulls me far more to the ocean. Ocean water good for me, three longteeth find me."

It was an impressive escape story. The wendigo might be the enemy, he thought, but he was a warrior worthy of respect. It was not shameful to be killed by such as those. Anyone who had seen them in action would need great courage to face them.

It was his fault, the arrows in the wendigo's back, and for the first time he questioned his decision to sing on Seketeme. Maybe he should row a little. Maybe he owed it to the wendigo. Maybe the wendigo would pass out from blood loss soon, and then he could turn the boat toward land, but until then, he had to respect those teeth. He put the oar in the water, and tried to match the wendigo for strength. While his own strokes moved the boat, he felt the boat surge at each oar-pull from the wendigo.

They turned south in the ocean, staying far out from the coast. The wendigo hoisted the small mast and sail in the boat, and they whipped southward. The windows of the Sub and Agora shacks dwindled off to their right. They were now entirely in the open sea, the shore invisible except for the lights of occasional fishing villages. Waves chopped against the boat, pushing it back and forth in the water.

Jalil was aching in his face, and he had a burning sensation in his neck, and his arms hurt from rowing, but they were still pumping along. He did not want to whine to the wendigo but he wanted a rest. The wendigo began whistling like a bird, except with rhythm and somehow Jalil's arms felt relieved, and he rowed on for a bit longer, keeping time with the birdsong. After another fifteen minutes though, he felt exhausted. He thought his arms might fall off, they were so heavy.

"Small man rest arms."

"I'm okay." Jalil didn't understand how the wendigo was still rowing so powerfully with three arrows buried in his back. He could keep up with a thrice-wounded wendigo. He rowed for a few more strokes, but the end of the burning in his arms was too attractive. He lifted the paddle and placed it in the bed of the boat. The relief was instant.

"Sleep in boat." The wendigo nodded at the floor.

Jalil paused for a second, considering whether he should sleep in the presence of his enemy. He realized that he was as defenseless awake as he would be asleep. In moments he was dreaming. When he woke, the sky was gray with the approaching dawn. He got up and took up an oar.

The wendigo said, "Where Hands and fat small man?"

He said, "They were going to go to Orpan's."

The wendigo nodded. "I forget you yell. Next time, you say first, 'I yell'. No yell without saying, 'I yell now.' Then I eat you. So no yell." The wendigo laughed quietly.

Jalil figured the wendigo was saying that he was willing to let the incident in AltUrba be forgotten as long as it never happened again. If it did happen again, he would eat Jalil. Jalil nodded, feeling queasy about making agreements with a wendigo. Yet he had to

220

admit that he had been saved twice. It was clear that he would be back in Aeternanox right now without this leafHead. Not only that, there was a big reward on his head in Urba, so leaving the city was necessary. The wendigo was probably saving him for the shore, where he would eat him. Jalil knew that he himself wouldn't forgive anyone who sang on him in the way that he had sung on the wendigo.

When the sun was cresting the horizon the wendigo turned the boat toward shore. Jalil rested his paddle on his knees while the wendigo's rowing redoubled, and the large rowboat shot like a shark through the ocean, and ground up onto the sand like a boat. The wendigo grabbed the bow and pulled the boat up among the trees. He pulled the branches of the trees around the boat. Jalil thought about running. He could get away from the wendigo. He had seen his teeth, and they looked ideal for ripping through a human body. Then he remembered how fast the wendigo had escaped from the Fels. Jalil was not fast enough to get away from him.

He sat down, awaiting the ripping attack of the wendigo's claws and teeth. Terror boiled in his stomach. The wendigo, however, had sat on the on the forest floor, and was gazing up at the intersticing branches like he was seeing heaven. "Ah," he said. Then he stood up and walked over to the Sub.

"Go ahead, eat me," Jalil said.

The wendigo laughed. "No eat you. You no yell, I no eat."

"I know you're going to do it, just get it over with."

"Wendigo no kill little person. Wendigo not like human that kill little person. I tell you I forget you yell. So wendigo and Jalil, we friend. Regnate there by Ornata. You tell him about they kill him. Come."

He pulled the boy up by the armpits and pushed him. They began to move through the thick forest. The boy had never seen this many trees in Urba. Thick trunks surrounded them on every side, reaching up into the sky, spreading their branches overhead, no sky peeked through.

It would have been scary except for the hard hand that held his shirt and pulled him forward among the trees. Even though their branches were knit together as tight as a spiderweb the two fugitives moved through barely brushing them. Jalil thought, "This way of going through branches is his magic. If he can bend the trees so that they don't touch them, he can also bend me. Maybe he already is; I'm doing what he wants."

When they had traveled for an hour the only sounds were small things hooting and rasping into the morning. The wendigo stopped by a tall tree with hints of yellow in its leaves.

"This ash tree." The boy looked up at the sprawling bigness of the tree. "It make bow."

The boy sat down on the leaves. In a moment his head was on the floor of the forest, and his eyes were closing. He thought he heard the wendigo whistling like the wind in the leaves, with his back against the trunk of the tree. It was as if the tree moved in response to his whisperings.

When Jalil woke the forest was bright. Sunlight shone through the leaves so they glowed in various shades of yellow and green. A chorus of chirped tunes burst from the branches, and small furry things hopped through the bushes. It felt as full of life as market day, but without people. He looked at the tree trunk. Three arrow shafts stuck out of its bark. The bark pooled around them, as if it had grown around them the way trees will grow around rocks. It looked like the tree had pulled the arrows out of the wendigo, but how the bark could grow that fast was a mystery.

Next to him the wendigo plucked a bow. Jalil got up and looked at it. It was smallish for the wendigo, but formed perfectly, with a thick middle and thinner ends with thick nubs of wood making notches for the string. Jalil knew bows, he practiced whenever he could, but this one was different. Even though it was perfectly shaped, there were no knife marks on it, and it was covered in black bark, as if it had grown that way.

"How did you make this? It's amazing."

"I wendigo. I treeHead, right? Here."

"For me?"

"This my bow." The wendigo reached down and pulled another bow, far bigger, from the ground. He took a strand of braided grasses and tied a loop in it. This loop he slid into the notch on one end of the bow, and then he stretched the length of his bowline to the other end. He pushed the bow into the ground so it bent, enabling him to tie the string to the other notch. The bowline went taut when he released it, and he tested it by plucking it. It twanged soulfully, and a lazy smile spread across Seketeme's face.

He walked over to the trunk and put his hand on it. He stood like that for a long time. Jalil somehow knew that he was not to speak while Seketeme had his hands on the trunk. It was as if Seketeme and the tree were in conversation.

Seketeme said, "My grandfather, Ahilensu Xinkwelepay, have best bow, Alankwelait, means, Star Hunter." Jalil knew that the bow in his hands was already far better than anything he had ever held in the Sub, and he wondered what kind of bow Alankwelait must be to so impress this particular bow maker. Seketeme continued, "He go deep into trees of Mishipeshu place to find it. They say, but he no talk, he wrestle Mishipeshu and live, to get that bow. It Star Hunter because it shoot far far. Very nice bow."

"What is Mishipeshu?"

"God in forest."

"You see him and stuff?"

"One time."

"What does he look like?"

"All animals." Seketeme paused, aware of how strange and unhelpful this answer was. "You no say what he look like, only see."

Jalil knew that Shyheem said he talked with Illumen, but did he really speak? Jalil had never heard him. It was far easier to understand the Bellumites, who said that the god Bellum helped you only if you helped yourself. That way it was almost like Bellum wasn't there, it was about you, not the god. Jalil didn't really worry about the gods, but if you could see Mishipeshu then he was real.

They continued through the woods. The wendigo would jog for a few minutes, and then walk until they came on a little meadow in the middle of the trees. There were long hard grasses growing. Atop them, golden flowers bloomed, dotting the field like trash dotted the market. The wendigo pulled a handful of the flowering grasses.

"Goldenrod. For arrows." As they walked, he sang to the goldenrod. It sounded like the birds, and it sounded like the wind in the trees, and it sounded like the wolves howling in the night. While he sang the goldenrod folded itself tightly around on one end forming hard points, while the other end dropped its blossoms.

"Now feathers."

The wendigo screeched. The sound was ear splitting and horrible, and Jalil jumped and looked at him. A screech answered, from high up in the sky. Diving down came a brown falcon, which landed on the wendigo's shoulders. The wendigo took a feather from its tail, and one from each wing. The bird looked scornfully down its hooked beak at the boy, but waited patiently while the wendigo harvested its plumage. The wendigo called two more birds.

In Urba they always said that wendigo were evil witches. They could control your mind, and mix poisons that would drive you mad. Jalil saw that the actual magic of the wendigo was different than any of this. It did not seem like the magic of the Bellumites, which came from nowhere, and caused everything around it to dim. Instead, the wendigo's magic was just talking, knowing the language of the trees and the animals.

They covered a few more miles, and then the trees ended, and they were looking out on a lot of flat land full of wheat fields and cornfields.

The wendigo said, "Night, we go there. Now, eat, sleep." They tracked back, and found a mossy spot. "Good for a bed." The wendigo lifted a finger to his lips and pointed. Hopping out of a group of ferns was a small rabbit. Its ears twitched toward the boy's loud breathing for a moment, before it turned its quivering nose toward the grass and nibbled. Seketeme reached slowly and smoothly over his shoulder and found an arrow, which he fitted to the string of his bow. His thin bluish lips moved without sound as he aimed. A twang and the rabbit was pierced; the shaft went all the way through.

The wendigo went over to the rabbit, and pulled the arrow out. He held the small animal in his hands and spoke in his language.

He turned to the boy, "Food."

"Should I make a fire?"

The wendigo sighed. "Eat raw."

The boy said, "What?"

224

The wendigo tore the carcass open and with his nails cut the furry skin away from the body. He twisted a haunch off and popped it in his mouth. He bit down, cracking bone, swallowing it all. He smiled, and whispered something. Then he twisted off the other haunch and handed it to the boy. Jalil looked at him and shook his head.

"I can't," he said. The wendigo shrugged and finished off half the rabbit, his sharp teeth cutting and pulling the meat off the larger bones.

"Good!"

The boy did nothing but look mournfully at his half, until Seketeme relented.

"Maybe small fire."

He was not joking when he said small. He found dry wood, and lit it, and had the rabbit over it, in a moment. He turned it around two or three times, before he extinguished the fire, and decided that it was time to eat. The boy ripped into the meat, realizing that he had not eaten since the prison. When they had finished, the boy lay on the grass, but the wendigo got up.

"We move, this bad place. They see fire."

The boy groaned. He only wanted to sleep for a moment. He let his eyes close. The wendigo reached down, and twisted the boy's ear, at first gently, and then more painfully. At first the boy was just annoyed because he couldn't sleep, then he was annoyed because it hurt, then it just hurt, and he jumped up and swung at him. The wendigo turned aside his blow with a forearm, and began walking. The boy chased after him. A moment later they heard the crunch of boots in the foliage behind them.

The wendigo sprang up into a tree, reaching down and grabbing the boy by his arm, and swinging him up. They climbed quietly through a few more branches, and watched a platoon of twenty men marching into the clearing were they had just been. Three of the men were Fels, the others wore the sky blue of the Guard. One of the Fels came forward toward the blackened ring of the fire. He kicked the smoking coals.

"Still hot."

"Look for the trail." The group spread out around the small clearing, and found a few signs of their passage under the tree in which the two travelers hid. The wendigo gripped the boy's arm, his claws cutting into flesh. Jalil did not want to sing out and betray the wendigo this time, but he knew if he did, he would be ripped to pieces long before the soldiers reached them.

The Fel Sergeant barked orders. "You two, go to one of the farms and get us some dogs." Two guards set off jogging.

"You, go to the vice regnate. Tell him we've got traces of what might be them in Quadrasylvania near the border. They need to send all he can to flood the area. We will grind the bones of that wendigo." One of the Fels set off jogging after the Guardsmen.

The wendigo smiled at the shaking boy as if to comfort him. This was not that bad. He ascended the tree as smoothly as a cat until he reached a higher bough, and this he swung himself along, his hands hooked over, his feet dangling in the air. With his head he motioned for the boy to follow. Jalil was tired, aching through his whole body, but he figured he could do it. He got his hands over the bough and started inching along. The ache came back into his arms, worse than when he was rowing, and he looked down, considering where he might fall.

He felt his hand give way and he fell. A strong hand, the wendigo's, caught his foremost arm and swung him through the air, so he landed in a fork of the next tree. The wendigo swung atop the branch and ran to him.

They went from tree to tree, using the branches as walkways. They were getting further from the clearing where the soldiers were walking in circles kicking through the underbrush. The boy found himself shaking with fatigue or terror, he didn't know which. The wendigo muttered into his ear some of his singsong, and Jalil found all the jangly nerves flushed out, his body calm and ready. The wendigo pointed out a route up their trunk and across a broad branch. Jalil found this route easier, with his feet on the tree, and plenty of handholds. The loud soldier talk from down below helped disguise the sound of shaking leaves. Soon they were five trees away from the clearing, and they moved toward the ground. The wendigo whispered into his ear.

"The dogs, and more come soon. We run far now."

The wendigo dropped to the forest floor, and the boy marveled that he landed noiselessly, as natural and soft as a leaf. Then he lifted his hands and the boy dropped into his arms, and was lowered to the forest floor. They bent low and scurried. When they had gone two hundred yards, they stood up and ran, the wendigo loping in a long stride, the boy running more heavily, but keeping up, and they ran until they reached the edge of the wood.

There were farm fields in front of them. To their left, on a road that ran into the wood a large group of soldiers marched. Their redcoats flapped, their leather rustled, as if some stone lizard was moving that way. As the fugitives watched, the soldiers split into two groups, with their eyes on the trees. The one group went toward them, and other went north, along the edge of the wood. The wendigo ran along the edge of the wood parallel to the marching soldiers. Jalil followed. After about two hundred paces the two fugitives reached a small stream that ran through the fields into the wood. The soldiers were near, the sound of their loud talking carrying to them.

"Here," said the wendigo, and began to run away from the woods, up the streambed. The boy followed, almost crawling, slowed because of the stones in the bed of the creek. At any moment the approaching soldiers could spot them and let up a cry, and then they would surely come to a bad end. They climbed up under a small wooden bridge.

"Now," whispered the wendigo, and he jumped behind a small tree where his head leaves blended in, but the boy had no hiding spot. He tried to duck behind the rock next to him, but half of his body was still in view. At the last moment he slipped into the small pool of the stream. He sunk down and gulped a big breath before his head dipped below the surface. Through the water he saw the sky blue uniforms of the Guard. They marched over the bridge looking toward the forest watching for the fugitives. Jalil let bubbles out, one at a time, and then he needed a breath. He tried to think about how cold the water was, but he was back to thinking about breath in a moment. He needed to breath, and the soldiers were still there, trotting across. He couldn't wait. He brought his head above the water, and silently sucked in the air. The soldiers were still looking the other way, searching the forest for the fugitives. He dipped back under the water.

When the last soldier had passed, the boy emerged, gasping for air. The wendigo laughed quietly. "You no boy. You tadpole!"

Jalil smiled. Despite himself, he liked the wendigo. The creature was ready for everything, a better athlete than any man. Not only that, he was kind to Jalil. Jalil knew that he would not be able to betray him again, that somehow he had gotten sucked into something he did not want to be in, and it involved this wendigo, and trying to tell the regnate something about how his own soldiers were trying to kill him. He wondered what his dad would think, but then he thought that his dad had never really known wendigo. His dad fought because he was told to, but if he'd known that the wendigo weren't mind-bending baby-eaters, they were actually great warriors, his dad would have understood that Jalil had to be loyal.

They continued up the creek bed. Around them were farms, big fields of golden wheat and barley. Jalil saw in the distance the men working, cutting the grains with sweeps of their scythes. He didn't see much, because the wendigo kept them in the creek bed, or in small copses of trees.

Once they climbed a small hill to get around a waterfall. Atop the hill they found a long slow moving passage of the creek and a farmer up the bank, watching as his cattle moseyed up to the bank and took long lapping drinks. The wendigo pulled the boy back down behind the cover of the hill and waited. The boy fell asleep, and was annoyed by the hard hand over his mouth that woke him. The wendigo was looking down at him, his leafy head framed by the night sky. He nodded onward. Jalil shuffled up and stumbled along the creek bed. They went a few more hours before they came to another large farm that stood close to the creek. The wendigo sniffed the air. "Dogs."

They climbed out of the creek on the far side of the house, and walked in a semi-circle around the house. The hunger grew as the memory of the rabbit faded. The wendigo plucked spiny leaves that grew by the water as they walked, and chewed them. He offered some to Jalil, which he tried, but the spines were grainy and the

228

taste was bitter and he spit them out. The wendigo insisted Jalil eat them, and finally he did. Though it was stringy and disgusting his hunger disappeared, and the fatigue vanished from his limbs. "Green Youth," explained the wendigo.

The wendigo showed him how to pluck the heads of wheat and grind them around in his hands until the grain and chaff were broken apart. One breath blew away the chaff, and then he could chew on the grain. It wasn't good, but it was food. After a few hours the fatigue returned. Jalil said, "Let me rest, just for a bit."

The wendigo growled, "Rest then die. They look for us. Dogs, soldiers."

Instead of resting they had to run. The boy thought about the kiMarket Day races they had through the Sub, from one end to the other, hundreds of boys, jumping the fruit stands and dodging through the wagons. It was a three-mile race. His legs had bounded over the cobbles and clay with relentless power, his lungs over and over sucking and pushing, and he had outstripped every Sub under fifeen and won. They had thrown him in the air, and then in the river. He was the best distance runner in the Sub his age, but that did nothing for him on the plains, running with a wendigo.

The wendigo hit the earth with his toes and bounced, his jogging fast, but seemingly effortless. When he realized how slow Jalil was, he coached him, encouraging him with his rhythmic babble. Somehow, when he made those forest sounds, more air was in the boy's lungs.

The sky was gray again, and they found a group of trees and rested. They went on like this for days, running through the night, and sleeping and creeping in the day, living off what they could scavenge. The boy was always exhausted, but even tired, he had to admire the leadership of Seketeme, who made sure the boy was fed, and kept pushing him.

On the seventh night in the woods they found the houses were getting much nearer together. In the distance they could see a walled town. The houses were painted blue, yellow, and green, and sat on carefully cut lawns. On the western side of the town, which was the furthest from the fugitives, they saw many tents, and the flag of Regna flying over them.

The wendigo went into the belt of trees that grew to the south of the town, surrounding the stream. It was not deep cover. Cows and chickens wandered through the trees. Humans were close, and the houses could be seen through the branches. They moved from tree to tree until they came to a broad highway that bisected the woods.

The wendigo stopped him and they watched as a girl passed, leading a cow into the town. A group of Fels was stationed in the road. They asked the girl if she needed help, but she ignored them. "What, you too good for a soldier?" She kept walking.

A Fel said, "Two cows going to town."

The wendigo said, "We need to cross road." It was impossible with the Fels guarding it though so they hid among the thickets. As the sun set Jalil watched the soldiers hoping that they would leave when night came, but instead they lit a series of torches, which they spaced out along the road. Then a fresh squad arrived, and the day shift left. It looked like there were Fels posted there all the time. The fugitives couldn't just wait for them to leave. The night squad appeared serious, walking up and down, but after two hours seven of them set up bedrolls and went to sleep. Three sat down to a game of dice.

The wendigo had been snoozing himself, but Jalil was awake watching them. Jalil reflected that he could easily give away Seketeme that they could already have chains on him when the wendigo awoke. He didn't want to do that. He was embarrassed to think he had done it before.

When Seketeme woke and saw the night shift mostly asleep and those awake locked in a game, he nodded. He pulled an arrow from the quiver he had woven from field grass. Jalil copied his easy movements and fixed an arrow to the string. The wendigo missed all the soldiers with his first arrow, which flew by them, and snuffed out the furthest torch. He pushed down Jalil's arrow with his hand, and waited. After a few minutes the most alert of the dice players saw the extinguished torch.

"Torch's out," he announced.

"You saw it," said another.

"I always get them."

"I don't care if they stay lit. You're the one who's always worried about it."

The alert Fel stood up grumpily, and headed off down the line of torches. "Now," said Seketeme. In a moment he was up, running lightly and quickly across the road with Jalil right behind him. The Fels watching their conscientious fellow tromp the opposite direction didn't see the fugitives.

The fugitives hid themselves behind the trunks on the far side of the road, and turned back to the Fels. The one was using a lit torch to relight the extinguished one, and the others were arguing about a throw. The boy and the wendigo moved back into the woods, finding a thicket not far from a tall stonewall. Seketeme said, "Last part worst. Segunda plains open, many soldier, but we get help. Tomorrow I teach you ride wapiti."

Seketeme said the word 'wapiti' with such joy and wonder that Jalil had to know what they were, and he asked Seketeme, but the wendigo only smiled and said that he would see.

21. Ornata

Somewhere in Regna, around the time of our story (so not that long ago) a Fel sentry prompted his horse with a half-hearted dig of his heels. The mount started another circuit of the field that separated the North Ornatan Outpost from Ornata itself. The soldier turned his eyes at the darkness under the low hanging boughs, willing himself to see enemy eyes there. There had been no fighting for the Fel, or any of his one hundred and ninety nine fellows posted there. Some of them, especially the Guardsmen, were happy with so little action. The Fel hated it; he wanted to pull out his lance and run one of the leafHeads through, to get in close and work with the sword. He didn't come out here expecting to ride a horse in circles for months on end.

Thinking these thoughts, he finished a full circuit, and rested his animal under the shadow of the outpost stockades.

"It looks like the leafHeads will be getting frisky tonight."

The Fel looked up to see the source of the voice. Just above him, peering out between the pikes was the bushy-haired head of the wagon driver who had delivered supplies that day. You might recognize him too.

"Great chance of that," said the Fel. "These wendigo are lulus. We haven't seen any action."

"Drink?" The wagondriver enthusiastically extended a winebag toward the Fel, who shook his head. The driver shrugged, as if to say he did not understand refusing a drink but it was just as well, and tilted the liquid into his own gullet, greedily gulping it back. "I think I hear them."

The Fel listened but heard nothing. Why was he listening to the drunken ramblings of a fearful civilian?

"Listen, they're running."

The Fel listened one more time, hearing only the rustling of the long limbs of the trees. He thought he heard something, no, it was

232

just the trees, wait. Was that running? It was running, he could hear bare feet slapping the forest floor, one, two, right left.

"Go grab the rest of the sentries. Charge the leafHeads!"

The drunken driver had put the Fel's idea into words. He blew his horn. In a moment two mounted Fels were galloping toward him, "They're coming, we'll meet them at full gallop."

The green-eyed driver settled himself between the fortifications, like a boy at a show, and remarked, "This should be good."

Shortly after the events in the lake Shyheem found himself bouncing on another wapiti, clutching the shaggy fur about its neck and peering through its huge set of antlers as the fat trees of Magnasylva whizzed by. Riding with him was Askasktuhon, the sachem of Ornata, about fifty longeyes, Kwenemuk the mindscout, and Angen. Angen told him they were going to Ornata, the front line in the fight between the humans and the wendigo.

Angen explained that a lot had happened at the High Seat after he was taken away. The Ornatans had asked for reinforcements. Tenaxen had refused help. It appeared that he'd been listening to the messages of the Arch Bellumite, and believed that the battle was not winnable for the wendigo. Shyheem agreed with this; after all, Illumen was on the side of the humans. Angen told him that Askasktuhon had only agreed to take Shyheem because he was desperate, shocked not to get more fighters from Magnasylva.

Shyheem only half listened as the castOut talked. He was remembering the incident in the lake. He knew he needed to talk with Illumen. He should not have been so afraid, calling out without faith, believing that death was inevitable before the monster of the forest. He was a servant of the Light Bringer gifted with hands of fire, and he had feared the wendigo god, which was nothing more than a monster.

He said, "They told you what happened in the lake?"

Angen said, "They told me that the Mishipeshu came and took you, but then you turned into a ball of blue flame while under water, and Mishipeshu decided he wouldn't eat you. The Ornatan wendigo took it for a sign that you had some use. Me, I figured that Mishipeshu figured out that you were a nasty, sour boy."

"Don't you see? It was Illumen against the god of the wendigo, and Illumen overcame. You keep saying that Illumen wants to help them. Why did he send his fire to fight the Mishipeshu?"

"It's true the wendigo worship Mishipeshu. It also true that Mishipeshu, whatever it is, is not like Illumen. It eats the wendigo sometimes, and they try to keep it happy however they can, believing that somehow that protects them, but it doesn't. It's a monster, not a god. However, people are not only what they worship. It's not an argument against the rightness of their cause."

Shyheem snorted. It was a waste of time trying to tell truths to a castOut. He recited silently to himself the Truths because people of darkness surrounded him. He alone could keep his connection with Illumen open.

Light shines forever. Illumen is light.
Light penetrates all darkness. Illumen is light.

They rode throughout the day, going hard, until the rising and falling of the beast beneath him made his behind ache. They reached a lake that stretched beyond sight. They released the wapiti and got into four big canoes. He was placed in a canoe with Angen and a longeye. All the Ornatans had five-pointed leaves on their head. Some were yellow, and some were red.

They heard a sound like thunder from behind. They looked and saw a string of Magnasylvan longeyes galloping after them, the brown jagged leaves of their hair flying behind them, their heavy spears bouncing with the movement of the great shaggy steeds, the riders light brown eyes peering between the formidable antlers. Leading the troop was Aihum, his strong frame tensed over a mount that was tall even for a wapiti. The Ornatans tensed, reaching for the bows, and handling their spears. Aihum pulled up and his wapiti leaned back its great head and sent up a bugle call, long and sonorous.

Askasktuhon stood in his canoe. "What do you want, longeye Aihum?"

Aihum spoke, "We come offering reinforcements."

"Sachem Tenaxen has changed his mind?"

Aihum shook his head. "No. We come despite him. We will fight for the wendigo, in the battle of today . . . though it will cost us something with our sachem, wendigo are free people. As the saying goes, 'Shall the tooth of Mishipeshu not sink into flesh?'"

Askasktuhon bowed deeply, for the first time since Shyheem had seen him, something like a smile flitted across his face, and said, "Ride quickly, the need grows greater and greater with every moment. We thank you. Let no one say that Magnasylva has no heart, though it has lost its head."

They watched the Magnasylvans ride west along the bank as they rowed into the lake. When they had rowed for a whole night they saw mountains rising from the far side of the lake. They were immense and blue with caps of white. After a long morning, in which the longeyes rowed hard enough to have sweat roll in streams down their spines, they reached the gravelly shore. They dragged the canoes up the beach of jagged black stone, and started climbing. Shyheem talked about how hard the climbing was until Askasktuhon dropped back and started commenting.

"Pray to the Light God to give you strength, little holy man!"

Shyheem said, "Illumen doesn't want me to do this."

"Yet he allows you to still continue. You must either disbelieve in his power or his will. Is he unable to free you from us, or does he not want to?"

Shyheem had no answer to this, and added more vigor to his stomps. This helped him keep up for a few minutes. Then he found himself fifty paces behind again with the longeyes stopping to watch him, wry smiles on their faces. This gave him an idea. Why should he support this mission? If they wanted him to go on they could carry him. He sat down.

After a few minutes Askasktuhon walked back to where he sat. He nodded his head to the slope and muttered. "Come."

He said, "No. I'm not going to help you go kill people. I'm staying right here."

Askasktuhon was silent for a long moment, then he dropped close to the boy, his lips peeled back in a growl, his sharp teeth pressing toward the boy. "I will carry you in my stomach."

Shyheem said, "I would rather feed you than enable your dark cause."

Askasktuhon waved up the mountain. His longeyes took the cue and resumed their even lope up the mountain. He said, "We wendigo have many rules about our secrets, but I have seen your power, and I am hopeful that you will reach understanding, so I will break those rules and share some of those secrets with you." He turned to Angen. "You must go on, for by telling one human, I already invite the wrath of Mishipeshu upon me. You too, Kwenemuk, go ahead. I can speak his language."

Angen and Kwenemuk climbed after the longeyes.

Askasktuhon said, "For human, parents human. But wendigo not like that. My parents trees. A LongBough, that what we call the trees in Ornata. I large seed from the up branches of LongBough."

Shyheem just looked at the Sachem of Ornata. What he was saying was so weird he couldn't respond to it.

"I can show you when we reach the forest. Our babies are the fruits of the trees."

Shyheem said, "You think I'll believe that?"

Askasktuhon said, "Why I lie? I want you to see that humans cut down trees they kill our parents. That why we fight them. These trees just trees to you, but they speak to us like your mother to you. They pass stories from past on, they teach us."

"I never knew my mother."

"That something you wish for other?"

Shyheem said, "I'm supposed to believe that the trees are your mothers! Even if it was true, it would be an abomination."

Askasktuhon stood up. He shook himself. "You like vinegar to talk, Shyheem of SubAgora. Angen tell me that the Light God you worship younger brother who protects who need protection. You think about things I have said, because if you fail to do what your god wants you become his enemy. You are one that showed me the power of your god, blue flame that even Mishipeshu fears."

Shyheem wanted the blue flame turned against Askasktuhon and prayed briefly to check if it would work, but nothing happened. "Come." The wendigo leader launched himself up the mountain, leaping by Angen and Kwenemuk.

"We must travel quickly, LightTalker."

Angen said, "I know."

"I will leave you with mindscout and one longeye. The rest of us must push on. Boy cannot keep the pace."

The sachem leapt up atop the rocks closing the distance between himself and his longeyes, who were already small specks way up the mountain. The two humans, the youngest longeye, and the mindscout climbed more slowly. Back behind them the lake stretched further toward the horizon the higher they climbed, until a gray mist swallowed its far reaches. Shyheem huffed and puffed, and stopped every few minutes.

Kwenemuk said, "Should I tell the story of how the wendigo were made? It is a long climb, and the story will take our minds from hard work."

The longeye grunted her assent, and Angen said that it would be interesting. Shyheem said, "I don't want to hear a story from a baby eater."

She went ahead anyway. "When the Golden Eagle was making the earth, he started with Plant. He said, Plant, go spread your children all throughout the earth. So Plant went and spread his children throughout the earth. Then Golden Eagle said, "This is so green, and the Plant's children keep growing. Soon Plant's children will cover all my earth."

"So he made Plant-Eater, and said, Plant-Eater, go and spread your children throughout the Plants. Plant-Eater's children spread, eating plants, and soon Plant asked Golden Eagle why he gave Plant children, if they were just going to be eaten.

"So Golden Eagle Spirit made Animal-Eater, and told him to spread his children over the earth. So Animal-Eater sent his children out on the earth, and they ate Plant-Eater's children. But soon Plant Eater came and complained to Golden Eagle. Plant and Animal-Eater complained too. Each felt that things were not equal, that there was not enough food for their children, or that their children were eaten too much. He tried to explain that things were equal, but they would not listen.

"Golden Eagle Spirit grew tired of hearing them complain so he made humans to rule Plant, Plant-eater, and Animal-Eater's

237

children, and they wouldn't keep coming to him with their complaints. But soon after he made Human, he saw that Human did not listen at all to Plant, Plant-Eater, or Animal-Eater. He walked around eating Plant, Plant-Eater, and Animal-Eater's children, without even stopping to say thank you.

"Golden Eagle said, 'I will make a creature that can hear Plant, Plant-Eater, and Animal-Eater, and talk to Human.' He made the wendigo. He made the wendigo the children of the Plant, and they were also Plant and Animal Eaters.

"Then for a time the earth was right. But still sometimes Golden Eagle got complaints. Sometimes they came from wendigo. Sometimes from the Human, and sometimes from Plant, Plant-eater, and Animal-eater. So Golden Eagle said, "I'm tired of these complaints. I will now make a spirit that will teach my creation that they are but creatures. They must rejoice in their good, and accept their sorrow, for that is what it is to be a creature.

"And he made the Mishipeshu, the spirit that is sometimes beautiful, and life-bringing, and other times terrible, bearing death. Humans and wendigo learned that they should not always complain to the gods, but sometimes they must run, like ants run from the tread of the moose. That the story of creation."

Shyheem thought that the story was full of darkness. Theom was supposed to know everything, do everything perfectly, but the way the wendigo god Golden Eagle made the world, he kept adding after-thoughts. That meant that their creator was not all knowing, which made no sense. How could he make everything perfectly but still have to make changes?

Angen asked, "What do you think about the wendigo version of creation, kaWick?"

Shyheem shook his head. "You people are twisted. You worship a monster that eats you."

Kwenemuk said, "You worship a strong god, Shyheem, for you survived the attack of Mishipeshu. The only other living person to do that is Ahilensu Xinkwelepay, sachem of Southern Ornata. Still, you must have seen how powerful it was. We do not choose to worship, rather we fear what is fearful, and appease it how we may."

238

"That is all the humans are doing," said Shyheem, "when they fight you, fearing what is fearful."

Kwenemuk shook her head sadly.

The castOut said, "You don't really know the history here. First, a group of supposed farmers showed up and went to work on the Ornatan trees. The wendigo attack, and the farmers all have armor on underneath their clothes. They were Fels. That wasn't the report that reached the Urba, but that was what happened."

Shyheem said, "Even if all that was true, it doesn't change the fact that they are murderers! Jalil's dad was killed by Ornatan wendigo."

"Yes, they have killed soldiers. They are under attack, and they defend themselves. But you have to ask yourself is there a conflict in which Illumen has called a manusignis, where there was a perfect innocent? Isn't it in all of our natures to respond to violence with violence? What do you expect them to do? Allow their families to die? Are you better than them? Does Illumen not care about the oppressed, just because they fight back?"

Shyheem said, "I'm not listening to you. You got castOut for these blasphemies."

Angen roared, "CastOut? I cast them out, the dusty-minded old power seekers. They couldn't hear the voice of Illumen if it shouted in their ears. There shall come a day when North Temple wished that they had heard the voice of this torch, had seen how I burned in the midst of their darkness, a late chance at turning back for those who have smothered his light! Then they will cry out, and they shall not be heard."

Shyheem looked at the reddening face of Angen, and laughed at him. The castOut was paraphrasing the Writ of the Torches, but very wrongly. "More blasphemy," Shyheem said.

Angen ignored this, allowing himself to calm down before he continued, "The worst thing is, he has given you the gift of the manusignis, and you only need try to use it in the path that I have suggested, to determine which of us is right. If you pray for their cause, and you light up, you know where he wants you. And if you don't, you know I'm wrong. You won't even need to argue."

Shyheem stomped on up the mountain. He did not answer because he was too angry. He knew that he couldn't even try to pray for the wendigo. They had tried to feed him to the Mishipeshu. They had killed Jalil's dad and they weren't sorry about any of it. Not that he thought Illumen would help them, but even if he would, there was no way that Shyheem could pray the necessary prayer.

They had climbed high. The lake was masked by a scuddy cloud, and the rocky humps of the mountains rose in front of them. To their left was the beginning of a forest that climbed up the side of the mountain. They stopped for a lunch of sundried venison and some roots.

They began the climb again. Time and time again, Shyheem had to stop and catch his breath. Angen tried carrying him once, but he was human, and was not capable of much more than keeping up with the wendigo. Shyheem was winded, and the muscles in his legs ached. He sat again, wheezing.

The young longeye looked at him with distaste. "Perhaps we leave you for the grolf."

Shyheem said, "That's fine. That would be better than staying with you all."

The longeye walked over and pinched the boy with her claws. The pain started him up, and he scampered up the mountain. The longeye grinned and sprung after him. Whenever Shyheem got winded and slowed down, the longeye caught up to him and pinched him, and it hurt so badly, he sped up. Shyheem saw this torture as further proof of the Bellumite nature of the wendigo.

At dusk, they had reached the ridgeline. The sun had dropped to the far side. There was a small plateau toward which the longeye nodded. Small bedrolls made of woven grasses and furs were tucked under an overhang in the rock, and a neat stack of wood was ready. Kwenemuk explained that the wendigo had such places along their trails, inns of the forest.

"This is an inn?" Shyheem asked sarcastically. He had forgotten the shack where he lived only a few months ago.

Looking up at the stars from the comfort of the bedroll made with the fur of some fluffy forest creature, Shyheem tried to pray

240

the prayers of a manusignis. He could not even produce a faint glow. He prayed the thirteenth Canto, "Do not forget your servant, my god. I am close to death, and my enemies surround me. They say, 'Illumen has forgotten him, and the time of his despair is near. Surprise them. Rescue me from the pit, and crown my hands with your light." His hands were cold, and the mountain murmured. The creeping and hopping things lifted up their strange songs from the bush.

He heard a voice in his head, "Wake up, Fire Boy."

He looked up and saw the round eyes of Kwenemuk looking down at him. The smell of something good reached his nose and he rolled over. The longeye had some small creature roasting over the fire. It smelled a lot like pork, and this encouraged Shyheem to get up. He went over by the fire.

She gave him a piece on a stick, saying only, "Parter."

Shyheem tried it, and discovered that he liked it. He finished that and put out his stick. The longeye pointed out where he should stab. Another muscle of the juicy meat pulled off, and Shyheem scarpered it down.

After they had all eaten they took off again. They went along the ridge at the top of the mountain. To their left down the slope of the mountain, the forest widened. The leaves in the first month of fall looked like a yellow carpet.

The mindscout said, "Ornata." There was pride in her voice, like when Burt described his father's recipes.

They marched along the ridge. The longeye hummed an unpredictable melody as they went. Kwenemuk was quiet, her face was turned to the trees, and Angen was through with talking to him. Shyheem liked this silent traveling much better. The path was undemanding compared with the climb. Sometimes it was up, and sometimes it was down, but more often it was close to level. It was also nice to march with a proper breakfast in his stomach. The forest below was nice looking. Streams flowed down the ravines taking in rivulets before heartily crashing in under the yellow leaved trees. Butterflies fluttered atop the trees, and hawks, below them and above the forest, cut great circles in the sky.

A great roar jolted his eyes forward. There stood a white-gray-haired beast, his dark eyes hidden in the tufts of gray fur. He was facing them, his forelimbs held aloft in a position of power. Out of his head awesome horns curved like a mountain goat's. The longeye reached back taking an arrow and stringing it to her bow, and then she spoke. Her words were a guttural rumbling.

We honor you, Mountain King. We are sorry to trespass through your territory. The ironclawed will kill us if we go by the plain, and we have need of speed. It is difficult for us to move on the great height of this mountain. Our breath is short and our legs ache. We are not built for such places. We are not good food for one such as you, brave one, for we are stringy and fearful.

The grolf rumbled back at the longeye. *Not hungry today. Pass.*

Kwenemuk started moving. Angen followed her. He saw that Kwenemuk trembled. They walked right by the grolf, ducking their heads to show respect. Shyheem watched the monster, which stood on four shaggy limbs, watching them. The wick saw the points of the burnished horns, and he shook as he went to move by it; he smelled the earth and sky that were mixed into its fur. Behind them the longeye followed, keeping her face toward the grolf, and her arrow on the string. She began to breathe again after they had gone about one hundred paces, and at five hundred she put away her arrow and sheathed the bow.

Shyheem said, "What was that?"

Kwenemuk said, *We had to show respect.*

Shyheem said, "What about the arrow?"

She laughed. *It's still a grolf.*

Shyheem said, "What if it attacked us, what would we do then?"

The longeye laughed, "I would kill it!"

Shyheem said, "Why is she laughing?"

Kwenemuk said, *I do not know. It may be joy at the thought of such a conflict. Maybe she thinks it is unlikely that she would overcome.*

"So we could have died up there?"

It was a grolf. Kwenemuk did not elaborate. Grolfs were capable killers and voracious eaters of meat. Once again, this struck him as an outrage. He had been comfortable in North Temple, and now through torture and kidnapping he was forced to climb mountains and dive into lakes with monsters.

They continued along the ridge. The wendigo assured the humans that they would not see another grolf for a long time because they were solitary beasts. Where one was, you would not find another for at least a day's march. Below them the forest changed. In the distance there was an earth colored clearing in the trees. In the middle of this clearing was a stone fortification. The group had stopped and looked at the far away clearing.

Shyheem said, "Are those the homes of the wendigo?"

Kwenemuk turned away from him. The longeye was snarling in her throat. Her jaw was set; her teeth ground against one another. Shyheem looked again, and saw the stumps in the far clearing, the earth gashed by the wheels of wagons, and other great machines so that great swathes of water stagnated there. He knew that this was the work of the Regnan army. Angen had bowed his head, and he spoke in Wendee, comforting them.

The longeye replied. Kwenemuk wasn't translating. Angen murmured back.

Shyheem said, "What is she saying?"

Angen said, "Mainly that she doesn't like us. This is the first outpost of Regna. You can see that they have cut the trees back all around it, and with them they have built these forts. It's called the Northern Outpost."

They climbed down the ridge into the forest. The trees had looked like any other from above, but from below he saw how they got their name. The leaves were a shell above the trees, which spread several limbs far apart to lift themselves toward the sun. The branches reminded him of the beams that held aloft the high ceiling of the temple hall.

They made camp again. Dinner was weeds in a pot, and Shyheem wanted to refuse it, but his stomach insisted. It tasted bitter, but he felt full enough to sleep. He bedded down right after the meal so Angen wouldn't try to talk to him. He stared at the moon and tried again the prayers of the manusignis. It didn't feel right, like he was talking to a rock wall. He couldn't break through to the place where the sky was up close, the blue giant listening to his voice like Shyheem imagined parents listened to their children.

Perhaps Illumen was not giving him prayer, and the flame that came with it because he was not following the god. He was letting these wendigo and this castOut cart him across lakes, through forests, and over mountains, without even resisting. What he should do is run, and tell their secrets to the Fels at the Northern Outpost. As he acted for Illumen, Illumen would send him the flame.

This idea brought him fully awake, and he lifted his head to check the rest of the party. The castOut's breathing was heavy and clear in the mountain air. The wendigo were nowhere to be seen. He sat up slowly looking for them. He stood, leaving the blanket, and started to pick his way down the mountain as quietly as he could.

22. A Clearing in the Thickets

If he could reach the earthy clearing, he would be free. He could tell the Guard about the Magnasylvan reinforcements. He could warn them that the castOut was there in the woods, advising the wendigo. He would let them know how deeply the tree cutting was striking the spirit of the wendigo. Then, the very kidnapping that the wendigo had sought to use against Regna would be used against them.

He found this idea energizing, and picked his careful steps more eagerly. He worried that the longeye would hear him. Maybe she was hidden behind one of the bushes. Illumen must be with him, because he found a well-worn wendigo path. The descent became easier, and after an hour he thought he must be close to the clearing.

The moonlight made its way through the Ornatan trees and he was able to see the path well. He began to jog along now. He knew he was only a short distance from safety. The branches of the wood looked strange. They were curved like arms, and they wound in among one another without touching, like the arms of dancers. This eerie place was the home of these monster-worshippers. His feet sped up another notch. He was now close to a sprint. Perhaps it was his speed on a moonlit forest path. Perhaps it was that the forest itself was aligned with the wendigo. One of those arm like branches reached out to trip him.

He skidded along the forest floor, and into a sort of thicket of thorns that caught in his skin. When he tried to get up, the thorns hooked into him. He stopped and pulled off one stem, and reached for another. The first fell back into place, its hooks latching again as if the bush was willfully holding him. In terror he thrashed forth from it, carrying a dozen thorns with him, but he had no time to stop and pull them.

He continued running, a little slower, and very aware of the branches around him, but still getting closer to freedom. Then he heard running behind him. It was swifter than his own, for though the steps sounded far quieter than his own, they grew in volume with each single pace, and then he heard the mindscout, *Shyheem. Wait. Shyheem, slowly.* He ran harder.

He burst through the last set of branches with a shout. The moon was bright, the fort less than three hundred paces away. He saw three horses were riding toward him. He permitted himself a glance back, and saw Kwenemuk was right behind him. Shyheem was happy she had no bow or spear with her. Otherwise, she would have been able to kill him moments before he reached safety. The thunder of the horses' hooves was like music. This was justice.

The nearest rider rose out of his saddle, holding aloft a great lance. Shyheem waited to see him spike the wendigo into the ground, but when the lance came down it was directed at him. It cut into the flesh of his thigh and pushed him into the ground. He looked down at the shaft in his leg in shock. He couldn't hear the sound of the horses tramping out a circle, preventing the wendigo from flying back into the trees.

Kwenemuk called out, "Shyheem!"

The boy looked back and saw them, the one with his sword drawn, the other two with their lances held aloft. One launched his lance, but the wendigo leapt to the side. She stuck out an arm, reaching for the weapon that quivered in the earth, but a slash of a sword forced her to pull back.

"Shyheem!" The mindscout called despairingly.

One of the riders stood over him, his lance hovering over the boy. Shyheem felt a sense of powerless despair. The soldiers, the Fels were attacking him. From his posture of helplessness he spoke, "Oh, Illumen."

Instantly he was crowned in a blue brighter than the moon, and out of him leapt three distinct jets that fell and seized the three riders as eagle's talons drop upon a fish. The flame burnt brightly and briefly before the mounted Fels slumped and fell from their mounts lumpy like potato sacks. The mindscout stood still, looking in amazement at the boy and the fallen Fels. As an aftershock of the flame, the boy experienced its heat in his veins, returning into his core, and he screamed.

The wendigo recovered her wits and ran to the boy. She looked down at the injury. The lance had passed entirely through the leg and lodged in the earth. The boy was tugging at the weapon, but the wendigo stopped him, pulling his hands away. She stooped and cradled the boy, pulling him up, pulling the lance from the earth. She stumbled toward the forest.

From the fort they heard cries of amazement. "What in Sheol was that?"

"You guys okay?" Nobody answered.

"Looked like an explosive of something. Send out another five."

"I'm not going out there."

Another voice shouted, "Fireworks!"

Kwenemuk got Shyheem under the canopy of the trees. The branches seemed to close behind them like a door. The longeye met them there, taking Shyheem from the mindscout. The shock was gone and Shyheem felt the pain of the wound growing in his thigh. With each step the lance wobbled, and more blood bubbled out, and screams shot along his nerve lines.

Weariness washed through him. It was stronger than it had ever been at North Temple. He had never produced that much flame, except against the Mishipeshu, and that time he just passed out. Now he felt that each of his limbs were like stone except his right leg, which burned like fire.

He was close to passing out, but the seismic events in the clearing kept him conscious. He had prayed as an afterthought, just the name of the god. Then the fire was there. Shyheem could not deny it. Illumen's flame had risen against the Fels of Regna, the soldiers of the regnate. It had skirted, even protected, the wendigo.

He didn't like being wrong. He didn't want to say to himself that he had been, since Angen stole him, unable to hear the truth of Illumen, because of his own pride. But there it was. If he really was an Illumenist, if he really was a manusignis, he had to admit it. He had to follow the light god.

He said to himself, "Shyheem, you are full of pride, and you missed the light. You've been cursing these wendigo with the fury of your god, and they are the ones he wants you to fight for."

They were passing through the forest, under the curving limbs of the LongBoughs. The bushes, which had seemed to reach for Shyheem during his escape, melted before the longeye's swift feet. The boy closed his eyes, and spoke with his god.

The longeye reached the campsite. Angen ran to the boy, seeing the red splashes on his robe. He began to make a sound, a blubbering. Kwenemuk, reaching the site just after, gushed forth a stream of Wendee, which she was too shocked or weary to mind-translate. Angen said to the longeye, "We need a Desiccan healer." The longeye started up, still out of breath, and took off running.

Shyheem murmured, "I was wrong, Angen. You were right. I've been so dark-minded. I don't know if Illumen can forgive me."

The castOut shook his head. "He already has. He sent the flame the second you asked for it. He is a gentle god."

Shyheem knew Angen was right again, and he felt a sense of peace that overwhelmed the exhaustion from the flame and the pain from the lance. Illumen was gentle, and ready to forgive. He didn't just know this because he'd read it in the Writ. He knew it because he was still alive, and the flame of Illumen still burned in him. The god had chosen him to light the flame for the wendigo, even though he'd been acting like an altic Bellumite.

He went to sleep. While he slept, the healer arrived. Small, and gray-skinned, with braided vines on his head, the healer pulled the lance and applied herbs that Shyheem felt burn even in his sleep, before lifting the boy, and dropping him into the cradling limbs of a LongBough. Then Kwenemuk sang to the tree, and over a few hours a hard layer of bark crept around the boy's leg, staunching the wound, pushing the tendons back where they belonged. The castOut watched in wonder. He had heard of woodwarbling but the truth of it was more wonderful than he could have believed.

When Shyheem woke, there were four longeyes there with a stretcher made of branches. They had shifted him to this, and told him to be strong. They were mostly gentle, running smoothly on their toes, but occasionally he bounced, and then the pain announced itself again, and he squirmed, and grunted.

He heard voices around him. They were slow voices, their timbre resonant, and they spoke the same as Kwenemuk, into his head.

This is the boy?

Yes, this is the hope of Ornata. They say that he has the fire of the LightTalker's god. He is a mindscout, speak to him.

Welcome, child. Ornata welcomes you. It was the trees. He could hear them, he knew which trees were speaking to him. This smaller one had a faster voice, *You can save us!* Then he was passing through a small clearing in which a great tall tree stood.

Child. Your mind is open, and now your heart is strong. The trees will tell you that hearing first, and talking second is the first step to wisdom, or truth, as you LightTalkers call it. The voice was deep, matching the great height and graceful sweep of the branches of the tree.

He examined the hard cast of tree bark around his leg. It had grown all the way around, making a cylinder of wood. He was able to move his leg, though the Desiccan Healer told him not to do this for a while. He was traveling to the center of the forest, where Askasktuhon waited, where he would offer the flames of the LightGod in service to the sachem of Ornata.

23. An Offer

The tiny brown bird pounded its wings, propelled itself through the air, out of the city, across the plains of Segundawick. A red-tailed hawk spied it and dove. The bird found refuge in a thicket outside of Segundaton. When the hawk gave up, the bird continued on, determined to deliver its message. It saw the thick walls of Fort Ornata, and buzzed its weary wings one last time before spreading them to glide the last two hundred paces.

A crack, and a fire burst caught it, crackling all through its brown feathers. In a moment they were black, and the bird's fine flight turned into a spinning dive. The bird thumped into the earth. The paper wired to his leg was gray ash that blew listlessly in the soft breeze. A red-robed man shouldered his thunderPipe and walked over to the carcass. He nudged the bird with his foot, noting the wire and burnt paper, satisfying himself that it was completely dead.

"Weak, stupid little bird."

It was early morning, the sky just gray when Hands, Burt, and Vermont awoke to a bang. They looked around and saw that the trapdoor had been slammed open. Two Fels sauntered in, and threw a ragged pair of pants at Hands. After he got them on, they helped him to his feet and prompted him toward the door.

"Just me?" asked Hands.

The Fels grunted assent, while one of them kicked Percy in the stomach, and remarked, "Lulu."

Hands was directed back down the stairs into the vice regnate's war room. The man nodded to the Fels, and they unshackled the boy, whispered a few word in the vice regnate's ear, and walked out. He said, "Well, little Sub, I thought we should talk."

Hands looked around the great room. The table was littered with drawing instruments and small figurines in blue, red, and green. He recognized them as Guardsmen, Fels, and wendigo. Near him, atop a stack of papers, was a small golden letter opener. He was careful to not let his eyes rest on it.

He said, "What do you want to talk about?"

The vice regnate said, "You are no common boy." Hands thought if he reached out quickly, he would have the golden knife in his hands, but it was a long way over the war table, and the man had fast reflexes. "It takes skill to escape Aeternanox, and it takes a different skill for a Sub to get a Citan to do what he wants. You have WickBaron Vermont doing your bidding.

"However skill in itself is not enough. WickBaron Vermont is quick-witted, and good with the sword, but he is still only a servant of others. You are different; you refuse to be ruled. A small fraction of people think that way, and it is the true sign of greatness. Even now, as I have you in prison, you aren't giving up. Right now you wonder, 'Can I get that knife and stab him?'" Hands looked at the man in surprise. "Go ahead. Give it a try."

Hands shrugged his shoulders as if to say, "What's the point," and a moment later he was up, his fingers closing around the handle of the letter opener, leaping across the map strewn table toward the vice regnate. The vice regnate was smiling as the boy swiped the blade toward his windpipe. He caught the Sub's wrist, and with his other hand lifted the boy and slammed him on the table. Hands gasped for air.

"Good try. But I'm not WickBaron Vermont, and you will not catch me napping. I, like you, have many skills, and insist upon my own power. I won the approval of the other Citans and got them to elect me as vice regnate. Soon, I will take the position of regnate."

Hands nodded. Well, he tried to nod. It's not easy to nod when your neck is being pressed into a table. He understood what the vice regnate was talking about. "Seeing your will, I think you should reconsider your mission. The regnate does not care about you. I, however, would be willing to tutor you, to bring you along. I offer you this deal. I teach you, and you help me. At first you will be no help, but with time, you will be able to repay me and even hold a position of power yourself."

Hands stared up into the eyes of the vice regnate, who held his gaze. He believed that the offer was sincere. He imagined it, waiting on this man, learning to use a sword like a Citan, learning to ride like a Citan, helping the vice regnate kill the regnate and assume the regnateship. He would make Burt his servant, Shyheem his lamp, and Jalil his dog. The First Child would not be able to laugh at him. She would have to respect him.

He would be betraying them, though. Burt would say it was wrong, and the regnate was Clarie's father. Would she be able to like him if he helped the vice regnate get rid of her dad? She would never know. The vice regnate had sent her to bed before he arrested them. He owed the Subs nothing. They always made fun of him for stealing and being hungry. Clarie mocked him also. She thought that she was better than him, and the thing he wanted was to show her that not only could he ride like her and beat her with the sword, but that he could dress like her, talk like her, hold authority like her. He was better than her.

The thought of it all lit a red ball of excitement in his belly. He imagined himself at the forefront of the Bellumites and the Fels, the drumbeat of their march letting the world know his power.

The wagon driver popped into his head then with his wry smile. Even the wild cluriKin had fled before him. He had already promised Hands that the Sub was special, and that things would work out. When he said that, Hands had felt a peace. He believed that there was some power that was looking out for him, and with that mindset, he had been at peace even with WickBaron Vermont. But the wagon driver, and his help was nowhere now. He had left Hands at the inn, and how could the wagon driver get into the vice regnate's guarded estate?

"I'm going to stay with my hoodBos. Somehow we're going to get you." Hands hated himself when he said it. He'd just passed up his one chance at greatness, so he could go die in a tower with Vermont, who would be trying to clean his nails, and Burt, who would be crying about his hunger. They weren't real hoodBos.

The vice regnate frowned. "I thought you were smarter than a bauble boy." He flicked his hands, and Fels re-entered the room, grabbed Hands, and propelled him back toward his prison.

Hands didn't know what he was doing. He was complimented by the offer, but somehow he believed that Burt with his fearful advice, Percy with his inept leadership and apologies, and the wagondriver with his strange pronouncements offered true friendship. Clarie with her fake yellow hair.

And sometimes there are choices we make that we cannot explain in their goodness. When we examine Hands' heart, we do not find someone who, before that moment, had fought for anyone but himself. Perhaps, in the course of this adventure, he had met others who fought for him, a wendigo, a grolf, and a wagondriver, and he had come to believe in friendship. Perhaps the younger brother god can shine light from the inside.

When Hands was shackled back in tower, Burt asked, "What did they do to you?"

Hands shrugged. "They asked more questions. You're probably next."

An hour later trumpets blasted, and the encamped Fels moved out. The vice regnate, fully armored, rode at their front. A purple cape flapped from his shoulders, and he rode as one with a white stallion. The steed shivered with energy, stepping lightly in front of the host of warriors. The standard bearer and the bald Bellumite followed close behind him. According to Percy, the Fels who followed after numbered five thousand, with hundreds of thunderPipes among them.

Hands tired of watching the endless stream coming out of the town. He stooped and picked up the Eire stone with his shackled hands, and using a sidewise jump, threw it, hitting Percy in the merdup with it, but Percy was absorbed in counting soldiers and weapons. He did it to Burt, who whined once.

Bored he went to the back of the tower and looked out at the South. There was a high stonewall marking the edge of the steward's castle, and beyond that was a belt of trees. He turned around and placed the stone on the ledge. He thought it glowed for a moment, like Shyheem's baubles. When he looked more closely, he realized it was nothing but the sun reflecting off the rugged rock. He shrugged, staring glumly at the wide farms of Segundawick.

Burt said, "It doesn't look good for the regnate."

Percy said, "I'm the worst wickBaron of all time. I got the First Child involved, and now she's in the vice regnate's hands. If the regnate dies, he will be able to control her completely."

Hands said, "That's the first intelligent thing you said in a while."

24. High Wire

Seketeme woke with the birds. The smell of the trees around him lifted his head. He found a tall tree, an oak, and sprung up, catching the bottom-most limb in his two hands. He pulled himself up and climbed through the branches. When he had reached the topmost branches, which swayed under his weight, he looked out at the surrounding countryside. He saw the numberless redcoats marching out, and his heart dropped. They were bound westward toward Ornata, his home.

He turned to look at the castle. A small movement, a flash of blue light in the topmost room of the high tower caught his eye. He saw somebody at the window in the tower. He trained his eye on the narrow window, until he made out the person. It was a short dark skinned boy. It was . . . He looked again to be sure, but he knew he would never forget the face of the boy that had freed him from his chains and the darkness of Aeternanox. It was Hands. He could see that the boy's arms were shackled behind his back. He descended the tree and went back to where Jalil was sleeping.

While he considered what to do, he moved through the wood, pulling up small grasses that he knew to be edible. Some he stuffed in his mouth, and slowly chewed, and others he collected and brought back to the sleeping boy.

They would free Hands. That child had given him these last seven days. They had been days of running, but he was once again under the sun and the moon and the branches of trees. They were not LongBoughs, but they still heard his voice, raised their old branches to salute him as he walked through them. He felt like a sachem's grandson again.

His mind turned to possibilities, ways that he might try and get in the walled house. He did not like their chances of storming it. He guessed that three companies were stationed there, around one hundred and twenty soldiers. Seketeme knew that in a wood he was a match for ten soldiers, but in the open or in a castle he didn't think he could take on more than three. Jalil was good for about one. The odds weren't even close. He remembered how Hands had picked the famous locks of Aeternanox, and wondered if that would work again. He had seen the way the boy's arms were drawn behind him. He guessed that whoever imprisoned him now had full knowledge of the boy's skills, and that was why he was shackled.

He sent out a whistle that the human ear could not hear. Jalil woke up, "Seketeme?"

The wendigo spoke quietly. "There is your breakfast."

Jalil tried to eat the handful of greens. By now he knew that a handful of green stuff from Seketeme would make him feel strong and hopeful, no matter how bitter it tasted. He stuffed them in his mouth. He knew to chew quickly, and swallow, before the harsh flavor made him gag.

The wendigo said, "Hands in tower prison." He pointed.

Jalil said, "How do you know?"

"I see him."

"You can see that far?"

"Yes."

Jalil knew that they were going to try and break out Hands. He didn't look forward to seeing Hands. Burt he would like to see. Burt would forget about the other night, the thing he had done. Hands, though, would revisit the betrayal. Jalil had grown first to admire, and to trust, and even to like Seketeme, and he didn't want to be reminded, over and over again, of how he had treated the wendigo. Worse, he knew he would have to tell the pickpocket that he had been wrong.

Jalil said, "Okay. What do we do?"

The wendigo explained his plan. Jalil thought it was clever, and it had a chance of being successful. It was a risk, of course, and if they failed, they could end up imprisoned or dead, but Jalil knew that Seketeme had no problem risking that, since Hands had saved him. He thought bitterly how different that was from himself, who had betrayed the person who freed him, only to be saved a second time.

First they needed some supplies. They went southwards until they found a big fenced-in farm. The boy went around to the front door and asked if he could have some work. The big woman who answered the door was wearing an apron. She looked at him suspiciously.

She said, "What are you doing around here?"

"I wanted to see the country. Get away from the city."

She said, "Well, that wasn't such a good idea. You don't belong here."

Jalil said, "What do you mean?"

She said, "I can see you're a Bugiri man. We don't like your kind in these parts. Stay in the SubAgora where you belong."

Jalil said, "I'm just looking for a little work. You don't like that, I guess I'll move on."

She said, "We'll see what the dogs have to say about that." She yelled, "Homer, Dasher, Argot, get' em."

Three baying furies of fang rushed past the woman. They were each about the size of the boy. Jalil vaulted the porch railing. They rushed through the gate after him. His more direct route over the railing had given him a few yards lead, and he was running full out, but the dogs were right behind him and closing. They had four legs to his two. It was a long distance, some three hundred yards to the woods. He felt the saliva of the foremost, a big black Humbershire sheepdog on his heels. The beast would have bit him, if it had not tripped on a rock, and the other stumbled over the dog's sprawling body. They were back up in a moment, but he had a couple paces lead again, and the woods were closer.

Meanwhile the wendigo had snuck around back into the tool shed. A gray-muzzled dog was sitting in the sun in the middle of the yard. It discovered the wendigo and let out a brief bark, but a few syllables from Seketeme put the dog at ease. It lay down and watched as the wendigo slipped into the tool shed, and found three strong ropes coiled around a nail. He found a bit of wire as well. The wendigo peaked out. The woman was feeding the chickens, holding a club in her hand. He eased his body out of the shack, while her back was turned, and slipped around it, his body merging

257

with the shadows of the trees and fences, until he reached the wood. He ran toward the sound of baying.

Jalil had not made the wood, but had leapt into a short tree some forty paces from its edge. The sheepdog had got his pant leg as he leapt. He shook his leg until the dog released its hold and dropped off. The branches he clung to might break at any moment, as the thin trunk shook with his weight. The dogs circled and leapt at his feet, which he pulled out of the way. This was how Seketeme found him.

The wendigo growled at the dogs. The dogs turned to him, instantly silent. His teeth were bared, and he moved toward them. The sheepdog bared its teeth growling back. They circled each other for a minute, before the wendigo leapt, dodging the dog's snapping teeth and catching him by the neck. They rolled together, with the wendigo landing on top, his hands pressing into the throat of the dog. In a moment the dog went limp, his muscles untensed, his tail wagging.

Seketeme growled, "I fight wolves in Ornata. You Segunda dog very weak."

The wendigo stood up. He looked at the other two dogs, who wagged their tails as well. He barked once, and all three of them ran off.

Jalil said, "You're not going to shoot them?"

"It no they fault. Master has hate, dog has hate."

"Well, shoot the master then."

The wendigo smiled, but did not unshoulder his bow. He led the boy back into the far side of the little wood. A small herd of wapiti loped up to him, and nudged him with their noses. He felt along the tallest's coat, and found that he was indeed a strong animal that would carry him as fast as most horses. He whispered to them for a moment.

———————

Percy suggested that they start yelling out the window. They could tell Clarie that the vice regnate was the bad guy who was plotting against her father, and that she needed to get away.

Burt said, "It's not worth getting beaten over."

258

Percy said, "Look, I'll tell them I shouted."

Burt nodded, "That's going to make a big difference, because they are really trying to be fair to us, aren't they? They'll say, okay, you and you only deserve a beating."

Hands said, "Maybe we should tell Clarie. I don't think she should have to marry that guy."

Burt said, "You're just in love with her."

"I hate her altic Citan face with her dyed hair," Hands protested.

"It's not like you'd have a chance with an alta anyway."

"I just said that I hate her."

"But you want to get a beating so we can save her," Burt teased.

"Fine." Hands agreed. "We won't yell. Sitting here is so much more fun than being beaten."

Burt said, "Look, can't we just do it tomorrow, guys? My body hurts from these stairs and all those times these Fels already hit me. Just give me a break for a minute." Percy made eye contact with Hands, and they both were quiet. They heard the desperation in his voice, and decided to let it drop.

The window was suddenly full of feathers, great golden wings that slapped the air, and then they saw a huge bird standing on the sill. It pulled its wings in for a moment to sidle through the narrow opening before unfurling them and fluttering to the middle of the cell. It turned its commanding eye on each of the inmates in succession.

Percy said, "A golden eagle."

Burt said, "It's got something."

In its talons it gripped the end of a rope that stretched back out the window, and a piece of bark.

Percy said, "Someone is trying to help us."

Hands said, "Yeah, now we got a rope, so we can hang ourselves."

Percy was at the window, looking down into the dusk. He saw the rope stretch down into the woods beyond the stonewall. He said, "The rope goes into the forest back there. If we can get out of these shackles, we can use it to escape. Some houses in the Citadel have these slide-lines. You take a rope to a high point, and put a chain over it, holding both sides, and slide down. It's fun."

The golden eagle lifted a talon and pushed the bark toward Hands. Inked into the bark was a jagged S, out of which curled a downward pointing arrow. It was the symbol that Subs scrawled on the rocks whenever making illegal forays into AltUrba to challenge both the Fels and the AltUrban boys.

Burt said, "Is it Jalil?"

Hands said, "He went back. He doesn't care about us, remember?"

Burt said, "Whoever it is they're from the Sub, so I say they're friends."

Dug into the piece of bark was a little circle of wire. "See, it's someone that knows us. They know you can pick locks."

"Hold on. I can't pick a lock with my hands behind my back."

Burt said, "Hands. You can pick the locks off a grolf, you can do this."

Hands shrugged and moved crabwise so that his hand landed on the piece of wire. He twisted it straight, and tried to insert it into the lock. It took a couple tries just to find the keyhole.

Burt stood up. "You can do it, Hands."

"Shut up."

Hands was good at picking locks, but he had never picked a lock without being able to see it nor had he ever picked a lock with his hands locked behind him. At first he didn't think he could do it. The wire tinkled around in there, he couldn't feel the tumblers. No, this was the opportunity to get out and be able to see the vice regnate again and tell him how pretty his red hair was.

He tried harder, picturing the lock behind him, as he felt the wire press against the insides of the lock. He pulled the wire back and made a bend in it. He pushed it back in again, feeling the curves of the pins. Again he pulled it out, and bent the turns into the wire. He stuck it in, and tried to turn it. He felt the lock almost engage, but it slipped. "Merd," he cursed. He pulled it out. He adjusted one bend, and stuck it back. This time he felt the mechanism engage, and listened as he twisted gently. Click. The shackles fell to the floor.

260

"Yeah! Hands!" Burt was ecstatic.

Hands said, "Shhh!" Burt shut his mouth, looking chagrined. After the challenge of picking the lock behind his back, the other two were easy. In two minutes, Hands had freed the arms of Burt and Percy. The three of them shook their arms, trying to get circulation back in their arms.

Percy took the rope from the eagle, which hopped to a window and dropped out of it before spreading his wings and soaring away. Vermont tied the rope to a rafter and hung from it.

Just then there was a loud grating as the bolts to the trapdoor slid back. Hands threw his arms behind his back and sat down. Percy and Burt followed his lead. In a moment the door swung open, and an unhappy looking Fel pushed his head up. Right above his head, the rope was tied to the rafter, and to his side, it went out the window. Each of the three prisoners trained their gazes on him, hoping to hold eye contact. He dropped a plate of hard bread where the eagle had just stood. He looked at the prisoners, and said, "If you weren't here, I'd be going to war, but now I get to watch some stupid Subs."

Hands said, "I'm not stupid."

The Fel stopped, shook his head, and stomped up the last few stairs into the room, and went over to the boy. He slapped him. "Don't talk back," he said. The slap sort of knocked Hands around, and the soldier saw Hands' eyes go wide. Hands was terrified that the soldier would see that he was out of his shackles. "You scared of a slap? I'll slap you again." He reached out and grabbed the boy's arm, meaning to pull him up, but the arm, not the boy came up. He saw the shackleless wrist and exclaimed. Percy sprung up and drove his fist into the Fel's jaw, and the Fel dropped. Burt grabbed the shackles, and clipped them around the soldier's wrists. They had to rip a portion of Hands' pants to stick in his mouth.

The three prisoners breathed a sigh of relief.

Percy explained how one took something, in this case the chain from their shackles, put it over the rope, grasped both ends, and dropped. They would zoom down the rope, over the wall, to freedom.

Burt said, "I don't know. What if I let go?"

Hands said, "Don't let go."

Burt stood out the window. It was a long way down. It was far enough that he wasn't going to bounce if he fell. Percy, thinking they could use some more clothes, borrowed the pants of the Fel, and tossed his undershirt to Burt.

Burt was still staring down. He said, "I don't know if I can do this."

Percy said, "Hands, you go first. Then he'll see how easy it is."

Hands got up in the window and flipped the chain over the rope. He looked down in the yard, dropping his weight onto the line while keeping his feet on the ledge. It was mid-morning, and no soldiers were visible. He bounced and jumped. He glided down the line, zooming over the garden. He slowed as he neared the wall, and had to lift his legs to clear it. He slid down through the tree branches, slowed and stopped, hanging five feet above the ground.

"Let go," someone said. He dropped to the ground, spilling onto his bottom. Above him, smiling, were Jalil and Seketeme.

"You're alive," he said. He found himself hugging the wendigo. "How? How did you get away?"

The wendigo smiled, his hand on Hands' shoulder. "You save me, I save you."

"Why're you with him?" Hands turned toward Jalil.

Jalil kind of ducked. "Hands, I'm sorry. I was wrong. Seketeme saved me again. They caught me, when I got back to Black Way. I thought he was going to eat me, but he brought me all the way here, and I know I was wrong."

Hands looked at him, not sure what to say. He had been glad when Jalil went back to the SubAgora. He had thought he would be back in Aeternanox, a fitting punishment for betraying Seketeme. Seeing him here, repentant was a lot to take in. Hands told him, "What you did was lulu."

Jalil nodded, "I know. You did so good, and then I messed it up." Hands didn't know how to process all of this. Jalil and he usually argued, and everyone said that Hands was a merdFace. Jalil saying he was wrong and Hands was right was like opposite world.

25. Wapiti Run

Maids surrounded Clarie. Two were working on her nails, another was shampooing her head, and another was offering her a plate of fruits from Bugiri. Vice Regnate Nickson had told her she had to get back to Citan standards for altaship. She looked out the window, longingly.

The road had been fun. She always thought she was better made to be a soldier than a First Child alta. She loved sword fighting, and she loved seeing the world. She knew that the world offered fights, and all sorts of adventures. Following Vermont, they had met the Subs, and fought the wild cluriKin, and it was awesome. Now she was back where she started, getting primped, not allowed to go on adventures. The vice regnate had told her she was staying there and the Subs and Vermont were leaving with him.

The boy Hands was fun. He didn't care that she was a Citan. He insulted her and fought her. She admired him when he stuck up for himself and stole the wickBaron's drink. When he sulked and sat staring straight ahead, that was boring. When the vice regnate had made a big deal about her she was annoyed. She worried that the Sub would find out that she was the First Child, and he wouldn't make fun of her or fight her anyway.

Her thoughts were interrupted when she looked out the window and saw Hands zooming through the air, shirtless! She saw the taut rope after he had passed. She thought they'd gone with the vice regnate to Fort Ornata, but actually they were zipping off high towers without her. She ordered the waiting women to leave at once; she wanted the room to herself.

"I need my beauty rest," she declared. They hurried out, exchanging worried looks. They did not want to have to tell the vice regnate that they had displeased the First Child.

When the door closed she raked her wet fingernails across the bedspread, streaking it with ten red stains and started toward the window. She examined the wall. She was two stories up, but there was plenty of ivy.

"Forget this merd," she said, and popped a leg shrouded in frills out the window.

Back in the tower Percy was trying to convince Burt to jump. They had just watched Hands glide over the wall.

"Look," he said, "Hands made it fine."

"Hands is lighter than me." Percy couldn't argue with that.

Percy said, "I'm heavier than you." This may or may not have been true.

"You haven't gone yet."

Percy looked down at the chunky Sub, who had moved away from the window and was sitting on the floor with his arms crossed. The wickBaron stood up straight and made his voice authoritative. "I order you to go."

Burt said, "I thought you agreed to stop acting like you're in charge of everyone."

Exasperated, Percy shouted, "You want to die up here?"

"I don't care what happens. I'm not going on that thing."

Percy went over and grabbed Burt, trying to pull him up. He got him about halfway across the room before the boy struggled and slipped out of his hands. He retreated to far side of the cell. The sound of the guards' steps climbing reached them. Percy shrugged, and got into the window opening himself.

"I'm getting out of here. Maybe after you see me you will get some guts."

Burt watched as the wickBaron jumped and disappeared. He heard the steps of the guard get louder as they got closer to the trapdoor. He shuffled over to the window. He got himself into the opening and slipped his shackles over the rope, but when he looked down he froze. He clutched the chain and whispered to himself, "No, no, no."

Down in the forest, Percy found himself facing a wendigo and a muscular Sub. He knew by the enthusiastic way that Hands

264

looked at him that this was the wendigo that escaped from Aeternanox.

Hands said, "Seketeme, this is Percy Vermont. He thinks he's in charge of everything, so he might try to arrest you, but he's with us."

Percy said, "Thanks for freeing us. I owe you a lot."

Seketeme said, "You no yell us to Fels?"

Percy looked confused.

Jalil explained, "You're not going to betray us?"

Percy said, "Oh no, just tell me what to do."

Hands said, "Where's Burt?"

Percy told them how he'd struggled to motivate the boy, and finally just jumped, hoping that watching someone bigger than him ride the line would convince him. Jalil and Hands knew that courage was never Burt's strong point. They both worried that they might never see Porkchop again.

Meanwhile, Burt stood petrified in the narrow window, listening to the climbing steps of the guard. He heard the lock unlatch, and watched as the trapdoor banged open. The guard poked his head up, looked around and saw the shackled and gagged Fel who nodded vigorously toward the window. He looked where the Fel was nodding and saw the chubby kid in the window. He jumped up. If he had better hands he would have grabbed Burt, but instead, he managed to bump him. Burt tottered out down the line, as stiff as a stone statue, gripping the shackle line tightly, before he picked up some speed, and started to zip down. He closed his eyes, whispering, "Please, Illumen, I don't want to die." With his eyes closed he didn't see the stonewall coming up and slammed into it with his knees, which hurt enough for him to release his hold on the line, so he toppled over the wall and fell into a bush. He started screaming. Jalil covered his mouth. "Burt, it's me!"

Burt looked up and said, "I want to die."

Jalil said, "I'm sorry about what I did."

Burt said, "My knees!"

Hands said, "You're fine."

A shout went out from the tower. "The prisoners have escaped!"

265

Percy said, "The First Child. We need to save her."

Jalil said, "What?"

Percy said, "The First Child of Regna is in there and he's going to make her marry him, if we don't save her."

Hands said, "We have to get the First Child."

Everyone else just stared at them.

Finally Jalil said, "That place is full of soldiers."

Percy started saying all sorts of things about duty, honor, an oath and all for Regna. Hands chirped, "Clarie," every few seconds.

They heard a call in the castle, "They're in the woods to the South. Move out."

Seketeme whistled at the woods and the wapiti emerged. "No time."

Percy shook his head. "I can't go. I have to save her."

Seketeme said, "You want go back, go. We escape."

At that moment someone said, "Hey, sillies." They all turned and saw the Clarie's blonde head atop the wall. "How come nobody told me about the slide-line. I thought you guys were going with the troops."

"Hurry up, get over that wall," said Hands, beckoning vigorously.

"Come on, come on," they all said.

The First Child climbed over the wall and jumped to the ground, landing lightly on two feet. "What's going on? How come Burt's in a nighty and Percy and Hands have no shirts? Is that a real wendigo?"

"Oh, Theom, thank you, thank you." Percy was kneeling on the ground.

"THE FIRST CHILD ESCAPED!" They heard someone roar from the other side of the wall.

Seketeme said, "NO TALK. Listen." He whistled softly, and they watched as giant deer like creatures moved out from among the thickets. How these creatures, with antlers as wide as a man could reach moved through the forest was a mystery. One of them moved toward Seketeme, and he gently scratched its head. "This wapiti, king of forest," he said. "He wild but he respect me, so he

266

let you ride. Hold his neck fur, if you gentle, you pull one way he go, but maybe not. Remember, not horse. Of forest."

They mounted the wapiti and took off through the woods going west toward Ornata. In a moment they had passed out of the wood, and were in the plains. They headed south, keeping the small wood between them and the estate of Nickson. Hands saw that Seketeme's head leaves had changed. In Aeternanox they had been shriveled and brownish gray, but now they were reddish, with a tint of green. He also saw that the wendigo looked stronger, more complete.

Burt said, "I think I broke my knees." It was true that under the dirty white nighty, Burt's fat knees were a dark purple brown. He could use his legs, though, and Hands was unsympathetic.

"Stop crying," he said.

It was actually not the time for crying. A horn sounded, and someone cried, "South!"

Seketeme made whistled drily, and herd of wapiti turned west. Now that their position was known, it made sense to make a beeline for Ornata.

They looked back and saw horses pouring out of the gate of the estate, maybe one hundred Fels. They had maybe a half-mile lead on their pursuers, who could see them clearly across the flat fields of grass. Seketeme called out, a strange bellowing from his mouth, and the wapiti quickened their pace to a run. Behind them the horses ran in pursuit. After a few minutes Seketeme looked back and saw that the horses were walking, and he bellowed again. The wapiti slowed in response.

Percy complained, "Let's keep running."

The wendigo shook his head. "Run long, tired, stop. Then men catch us."

Hands felt the heavy breathing of his mount and realized that the wapiti, like the horses, could only run for a short distance. Then they needed to walk and catch their breath. The distance between the groups stayed the same with Seketeme urging the wapiti to run when the horses galloped, and bringing them to a walk when the horses walked.

Clarie pulled her mount up next to Hands and Burt. "What's going on? Why are we running from the Fels?

Hands told her about the vice regnate. She said, "I never trusted him. He acted like he was the only thing on the earth, even when he was following my fathers orders."

Hands laughed, "Sounds like you two would be a perfect match."

She reached over and punched Hands in the shoulder, but she was smiling. Hands rubbed his shoulder and tried to sidle his wapiti toward her.

Percy said, "No hitting the First Child."

Hands said, "What are you going to do about it?"

Seketeme with a growl, "No play. Long journey tonight. Much danger."

Clarie waited until Seketeme was further away and asked Hands, "Who are the other two?"

Hands told her about Seketeme and Jalil. She said, "The Sub has big muscles."

Hands said, "Yeah, but he's lulu. I beat him up all the time."

Burt snorted, but said nothing. His shins hurt. He had got a bunch of scratches from the bush he landed in. His head still ached from being banged against the tower wall. He doubted he could walk after slamming his knees into the stonewall. This life on the road was terrible. All he wanted was a bowl of stew.

He called, "How far, Seketeme?"

Seketeme said, "Far, maybe two days."

Burt shook his head. They were going to be captured, and he was going to be beaten again, and then he would die. This brought him close to weeping.

Jalil pulled up next to him. "How you doing, PorkChop?"

Burt said, "I don't want to talk about it."

Jalil said, "It's not that bad. We slept on the ground for eight days." He told Burt about how Abierto and Shawnee had been so concerned about Burt, and how Abierto had tried to save Jalil from getting caught by the bounty hunters.

268

Burt knew that Jalil was trying to encourage him, but thinking about his dad and sister and the warm inn, with its good food, just made him feel worse. He would never see them again.

Soon it was dark, the stars distant pricks of light. They had a few hours of dark before the moon rose. The wendigo led them as they intermittently trotted and galloped in single file. They could feel the wild energy of the forest creatures, their heads erect, their feet picking precise places.

"Let's lose them," suggested Percy in a hiss. "Turn. They'll never know."

Seketeme shook his head. He pointed back with a wag of his head and said, "Men wide line. We turn, we lose lead."

The dark had this disadvantage to Burt. He could not know how far the enemy was behind. They might be only ten meters away. He did not like not knowing, and when he tried to talk to Jalil, the wendigo silenced him. At some point, the wendigo dropped off his wapiti, and melted into the plain. His mount loped on, as did the rest, the only sound the faint clop of the horses behind them, an occasional hiss as the men communicated. The wapiti walked silently.

"Bernie? Oh merd!" The men erupted in shouting. Some pledged loudly to get revenge.

A minute later the wendigo emerged from the darkness, sprinting. He leapt onto his wapiti. Burt imagined that the wendigo, whom Burt admired but found a little intimidating, had leapt from the shadows, and with his bare teeth, killed a Fel.

They kept on. After six hours, Burt almost lost his handful of fur more than once. Jalil, who was riding for the first time, had a hard time with the bumping. He found the movement of the beast under him required the use of muscles in his back and behind that he didn't know he had. He whispered a request that he walk, but the wendigo said he couldn't.

It was then that the moon made an appearance on the eastern horizon. It was only a sliver, but in a few short minutes half of it had crested the horizon, and the plains turned from black to gray. Looking back, they could see the redshirts only a quarter mile behind. They had spread themselves out wide like a net.

269

They heard them shout. "Wait, Subs, we have a question."

The wendigo bellowed again; the wapiti ran. Behind them the thunder of horses' hooves followed. The gallop lasted a half-mile before the winded horses slowed to a walk. The wapiti returned to a walk as well. They glanced back and tried to figure if the distance had shrunk or grown between them. Burt was sure it had shrunk.

They didn't stay at the walk for long. A bang cracked the air. A Bellumite was reloading a thunderPipe, and this he also heaved into the night sky.

The wendigo called out and the wapiti again ran. They couldn't get out of range though. The second explosion landed right in the middle of them and Hands and Burt would have been fried if not for the dexterous feet of the wapiti, who sprang aside just before the ball of flame swooshed in and exploded against the plain.

Calls reached them through the night. "These are some tricky Subs."

"All Subs are tricky."

"That's why we lock them up."

Laughter went up and down the line. The wapiti had slowed again. They were not beasts of burden, and they were unaccustomed to the weight of a man. All the wild strength of their limbs was taxed by their burdens, and though their hearts yearned to the haunting yodels of the wendigo, their muscles could not keep pace forever. The horses were gaining.

In front of the group, Seketeme dismounted, and jogged alongside his wapiti. Jalil did the same, for he was a runner. Burt didn't even try and Hands only kept up for a bit before he had to get back up. Clarie ran for a little longer, but soon she was out of breath too. Percy jogged by his shaggy steed for longer, but when the redcoats realized what was happening they shouted and started to gallop again, and the three runners had to remount their wapiti and run again. The beasts of Hands, Burton, and the First Child lagged behind because they had had no break.

The wendigo moved Burt onto his wapiti, and dropped down in the grass of the plain, sending the unmounted wapiti along with the group. He pulled an arrow from his quiver, and notched it. He released. He sprung up and sprinted back toward them. Behind they

270

heard a cry, and Jalil said he'd seen one of the Fels fall from his horse.

Burt didn't think he could stand the ache on the inside of his thighs any longer, and he found fatigue working through him. His eyes seemed to sag, and he thought about falling off the wapiti, and lying down, waiting for the Fels to kill him. As long as he was resting, this would be fine.

A half hour later, and the sky turned gray. The sun rose behind them, and they were still closely pursued by the Fels. The distance was shrinking, it was only two hundred paces. The escapees were very tired, when Seketeme stopped by a low boulder. He said, "We must stop and fight. Jalil, you Citan, stop here with me. Hands, Burt, girl, go on. We come later."

Hands looked at Seketeme. He watched as Jalil dropped from his mount ready to fight by Seketeme's side.

He said, "I'll stay with you too. I'm ready for these redcoats."

Seketeme shook his head, "You have no bow, no training. Go." He added a snort that was directed to Hands' wapiti, which turned and galloped on.

Hands looked back at Jalil, who had a bow, a miniature version of the one Seketeme carried. Seketeme must have taught him how to use it as they traveled through the country. Just like always, Jalil was showing off, making everyone like him and forget about Hands. The First Child saw his scowl. She said, "Can you ride with me?"

He turned and looked at her. Her cheeks were flushed with the effort of riding, and the excitement of the trip. She was smiling at him, and he found the edge of his anger dulled.

Burt looked at them and saw her smiling. His tiredness was so great, it reached him from far away. He had thought only SubAgorans would be able to tolerate the pickpocket. Actually, they didn't. He himself had been surprised that Hands was a friend. None of that would matter if they fell off their wapiti now. He turned his eyes to the end of their ride, a red forest on the horizon, and flexed one hand, then the other before gripping the shaggy neck fur again.

271

Percy dropped down with Seketeme and Jalil. "I've got no weapon," the wickBaron said.

Jalil said, "And no shirt."

Vermont said, "What do I do?"

Seketeme said, "First one come, I kill. Then you have weapons."

Jalil added, "And some clothes."

Percy said, "Do they give classes on being a smart mouth in the Sub?"

The redcoats were riding toward them, keeping their wide formation. Soon they could hear them.

"Where is the wendigo?"

"Running with it again."

"We're going to have to make a last push. We're only four miles from Ornata. If they get away, he'll kill you."

"He'll kill all of us."

Seketeme stood up and released an arrow, which struck the neck of the nearest redcoat. He went down. Jalil stood and released an arrow at the next one, but missed the man and hit his horse. The horse reared, throwing the rider, and then took off, causing the other horses to skitter step as he thundered by. Vermont ran out and took the spear from the fallen Fel, and waited for the nearest to charge. The Fels still didn't realize they had been ambushed from behind the boulder. Their superior numbers made them believe that retreat was the only thought in their enemies. They were the soldiers. It was hard to understand why two of their number, now three, for Seketeme's bow had twanged again, had fallen from their horses.

When a quick-witted sergeant realized what was happening he charged toward the boulder, his sword ready to slash down. As he reached the boulder Vermont rolled out and planted the spear's butt in the earth, training its point at the stomach of the charging sergeant. The Fel was skewered.

The Fels were shocked. Their company was not made of shock troops, the lovers of battle and bloodshed. They were custodians, men who liked the job of soldiering because it meant they got to eat well, and tell other people what do. They had volunteered to remain

272

at the vice regnate's castle, where it was safe. What they didn't like was the possibility of death, and when they realized a number of their colleagues had just died, their first instinct was to gallop out of arrows' range, which they did.

They bunched up, and talked. They figured out who had fallen. They said, "That's only six down. We've still got way more than them."

The Bellumite, who had stopped to prepare his thunderPipe, caught up with them and said, "Turn and charge that rock. If I see one of you lag, I will kill you myself."

They turned and charged. The Bellumite threw a metal-cased bomb toward the rock, and hit its front with his first blast. It pushed the whole stone back, cracking it down the center.

The three took off running for the wapiti, and the Fels let up a roar and spurred their mounts on. Their horses galloped, closing the distance. The archers among them released arrows, and the Bellumite continued to fire his thunderPipe, his confidence growing with every explosion.

Burt, Hands, and Clarie were ahead of them, approaching the wood. Burt said, "We're supposed to go in there?"

Clarie said, "There are going to be some unhappy wendigo in there."

Hands said, "We're friends of Seketeme."

Clarie said, "They don't know that, do they?"

Hands said, "I think if we come peacefully, they'll let us live long enough for Seketeme to get here and explain we're on their side. Besides, those guys back there need the help from these wendigo."

Burt grunted something, and Clarie seemed surprised to hear that they were on the side of the wendigo. Hands continued on with such resolution that the other two followed him. They rode among the boughs and found themselves grabbed and pulled further into the woods. Hands was shouting, "Seketeme, Seketeme, Seketeme."

The wendigo looked at him curiously. He pointed back toward the plain, "SEKETEME. SEKETEME."

Meanwhile the fighting contingent continued their retreat. The mounted Fels closed quickly on the footbound escapees. Then, starting out of the long grass were the wapiti. They grabbed the antlers and swung up. The animals surged under them.

Soon they realized that the great animals were tired. The Fels were catching up to them. Vermont wheeled there. The wendigo rode on, pushing the boy's mount ahead of him.

"Vermont, come," he shouted.

"I've failed the regnate too many times." The young man was waiting the charge of the Fels, moving his beast horizontally to their line so that their arrows kept missing. The first to reach him saw his sword fly out of his hand, and felt the staff of the spear smash into his head, before he crumpled unconscious from his mount. Percy brought his wapiti over to the riderless horse. He pulled himself onto the horse and shouted at the wapiti, and it took off for the forest. He sat the horse masterfully, and could direct it with the simplest of knee pressures.

He wheeled the horse finding himself already surrounded by four Fels brandishing their swords. His spear twirled, smacked and poked, and when they fell back, they were only two, and one of them saw his sword was in the hand of Percy, who spun the blade twice to get the feel for it. He launched the spear at the one still armed, and it slammed into his helmet, knocking him out. More were arriving, but they saw the way the sword danced in his hands, and they had seen him fight the others, and they were in no hurry to engage.

He was a Citan; he trained daily in the fine arts of spearwork and swordfighting, and they were no match for him. They pretended they were enjoying the moment of victory as they circled. "Not so tough now." Still they kept their distance. Said one, "Always wanted a chance to fight a Citan. Show them how we fight in Segundawick."

Vermont said, "Here I am, wheel out your horse, and try your Segunda tool against my Citan sword."

The soldier had no choice but to enter the ring. He cantered in, wearing a sleeveless shirt to reveal stone hard muscles. He rode toward the Citan, and swung his great sword with a ferocious waist level swing. Vermont dropped down to one side of the horse, ducking the blow, and popped up, sliding his blade into the

274

underarm of the Fel, whose eyes opened in shock. The others groaned, still circling.

"Fight, you coward dogs!" The Bellumite galloped forward. He fired his thunderPipe and Percy felt nothing. He was only fifty paces away, reloading. Percy heeled the horse smartly. Then he felt a great pain, and looked down. A red slash was in his side. The Bellumite was not far behind, riding a superior horse. He reached into his bag for another bomb, a metal ball with a canvas fuse.

Meanwhile, the Ornatan wendigo looked strangely at the dark boy who pointed over and over back toward the plain, shouting, "Seketeme. Seketeme." The three humans befuddled the wendigo: they came unarmed to Ornata riding on wapiti but they were humans.

Percy was retreating at break neck speed, not far behind Seketeme and Jalil. "This one is mine," said the Bellumite, lighting the bomb. To kill such a warrior was a great honor for a Bellumite. He laughed triumphantly as he pulled back his hand.

A brief whistling noise interrupted his throw, and three arrows thumped into his chest. The bomb dropped from his hand, and a shout, something between the keening scream of the panther, and the barking of the fox, went up, and then the air was buzzing with arrows like a swarm of bees. The Fels yelled out, "Retreat!"

The dawn light showed a line of small figures under the trees drawing and shooting arrow after arrow. Percy breathed a sigh of relief. As the escapees closed the last hundred yards to the wood, walking and panting the wendigo saw Seketeme. One knelt and began to weep. Others shouted in amazement. One broke forward and grasped Seketeme, ruffling his headLeaves and punching his shoulder to guarantee that he was real. They spoke, exclamations of shock and joy.

26. Voice of the LongBoughs

The longeye stood by Sachem Askasktuhon, his body tense with news, his chest heaving with the effort of his run. The sachem wondered what it was now, how many of his longeyes had died.

"Sachem, the Mishipeshu stirs from the forest heart, and now moves through the woods toward you."

"He is hunting."

"No, Sachem. He looks at no creature and marches stately as the moose."

The sachem nodded and sent the longeye away with a flick of his hand. He remembered a story his father told of a sachem that was lazy. In his rings the treetenders had drank fermented ciders and slept in the shade, not tending the LongBoughs. The Mishipeshu emerged from the woods, and the sachem knew that Ornata sent its spirit in judgment. He was rooted to the spot watching the terrible grace of the Mishipeshu. It reached him, and with a brutal bite snapped his leafed head from the trunk of his body and turned back toward the heart of the forest leaving his body to feed the vultures.

Perhaps Askasktuhon had earned such an end. Under his leadership Ornata's trees fell and longeyes wilted. The treetenders retreated farther and farther from the forest edge. He had failed to secure the Magnasylvan reinforcements he needed, and he did not know how to fight the Fire-Warriors. His small successes, the LightTalker's FireBoy and the one hundred Magnasylvan longeyes, were like a longtooth shot at a buck from over sixty yards. If it struck, it would be glorious, but it was not likely to strike. He comforted himself that death would mean he escaped the desperation of losing a battle for everything he loved, little by little, day by day. Better to return to the floor of the forest and feed the LongBoughs than to fail like this.

He saw first a changing in the light among the trees. They began to glow themselves as if pouring out the sunlight that they had stored, illuminating the great creature that moved through, parting the LongBoughs back like blades of grass. When it emerged from among the trees it was in the form of an enormous brown grolf, which, though it walked on all four legs, was twice as tall as him. The sight of the Mishipeshu flooded his head with visions, a thunderhead sailing on high winds eating the blue, a deer quietly drinking from the placid murk of a forest pond. The pond erupted with the flash of long jaws, the alligator teeth seizing the deer and wrestling it down into the water, which bubbled and splashed for moments, before it was still again, an eerie quiet, a frog pumped through leaf browned water. The visions ended after a moment.

Astride the monster's massive shoulders rode a man. Like a wendigo rides a wapiti, the rider sat easy, his lower body rolling with the movement of his mount, while he held his chest and head erect and still, calmly surveying the Ornatan Meadow.

Askasktuhon knew this man. Three decades ago, this man had delivered the half grolf, half man child to their forest. Askasktuhon had found him surrounded by the longeyes, who were waiting for the word to rip him apart. The man said that the half-breed needed a home, and who better than the treepeople to understand a half-breed. Askasktuhon had disliked the man's confidence and authority, but then he saw the child. The boy wore hurt on his face, and the sachem could sense his beast-strength. The wendigo adopted the boy, and the man rode off with the woman weeping in the back of the wagon.

"Hey, Askasktuhon," the man said. "Long time no see."

"Who are you that ride the Mishipeshu like a wapiti?"

"I have many names. The wendigo of Faunarum call me Master of the Mishipeshu, which I always thought sounded pretty good. Others call me Wagon Driver. The name changes and I don't think it's that important. You will have some small visitors soon, friends of the FireBoy. They will propose to you a plan that will seem foolish. Do everything that they say, if you wish Ornata to survive."

Askasktuhon said, "What reason have I to trust you?"

"I will give you two. First, the last thing I asked you to do was to raise a boy. You yourself know what good that did this forest." This was true. The half-breed grew to be almost grolf sized, and he was loyal. Even now he was the wendigo's only source of information in the human city. "Second, the Mishipeshu listens to me, Sachem Askasktuhon. Who are you to not listen?"

The man turned the godMonster back toward the trees and prompted it with a simple tuck of his heels. It bounded off among the leaves.

———————

Two wendigo longeyes, bearing sheaves of arrows, carried Shyheem upon a stretcher woven from river grass. Angen and Kwenemuk walked beside the stretcher. Above him the trees five fingered foliage flashed by, held up by an infrastructure of curvy branches. The leaves only grew at the outer tips of the branches so that the space under each tree was like a dome held up by silver arches, with a roof of yellowing and sun-drenched leaves.

They walked into a meadow, where, though it was fall, small yellow flowers and larger violets dotted the green grass. In the center rose a LongBough that towered high over the other trees. Visible high up in this tree were places where the branches twisted and flared into a spherical spiral like a living nest. In one of these branch spheres Shyheem saw wendigo, small as ants because they were so high up, watching him.

Shyheem heard a voice in his head, *Welcome, Shyheem. I am a grandmother tree.* Though the tree towered above him, its great branches moving slowly in the high breezes, it looked gentle. For a moment he thought he saw the face of a mother, eyes turned down on her children in the leaves.

"Hello," he thought back.

Kwenemuk was skipping along next to the stretcher. Her mindspeech reached him like a babbling broke after the lake serene tones of the trees. *They all said you would never change, that it was a waste of time, and that Mishipeshu only refused you because you were too much like a glow-worm. But now, we have a chance. Three Fels burnt like leaves in the fire!*

278

Angen was reading through the ironbound writ at his side. He wanted to remember all he could about the manusignis. The boy would need more help than simply finding the right context to use the godFire. Every few steps he tripped over a root, but he kept on reading.

The trees greeted Shyheem as they passed. He learned all about them, how they knew everything that happened, though they were rooted to one place. They shared constantly with one another so news spread through the forest. They watched the young wendigo. The trees were the memory of the wendigo, sharing stories that the younger did not know. They spoke as though he was already their friend. He wondered then at the diversity of things Theom had made, and cursed his pride again. These gentle, wise beings were much closer to Illumen's light than he was.

A quiet thump interrupted the quiet greetings between the birds, and the rustling mindspeak of the trees. The faces of the longeyes grew solemn, their eyes strained forward, and the thumping grew louder. The trees around him neglected to greet him, their attention turned to the noises. He heard them in his head. "There is another one."

Shyheem heard a screeching noise that followed each thump. At first it was just screaming but then he heard the words.

Fire! Stop it, the fire!

Water! Water!

The volume of these cries increased as the stretcher moved closer to them. Shyheem tried to sit up and asked that they stop. Angen shook his head and they continued on. Shyheem found himself lifted off the stretcher and slung across the back of one of the longeyes. They were climbed one of the mother trees to the nests. In it, they perched him on the branches, and pointed at a clearing.

He looked out on a swath of orange mud marred by the wheels of machines and the iron shoes of beasts of burden. An armored horseman with a mane of red hair and a purple cape rode among an army of Fels. The Fels cheered as four men dipped their hands into bags, pulling out their ironwrapped bombs. They dropped these into a small catapult, and them launched into the forests. Three of the bombs crisped some leaves and passed through, to explode on the forest floor, but the fourth hit a LongBough at its base.

It exploded, the orange red flames seizing the trunk and running up the branches, turning the leaves to ashes in a moment. Shyheem heard the tree scream *No! The flame!* Then it was wordless, weeping and moaning.

Shyheem shook his head, and watched as the four Bellumites released the catapult again, loosing another barrage. The bombs crashed in among the trees, and with each explosion, new voices joined the screaming. He did not want to hear these good parents whose words were their best gift reduced to wordless screams. He covered his ears, and closed his eyes, but this only stopped the sound and sight of the bombs, the screaming went on in his head.

"Where are the longeyes?" Shyheem couldn't understand why no one defended the trees.

Angen said, "They are waiting. It is hopeless to attack right now."

"And the trees just die?"

Angen said, "You can hear them? What are they saying?"

Shyheem said, "Only screams."

Another tree was hit directly. Its leaves curled, erupted in flame, and waved and blew in the wind, ash. After a gasp, its spoke, its words strained.

Goodbye, sun and rain. My children!

Then anguish born groans. Angen looked at the boy, and his hard face carried a look of concern. Shyheem started to pray, desperate and angry about the slaughter he was watching. In a moment blue flames two hands high were running across his shoulders and spurting out of his eyes. Angen told the longeye to pick him up. The longeye was staring at the flaming boy in shock. Angen grabbed the boy himself. He felt the edge of the flame, but it skirted him. He descended the tree and jogged toward the center of the wood, away from the dying screams that he could not hear. Around him the angry murmur, the thousand condolences of the trees ran on.

Shyheem murmured, "Does it hurt?"

"Still trying to burn me, kid? It won't work." Shyheem could see the twinkle in the castOut's eyes. He said, "You're ready now, kaManusignis."

Regnate Grant sat Nickson right next to him, and began prattling on about the efforts against the wendigo. Nickson barely heard it. He already knew that Grant would go soft and mince about talking about his soldiers' lives. If he asked, Nickson would tell him that Regna had the numbers to just march into the forest and take it over. That would save lives in the long run. Probably.

Grant put out a heavy hand, grabbed Nickson by the shoulder, "I'm glad to see you're here, John." He saw Nickson as his number two, his right hand man. There was a time when Nickson's conscience would have pricked when the ruler put him at his right hand, ready to share the plans with him. Potens had taught him that conscience was weakness. So he smiled, and nodded, thinking that his men would need to create a skirmish. Then the regnate would take the field. There he could die killed by a wandering arrow, nicely fitted with wendigo leaf fletching.

27. Ornata

The Subs and their Citan friends stood a few paces in under the trees in the orange glow of the dawn. The humans take in the strange, wiry creatures. They have never, or only briefly, seen the wendigo. The wendigo stare back, with less interest and great antagonism. One reaches out and rakes a clawed hand across Burt's face. The others looked ready to go further, but Seketeme interposes, growling and roaring. The other wendigo back away, but begin to speak, their anger and disdain leaking from them though the humans do not understand the words. After a lengthy argument Seketeme turned to the humans.

"You wear vines. To put ties on boy who take my irons . . ." and he trailed off. Hands patted him on the shoulder. He wanted to express that Seketeme had earned his trust, and saved Hands life at least twice. He wanted to say things that he had no language for, about finding family in that strange moment in the belly of the earth when he had trusted a creature he knew nothing about.

The wendigo produced some vines. The humans found their eyes covered, and their hands lashed together behind them.

Burt said, "Think you can spring this one?"

Hands replied, "Doesn't seem to be any locks."

Jalil said, "You would think that would make it easier." They laughed until one of the wendigo barked.

Seketeme translated, "They no like men. They no want you talk."

"Sorry."

They started off through the woods. The boys knew that they were under the trees because they could hear the birds and other animals calling out through the branches, and they heard the wind stirring the branches.

Burt said, "Are they going to kill us?"

Hands said, "That would be a shame. So many people already failed."

Jalil said, "They seem to respect Seketeme a lot. He won't let us die."

Hands didn't like Jalil talking about Seketeme like they were best friends. It wasn't fair because Hands had saved the wendigo, while Jalil had tried to betray him, and now Jalil got to run across the country with Seketeme, and learn all about him and the wendigo ways. Hands said, "How'd you get to know him so well? Last I remember you tried to get him killed."

Jalil said, "Well, I thought he was going to eat me at first. That's what I deserved, but Seketeme was too dollar."

One of the wendigo barked, and another pinched Jalil's arm. Another began to talk angrily to Seketeme.

Seketeme dropped back. He said, "These wendigo think humans no good. Humans come here, kill us for long time. You follow what they say, we talk to sachem, he say, you can lose the blindfolds and ropes. Now, no talk."

They walked on for a long time, tripping over the feet. They had not slept in days, and they weren't supposed to talk. Finally they were stopped, and a quaking voice cried something out. Their blindfolds were removed. They saw that they were in a clearing dappled in morning sunlight. In its center grew a tree. In all of Urba, there was no tree that looked anything like it. They had to crane their necks to look up toward its foliage, as high as a cloud above them.

Seketeme walked toward the center of the meadow. There was an old wendigo sitting at the base of the tree, covered in small blue butterflies. The old wendigo croaked as he saw the Seketeme. His leaves were not red, but brown, and shriveled. He struggled up with the help of a staff to his feet, the blue butterflies all fluttered away from him, and threw his arms around Seketeme. The two wendigo stood like that for a long time, and the butterflies settled on both of them. When they released their grip, it was slowly, and the four winged blues stayed put.

Seketeme helped the old wendigo to sit. They continued to talk quickly, their tone familiar and full of joy. After sometime the old wendigo beckoned and the wendigo guards pulled Hands toward the middle of the meadow. "Hands, this is my grandfather, Xinkwelepay, sachem of Southern Ornata."

The old wendigo searched the face of the boy through the tears in his eyes. Then Sachem Xinkwelepay spoke, his voice almost a whisper. Seketeme translated. "He says that he lose hope of seeing me again, he thinks I dead. Now he die happy. He thanks you beyond his words, he no know you, you like his best friend."

Hands said, "Tell him you saved me too, so it's even."

Seketeme rested a hand on the boys' head. "I told him. He says it is you, with your city fingers, who release me, make me free, and gave me back the wendigo way, oneness with the rain and sun. This chance to do great things. He wants you to have thing. This his most valuable thing. When he young, he foolish, proud, he goes into the dark grove where Mishipeshu lives. Mishipeshu comes, he wrestle with it. Mishipeshu bites his hand." The old wendigo held up his left hand. The pinky and ring finger were missing, scar tissues criss–crossed where the fingers should have been.

"He does not know if Mishipeshu has mercy, or think of something else, or maybe he as young man so strong, but Mishipeshu stops, lets go, and goes away. My grandfather sings this bow from a tree in that grove, and now bow a legend. The bow has the power of Mishipeshu. Name Alankwelait, StarHunter."

The old wendigo extended the bow to Hands. The boy took it. "Thanks," Hands said shyly. The bow was intricately carved with the roaring beasts and gentler faces that Hands could not identify. He ran his hands up and down it, feeling the strength of it. It seemed to him like the bow felt him and spoke to him, offering him service, showing how it could make him a great warrior.

He looked again at the old wendigo, who was smiling at the boy, his old eyes crinkled almost closed. Hands felt a bubbling warmth spilling through him, overthrowing his exhaustion and his frustration. This was what it felt like to be appreciated. He wanted to stay here, under the smile of Xinkwelepay forever.

The wendigo guarding the others interrupted the moment, shouting something to Seketeme. He stood lightly, his movement graceful and quick in the forest. He motioned for Hands to follow. Hands waved as he left, the bow clutched close.

Jalil looked at it with amazement, and the wendigo around them stared at the weapon in the boy's hand, talking excitedly.

Jalil said, "That was pretty awesome. I still can't believe you let that grolf out. I'm sorry I was such a Citan about the whole thing."

"Hey!" Clarie said, "What's wrong with Citans?"

"They're altic snobs," said Burt.

"Yeah," said Hands, "They go around on litters so their feet don't touch the ground, 'I'm too altic for the dirt.'"

"My feet are on the ground."

"You're not a real Citan." Hands pronounced this authoritatively, and while Vermont frowned, the smile on the First Child's face showed she was more than happy to be separated from her district in the judgment of the quick-witted SubAgoran.

Hands asked Jalil about his journey. Jalil told them how the bounty hunters had taken him from his mom's house. Hands and Burt grilled him about the Sub, and he told them the little news he had. He told them how Seketeme had saved him at the docks, about their flight by boat and cross-country run until he had seen them. They told him about their journey, meeting Orpan in Agora, heading down the main way, and stopping at the castle only to learn that the vice regnate was behind the whole plot to kill the regnate. They told him that the girl behind him was the First Child.

"Wait, you guys are hanging with the First Child?"

"Hands made fun of her the whole time."

"What'd you say, Hands?"

Hands said, "I told her that that's her natural hair color. Yeah, I said all Citans have gold colored hair, because all they think about is money." Jalil shook his head, chuckling.

Clarie said, "You're skinny."

Burt said, "Oh, wow, good wordSlap. Try me."

"You're fat."

They all laughed. Hands added, "They never told us who she was."

"As if that would have made you show ring respect," Jalil said.

285

Hands said, "No. I would have had better wordSlaps for her. Special for the highest Citan."

———————

The Desiccan healer, his head wreathed in vines, sang to the bark cast. It vibrated a little, then slowly peeled back in response to his voice. Beneath the bark, the scar was closed where the spear had gone in, the flesh monotone right up to the jagged red line where the skin had sewn itself back together. The healer applied a yellow paste, which smelled like peppermint, to the wound. He spoke rapidly in Wendee to Angen, who translated. "He says you can walk tomorrow, but today you still need to rest." The healer smiled at the boy, showing old teeth yellow and pointy. He pulled a gourd from the wicker basket and poured something hot and green down Shyheem's throat. The boy gurgled once, and then swallowed. A warm feeling washed over him, and he was asleep.

"SHYHEEM?"

"SHYHEEM!" He woke up to yells.

"I can't believe it's Shyheem!"

Dancing around him, jumping up on the thin branches, so the whole nest shook were Jalil, Hands, and Burt. They shouted a series of questions about his leg, how he got there, and what he was doing, and Shyheem found himself too overwhelmed by noise and happiness and the complete improbability of finding Subs, his Subs, there. Then they all jumped on top of him. "Merd pile!"

Angen lectured, "Get off him. Be quiet, can't you see he's healing?"

The boys sat back, chagrined.

Hands said, "Who's the beard monster?"

There was a lot of story to be told. They couldn't believe that they'd all made friends with the wendigo. They were more shocked to learn that Shyheem could make godFire, especially the Illumen kind, which they hadn't even known was possible. He told them that he'd tried to help them by using his only connection to go to North Temple, but the lamps weren't any help. If he was honest, he kind of forgot. They all instantly excused this, explaining that

286

nobody was letting them out of Aeternanox, and anyway, they'd gotten themselves out of that. Well, they had a little help.

All the Illumenists cared about was developing Shyheem's power, which, he confessed, became the only thing he cared about for a while. He was so intent on succeeding as a wick until he got kidnapped. "By this guy," he said, jerking his chin toward Angen. The boys introduced themselves to the castOut. "We're used to kidnappers. We've all been kidnapped at least twice."

Shyheem told them how the wendigo tried to feed him to the monster Mishipeshu, but Illumen wasn't having that, so some of the wendigo decided they were stuck with him, and he'd still have been against them, if it wasn't for that crazy night when he was almost killed, and that pretty much brought it all together.

Jalil said, "You weren't the only kaLulu. I sung on our wendigo."

They told him of their escape from Aeternanox with the grolf, and Seketeme. They told them about Orpan, and their escort. They introduced the Citans. "That's Percy."

"He thinks he's pretty special. He's a Citan WickBaron."

"And that's the First Child."

"Yeah, I saved her from being eaten by wild cluriKins."

Clarie said, "I saved you."

They told him that the vice regnate was the man behind the assassination plot. Shyheem recognized in their description the man who had ordered the attack on the trees. His hands flared blue as he thought about it.

Burt pulled his pants up past his knees showing the deep purple bruises on his shins. They told him how they hightailed it for Ornata, and barely made it, only to be welcomed with blindfolds. They were only a few miles from the regnate, but they were separated by no man's land, the dangerous place between warring peoples.

Percy interrupted, "I'm glad you guys are all catching up, but last I checked, our mission was to save Regnate Grant, and we definitely haven't done that." Hands looked at him, and wondered if he could manage the headbutt move if Percy's hands weren't tied up.

Then Clarie said, "Yeah, how do we warn my dad?" Somehow, this changed Hands' mind.

He added, "How do we tell the regnate?"

Burt said, "Maybe Percy can just march over and talk to him."

Jalil said, "I don't think the vice regnate will let that happen."

They discussed possibilities. Open war was a bad plan because the wendigo weren't able to fight in the open against the forces of Regna. They were outnumbered almost ten to one. The other problem with that the vice regnate was waiting for open war to kill the regnate. Shyheem told them that he wanted to help the wendigo. Saving the regnate wasn't his concern anymore.

Hands said, "The regnate can execute all the Fels that imprisoned us."

Burt nodded, "That's really important to me and Hands. They've done all this slapping and headWatting, and we really think they should be executed. We plan on watching and getting their heads as souvenirs."

Hands said, "Actually the vice regnate told me that he sent mercenaries to go across borders, cut down trees, and prompt the wendigo into attacking, and he hates the regnate because the regnate lacks the stones to really take the war to the wendigo. So if we save the regnate, he might listen to us and call off the attacks on the wendigo."

Jalil added, "Especially if we get the wendigo to help save him."

"Yeah. If we save the regnate, we can end the war," added Burt.

Shyheem said, "Your idea is that we say to the wendigo, 'Hey, save the regnate of the country that is burning your trees.' I don't think they're going to like that. They're pretty frustrated with humans."

"Oh, we know. We saved an important one, and bring him home, and the next we know, they tie us, blindfold us, and call us all sorts of mean wendigo words that we don't understand."

The boys pondered how they might convince the wendigo that their plan was a good one. There didn't seem to be any easy answer, but somehow they had a confidence about it. If they could just talk to the sachems. Everything else had worked out, even when it didn't seem possible, even when they didn't know what needed to happen for things to work.

A breeze moved through the tops of the trees, and the sun beat gently down on the outstretched leaves. Far below, on the forest floor, small furry creatures ran from tree to tree, hole to hole. The Subs looked at each other, trying not to smile.

The next visitor was Kwenemuk. She swung herself up into their ornament. Her leaves were unbound, and the red leaves fluttered about her copper cheeks. Her dark eyes flashed. She was the first wendigo their age that the boys had seen. She stood straight as a sapling, turning her smile on Shyheem's friends.

Shyheem said, "You look happy."

I am. I am Ornatan, in Ornata.

The humans who had come from the plain looked around in surprise. They heard the voice in their minds, but her lips didn't move.

I'm a mindscout.

"Careful," Shyheem remarked. "She can read your mind."

Jalil and Burton looked down, their brown skin flushing darker. Hands looked over at his tongue-tied friends. He said, "We need to talk to your boss. The big wendigo."

"Sachem," corrected Shyheem.

"Yeah, that's the one. We've got a plan. We're friends with Seketeme."

Is it true you saved him from the human prison?

"Yeah, I did that."

That was a great act, and the trees honor you for it. My great act has been to convince this one to help us. He insisted that he would burn all of us. Shyheem affirmed this with a nod. She continued, *I'm here to take to you the council. You'll talk to the sachems there.*

They descended the tree after her. Vermont and the First Child made to follow, but Kwenemuk shook her head. *Only the Subs and Angen are wanted in the Tree Council.* They tripped through the woods, vaulting streams, smushing the moss, and stepping between the roots.

They reached a clearing, only half-shaded by ten trees whose straight trunks shot past the other trees and rose above the forest before opening their canopies. The middlemost tree grew in the middle of a large stream. *Wemituhon,* said Kwenemuk pointing at the tree. The stream entered the meadow on the Western edge, crashing off of a small cliff of brown rock into a little pool. Then the water meandered serenely through the center of the meadow. A large herd of wapiti grazed the meadow. Many different wendigo were there too, gathering wood, carving arrows, gardening, and some were at the edge, singing to smaller trees. This was the center of Ornata.

They followed Kwenemuk to the stream where they hopped from stone to stone to the base of the great tree Wemituhon. They passed a longeye who measured them with his eyes before waving them on. Kwenemuk grabbed a ladder that grew in the trunk. While the others climbed away, following the steps of their guide, Burt stood on the ground. He got on the ladder at last, but after a few steps, he stopped climbing again. The longeye behind him barked something in wendigo, but all Burton could think about was what it would be like in another ten steps. He dropped down, falling into the longeye, and knocking him from the tree. They lay sprawling on the ground, the longeye barking at the boy. He rolled over and grabbed Burt, his lips peeled back revealing a sharp row of teeth. He thought the boy was attacking him. The boy's terrified expression, along with his hysterical blubbering, showed him his mistake, and he released Burt. Burt did not get up, but lay staring at the tree. He knew he couldn't climb it.

Jalil was enjoying the climb. Spreading out around him were trees and more trees, as they cleared the first fifty steps. They were still far below the tree's leaves.

Angen warned, "Don't look down."

Hands and Shyheem took the advice. They already felt far from the earth, strangely suspended in the wind. Jalil continued to peek down every so often. He trusted himself not to grow dizzy. After all, he could throw a rock and hit an AltUrban at fifty yards. The view below was stunning. The wapiti grazing in the meadow had shrunk to toys, and the stream that divided the meadow was only a ribbon of reflected sunlight. Then the dizziness grabbed him, and

290

he had no sense of up or down. He clung to the step he was on, staring straight at the tree, tremors running through his body. Slowly he felt balance return to him. He looked up and saw that the others were far ahead. After that he climbed carefully, not looking down.

Their arms and legs were already tired when they reached the canopy and found themselves climbing in among the leaves. The climb became easier, as they moved away from the trunk and found themselves stepping on branches that seemed to grow as gracefully as the other LongBoughs but still made a staircase of evenly spaced footholds. Jalil told them about how he had seen Seketeme sing to the tree, and how a bow had formed from the branches. Angen said it was called wood warbling.

As they climbed through the canopy, they found that they could not see anything below them but leaves, and they felt safe, as if the tree, which had grown exactly as the wendigo wanted it, would catch them with leafy hands rather than let them fall. As they got higher, the leaves around them grew thinner.

Their climb took them into an oval nest far larger than any they had found. It sat almost at the apex of the tree. The leaves were thin and they saw the forest spread around them. They saw the line of mountains to the West, and the plain far off to the east, and the scar of orange earth at the edge of the forest, where the outposts and the fort stood. To the south the forest stretched to the horizon. Seated around the edges of the ornament were wendigo. They saw Askasktuhon, the sachem at one end. Unlike the regnate and the wickBarons, he had no special seat, but crouched on an unornamented branch. The leaves in his hair had turned bright yellow. They saw other sachem, Seketeme's grandfather, seated on the other side of Askasktuhon. Seketeme was there, and Aihum, the Magnasylvan longeye eyed them from a firmer branch. There were around fifteen wendigo, and the four humans.

You are in the council of the sachem. The words of Kwenemuk echoed through their heads. *You will wait to be spoken to before you speak.*

A voice rose from the branches they sat on and resonated within them, which caused the humans to start up, which is a bit

291

scary when you are floating at cloud level. "It is time to talk again about those Regnan axes. For too long we have eaten their steel. The Regnans have begun this war, attacking us whenever they can find the younger outside of Ornata, and attacking the elders when they cannot. They have many more longeye than us, and even if we count one wendigo worthy of five humans in battle, we are still outnumbered two to one. The younger have fought from the elders' branches. Still the wood perishes. More reinforcements arrive for them, while we lose longeyes that it will take generations to replace. Thank the sky-god, thank Mishipeshu, new power has come to Ornata." The boys stared around, but no one was talking. Finally it dawned on them that it was the tree Wemituhon that was speaking.

Wemituhon went on, "The LightTalker's FireBoy offers his flame. The LightTalker says he may be able to overcome an army of Fels. We know that he burned three mounted Fels in a moment. Aihum has also joined us, bringing the most magnificent Magnasylvan longeyes. They ride the tall Northern wapiti, and prefer close combat, a tactical option not used by the Ornatan wendigo. My children shoot far and true with the longteeth, like clouds send out rain, but are not gifted with the spear, the club, and the hatchet. Returned to us is Seketeme, grandson of Xinkwelepay, one of our lion-like longeyes. He returns from the cold-iron evil walls of the human prison.

"With new resources comes a strange piece of advice that Ornata must consider. It comes from a man we have not seen for many years. His last visit, his wagon came rattling across the Segundan plain. We were surprised because he spoke Wendee, but he would not discuss the source of his knowledge. He explained that he was giving us a halfBreed, showed us the boy's horn nubs on his forehead. He said men could not understand the holiness of such things, that Mishipeshu had created a blessed child. We took the child, thinking it was a great burden.

"The wagon driver offers the boy as proof of his trustworthiness. Orpan grew not only strong but disciplined, and many longeyes can speak of his courage and the keenness of his nose, but we tall ones know him as a friend, respectful to elders. He sacrificed his freedoms to go to the city of man and be our eyes there.

"The wagon driver came to us this time, seeking conversation with Askasktuhon, mounted on Mishipeshu, which responded to his commands." There were gasps around the Ornament, as the wendigo heard that a man rode their god. "I saw it, the oldest tree in Ornata. I have never seen the like. This also makes him seem a friend, yet there are stories of evil men who have controlled Mishipeshu. I do not know. His advice was this. The brown children, friends of the FireBoy, would come to us with a plan. We ought to follow it."

The eyes of the wendigo turned to the Subs. Hands looked at Jalil, who looked down at the lattice of branches that made the floor. Burt hadn't made it up, and Shyheem shrugged when Hands turned an eye to him. Hands stood, making sure to hold a branch as he balanced.

"Look, we're just some Subs. In the city nobody cares about us; people notice us only to kick us. For some reason a dying man told me about a plot to kill Regnate Grant. We started trying to warn him, and we ended up here. I don't have any reason why you should listen to us. We used to hate wendigo, calling you mindThieves and babyEaters. Then we met Seketeme and we liked him a lot. I'm not saying I like all of you. Some of you bark a lot, and others always want to put vine ties on me. In general though, we're on your side.

"Also, we hate Fels. They've watted us pretty much everyway. The guy running them is the Vice Regnate John Nickson, and he is the one that started this war. He's just using all this as a context to kill the regnate. If we could talk to the regnate, we'd get him to end the war. You guys need to save the regnate. I'll help."

There was a disapproving rustle, as Aihum leapt to his feet. He was on a branch thinner than a man's wrist that bobbed under his weight. Yet he stood as easily as a bird perches on a twig. "These words stink more than the passings of the puma. The regnate has camped his armies here, brought steel to your woods, and killed the tall ones of Ornata. Any enemy of his is a friend of ours. This idea from the small human is insanity."

293

Hands said, "What's really crazy is having leaves for hair, and a tree for your dad."

"Hands," Seketeme growled, but the Sub kept going.

"I've got a brain in my head, not a pot for dirt. I might be the only one thinking in this whole tree." Aihum sprung into the middle of the network of branches, which swayed slightly at his quick movement.

Askasktuhon said, "Aihum, sit down. This is my meeting." The big longeye stalked back to his seat. Askasktuhon turned to Hands. "You are more disrespectful than the FireBoy."

Seketeme said, "Sachem, he does not know our ways."

Askasktuhon said, "Shall that excuse such words in the arms of an elder?"

Seketeme said, "I am sorry for what he has said. You must know, leader of our kind, that the ways of the humans are not our ways. This child knows nothing of respect, for when his parents died, he was not taken in by the voices of the elders, nor was fruit given him by the elders. He wandered in their streets, begging, and then stealing when not enough was given. Everything he has, he has taken, and these quick, harsh words are the voice of one without a mother or father."

The bass-timbered voice of Wemituhon drowned out Askasktuhon and Aihum's attempts to speak. "Seketeme, you have spoken with wisdom. Yet, it will not be as it has been for the boy. He is among us, and he must learn to use words with care. The discipline for his wrong words will be cleaning the pastures after the council, and you shall take him there."

Hands said, "Fine, I'm sorry. I was just wordSmacking."

Askasktuhon stood up. "We must continue with the discussion of the plan to rescue the regnate. Aihum has said that this man is our enemy." He sat, looking for who would speak next.

Xinkwelepay stood up. "Aihum, your words rise straight to the point, as the crocus faces the sun. Though I have a great personal debt to the little human, I cannot see how we should risk wendigo lives to save this sachem of the humans. It has been said that one of the humans is the daughter of the regnate. Surely this is our greatest resource, a treasure for which they will stop the war."

Hands rose at the same time as Aihum. The deep voice of the tree Wemituhon spoke, "Let the city child have his say."

"The First Child won't have any value after WickBaron Nickson kills the regnate. You guys are angry. I'd be angry too. But what options do you have? Can you push them back? No. Can you wait longer while your trees die? That won't work either."

Aihum spoke in response. "I have come far because I heard the sorrow in Ornata's sachem. I did not come to compromise, but to crush the cause of that sorrow. My spear is sharpened, and my war-club scratches the air. Should we not fight here with all we have, the strength of Magnasylva, and the glory of Ornata? Though their numbers are many, they will know fear. The men that survive will carry a tale of terror back to their city."

Askasktuhon stood. "Aihum, does not my heart long only for strength, to enter the field with war in my eyes, my proud bow, grown from this forest, singing the revenge of one thousand trees? But I am not just a longeye. My duty is to this forest. How can I save it? Your solution is the end of Ornata. We could repel them the way you suggest, but it would cost us everything. At least the boy's suggestion has a chance."

Xinkwelepay spoke. "To capture the regnate is not to commit to be his friend. If we hold him, and they still have allegiance to him, even though he will not change his orders, still the Regnan army must desist its attack."

Askasktuhon spoke, "This is true. If we hold the regnate, we can force the Regnans to desist their attacks. We will follow this course of action. We shall turn then to questions of strategy for which we do not need the children. Seketeme. Kwenemuk, take them out, and direct the SubAgoran Hands to his discipline."

They moved out, the eyes of the wendigo sachems either hostile, or neutral, watching them leave. Back down on the ground, Seketeme pointed toward a corner of the meadow covered in the droppings of the wapiti, fat as fists and blobby. "Pick them and throw them there." He pointed out the gardens enclosed with fences made of intertwining short trees.

"What if I don't?"

"I think Askasktuhon will have you fed to Mishipeshu."

295

"You mean that thing that tried to eat Shyheem."

"Yes."

"I would watt that monster right in the face." Seketeme smiled, and turned to leave. "You don't have a shovel?" Seketeme shrugged and bounded back toward the great tree.

Hands stared at the piles and piles of merd. Hands tried to pick up one of the wapiti droppings with a stick, but it broke when he stabbed it. He tried sliding a stick under it, but it just rolled off. He said some things about leafHeads using merd to fertilize their heads. He knew it was more trouble or doing this, so he shrugged, and he grabbed a big wapiti merd.

Jalil and Shyheem stopped and watched Hands pound the wapiti merd into the basket. Shyheem thought about how he had hated Hands in the Sub because Hands was so arrogant and selfish. He never thought about others or what was right. Shyheem had believed that he was different than this, putting Illumen first, and doing what was right. Now he knew that he had been just as proud, just as selfish living for his own light. Hands wasn't the enemy, but another child of Illumen.

Jalil meanwhile was thinking his own thoughts. Hands had always been a pain in the merdup, the only Sub who didn't recognize Jalil's ability. It hadn't mattered how many times Jalil kicked his merdup, Hands always believed he could win. Jalil had been frustrated by Hands' obstinacy, but now he had to be thankful for that courage. How else had Hands been able to stand up in the council of the wendigo, and speak his mind? The wendigo were just like Jalil, not believing Hands' arrogance, and finding him annoying but that didn't stop him.

Hands was wondering whether running into the Regnan camp and tipping off the soldiers about the impending attack was better than cleaning up the pen when he heard the squish of wapiti merd going into the basket. He looked up and saw Jalil and Shyheem, scooping up the smelly blobs. They were working hard, and the field looked smaller. A moment ago he had thought he was alone.

It didn't smell that bad. Old grass logs.

When they finished Kwenemuk took them back to the tree. Clarie and Percy asked a lot of questions.

Shyheem said, "Hands convinced the wendigo to try and save your dad."

Clarie grabbed Hands as he was coming up the ladder, and planted a large kiss on his lips. "Thank you, thank you! My dad is dollar, you'll see."

The afternoon slowed down, everyone waiting and wondering what would happen next. Would they be part of the battle plan, or made to sit in the nest, and wait? Jalil picked up the bow that Xinkwelepay had given Hands, and felt its string. He asked if he could practice with it. Hands was in a great mood, between the Subs helping him with the wapiti merd, and Clarie giving him a kiss, and he said, "Sure, have fun."

Hands taught Clarie a game called Slapsies. Hands beat her for a few hours, and she finally gave up, asking him, "How did you get so good!"

Burt and Shyheem questioned Kwenemuk about being a wendigo and a mindscout, and evening crept through the leaves as gentle as a mother lion.

Jalil returned smiling. "Hands, this is the best bow ever. I was practicing with the wendigo, they said this bow is Alankwelait, which means hunter of stars. It feels so good in your hands; it feels like it knows. And the power, it's kiDollar."

Hands said, "You want it?"

Jalil said, "You can't give this away, Sub. This is too good."

"I'm serious," said Hands. "You should have it."

Jalil looked at the bow, running his hand down its carved length. "I don't deserve this."

Hands said, "Just take it. You know you want it."

Jalil gave into a face-splitting smile. He said, "Thanks, Hands. This is dollar."

Angen interrupted all this, his shaggy head popping into the Ornament. "Shyheem, you need to be alone and talk to Illumen. They need your flame tomorrow." Shyheem nodded and closed his eyes. The other Subs grew quiet as well as their minds turned to the battle. For Jalil being a soldier was something that he had longed for since he could understand what that was. He imagined fighting with such skill that they made him an honorary longeye.

Hands was also excited, because it was a chance to show anyone watching that he was fearless. He imagined riding a horse in among the Fels, grabbing the regnate, and whisking him back to the safety of the wood, where Clarie waited.

Burt looked at them all, and saw the focus in Shyheem's eyes, and the excitement in Jalil and Hands. He saw the grumpy way that Clarie watched the others. Once again, Vermont had told her that she was too valuable to enter the field despite a lot of begging.

Burt wished that he was like them, happy to fight for something good, but all he could think about were the arrows, bombs, bullets and blades that would be flying around, and how much he didn't want one to land in any part of his body. He was even more scared that they would see how scared he was, and they would know that he was a lulu.

28. Regnate

Nickson stood on the walkway above the wall of the fort and looked in frustration toward the unmoving forest. The Bellumites had unleashed their bombs, and still the wendigo did not charge. He needed them to charge so that the regnate would ride into the field where arrows chanced the skies and blades were misthrust.

The regnate, standing next to him, said, "It is a beautiful place, don't you think?"

Nickson said, "A breeding ground for monsters."

The regnate shook his head. "You know, I never understood why you hate the wendigo. They follow their gods, and we follow ours. Two generations ago, we had peace with them."

Nickson looked sideways at the regnate. The regnate said, "I find it beautiful, regardless of the dangers."

He excused himself and found one of his Fels. "Tomorrow," he said, "order some Guard to follow you, and go into the forest with nine other handpicked Fels. Order the Guard to chop down a tree. When you are attacked, retreat, and blow the horns. We will make this war."

Shyheem and Angen waited in the shadow of the trees where the branches of the LongBoughs closed around them like a mother's hands. They peered through the five fingered leaves at the two outposts that sat in the middle of the muddy wound that the steel axes and churning wagon wheels had torn into the forest. The outposts were walled in with dead trees driven vertically into the ground, and sharpened at the ends. Fels and Guardsmen moved in and out, and the longeyes reported that around two thousand troops were camped in each.

Three quarters of a mile away in the plain's gray grass stood the fort, a solid stone construction with battlements tall as six men. The

Regna flag flew above it. The longeyes also reported that the four thousand Fels and the twenty or so Bellumites that had arrived with the vice regnate were camped in and around it.

On the far side of the clearing, over a mile away, a handful of Fels had set themselves up around a group of Guard that had been sent to chop the trees. The axe men chopped quickly. Their eyes were directed not at the trunks they chipped at, but at the shadows between the leaves that swayed around them. They had seen many men struck by fatal arrows while they chopped the trees.

They had gathered their armor and borrowed extra pieces, a collar guard, a pair of greaves. They knew how the wendigo arrows could outsmart armorers. Any chink or eyehole was a window for death to fly through.

Angen urged Shyheem, "Pray. Keep praying until you can't anymore, and then get back here. If you extinguish your flame before you are under the cover of the wood, they will kill you."

It was easy to pray right then. Shyheem's head was filled with the tree's screaming lament. The steel bit into the tree's flesh, cutting sap lines and rings of memory. The other trees spoke to those that were chopped, seeking to comfort them. Shyheem hated to hear it. He said, "Illumen, stop them, stop the axes."

On the opposite side of the clearing, Hands sat astride a wapiti behind a long line of mounted Magnasylvan longeye. Their tall spears vibrated with eagerness, their oval leaves fluttered showing jagged silhouettes. Clarie had wanted to be with them, but the wendigo had imprisoned her in a nest. She had tried to train Hands to sword work in the few hours they had, hoping he could replace her, but she gave up on him, crying in frustration that she wouldn't be able to help save her father. He had patted her back, wondering at the strength of emotion she showed for her father.

Next to him, mounted on the only horse in Ornata, Vermont said, "Follow my lead out there. We can't afford to have you hurt."

Hands said, "You're not my dad."

Vermont looked down at the boy who was staring forward resolutely, "If you get hurt, I would be sad."

Hands said, "Oh, yeah? Are you going to cry?"

"Probably."

300

Hands frowned but was unable to insult such a blatant confession of affection with his usual wordSlaps. Vermont turned his eyes to the tall figure of Aihum who sat silently atop his wapiti, his great spear clutched in one hand, his eyes directed to the field, awaiting the signal.

Jalil waited next to Seketeme. They were ensconced in the wide crook of a tree, only twenty yards from the chopping Guardsmen. He held an arrow against the string of Alankwelait. He had practiced with it for the last two days. It sunk arrows deep into the wooden target, and now he felt its wood like it was alive. To the right and to the left, hidden in the trees' branches and behind their trunks were the Ornatan longeyes. Their five-pointed red or yellow leaves mixed into the yellow leaves of the LongBoughs. They held arrows against the strings of their bows, relaxed and pointed down, but their eyes were watching the Guard who were chopping at the LongBoughs, their ears turned to the call of their leader. Like an eagle flying in wide circles, waiting to see its prey, the longeyes craned forward from the neck, their fingers waiting like stretched wings.

Jalil's mind turned to his father, a Guard like these whom he would be fighting. The Guard knew what was coming. He could see their fear, the furtive way their eyes darted among the leaves, and hear the forced volume of their voices. He admired his dad. Dad had wanted to defend the country, the regnate, and Jalil. He did what he was told as a soldier. He had put himself, just as these soldiers did, in great danger knowing he might die. His father thought he was fighting for the good guys.

His father had been wrong though. The regnate wasn't defending the country. He was invading another land, fighting a people that fought to defend themselves. Those people were not evil; the regnate was the bad guy. He was the one that fought from the security of the stone fort with the Fels and Bellumites around him while the SubAgoran Guard had to chop the trees within bowshot of the wendigo, and live in the makeshift wooden outposts that were surrounded on three sides by the woods. His father was a brown-skinned Guard. That was why he died.

301

Seketeme reached toward the branch by his head, where eagles, hawks, and vultures perched, turning their heads with quick jerks. He pulled an owl from the branch, and after saying a few words to the night hunter, threw it in the air. Its wings pumped, and it shot out of the woods into the blue sky over the clearing.

A moment after the owl turned a circle through the clearing, Jalil saw a blue flame start, the small beginning of a fire, under the trees across the clearing, and then grow up into a torch as tall as a tree. The flame moved out of the forest into the muddy clearing. It furled around the outline of a boy. The flameMonsterBoy marched toward the first outpost.

The Guard didn't know what it was. At first they expected the figure in the midst of the flames to fall to its knees and die. What living thing can burn like that and survive? But the blue giant continued to march toward them, falling into the ditches they had dug, and then scrambling out the other side. After a minute, one of the captains called, and organized a team of archers who let off a volley of arrows. Five of the arrows hit the figure. One of the archers called, "A hit. I got him."

Someone else screamed, half curiosity, half terror, "Why doesn't he burn up?"

The figure did not stop his forward march. Some of the soldiers yelled that it was a demon. The resourceful captain had a trumpeter blow the signal for a Fel squad. In a moment they were out running, ten hard men. Their boots crushed the ground; their spears were leveled toward the boy. From the walls the rest of the men cheered, even those that were a half-mile away, working on the cutting down the trees. The squad hit the blueFlaming giant with their lances.

The lances erupted blue with flame and the men dropped them, yelling curses. They unsheathed their swords, and closed around him. They sprung at the word of their sergeant. Ten swords simultaneously swung toward the boy wrapped in blue flame, but the swords rebounded, and the boy was still standing. He jumped to the sergeant and grabbed his arm. The sergeant was embroiled in a moment, curling flame blossoming off him in every direction. There was a burst, and half of the men were on the ground. Those still

302

standing stepped away. They looked down at their fellow fighters, burnt on the ground, and their courage left them. They ran back toward the base. One of the men on the ground screamed, "It burns!"

The men in the outposts did not like the sound of their fellow Regnan screaming. It made everyone nervous. They didn't like seeing the best foot soldiers get swatted like flies. The captain of the second outpost was organizing his cavalry. The trumpeters gave their signal, but they were far from ready. Their horses had to be let out of the stable, saddled, and then run out. Meanwhile the little blue giant had gotten close enough that most of the arrows were hitting, but none of them did a thing, falling singed and useless a pace short of their target. The archers rested their bows and watched his march in growing terror.

The gate to the second outpost swung open, and a line of horses swung out, rounding the outpost and galloping the short distance to the figure, their lances aimed at him. As they struck the lances were consumed by flame, and the riders wrung their hands in anguish. Two fell off their mounts, and were lit by the flame. A brief scream erupted and then silence fell.

The archers and watchers on the fort wall had a clear view of the figure. It was a boy, a thin boy, covered in a roiling blue flame that towered above him, but did not burn him. He arrived at the first outpost, and he reached out and grabbed the logs, and they lit up in flame. He withdrew his hands, and the flame continued. Each stake lit up, and the entire outpost was covered in the hungry blue heat. The men started pouring over the pikes, climbing over one another to get over the log wall. One snagged his shirt on the pikes, and dangled. When they hit the ground they saw the Fire-Boy was not their only problem.

The trees seemed to open, and birds poured out down into the field, their beaks hammering the Regnan's eyes. Seketeme stepped out from behind the tree, advancing, followed by a line of wendigo longeyes. Their longteeth flew through the air, as thirsty for flesh as the birds that swirled in the sky. The Guard screamed in terror as their vision filled with the feathered flurries, and their bodies filled with longteeth. Those who still could, broke and ran for the open ground of the clearing.

Jalil turned the power of Alankwelait on the running Guard. The shot he envisioned was the one he shot, the arrows seeming to follow the path of his eyes, and he sent merciful arrows that pierced thighs and shoulders, putting the Guardsmen down while keeping them alive. He marveled at the wood of the bow that seemed to live and think with him, teaching him as he held it.

The surviving Guard ran toward the first outpost, until they saw that it was ablaze in blue. Their panic grew, and they turned to the second outpost.

Burt was with wendigo tenders, those who normally watched the wood rather than hunted in it, but even they had been called to this battle. With them was a wolfpack, a herd of wapiti and four sinuous dashes of pale fur that hid among the upper boughs that the wendigo told him were kwenishkwenayas, mountain lions. When the longeyes unleashed their longteeth, the tenders urged the creatures and charged, accompanied by the bellows of the wapiti, the war yammerings of the wolves, and the eerie screams of the pumas. Burt did not follow them, but stood transfixed. He did not want to go out there where arrows and steel flew about randomly. He clutched the last tree trunk, and hoped no one noticed him.

In the outpost the captain was screaming at the Guard, ordering them to maintain formation as they retreated toward the second outpost, where they could regroup, but the soldiers, Fels and Guard, were running here and there, and many of them fell. Longteeth picked out those who strayed too close to the trees in their frenzy to get away from the blue figure.

They did not expect the wendigo to fight in the open. They assumed that the wendigo would always shoot from the cover of the trees. When they reached the second outpost they called to one another, trying to figure out which of their friends had survived. The flame monster continued his march toward them. The line behind him advanced as well, and the arrows now fell into the second outpost like rain. The soldiers tucked themselves under the walls, or got inside the little cabin-like structures. The braver soldiers were throwing rocks at the flaming boy, and one of these hit him, knocking him down, but he rose undamaged, flaming, and continued toward them.

"What is it?" The scream of some frantic soldier echoed into the starry sky. They had never fought such a thing, and though they talked in fear and hate about wendigo magics, never had they seen them. The thing, the fireMonster, was unstoppable. No weapon could strike it, and with a single hand it had burned down their whole outpost. Those that had run from the first to the second outpost felt no security. Why would a second wooden outpost form any more protection than the first? Soon a mass of them, shields crowded over their heads, sprung from the back door, ignoring the commands of the captains, racing toward the fort.

When the vice regnate and regnate, watching from the fort, saw that it was likely the Guard would lose both of the outposts, the regnate ordered the Fels and Bellumites to arm. A team of men heaved the great wooden gates open. The Fels organized themselves in a minute and were trotting out the gate. Behind them walked the dread Bellumites with their thunderPipes and bomb catapults.

The regnate ordered his horse saddled. Nickson went through the same preparations, taking care to keep pace with the regnate so that he could be beside him in the melee and slip his steel sideways under the his breastplate. He would remove his helmet and look the regnate in the eyes. "Hey, Grant. Looks like you missed something."

The Fels were a vast and solid square of red that swept across the wide clearing impervious to the pecking of the falcons. The wendigo longeyes had pushed back the Guard, stepping far out into the treeless space, and they were scattered and solitary. The Fels swooped out, surrounding them. The longeyes fought hard, but surrounded by spears and the long steel of the Fels, separated from each other, many were cut down.

The Bellumites loaded their thunderPipes and fired their bombs. The bombs they directed at the fireGiant. The red bombs hit the blue flame. Purples explosions resounded. The blue flame was not extinguished but the boy was knocked back by each powerful burst.

When Aihum saw the fort gates open and the Fels stream out, he whispered into his wapiti's ear and it leapt forward. Behind him came the Magnasylvan longeyes, galloping toward the open doors of the fort. The Fels who guarded it saw them too late, their eyes being turned to the Fel troops progress through the field toward the fireBoy and the wendigo archers. They fired a barrage of arrows toward the train of charging wendigo and yelled for the gates to be shut.

The Magnasylvan longeye force sped toward them, and the gate guard redoubled their effort, pulling on the massive gates, and shouting. Those inside heard only panic, and hastened their arming.

The Magnasylvans urged their wapiti to speed, and launched spears at the Guard struggling with the fort's gate. In a moment the wendigo arrived. Aihum charged into the middle of the unfortunate soldiers pushing the gate, his spear held aloft and plunging down, a hungry hawk diving for mice. The Fels had never fought a wendigo like this. He was large and strong, but moved fast and precisely like a cat. He smiled too, for the wendigo of Magnasylva loved close fighting, the heave of muscle, the grunting of effort, and the cleaving of flesh.

In the first charge, the vice regnate found himself separated from the regnate. Some Fels, not Nickson's, surrounded the regnate, fighting to protect him. They retreated as the wooden spears and clubs beat at them. They were trapped against the wall, the only avenue out the door into the tower.

Nickson yelled, "The regnate, secure the regnate." The double meaning would be clear to his own men.

The main group of Fels had surrounded the regnate, and was fighting the Magnasylvans in the center of the great courtyard of the fort. One of the Fels, a confederate to Nickson's plan, saw an opportunity. He moved toward the regnate, a dagger in his hand. He planted his foot so as to drive the blade up under Grant's breastplate and waited for a moment when everyone was distracted. Vermont, occupied with three Fels, saw the movement, and yelled, "Aihum, the regnate!"

Aihum saw the exposed dagger, and threw his heavy spear. The great point hit the helmet of the traitorous Fel, punching through the metal and ending the Fel's plan and any other thoughts in his head. The regnate, thinking the spear had been for him, darted through the door into the squat four-story tower that stood in the middle of the wide courtyard. The Fels followed after him.

Vermont yelled, "Aihum, I need to get to that door!"

The Magnasylvan surged, now working with a great club that shattered the swords of the Fels. The Magnasylvans pushed the Fels back into the rooms in the walls of the fort. The human soldiers melted back, jumping onto staircases toward the battlements. The Magnasylvans won their way to the door through which the regnate had retreated and turned their strong spears against the Fels. Vermont and Hands flung themselves at the heavy door. It was locked, but Hands was prepared, and while the grunting and screaming continued, he popped his wire into the lock, and worked his magic. Nickson screamed, "The regnate!"

Hands worked frantically, doing his best to keep his hand steady as arrows thunked into the wood all around him. An arrow struck the door by his face. He breathed deeply and stilled his nerves. His wire caught, he twisted, and the door sprung open. There were more Fels in the room thrusting spears and swords at them. Vermont stepped forward, his sword held at ready. With short strokes he knocked aside their blades, and stabbed them with incisive thrusts.

Vermont led the way up a stone staircase. Red coats filled the path in front of them. Their strength and training, however, were nothing against Vermont. The sword work of the Citan was exquisite, the blade a dancing multiplication of crescents, the setting sun reflected in wind blown water. His blade darted, probed, and bit, while their blades clamored and clashed and could find no flesh to eat. Behind him was Hands, wondering if he could go back to the shelter of the trees.

When they pushed by the last Fel, they were in a small stone room, facing a man with a white beard and small serious eyes. In his hands was a great sword.

WickBaron Vermont said. "Regnate, we are here to rescue you."

The regnate said, "WickBaron Vermont?"

"Yes. There is a plot."

"Explain to me." The regnate spoke with directness of someone used to being listened to, but also with a worldly experience, as if anything was possible. "What are you doing? You just cut down five Fels to get to me? The wendigo are attacking, and you are attacking my guard. Explain what is going on."

Vermont struck his head. "Regnate, there is much to tell, and no time. Your life is in danger here, and your only hope of survival is with the wendigo you have fought against."

"Who is it that is against me here?"

Vermont shouted, "Nickson. He corrupted the Fels."

Nickson, meanwhile, had run the length of the battlements with his Fels circling the fort to the back entrance to the tower. He had seen Vermont in the scrum and realized that the wendigo were not going to kill the regnate, but save him, and if Vermont got to the regnate, Nickson would lose everything.

On the second floor he looked around. His Fels watched him, awaiting his word. "The time is now. Kill him. One hundred dollars to the one that lands the killing blow."

In a terrible, treacherous moment, Fels turned on their loyal brothers, dipping surprising daggers into the throats of those too honest to consider assassination no matter the offer. The good Fels found their confusion multiplied, "Wendigo in the fort, my brother stabbing me." They died before understanding.

Inside, the regnate was still looking at Vermont, a puzzled expression on his face, when the door behind him burst open. A Fel nearly as big as a grolf popped through it. He heaved a spear at the regnate. For someone with white hair, the regnate's feet were quick, and he dodged to the side. The spear thudded into the stonewall behind him.

The regnate said, "You're telling me I should escape to the wendigo?"

Meanwhile his sword worked with authority. The big Fel didn't last long after he threw his spear. Vermont, who was facing in the opposite direction, trying to press two more redcoats back through the door, shouted, "They offer you sanctuary. I think they will

308

expect favors later, like the ending of this war, but it's better than dying here. Your people need you to live."

The regnate shrugged as if to say it was a lot to take in. He said, "These Fels attacking me argues your point most eloquently." He slammed and locked the back door in the face of two more charging red coats, and turned to the staircase. "Stand back, your regnate would pass," he shouted. The Fels, used as they were to listening to his commands, fell back.

Behind them Nickson shouted, "It's you or him now!" They remembered they were no longer obeying the regnate, and surged forward. They found their old master's sword sharp, and Vermont was not fighting with wood himself. They backed up. The regnate and the wickBaron advanced. Behind them, amazed to be in such a situation, was Hands, cowering behind the Citans.

Nickson saw three of his Fels go down before he shouted, "Fall back to the courtyard. We will overwhelm them with numbers."

The regnate and Vermont, knowing that their enemies planned to overwhelm them in the open space still pushed forward. They chased the retreating Fels out of the staircase door right into the swords of the others. The regnate and Vermont used this momentary confusion to great advantage, darting their blades about so that the cluster of red coats at the door sank to the ground pierced multiple times. They vaulted this first bunch, and they found themselves surrounded by ten more Fels. These Fels were not just armed with swords. Seven leveled long spears at the trio.

"A small challenge for your sword work, WickBaron Vermont." The regnate smiled as he moved in a circle. The two men used swords like magic wands, they spun and leapt and multiplied in the air, and the many Fels, trained as they were in the art of the swordfight, found themselves bewildered by the dexterity of the man they had protected for so long. Many Fels crumbled to the ground, caught by the stinging blades of their regnate and the wickBaron.

Nickson shouted, "Enough."

As the redcoats stepped back, Hands looked around. Slain, draped on the ground like the butcher's carcasses were the great wapiti of the Magnasylvans, and their longeye riders were spread out next to their steeds. The courtyard was full of Fels. Some were carrying bow and arrow, trained on them, others carried melee weapons. They totaled at least one hundred.

Nickson stood in the middle of the circle, facing the regnate. In his hand was a sword with a square end. He said, "I will show you how you fight a regnate. The first thing is mental strength. You must believe in yourself." As he spoke an orange light crisply lit his silhouette. Then he sprang forward, his sword a long rectangle with which he hacked and sawed. The two fell back before his onslaught. As they retreated, he kicked out, his heavy boot slamming into the thigh of Vermont and the wickBaron crashed to the ground. He turned his attention to the regnate. Suddenly red-orange flames flowed off his square blade. He heaved and slashed, three times, blows the regnate barely turned, before he broke off the regnate's blade at the hilt. The regnate backed up until his back was against the tower wall. The steward placed the square tip of his sword against the regnate's throat. The flames of the blade sizzled on the regnate's neck, burning the skin.

"You always thought I was all about serving you."

"I knew you were ambitious, Nickson."

"How I have longed for this moment. You always so authoritative, never dreaming that you should fear me, that I am capable of destroying you. Now you know."

"What about the other houses, Nickson? They will not give you any power when you killed me."

"No one will tell them about this."

The regnate shrugged. Out of the corner of his eyes he was watching the Sub who had come in with Vermont to rescue him. He regretted not being able to protect him, but dying in itself would not be so bad. It would be better than the responsibility of ruling, he thought, as Nickson's steel pressed against his throat.

Meanwhile, the flaming boy had reached the second outpost. At the first contact he had felt great thrills of exhilaration as the flames of the manusignis lit on him. He had chanted the Cantos. The god was real, he was present, he had taken up the cause of the abused, and his instrument was Shyheem. Like the blue flames that

310

washed over his skin, waves of joyful adoration washed through his heart.

Now, the exhilaration was gone, and he fought great blankets of exhaustion that covered him. The red fireballs that crashed into him endlessly were slowing him down. He did not feel physical tiredness, but a sadness, as if a great hole had opened up in him where his hope used to be. The power that he wielded seemed smaller than necessary. He felt it lessening, the heat and strength of the flames.

He called out, "Oh, Illumen, do not forget me. Do not forget these wendigo." Yet he felt it dwindling. It was going to happen. He would lose the flame. Then the fireballs would kill him. The wendigo, and their great forest would be cut down. The wendigo, like the Subs, would be made to work for the Regnans.

Seketeme had rallied a group of Ornatan longeyes to him back under the boughs of the trees. He saw that the Bellumite firebombs were weakening Shyheem. He cried a command, the Ornatan longeyes sprung forward, running after him. His long loping stride carried him onto the middle of the muddy clearing. Jalil ran after them.

They were headed straight for the Bellumites. The Fels who were marching around the perimeter of the clearing, trying to beat back the loose ring of longeyes, saw them first, and sent a squad to intercept them. Their leader, a captain, rose up in his saddle as they approached, his lance cocked back, but before he could move Seketeme sprang into the air and unleashed his spear like a snake striking, and the hard wood broke through the plate of armor on the captain's chest. In a moment, Seketeme was on the captain's tall black horse, galloping toward the Bellumites.

Jalil said to himself, "Seketeme eats Fels for breakfast."

He charged, along with the other longeyes, into the midst of the Fel cavalry. Because he was small, and his dark skin blended with the upturned earth of the clearing, the Fels missed him, and he was able to run out of the side of the big melee all in one piece. He had seen at least two wendigo who would not be able to do the same. He raced after Seketeme.

The Bellumites had seen the charging longeye and turned their thunderPipes toward him. The thunderPipes cracked, leaving trails of flame in their wake. Somehow Seketeme was able to urge the beast under him into tightly angled swerves so that the bullets just missed. He reached the first Bellumite and skewered him, but the spear would not come out.

One of the Bellumites smiled and pointed his thunderPipe at Seketeme's chest.

Jalil screamed, running to the side of the field, pointing, frantically miming the shooting of arrows and pointing at the Bellumites. The longeyes in the shelter of the LongBoughs saw Seketeme's situation, and diverted their longteeth toward the Bellumites.

Seketeme's attack had stopped them from bombing the Fire-Boy, but his exhaustion still grew. His flame faltered. The soldiers saw it and took heart. The fire monster was losing power. They shouted as he collapsed. He looked at them, and longed for the coolness of their steel cutting his heart and cooling his soul. He was hot through and through, and he just wanted to rest.

He felt a hand under his head and heard a familiar voice, "Manusignis. Pray. Only Illumen can save us. Younger brother god, these ones who have longed for your coming, whose hearts are lifted like the crocus toward the sun. As you have come, do not depart again. Your light shines with the hope of the people."

Shyheem did not want to fight. He wanted to rest, and he tried to ignore the voice. The hard voice called, "Manusignis, you are needed. Manusignis, pray."

He barely shook his head. "No. Over, please."

It said, "It's not over. Pray, manusignis."

Shyheem whispered, "Why is it me? I don't want to think about it anymore. It's too sad."

The castOut said, "The road to joy passes through Sheol, and in the maws of the grolf I found light."

Shyheem heard him from a great distance. He saw the field like it was in a fog, and knew why the man wanted him to pray. He didn't want to pray though. He wanted to lie there, until the heat was gone. He didn't want to fight anymore. The fire burnt him. All his failures, all his proud judgment of the wendigo, all the times he had told Hands to go to Sheol came back to him, and argued against him. He was not worthy of the flame.

Worse, he felt the force of evil in the world; he felt the hate of the wendigo, the hate of the men. He felt the lust for power that egged in men's guts, the greed for wealth that shackled the hearts. It was in him, it was everyone. Living was too much, like walking under the mountain. Fighting it. Why?

Burt was watching Angen bend over Shyheem from the trees. He saw three Fels who crept through the field toward Angen and Shyheem, their swords in hand. He thought to yell, to move, but the terror overwhelmed him and paralyzed him. They were close, and he knew they would strike soon and kill them both.

He yelled. "Angen!" Still the man was bent over Shyheem unaware of the threat.

Burt shook his head, angry with himself, and started running, bellowing, " For SubAgora!"

In his hand was a simple club, and the three Fels saw him and turned. Burt felt their hard eyes taking in his size, and weapon, his heaving breath as he tried to sprint. What was he doing charging three full-grown soldiers? The soldiers, seeing a round little boy brandishing a stick, started to laugh.

But he couldn't bear the thought of them getting Shyheem. He ran on, ready to die if it would save his friend. He reached them, and slammed his club into the first's knees.

"Ouch!" The other two looked on surprised. "Don't just stand there. It hit me! Kill it." They shoved their swords at him, but Burt managed to jump back. Then he tripped, and found himself grabbed. He looked up into an evil grin. He was going to die.

In another part of the field Jalil found himself within striking distance of the nearest Bellumite, and swung wildly. The Bellumite dodged, grasping the bow in his flaming hands, and threw it to the ground. "What is this? A Sub, so far from SubAgora? I think you should have stayed where it was safe." Jalil struck out, but the Bellumite caught his fist. The fingers flared red around his fist and it burnt, and the Bellumite smiled.

"Bellum is strength. Worship him!"

313

Jalil curled his other hand into a fist, and using the Bellumite's grasp as a fulcrum swung it down into that smile, once, twice. On the second impact, he found his hand released. He picked up the bow and clubbed the Bellumite's head. The flames faded from the priest's hands, the smile left his face, replaced by a dazed nothing look. Jalil wheeled to see that Seketeme had been joined by other wendigo, fighting the powerful flames of the Bellumites, too close now for the thunderPipes to fire.

In the fort, Nickson said, "You are too weak to be regnate."

The regnate said, "Ask the Fels that have tasted my blade about my weakness, if you can find one who still has the power of speech."

Nickson laughed, "Your weakness was in your heart. These wendigo should have been squashed completely. They are an infestation, and we have the strength to drive them out, but you dilly dally out here with lumbering the forest, and talking about possible peaces."

Meanwhile, Shyheem heard a voice from faraway, "Who are we, that you have called us? Are we strong, that you give us strength? No, we are weak. Are we good, that you give us goodness?"

Shyheem whispered heavily, "No, we are bad."

The castOut said, "Yet you have chosen us. We are made little by the way in which you make us great. Fill us with your light."

Shyheem thought along with the prayer, and found that he burnt anew, incandescent, the flame close to his skin and glowing, and he took off marching across the field.

The three Fels had lined it up so one would hold Burt, and another would chop through him. There had been a brief discussion about whether he could chop through such a chunky midsection in one blow and he intended to prove he could.

As he drew back his big sword with the chop, a blue flame seized him and burnt through in a moment, before catching the other two torturers. Burt dropped to the ground, breathing a big sigh of relief, and wondering if anyone had a spare pair of pants his size. He watched the blue giant stride on. He knew he had come at the right moment, that they would have killed Angen and Shyheem without his nearly suicidal charge.

The mounted Fels, seeing Shyheem, steered clear, for they had watched his earlier march, the scorched wake left in his passing. They were too slow to escape, for now great streams of flame spouted out, like dragon necks, and brought them down. The boy reached the fort and brought his hands up, heaving the force of his flame against the stonewall and it exploded, the rocks turned to dust by the heat of his flame.

The Fels jumped when the walls around them erupted, burning them with flying cinder. They turned and saw great fingers of flame swirling about, lighting on them, and they dropped their weapons and ran. Nickson jumped from the gust of blue flame, dodging in the smoke and dust, just to survive.

In a moment the regnate, Vermont, and Hands were isolated from the others by smoke. The men looked around amazed.

Hands was quicker to grasp the meaning of the situation, and he was up and running, thankful to be alive. "Come on," he called. He jumped through the hole in the wall. The regnate jogged after him, and in a moment they were in the open field. Hands and Vermont were moving toward the woods. The regnate said, "You're sure about these wendigo?"

Hands kept running. If the regnate wanted to try and convince more of his Fels that they shouldn't kill him, that was fine, but Hands didn't want to be around to see if he succeeded this time. Vermont said, "They will shelter you!"

"Why should they shelter me?"

"You have to trust me."

The regnate grimaced. It was not honorable, he felt, to ask for mercy or help from the wendigo, who were his enemies, and who had fought him with honor.

The solid column of over one thousand Fels headed toward them, firing arrows. Three Bellumites were stooped and running toward them as well, with one pausing to raise his thunderPipe and try a shot every few seconds. Grant had no choice. He followed the two rescuers. The great leafy boughs of the forest opened for him and he entered Ornata.

Seketeme was terrible among the Bellumites. His spear rose and sunk implacable and steady as the blacksmith's hammer, his teeth snarled like a wolf. The Bellumites were unable to fire their catapult with him in close proximity, and they found their fire fists weak before the fury of the wendigo. They called a retreat. The Fels that still marched in orderly formation saw that the fort wall was burst, and the Fels streaming from it, and suddenly their confidence was unsettled. They were the only Regnan forces left in the clearing, and they could not withstand the arrows coming from all sides, unable to shoot back, their vision obscured by the beating wings of flocks of birds. Their leader turned them toward the plain, away from the trees that belched warriors and beasts at them.

Angen carried Shyheem cradled in his arm. The boy was unconscious; his body almost too hot to hold. The castOut whispered prayers. He knew that some manusignis had died after using the flames. He rushed under the boughs of the trees bellowing in Wendee, "I need the healers!" In a moment one of the small Desiccan wendigo was with them, pouring green juice into the boy's mouth. The healer examined the boy, felt the heat of his body, saw the unseeing look in his glazed eyes and shook his head, murmuring in Wendee.

Jalil and Seketeme stood watching the soldiers running for the plains, escaping from the clearing and the shadow of the trees. Jalil was shouting in triumph, but Seketeme looked around them and shook his head slowly. They were surrounded by longeyes lying down, holding their life sap in with unsteady hands. Some already gazed unseeing at the distant stars. Seketeme stooped and pulled up a groaning wendigo, and carried him toward the forest.

When they got under the trees, Hands allowed the regnate and the WickBaron to get in front of him. Behind them the sounds of the battle instantly dimmed, as though they happened in another place. Ahead of them on the path stood the sachem. The crown of yellow leaves blazed on his head. By his side was Kwenemuk, smiling.

Sachem Askasktuhon spoke, "Regnate Theodore Grant, ruler of the free country, welcome to my forest. Though you have not been its friend, it offers refuge now in your moment of need. Such

316

is the grace of the forest. There is also great hope for us wendigo and for our woods that by this act of undeserved kindness, we gain an ally, a man who will end the onslaught of the axe against us and our trees."

The regnate knelt on the path. "If you do not kill me now that you have me in your hands, I owe you a great debt. I am a man of honor, and I will repay the debt."

29. Ornatan

If I fall on the paths of the mountains,
If the craggy tors—like grolf arms take me—
If Mishipeshu drags me down to the forest fountains,
Or sends his longteeth, the wolves and puma, for me—
If the humans angry and fierce from their stone inns,
If the metal men use their earthVeins to pierce me—
Do not bury me in the grolf's rockland;
Do not bury me in the humans' grassland.
Oh, please don't let them bury me in the townland.
Bury me in the grove of the Mishipeshu
Where dark heat breeds life out of death,
and I will feed the forest.

————————

Jalil felt someone shake his shoulder and opened his eyes to a lattice of browning leaves. A wendigo was barking at him. He sat up and rubbed his eyes. He was only a few steps from the clearing, burrowed down among the fallen leaves under a perimeter tree. Wendigo were moving about, and the one that had woken him pulled him up, and into the clearing.

Spread about him was a panorama of the effects of the battle, broken spears, dislodged stone blocks, seared logs, and coppered arrows mixed in with fallen wendigo whose head foliage withered, as their life-sap spilled from new holes. By them were dead men who stared straight ahead but saw nothing. Jalil bent his eyes away from their ghostly looks.

The wendigo were lifting corpses onto stretchers, and carrying them into the woods in a steady line. Jalil walked over to a stretcher, but another wendigo shouted at him, and he dropped the stretcher. The same wendigo pointed toward the other end of the clearing. Jalil walked that way. Soon he was helping to break down the remaining logs in the outposts. While he worked, he recalled the night before, the moments of glory, and the sadness that followed.

The clearing changed. The stray swords, armor scraps, pots, and wooden furniture of the soldiers were gone, and the dead wendigo had been taken away. The wendigo were digging a dotted collection of round holes in the clearing. They dropped things into the holes with gentle hands, filling them back over with dark loamy soil dug from stream banks. While they planted, they hummed faintly.

They worked without stopping, without talking. Every once in a while, a hint of promised Spring entered their song, but it was not long before the line of grass-woven stretchers re-entered their thoughts, and the melancholy returned. The clearing was the wendigo's again, but it had cost them many longeyes. The sun crested the mountains, and Jalil realized how tired and hungry he was. He walked back through the clearing, into the woods. The wendigo shuffled with him. A wendigo handed them some fruit. They washed the blood from their hands, and began to eat.

The sun was setting, and as it touched the horizon, a wailing went up, as lonely as the honk of a flockless goose. The Sub went to find who was wailing. When he got close, a longeye stepped from behind a tree, barring his way with his bow. He shook his head and pointed Jalil back the way he had come. The grasping cries continued long into the night, and it made the boy remember his father. The keening sought home like the wind among the mountain peaks. He went to sleep dreaming that the souls of the men wandered on into a different land, a place that was as full of light and dark as this one, but where the gods were closer, their faces as familiar as old friends.

He awoke to a hand on his forehead, and looked up and saw the thin cheeks and small, glinting eyes of Kwenemuk. *You fought bravely.* Her leaves were candescent orange with the early morning rays, and her copper face was smiling.

Jalil said, "Do you know where the others are?"

Yes. I was sent to find you.

They marched off into the wood, where the criss-crossing trail ducked under bushes, crossed streams, and wended its way up huge

319

rocks. Soon they found themselves in more familiar territory. They stumbled into a bump on the forest floor, which turned out to be Hands burrowed under a pile of the leaves. He looked dirty too and Jalil guessed he'd been recruited to the clean up as well. They woke him.

"Where's Burt?" Jalil asked.

Hands explained, "He's working in the sick groves. Shyheem is there too. He's pretty sick."

Kwenemuk led them to the tree where the Citans waited under guard. Hands sprung up the tree ladder. When he sprang onto the bouncy floor of the nest, Clarie shouted. She jumped across the small room and tackled him. She punched him in the chest twice before he pushed her off.

"What's your problem?"

"Dad's back! You got him."

Hands said, "Aihum, Vermont, and Shyheem got him."

She said, "They wouldn't have done it if you didn't tell them to."

He shrugged.

The regnate stood, bobbing on the thin-branch floor. He felt unsettled. It was a strange experience to be in the tree, a man floating among tree leaves. It was even stranger to find himself in debt to Subs. The Subs were bad mannered, outer-ringers, and dark-skinned, and the boy Hands had no respect, yet his daughter watched the boy with admiration. WickBaron Vermont also respected the brown-skinned Subs. The world was changing, suddenly. The very ringWalls of Urba were crashing all around him. Change was part of life. He tried to view the current situation with that same degree of cosmopolitan acceptance.

"Thank you, SubAgorans. Clarie has told me of your contributions in my service. I owe you everything."

Hands said, "You owe the wendigo everything."

Theodore Grant said, "I do not disagree with you. I think that it is possible for me to owe you and the wendigo everything. They have said that I am to call off the war. This for a long time has been my intention.

320

"I fear that it won't work. As we speak, Nickson is marching back to Urba, where he will gather the eight houses and get them to declare him acting regnate, claiming that I am either dead, or bewitched by the magic of the wendigo. Then his agents will be everywhere, and I will have no way to return to my place without facing assassination, and claims of mental incapability."

Jalil said, "So it was all for nothing?"

Grant shrugged, "The Regnan army has retreated and they will march all the way to Urba. The wendigo may have won little in my allegiance, for I am a regnate without a country but they have also won months to rebuild, and re-arm."

The regnate asked them to tell him about their adventures. It took a while, but he listened patiently. He had not known that SubAgorans were capable of such courage and cleverness, and he began to understand some of his daughter's admiration for the boys.

He said, "So you did all this to warn me, and then save me?"

Jalil said, "That's our duty as Regnans."

Hands said, "Not cause I care about you. I just wanted you to behead those Fels."

The regnate laughed. "Even that ambition has failed."

Hands shrugged, "I don't know, Shyheem got a bunch of them. Burning is fine."

The trees themselves seemed to bear the weight of the Ornatan casualties. Their boughs drooped, and their five pointed leaves turned from red and yellow to brown. The fall breeze turned old, blowing toward the dead months. Under the branches, among the injured wendigo, was one thin boy whose skin had gone from brown to gray. His eyes were open, but he was not in them. He twitched, and cried out, and his body was burning to the touch. The woodwarblers sponged his body and quietly poured their restoratives into his mouth but gagging spasms pushed most of the medicine back out.

By him was the black-bearded Angen. He shook his head and murmured, again and again. He had heard the stories, and he knew

321

that it was prayer that would work best. The luminology explained that the suffering after the lighting of the flame was the cost. The manusignis experienced the suffering of those whom he championed. Watching the boy's face twist and flinch, Angen realized how much of their suffering the wendigo held inside themselves. Their stories about the pain of seeing and feeling a tree fall were shortened, the emotion left out, their hatchet-straight faces a dam holding back a river of sorrow. He feared that the boy was close to death; he knew that it was possible to die from too much heartPain, the body relinquishing its hold on life like a hand releasing a hot iron. Certain stars said that death was a blessing. It was a weighty responsibility to be a manusignis. If the boy survived it would be far harder for him to ignite again. He would know how he would have to pay.

Angen questioned himself, looking down at the small beads of sweat popping out of the boy's forehead. He had brought him where his flame could spring to life. He had forced the child down the path. He imagined that the boy experienced again and again the axe against the trunk of his life, the Bellumite flames eating into the crevices of his soul.

Occasionally Burt stopped and watched his sick friend. The more experienced healers, Desiccan woodwarblers, focused on the fireBoy, but Burt stood back and watched, worrying, when he paused from washing a sick wendigo. Mostly he moved from bed to bed, mopping a brow, feeding the wendigo their strange stews and juices. There were no mindscouts in the sick grove to translate, but the head healer would nod and gesture the actions of feeding, washing, or redressing and Burt understood him. It was easy to guess since many of the tasks were regular in the sick grove. The healer, a short wendigo, with sparse leaves on his small head, scrubbed the boy's bristling head, his fingers hard as oak and Burt understood this to be encouragement.

Burt had a strong sense of purpose among the sick, his eyes scanning them for any need, watching the wood warblers and following their lead, speaking gently in his Sub dialect to the wood people. He learned to say, "Welaxen," to encourage them. He could tell what some of them needed, and he watched the administration of the different juices, and could predict who needed what when.

Hands, Jalil, and Clarie entered the grove of the sick, with its high serious trees, and soft ferns, and saw Shyheem, his body seemingly smaller and thinner than ever before, his limbs lying like rags on the thick moss. He lay in the rows of injured wendigo. Their friend had done far more than they; he had been the main weapon of the wendigo attack, and now he was sick. They asked Angen what was wrong.

Angen patiently explained, though his voice was weary, how Shyheem entered into the suffering of those for whom his flame burned. When they asked when he would get better, he said that he didn't know. He could only ask Illumen to remember his servant and show mercy. They should do the same.

Burt said, "If he's serving the Illumen, how come Illumen makes him sick?"

Hands said, "It's stupid."

Angen said, "I do not know why but only that it is."

Clarie shook her head and punched Hands in the lower back, as a way of expressing her disapproval. Hands, for once, did not respond.

A feast was called, for though many had died, the armies of Regna were pushed back from the wood, and the wendigo now held the regnate. Spread out in a meadow amidst the trees were woven mats, with red and yellow fruit, and a series of fires straddled by roasting meats, covered in herbs that only the wendigo know how to find. They had been cooking since noon, and the meat flaked off the bone. The wendigo fed them the fruit, which burst in the mouth, juices pouring out, and the meat, which melted against the tongue until the Subs could eat no more, but lay contented on the grasses, staring up at the wind-waved branches

Clarie had got a handful of raspberries, which she periodically forced upon Hands. Kwenemuk came across the field to sit with them. Two narrow straps held up her shirt of bark. Her dusky shoulders shone in the evening light, and Jalil found himself wondering whether her skin was yellow or green? Maybe copper? It was a fascinating color, a shimmery multi-flection like the sun among the wind blown tree leaves.

I'll translate for you?

"Yes, please." She sat down by him, and he moved a little as she sat until his arm touched against hers. She didn't move away.

Askasktuhon said, *These braves held their spears like candles, and ran into the heavy wind, which rained down longteeth on them. Those longteeth have bitten their hearts. Though we are heavy, though the leaves of the trees remember them with their color, yet we shall not overlong be heavy. For that which dies, brings life, and the forest lives on. Our enemy has no heart, and will not stop in his iron schemes, and we must remember that these longeyes died to protect Ornata, and this is the best reason to die, and we must carry on their fight. In a way, this sadness is not sadness at all, but happiness. Those who have fallen would not change what they have done, and we should not wallow too long. One battle has been won, the war will go on.*

The gathered wendigo murmured in response, their applause sounding like the wind among the trees.

We have among us three boys from the lowly places of Urba, what are called beggars in their city, their regnate tells us.

At this, Burt whispered, "I'm not a beggar!"

Hands said, "I'm a thief, not a beggar."

Sachem Askasktuhon continued, *They discovered a plot to kill their sachem, and have since, in the effort to find and warn him, fallen into the hand of the assassins, been ensconced in a prison deep under the earth. From there they freed not only themselves, but our own son, the son of Xinkwelepay, the longest-eye Seketeme, and a Northern grolf. The chaos of the wild was unleashed into their dungeon, and Seketeme escaped, and is returned to us.* Great applause greeted this, the trees shaking a million leaves.

The one who freed him they call Hands, for he was a thief in the city. Hands nodded and smiled around at the group. *He is the one who advised us to capture the regnate. What that means for the future of this war is still not clear, but we have shown strength, for we have captured their ruler, and sent them running across the plain.* Many of the wendigo were up, cheering. *We name this SubAgoran Nahenemuk, the clever raccoon.* The wendigo cheered and Clarie jumped up and shouted.

324

Also in his group is one they call Burt. This one we also honor, for while he fought by the tree-tenders, he intervened at the moment of need, risking his life against three human soldiers to save a friend, a friend whose warFire is more powerful than ten grolfs. Of him I speak later. He has also served us in our sick grove, ministering to the sick wendigo as carefully as a grandmother. Him we give the wendigo name Munhake, the groundhog, for he loves comfort. The wendigo cheered, especially the group of Dessican wendigo who had been working alongside Burt in the sick grove.

Lastly, we recognize Jalil. This one has learned to love the wendigo ways, though his father died in the war against us. In his quick feet and strong fists, in his fearless fighting, and biting use of the great bow Alankwelait, we see a longeye in the making. Him we name Temetet, the wolf pup. The longeyes were heard loudest now, uttering jubilant war cries.

Meanwhile another of their group was taken to North Temple, to become a FireBoy. He studied there, until Angen saw him. Angen was then our only friend from all the Regnan lands. He stole the boy and carried him over the Appalacha Mountains to Magnasylva and from thence to here. You do not need me to describe the power that this young one wields, how the forces of Regnan have left Ornata, and run terrified across the barren openness of the Segundan plain. They fear to speak of the thing that they have seen, the fingers of their god reaching through this little human toward the dark-hearted.

Yet now he is close to death, overwhelmed with the faith he has spent in our cause. Mishipeshu, do not let him die for good. Golden Eagle Spirit, see him. We have more battles to fight. Here Askasktuhon paused allowing time for his words to travel to the gods. The wendigo tilted their heads back, looking toward the hollow expanse beyond the shelter of the trees, hoping their thoughts reached the All-Seeing One. Then the sachem continued. *Him we do not presume to give a wendigo name, for he belongs to the light god.*

He drew his breath, and continued. *We will honor these far-travelers now by making them honorary members of the Ornatan wendigo.*

A group of longeyes came up from behind and hefted the boys onto their shoulders. The trees clapped a furious crescendo. The boys were sat on the long log from which the pacing sachem spoke, and told to strip their shirts. An old wendigo moved forward, with a large wooden palette. On it was a long needle cut from a river reed, and two pools of dye. It would have hurt if they had not been handed gourds full of hot burning stuff that they were forced to drink by the cheering wendigo. Drinking it they felt stronger and wilder, and the needle in their backs was only a scratching. They could watch the art appear on the backs of their friends. The raccoon tattooed on Hands' back shot a knowing look through his bandit mask, three of his fingered paws planted on the earth, while it held one dexterous fore-paw ready for whatever puzzle or trap came next.

On Jalil's back a small sized wolf emerged as the artist plied his needle. The wolfpup's head poised close to the ground; its legs wound up under it; teeth bared. It was a powerful, elegant looking animal, holding in tremendous energy. Burton was decorated with a thicker animal, a woodchuck in the midst of the grass. The animal looked like a caring friend with warm fur. As the work was going around, wendigo gathered behind them, encouraging the artist and advising him. When it was finished the sachem leapt to his place again.

I present three new Ornatans. Great cheering erupted, their wendigo names chanted.

Then the wendigo got up to dance. There was a beat, like a thousand tiny cymbals beating, and another, a stomping bass. The bass came from the landing of the longeyes' feet, and the cymbals were the leaves of the tree, shaking to the song. They danced with hands up, their heads swiveling slowly, as if they were trees shook and thrown about by a mighty wind. And their feet moved with power, together, stomp, stomp, and their hands flailed against the evening sky. There was no singing, or any song, but the beat alone.

Kwenemuk took Jalil by the hand, and pulled him up. He tried to sit back down, but she laughed and pulled him into the middle of the dancing throng, and the rhythm caught him up. He tried to imitate the willowy moves of Kwenemuk. Hands joined in and so did Clarie. They put their hands up, and waved them slowly then quickly, ignoring the disturbed eyes of the regnate. Even Burt wasn't able to resist the powerful beat, and found himself throwing his arms up. They danced for hours until they fell down, breathing heavily, and then the wendigo sang, only a few at a time, and though Kwenemuk was asleep, her leafy head resting on Jalil's

326

shoulder, they knew that the song was about the lost longeyes, how hollow the tree hearts of Ornata were, where the birds no longer sang, and the flowers refused to bloom.

In the weeks that followed, Shyheem started to close his eyes, and breathe slowly and evenly. When he was awake he still spoke in a disjointed mumble about axes, and warriors dying, and hands of fire. In another week he was mostly conscious, but his heart was heavy, and when the boys visited him, his eyes were glazed, and their chatter sounded like birds in the trees. It was nice and cheerful, but had nothing to do with him.

They thought they would cheer him up by telling him how awesome the arching burst of blue fire had been. They described the looks of terror on the faces of the hardened Fels. It was really dollar to have such a power. But when they spoke, no smile returned to his face. Instead his mouth twisted, and his eyes closed, and when they said it was dollar, he reared suddenly, grabbing the bowl at his feet, and retched, his thin body convulsing, but nothing came up but a bit of bile. Angen pulled them away, telling them that Shyheem needed rest.

Angen spoke with him quietly. He told him the way of his suffering, and the boy understood, and sought to pray, and there, in those long and vivid night conversations with the god he could not see, he came to feel that the pain that he felt was not just the pain of the people of the woods, but it was the pain of the world. The evil was not the pain, but the things that caused the pain, and his experience of it was because he had fought it. Then he was able to walk again, though he walked heavily as an old man.

Wendigo scouts returned to the great meadow after talking to the birds and the small beasts. They reported that among the Guard, the regnate was believed to be bewitched by wendigo magic, as good as dead, and the vice regnate had assumed authority, and was moving up to the White House in Citadel. Everyone expected that once there, he would marshal the country to a great war against the wendigo. Already new recruits were being pulled from the SubAgora to fill the decimated ranks of the Guard.

327

The boys were enjoying the woods. Shyheem wandered with them, though he was reserved and shy working through his own thoughts. Kwenemuk led them through long mountain paths, and showed them the beasts of the wood, the bears, the wolves, and the deer. Once they heard an eerie scream, like a woman whose man has died, and she said it was a puma. She pointed toward the dark inner groves, which grew over clefts and hills, out of which breathed a hot dark smell. "That is the home of Mishipeshu." The boys shrunk back from the wrapping mist knowing that it was no place for city boys, and even the wendigo feared it.

There were many happy places in that forest where they could go, and always, Kwenemuk and Shyheem were speaking with the trees. They might have been happy living their life there, learning the wendigo language, and practicing archery with the young longeyes, if not for their sense that they were on a the journey that had just begun.

Everyday, the regnate, Vermont, and Angen climbed up the great tree and dwindled to toy-size men on the ladder in its trunk before they disappeared among the foliage. Seketeme went to the council meetings, too. The Subs knew that the sachems and men discussed what was next because Nickson would return, intent on destroying the regnate and wendigo.

One day, Hands was recounting their journey again, discussing the man Eire. "He saved us, Clarie included."

Clarie said, "He was weird."

Burt added, "He gave me the spooks. The way those wild cluriKin listened to him wasn't right."

Hands said, "I liked him. He gave me a bauble." Hands produced it, the rough rock, which was faintly blue in the forest half-light.

Shyheem was normally in his own thoughts, talking with the trees, or his god, but what Hands said interested him. He asked to see the bauble, which Hands passed to him. Shyheem spasmed as it hit his palm, feeling the jolting charge of prayer in the bauble. "Where did you get this?"

"A wagondriver named Eire. He said someone was watching over me."

328

Shyheem shook his head, remembering the wagon driver who had brought him through woods, and warned him against the rigid luminology of North Temple. "Did he have curly hair, like a mop? Green eyes?"

"Yeah? You know him?"

When they had exchanged stories, the two boys were amazed. Somehow this strange man had been there and helped, said the vital thing, at the right moment for both of them. Jalil, who had not been with them at the Red River pass, or in Faunarum, still felt that he recognized the description of the man. Without the driver, Hands thought he would have joined with Nickson. Shyheem would never have spoken with Kikishimenshi, the sachem of Faunarum without Eire. Shyheem said, "Illumen used him to watch us."

Hands said, "He's hoodBos with Illumen, definitely."

Shyheem said, "He has Illumen's power. I can feel it in the bauble."

Hands said, "Well, I'm a little bit of an Illumenist myself. I mean, Nickson is in Citadel, and we're not done facing him, but I feel like he won't last, and not cause we're tougher or smarter. Somehow, when it seemed impossible, things worked out. It feels like it might keep going that way."

329

30. Eire

Nickson and Potens had settled themselves in the carriage for the long ride to Urba. Nickson recited the events of the Ornatan battle, beginning with his easy defeat of the regnate's sword, interrupted by the roaring, how the fire picked him up and threw him.

"All my training, it was nothing, before that roaring flame. Why did it not consume me?"

Potens said, "You are protected by our secrets."

Nickson nodded. "Also: I was afraid."

Potens said, "Fear is wisdom. Cowardice is not fighting. The knowledge of other power motivates me to get more; the only protection of my only life."

Nickson was silent, rechewing the dictums of their way. The topic moved on, and Nickson explained how the regnate's escape into the woods was just as good as the regnate's death. Nickson's confirmation as regnate was inevitable, "Which of the eight families will resist me? WickBaron Vermont is stuck in Ornata with Grant, and the rest of the family is too old and weak."

Potens nodded. "Nothing important is ever easy. You must remain vigilant and ruthless."

The carriage halted. When it stayed halted for a few moments, Nickson put his head out of the window. "Driver, who told you to stop?"

"I'm sorry, WickBaron, some idiot shepherd has got his stupid sheep all in the middle of the road. It's out of control."

"If he is slowing us down, the Fels will have to punish him."

Outside the carriage the Fels stooped and dragged bleating sheep from the road. They laid hands on the shepherd, punching him so his bushy hair shook and bruises were raised on his sun dried cheeks, but he bore the blows without protest so that there was not much fun in it.

Finally the flock was deposited on the side of the road and the column was able to move on. The shepherd's green eyes watched the war carriage roll past, eyeing the two men inside. He shouted as they marched by, "Think you're tough? You better watch yourselves!"

The soldiers laughed at his rantings. One shouted, "Whatever you say, bushy top."

He whispered, "You, Nickson. You won't just push the little people around forever. That merd don't fly.

"You're going to get burnt by the sky's veins.

"Silent war between mishipeshu will turn the blasted trunk straight as golden rod.

"From the dark docks and iron hearts, a king of the thieves comes who will rule with righteousness and justice. The rings in which you have hid your lies and your treasure, will be broken up."

He yawned, looked at the bunch of sheep wandering up and down the road. "I could go on, but I've got to herd these dumb animals."

331

Glossary of Terms

Regnan Words
Citan- person from the innermost ring of Urba
AltUrban- person from AltUrba, second innermost ring
SubAgoran- person from SubAgora, last human ring
Regnate- ruler of the country
WickBaron- ruler of a wick
Baron- landowner
Bellumite- devoted follower of Bellum
Wick- one of the eight regions of Regna

SubAgoran Slang
Altic- proud, or related to the upper classes
Sub- person from SubAgora
Watt, FistSlap- punch
Ka- prefix meaning small
Ki- prefix meaning giant
Dollar- good, great
WordSlap- to insult, an insult
Rah- strong sense of self
Grimey- to steal

Illumenist words
Lamp- leader in Illumen's temple
Wick- student training in a temple of Illumen (also a name for
the regions of Regna)
Torch- traveling lamp
Firmament- seven stars who preside of Illumenists
Star- a member of the Firmament
Shining One- the leader of the Firmament
Manusignis- one gifted with hands of fie
Parwa- a wick training to become a manusignis

Wendigo words
Longtooth, longteeth- arrow, arrows
Longeye- wendigo warrior

Woodwarbler- one who can control treegrowth
Mishipeshu- monster/god of the wendigo
Mindscout- a telepath
Ornata- Southern forest
Magnasylva- Northwestern forest
Faunarum – North Central Forest
Desicca – Far Southern Forest

About the Author

J. Shepard Trott grew up in Philadelphia, and attended that city's schools all the way through college, at which point he ended up teaching literature in rural Uganda for two and a half years. He returned to Philadelphia to get a Masters in Education.

With this degree he began teaching in the public schools of, you guessed it, Philadelphia.

Currently he lives in the Kensington section of Philadelphia with his wife Lydia and sons Jem and Zeke. When he is not inventing elaborate stories in fantastical worlds, he's teaching English at Central High School of Philadelphia, or passionately watching, and coaching soccer. Another Trott book is *Nobody Says Hi Anymore*, a book set in a zombie-infested Philadelphia. Look for the sequel to *Illumen's Children* in the fall of 2016, *The Sons of Rasheen*. That book takes place back in Urba, as Hands, Burt, and Clarie, assisted by Percy Vermont, the regnate, and Orpan, go underground to undermine the rule of Nickson.

Turn the page for the start of the sequel!

Excerpts from The Sons of Rasheen

Chapter One: Clarie

In dark times like these, when assassins live in the
White Manson, and the rightful ruler and his daughter, me,
hide in Agoran attics, justice arrives with the slash of the
sword and leadership sounds with the boom of the
thunderPipe. In the forest I trained myself to be a warrior
regnate.

I swung the sword against the Subs and Vermont,
until I couldn't lift my arms, and my hands bled. I got
knocked on the helmet, bruised on the thighs, so I could
become a warrior. I thought we'd mount the wapiti and
attack. Instead we snuck into the city and Dad stuck me in
this one-room attic, hiding with the dust bunnies.

I had to exchange the wooden practice swords for
jeweled hair pins. He made me suffer a corset and sweat in
heavy brocaded skirts. It was weird because I used to have a
servant to pull the cords, but in the attic Dad did it. When I
told him I couldn't breathe, he said, "Learn to take little
breaths. This is the way of a Citan alta, and that is what you
are."

Once I was watching while the Guard lined up and
tried to practice spear thrusts and lancework. They thought
they looked good but I knew I could beat them with a short
sword. Not all of them at once, but half a squad, no
problem.

They had a big grolf chained up in the middle of
them, his roars were shaking the whole city and his long
gray fur flew as he swung and pulled against the chains with
links as thick as a man's thighs. They kind of poked at him
from way beyond the reach of his chains and then ran back.

Then they congratulated each other with shouts. Good thing those chains didn't break. Idiots.

All of the sudden Dad grabs me and yanks me to the floor. "What are you doing?" he hissed.

"Watching the army!" I was kind of yelling at him.

"Someone might see you!" He didn't have to explain the rest. How there was a reward being offered for us, how Nickson would send his best, merciless Fels, thunderPipe strapped Bellumites through the door, and they would throw Dad from the window and me too. I'd heard it before, trust me. Any time I raised my voice above a dry whisper. Anytime I half giggled, the lecture got launched. Last hope, be quiet, blah blah blah. How are we the last hope if we're sitting in an attic, doing nothing?

. . .

Chapter Two: Hands

Yo, I can't lie. It was kiDolla to be back in the Sub. Now, you know I missed Seketeme, and the woods and all the non-stop fun we had woods-romping. I missed Jalil and Shyheem, too. I mean, not that much, cuz those Subs be on themselves, but I missed them. On the other hand, being back was rahLife. See, I ran out of this city a kaLulu that every half grown Sub and double sized Fel fistSlapped and wordSmacked. I was a thief. I got my merdhup footSmacked on the daily from the AltUrba Wall back to the Apia Gate.

Now, I'm grown. I was eating meat every day up in Ornata, drinking wendigo health drinks that tasted the same as dirt. My shoulders popped out like bell mushrooms after a summer rain. Meanwhile I trained, learning how to fight like a Citan and a wendigo. Like, I can make my sword twinkle, and I can kick you in the face. You think I'm going to hit you one way but the second hit is coming from somewhere else.

We smuggled ourselves back into the city. They looking for us everywhere, the Fels had a mandate and merd. Probably had daily meetings describing us, public enemy number. Clarie, Percy and Theodore dressed in all these robes like lamps. Burt and I were walking ahead, acting casual. Acting like we didn't know them. The plan was that if we saw anything bad, we would touch one another, like a punch or slap or anything, as a warning. There was a little Fel squad at the gate, and they said some stuff about Subs. I decided to distract them, so when we were passed I screamed some merd about they moms and they took off after us.

Porkchop was breathing heavy in a second, I mean, he wasn't as fat as he was when he lived with his dad but he was still Porkchop. I checked him hard so he somersaulted into a pile of hay and kept running. They knew I was the one that wordSmacked on they moms so they left Burt and came after me. After we ran through a couple small markets, most of them got tired as I shredded some ground, but two of them, young and real in love with their moms, kept up. I had run from Fels my whole life. They usually caught up and gave me a beat down. I didn't need to run anymore though. I stopped, looked around. I was in a little market. I borrowed a sword from a graz's stall; he hissed, "Thiefs," and threatened, "I goes for Fels."

The merchants in the neighboring stalls were also glaring at me. I said, "I'm trying it out. Maybe I'll buy it."

They frowned at me, saying with their eyes, "This Sub don't have a brownbit on him, how he going to pay for that sword?"

I'm thinking I didn't know I was this famous, all eyes on me.

Then the two Fels thundered into the square. The graz sword-monger looked happy to see them pointing a claw at me and announcing, "Thiefs. My sword!"

Their swords were already out. They saw I was a kaSub and assumed I wouldn't know what to do with a sword. They charged me and thrust. I stepped to the side, bringing the dull edge of the blade into the near guy's helmet. It rang like a bell and he collapsed. Could have killed him but I didn't want the kind of hunt that comes from being a Fel killer. The other was backing up, in a wary stance.

He shouted, "Fels. Fels." Some kind of rallying cry.

I said, "You want your friends now?"

That pissed him off and so he jumped in. I slipped a foot out and rammed it down into his knee, and the thing cracked sideway. That trick, use of feet, was wendigo style. He fell to the ground, clutching his leg. For good measure I smacked his gaping mouth with the flat of the blade. His mouth popped blood like a blueberry pop juice. "No, no," he said.

I said to the graz, "Weight's wrong," and chucked the sword back on his table, and I got out of there. You see what I'm saying? It's good to be back home, now that I'm a kiSub. The distraction worked too, the Fel who was left hadn't bothered with making the Citans lift their hoods and they'd walked their horses right through and into Orpan's stables.

Made in the USA
Middletown, DE
05 February 2023

23077013R00208